The Bradshaws of Harniss

THE BRADSHAWS
OF HARNISS

BY

JOSEPH C. LINCOLN

Grosset & Dunlap

PUBLISHERS   NEW YORK

Copyright, 1943, by

D. Appleton-Century Company, Inc.

C. 16

BL AUG 1 3 74

Chapter 1

DOCTOR STEVENS was leaning back in his desk chair and looking at his patient through his spectacles. The doctor was of medium height, gray-haired, plump, and florid. His left hand was thrust into a pocket of his pepper-and-salt trousers, and the fingers of his right toyed with the watch chain spanning his ample waistcoat. The expression on his good-natured face was more serious than usual.

"So that's just about it, Zenas," he said. "I've told you the truth because that is what I took it for granted you wanted me to tell you."

Zenas Bradshaw, the patient, was standing at the other side of the desk. He also was of medium height, broad-shouldered and thick-set. Practically all the Bradshaws, beginning with Zenas the First, who came to Harniss in 1816 and founded Bradshaw's store in 1817, had been "chunky." In fact, there was a strong likeness between the oil portrait of Zenas First, hanging over the mantel in the home of Zenas Second, and Zenas Second, himself, who was standing by Doctor Stevens' desk at that moment. The sole exception to the family "chunkiness" was in the person of Marcellus Bradshaw, Third, who was Zenas Second's grandson. Marcellus— every one called him "Mark"—was slender, and his hair was brown, instead of the Bradshaw red. Mark took after his mother's people in looks. She was a Pierce, one of the West Ostable Pierces.

Zenas—the present Zenas, that is, and the only Bradshaw of that name alive in 1940—had just risen from the chair reserved for consulting callers. He had picked up his hat from the couch where he had tossed it when he came in and was holding it in his hand. Now he nodded.

"Um-hum," he agreed. "That's just what I wanted. If I wanted something different I'd have gone to another fellow. Just one more thing I want to be certain of, Ben. What you've told me is the truth, I don't doubt —but have you told me all the truth? Are you holding anything back? If you are, you mustn't."

Doctor Stevens shook his head. "I'm holding nothing back, Zenas," he replied. "There's nothing seriously wrong with you; in fact, you're in pretty good shape considering your age. But that's just what you've got to consider—your age. You can't go on as you have done, down at the store every morning at half-past seven, staying there every night but Saturday night until after six and Saturday until after nine. Carrying all the responsibility of the business on your own shoulders, doing all the figuring—"

Bradshaw interrupted. "Don't do the figuring," he protested. "Elsie Burgess does that and does it first-rate, too. A smart bookkeeper, Elsie is."

The doctor snorted, impatiently. "Nobody ever said she wasn't, far as I ever heard," he admitted. "She makes out your bills and keeps your account books, that's what you pay her for. But when she goes home and the store is shut up, her job is over for that day. Yours isn't. You've got to think of to-morrow and the day after, and the next week and the weeks that follow along. You do all the buying; you see that the stock's kept up; you take care that the bills she sends out are paid—"

"Not all of 'em, Ben, not all of 'em. There's some so far behind that you couldn't sight a payment with a spy-glass."

He grinned as he said it. His friend did not even smile, because he was too deeply in earnest. "That I don't doubt in the least," he declared. "And that part of the worry is yours, too. The store is on your mind day and night. And, besides that, you are a church trustee and member of the Town Improvement Board and—oh, I don't know what all. You can't do it, Zenas. You just mustn't do it. You are getting to be an old man."

"Here, here! You told me that once before. I ain't but five years older than you are. Don't forget that."

"Humph!"—dryly. "I'm not likely to forget it any more than I forget that I am sixty-three. Zenas, you and I have known each other for a long time, and that is why I can talk to you as I have been doing. You are as close a friend as I've got, and I don't want to lose you. I don't want to see you drop down dead, as Nathan Kelley did last June, or break up and get to be the half-paralyzed wreck that Sam Crowell has been for the last eight months. You don't want to be like poor Sam, do you?"

"Wouldn't say I did, now that you mention it: no."

"Then you've *got* to take things more easily. Make that grandson of yours carry his share of the load. Make him stop spending half his time over at the flying field, or chasing to dances and summer people's beach parties, or girling around from Bayport to Denboro and back.

3

Set him to work and keep him at it. That's what you've got to do, for your sake and his own. He—"

Zenas Bradshaw was showing signs of uneasiness. Now he broke in.

"Mark is a good boy," he said, briskly. "He loves to fool around those flying contraptions, and you can't hardly blame him. Papers are full of what's being done with them in the war over across, and it gets ahold of the young fellows. Would me, I guess likely, if I was his age."

"But you're not his age. And he is old enough to realize—"

"There, there! Well, Ben, I'm much obliged to you. You can take the thanks now and put the rest of what I owe in your bill. Matter of fact"—he hesitated momentarily—"I—well, I've been thinking somewheres along the line of what you've told me for quite a spell lately. I used to say that I was going to give up real hard work when I got to be seventy. Seventy sounded a long ways off then, but it's right around the corner now. I always figured that Mark would take hold of the store and—well, he will, of course. I'll—er—I'll have a talk with him. He's a smart boy, Mark is, and a good boy, too. Little careless, maybe, and—and doesn't always take time to think ahead, but that's natural at his age."

"Humph! You speak of his age as if he was sixteen. He's twenty-one, isn't he?"

"Eh? Oh, yes, yes! But he hasn't been twenty-one more than a couple of months. . . . So long, Ben. See you again pretty quick."

"If you don't I shall make it a point to see you. And remember—"

"Yes, yes, I'll remember. Just now I'm remembering

4

that I ought to be in the store this minute. Good Lord, it's 'most ten o'clock!"

He hurried out of the office. Doctor Stevens accompanied him to the front door and then walked slowly back to his desk, shaking his head dubiously.

Bradshaw's Store was one of the institutions of Harniss, like the First Meeting House, or the old Sears house on Wharf Road, which had been built by Captain Ezekiel Sears in 1762 and was now owned and used by the Harniss Historical Society. Bradshaw's—the business, but not in the present building—was founded in 1817, and it had been carried on ever since by one Bradshaw after another. Zenas Bradshaw, First, was born in 1775, served in the Navy during the War of 1812, came to Harniss in 1816, and opened his little "general store" on the Upper Road a year later. If one is interested sufficiently to visit the Harniss Public Library and consult the files of the Ostable *Banner* of that period, one will find occasional small advertisements reading in this fashion:

MR. ZENAS BRADSHAW desires to inform the residents of HARNISS and vicinity that *he has just received,* via New Bedford and Boston packet, the following consignment of merchandize: 2 Hogsheads prime West Indian molasses; 1 Hogshead first quality West Indian brown sugar; 25 lbs. Malaga currants; 2 barrels best quality fine wheat flour; 5 lbs. best citron; 50 yards figured calico; 100 yards white cotton cloth, suitable for sheeting; 50 reels silk ribbon, various colors. These, together with a large and varied assortment of groceries, dry-goods, and staples, will be found on sale *at reasonable prices* by Zenas Bradshaw at BRADSHAW'S STORE on the Upper road in Harniss. *Early inspection is recommended.*

Zenas Bradshaw, First, died in 1865. His son Marcellus worked for and with his father, at first as a clerk and then as a partner, except for a brief interval when he served aboard a troop transport in the War with Mexico. During his lifetime the business grew and prospered. Marcellus died in 1880. His son, Marcellus, Second, born in 1844, served through the whole five years of the Civil War, settled down as partner in Bradshaw's, succeeded his father as head of the store when the old man died, and died, himself, in 1920. His son Zenas, Second—our Zenas—was born in 1872. It was during his partnership with his father that the store moved to its present quarters on Main Street, opposite the post-office. By this time it was no longer a "general" store, having given up its dry-goods and notions, but was selling only groceries, hay, grain, and meal. It had become one of the best-known establishments of its kind in Ostable County. Zenas married in 1894, and the marriage, true to Bradshaw custom, produced another male child, Zenas, Third, who would, in the regular course, have carried on as partner and, later, head of the store.

But then followed the greatest tragedy of the Bradshaw line. Zenas, the younger, enlisted as a volunteer in the American Expeditionary Force of the first World War. With his family's full consent he married when he was but twenty-two, before joining the army. He was sent overseas and was killed, in the Argonne, in the fall of 1918, just before the Armistice. His wife, Ellen, died in childbirth a month later. The baby, however, lived, and Zenas, the grandfather—our Zenas—took him to the Bradshaw home on Pond Road.

"Looks as if you and I had another young-one to bring

up, Susan," said Zenas to his wife. "Haven't forgotten how, have you?"

Susan Bradshaw replied that she should hope not. There was a little discussion as to what the child should be named. Susan was in favor of naming him for his father and grandfather, but her husband objected.

"That would make a big Zenas and a little Zenas in the family," he said. "We had that same thing when his dad was little, and you remember how the children used to plague him hollering 'Teeny weeny Zenie' after him. Had two or three fights over it, he did. No, let's switch back to Marcellus. That's a good Bradshaw name, too."

Little Marcellus thrived and grew. When his grand-mother succumbed to pneumonia, Zenas and the boy carried on, with the help of a housekeeper, in the Pond Road home. Mark graduated from the Harniss grammar school and the high school. Then, largely because he announced that he was tired of "school study" and did not want to go to college, he entered Bradshaw's Store. He had been a good-looking youngster, popular with the boys and girls, particularly the latter, and as he reached manhood his good looks and popularity re-mained with him. The old ladies liked to have him wait on them, and the younger ones offered no objections. Mark Bradshaw made a good groceryman, when he kept his mind on the job. That mind was, however, likely to be busy with other matters. It was of this tendency that Zenas was thinking as he walked away from Doctor Stevens' office that April morning in 1940.

No doubt about it, he would have to talk with Mark— and seriously. The boy—Zenas never thought of him as anything but a boy—was twenty-one. He was a man,

7

as far as years went. And, as a man, he ought, as the Bible phrased it, to put away childish things. Girls were all right, and dances and parties and automobile rides were all right, in their place, but those places should be, by this time, in the second row, not the first. By Zenas Bradshaw's rating there were but two all-important items in that front row, Mark Bradshaw's future welfare —and Bradshaw's Store. One depended upon the other.

Generations of Bradshaws had kept that store alive and solvent. He—Zenas Bradshaw—had clerked in it and worked with it and planned for it ever since he was fifteen, had prospered with it in good times and fought with and for it through hard ones. It was still doing pretty well, even with the competition from the new "chain store" farther up the street, but it needed constant attention and careful watching and tactful management as much as it ever had, and perhaps more. And he, Zenas, would be seventy years old in two more years. Seventy! It didn't seem possible. He felt—why, he felt as young now as he had when he was fifty. Eh? Well, no, maybe not quite as young. He didn't sleep quite as well, and those pains in his leg, the leg which had been crushed by the sugar hogshead in '98 and which had made his volunteering for the Spanish-American war an impossibility, were a little more frequent and a trifle more serious. But he did not feel old. Hang it all, he *wasn't* old. He ought to be good for a lot of hard work yet.... But he was sixty-eight, and Mark was twenty-one. And if Mark was—well, if he was to be left with Bradshaw's Store on his hands—er—some day, he must straighten out and settle down.

Over Zenas's head, a thousand feet up, an airplane hummed and droned. Zenas looked up at it, squinting in

8

the sunlight. A winged silver sliver glistening against the blue. Came from Frank Seymour's landing-field over at South Harniss, it did, of course. Seymour was chauffeur, caretaker, and general outdoor factotum on Ex-Senator Buck's fine summer place on the Beach Boulevard. He was an adept mechanic, could repair an automobile as well as any garage man in the county, and, even when airplanes were still a novelty and a marvel in Ostable County, Frank Seymour bought a small second-hand plane from an exhibitionist at the County Fair, took its engine to pieces, put it together again, and learned all its tricks and manners on the ground. Then he attended a flying school in the city and, for several years, had been a licensed air pilot. In 1935 he contracted for a few acres of cheap flat land in South Harniss, withdrew his savings from the bank, paid for the land, and had it cleared and scraped. Then he built a makeshift hangar, largely with his own hands and in his spare time—as the Bucks occupied their Boulevard home only for three months in the summer, he had much spare time—and opened the Seymour Flying Field, where private planes might be stored and cared for and where lessons were given by a competent instructor—namely, Seymour himself.

Now, in 1940, a few planes were kept there by their owners during the summer months, and at least two of Harniss's young men had learned to fly and had earned their pilot's licenses. Seymour's field was not exactly a busy place, but it was by no means a deserted one.

Mark Bradshaw was a friend of Frank Seymour's, and he spent a good deal of his time at the field. Flying, its thrills and its risks, appealed to him. He went up with Frank often, and sometimes, just how often his grandfather did not exactly know, was permitted, while in the company of the instructor, to handle the machine in the air. Zenas Bradshaw did not strenuously object to this. He knew perfectly well that, if he were twenty-one, he would probably be doing the same thing. Beyond warning Frank to be careful and occasionally hinting that the grocery business was on Main Street and not up in the clouds, he said little. Of late, however, he had been thinking a good deal, and now, this morning, his thoughts were serious, very.

Bradshaw's was a rather old-fashioned store, in fittings and appearance as well as in its business methods. There were two signs over its front door: one, the uppermost, was small, battered, and time-worn. Its letters were white on a black ground. This was the sign that Zenas Bradshaw, First, had put up over the door of his two-room shop on the Upper Road in 1817, one hundred and twenty-three years before. Below it was a far bigger, modern one, its letters raised and gilded against a red background. There had been other signs, a dozen of them, but each had been discarded to make room for its successor. The old sign, however, the original, had never been taken down, except when it was moved from the Upper Road to Main Street. It was a landmark, something to be pointed out to tourists. Harniss was proud of that sign.

The interior of the store was a combination of old and new. Plate-glass show-windows, but old-fashioned fittings, shelves, and counters. Clean paint, clean floors, everything dustless and orderly, but no nickel or glitter in the appointments, a marked contrast to the new "chain store" up the street. A homy, friendly sort of place. Feminine summer residents described it as "so delightfully quaint." Zenas Bradshaw did not mind that: it was good advertising.

When he entered its doors this morning he gazed about, giving the establishment his customary appraising glance. Abner Hallett, the chief clerk, who had been a part of Bradshaw's since he came there as a boy in 1892, was leaning over the right-hand counter deep in what appeared to be an argument with Mrs. Amelia Fellowes, who lived over on Front Street. Front Street was called "Uncle Percy's Road" in the old days, but few called it that now. Mrs. Fellowes certainly never did. She was a well-to-do widow, built on ample lines, moving with the majesty of a battleship and delivering her opinions with the forceful finality of broadsides. She was a member of the Board of Trustees of the Harniss Public Library, President of the Women's Club, and extremely active in social matters connected with the Universalist Church. Between her and Mrs. Abigail Simons, who handled the social activities of the old First Methodist Society, there was bitter competition and rivalry, no less bitter because the two ladies always kissed each other when they met.

Zenas did not like the expression on Mrs. Fellowes' face as she talked to Abner Hallett. Abner did not look very happy, either, so Zenas thought, although he did not seem to be doing much of the talking, probably because he was not given the opportunity.

Elsie Burgess, the bookkeeper, was waiting on another customer. Elsie should not be doing that: she should be in the small office enclosure, at her desk. Mark ought to—but apparently Mark was not present; at least he was not in sight.

There were sounds of activity in the room at the

11

rear of the building, where the orders were put up for delivery to customers, and Zenas went out there. Willie Snow, the driver of the Ford delivery truck, was busy with his bundles and baskets.

"Where's Mark, Willie?" was Zenas Bradshaw's first question.

Snow shook his head. "Don't know, Mr. Bradshaw," he replied. "He was in here about nine, but I ain't seen him since. He went out 'bout as soon as he come in. Never said where he was goin', just that he'd be back later along."

Zenas made no comment on this statement.

"What's the matter with Millie Fellowes?" he asked. "Put out about something, is she?"

Willie Snow grinned. "Put out ain't no name for it," he declared. "She's sorer than a blister. Seems that bread we sent up to her place last night was stale, so she vows. She was givin' Ab hark from the tomb when I was out there just now. Vowed and declared she was going to take her trade to the chain store. Going somewhere that could be depended on, she said. Shouldn't wonder if she meant it, too." His grin became a chuckle.

Zenas Bradshaw was not amused. "Bread?" he repeated. "Why should we send her stale bread? Enough fresh, wasn't there?"

"Not last night, there wa'n't. She give us that big order yesterday, don't you remember? She's having a big blow-out at her house this noontime, sewin' meetin' and luncheon for the County Universalist Women's League—some such name. Women folks comin' from Bayport and Orham and all over. I fetched her up a ham and some chickens and a lot of canned stuff and

12

coffee and the dozen loaves of bread and a pound of tea and—"

"I know, I know." Zenas remembered the order. Mrs. Fellowes had given it to him, personally. It was a good-sized order, and Millie Fellowes was a good, if overfussy, customer of Bradshaw's Store. She had been particularly fussy about this order, and he had offered suggestions as to additions which she had accepted. The bread must be *very* fresh, she had insisted, because, if she did say so herself, she had always been famous for her sandwiches. Mrs. Cabot, wife of the Honorable Samuel Cabot—"The Ostable Cabots, Zenas, you know *them*, or of them, anyway"—had told her, Mrs. Fellowes, with her own lips, when the last Harniss meeting of the League took place in Amelia's home years before, that she had never tasted such sandwiches in all her life. "So you see, Zenas—"

Zenas had declared that he saw, perfectly.

"*Was* the bread stale, Willie?" he asked, sharply.

"Not the whole dozen loaves, no, Mr. Bradshaw. But we had that other big order, the one from the Methodist folks, and there was a lot of bread in that. Mrs. Abbie Simons is having a time to her house, too, and the Simons's order was put up first. So, when—"

"Wait!" Zenas had forgotten, for the moment, that the Methodist Ladies' Aid Societies of Harniss, Denboro, and Orham were gathering at the home of Mrs. Abigail Simons that same day, and the last-named lady had been as particular concerning the items in her order as Mrs. Fellowes had been with hers.

"Did Abbie Simons get stale bread, too?" he demanded, even more sharply.

"No, sir. I was just going to tell you, Mr. Bradshaw. Me and Mark put up both orders this mornin'. I'm just back from deliverin' 'em. Well, we put up the Simons one first, and when we got around to the Fellowes, there was only about six fresh loaves left. So—"

"The bread delivery cart comes to-day, doesn't it?"

"Yes, sir, but it don't come till after twelve. Well, as I was sayin', Mark and I see that we're six loaves short on Millie's—I mean Mrs. Fellowes's lot. So Mark, he says to me, he says: 'What's them loaves over yonder?' says he. 'Them's staler than a last year's bird's nest,' I told him. 'Never mind,' says he, 'put 'em in with the others. The old girl will never notice the difference, and I want to get away this forenoon.' So he done it and—"

"Stop! Heave to! Let me think." Zenas stepped to the door opening into the main store. Mrs. Fellowes and Abner Hallett were still arguing, apparently, although the lady, very red-faced and straight-backed, seemed to be on the point of departure, and Hallett, who had come out from behind the counter, was evidently still trying to explain. Zenas Bradshaw turned quickly back to his delivery desk.

"Willie," he ordered, "listen to what I'm telling you. Before you do anything else, put up a whole new order for the Fellowes's, a *whole* new one, understand?"

"But—but Mr. Bradshaw, there wa'n't nothin' the matter with the ham and the chickens. No, nor the tea nor the canned stuff. They was all right. It was just the bread that—"

"Don't stop to talk. A whole new order was what I said. Put it up, and do it this minute."

"But there ain't no bread, Mr. Bradshaw. Not even the stale kind. You see—"

"Shh! Put the rest of the order up, get the baskets aboard the car, and get going. Drive fast, and, first of all, go over to the bake shop at East Orham. Buy from them—here's the money—a dozen loaves of the freshest, best bread they've got. When you get those loaves put 'em in with the rest of the Fellowes order and rush the whole business up to Millie's. And don't lose one extra second. Got that straight, have you?"

"Yes, sir. Shall I tell them at the Fellowes's that we're sorry about the stale bread, but 'twas all we had on hand and, knowin' they was in a hurry—"

"No, no"—with emphasis. "Don't tell them anything except just what I tell you to tell them, and that's this: say that you had another big party order to deliver and you might possibly have got the two mixed."

"But I never. I put up Abbie Simons's order myself and—"

"Shh! Say just what I've told you to say and no more. If the Fellowes hired girl, or cook, or maid, or whatever they call 'em up there, asks any questions, don't answer 'em—change the subject. Then get the things in the order you left there before and bring that first lot straight back here to the store. Sure you've got it right, now?"

"Yes, sir. I guess likely so. Only—"

"Hush! You and your 'onlys.' Never heard, did you, of the fellow that might have won the swimming race, only—"

"Eh? Only what, Mr. Bradshaw?"

"Only he couldn't swim. Now jump and fill those baskets."

Willie Snow "jumped." Zenas Bradshaw hastened out into the main body of the store. Mrs. Fellowes's hand

15

was on the latch of the street door now, and her features were, as Elsie Burgess said afterwards, like the stern and rock-bound coast the Pilgrims landed on in the poem. Abner Hallett looked as if he was sinking within sight of that coast.

Zenas saw all this, but his expression was smilingly serene. "Why, Millie," he hailed, "aren't leaving without giving me a chance to say good morning, are you?"

Mrs. Fellowes turned, looked, glared, and spoke. "Zenas Bradshaw," she said, "for twenty-five years I have traded at this store."

Zenas broke in with a smiling protest.

"Oh, now, not so long as that, Millie," he said. "You must have been more than fifteen when you began trading here."

As a usual thing any flattering, if exaggerated, hint concerning the lady's youthful appearance was graciously and simperingly received. This time, however, it was a wasted effort. Mrs. Fellowes did not even wait to hear the end of the sentence.

"Stuff!" she snapped. "Zenas Bradshaw, do you know where I'm going this minute? I'm going, straight as I can go, to the chain store. That's where I'm going."

"Is that so? Well, well! Quite a nice-looking place they've got there, that's a fact. And I hear they're beginning to pick up some trade. Saturday nights, when the Fish Village crowd gets its money, they do pretty well, I don't doubt. Glad to hear it. I wish 'em luck. There's room enough for two stores in this town, and I always said so."

That this was not precisely the effect Mrs. Fellowes had expected her announcement to produce was evident; also that the reference to Fish Village was not

16

too welcome. Fish Village was the local term for that section of the Harniss outskirts populated by the Portuguese trawlers and dory fishermen. It was distinctly not an aristocratic locality, which was probably why Zenas Bradshaw mentioned it. He was not a snob, but Millie Fellowes was.

She was thrown on the defense by it, and she was not one to retreat without a fight. Her grip of the latch relaxed, and she swung about.

"I am going to that chain store," she repeated with withering finality, "because, wherever I give my custom, I expect to be honestly treated. Which I have *not* been in—in some other places. If you don't know what I mean, Zenas Bradshaw, you ought to. I should think you would be ashamed, but I don't suppose you are. After all these years! . . . Well, this is the final straw. Good-by."

She was reaching for the latch again, but Zenas's hand reached it first.

"Here, here!" he expostulated. "What's all this? Straw? Did you sell Mrs. Fellowes any straw, Abner?"

Abner Hallett, who had been hovering uncertainly in the background, like a flustered chicken, stammered an explanation.

"She didn't mean straw, Mr. Bradshaw," he sputtered. "She means—er—bread, that's what she means. Seems that bread we sent up to her house last night wasn't— well, 'twasn't quite as fresh as it ought to have been. She says—she says—"

Mrs. Fellowes said it herself. "Fresh!" she sniffed, scornfully. "It might have been fresh in George Washington's time, maybe, but now—well, if I heard it came out of the chip pile I shouldn't be surprised. The idea of sending stale, dry stuff like that to me! One of the oldest and best customers you've got, and my father and grandfather before me. I gave that order to you, yourself, yesterday, and I told you then that I was having a very important and—er—distinguished lunch meeting at my home this noon and I was extra particular. Naturally I would be, with some of the finest women in Ostable County, the very finest. And, in spite of that you—why, you—"

She was a bit short of breath by this time, and Zenas Bradshaw took advantage of the shortage to surprise her. He should have been—she expected him to be—distressed and humiliated and alarmed. Abner Hallett had been, but his employer apparently was not. On the contrary he seemed to be relieved—yes, even pleased.

"Oh!" he interrupted. "O-oh, I see! Yes, yes. When you said 'straw,' I was afraid there might be something else. You didn't know about the mistake, Millie? No, of course you didn't, but you will when you get home."

"Mistake? What mistake? If you mean you thought I would let you palm off that old dry bread on me and say not a word about it you *have* made a mistake. Yes, and your last one, so far as I am concerned."

"No, no, no"—soothingly—"I mean the mistake in delivering the two orders. There is another big women's party in town to-day and—well, it might be that the two orders were switched around, got delivered to the wrong houses. Lucky I found it out in time, a few minutes ago. Your order, the right one, is up in your kitchen by this time—or will be before you get there. Too bad you had all this trouble, Millie. I *am* sorry. I don't blame you for feeling upset, I declare I don't."

Mrs. Fellowes' expression was slowly changing. She

18

knew all about the other "party." It was the meeting and luncheon of the County Methodist Ladies' Aid Society at the home of Abigail Simons. The two dates had conflicted, and were any other two ladies in Harniss involved, one gathering or the other would have been postponed, but not by Millie Fellowes or Abbie Simons. Neither would even dream of such a concession. Another thought flashed to Mrs. Fellowes' mind, a thought almost too good to be true.

"Well," she said, a shade of doubt still lingering, "if that is so . . . But, if you had enough fresh bread on hand, why did you send that awful dry stuff to—to anybody? Nobody could possibly order it."

Zenas solemnly shook his head. There was a twinkle in his eye, however, and the lady noticed it.

"Everybody isn't as particular as you are, Millie," he observed. Then he added, with apparent irrelevance, "Stale bread is considerably cheaper than fresh. Goes just as far, too."

The last vestige of a frown left the Fellowes brow. She almost beamed.

"I see," she said. "I—see. Well, of course, if it was just a mistake, and you're sure the good bread will be at my house in time—"

"Shouldn't wonder if it was there this minute."

"All right, then, I won't go to the chain store. I should have felt dreadful to do it, anyhow. As I said, after all these years. Good day, Abner. Good day, Zenas."

"Good morning, Millie. Oh, by the way, we've just got in some especially nice bottled ripe olives. I forgot to mention 'em to you yesterday. Ripe olives are first-rate with a luncheon, don't you think? When I was a young fellow there was nothing but the green ones, in this store or any other."

Mrs. Fellowes said she guessed she didn't need any olives. Then she said that she might look at them. She left, five minutes later, with a smile on her face and two bottles of the olives in her hands. Zenas Bradshaw accompanied her to the door.

Abner Hallett regarded him with awed admiration.

"Well, I do declare!" vowed Abner. "I never saw anything like that in my born days. I couldn't do nothing with her. She about snapped my head off. And she *was* headed for the chain store. She was, she meant it. How you can handle 'em, Zenas! I vow I'm proud of you."

Zenas grunted. "Nothing much to be proud of," he retorted. "Willie told me what had happened, and I sent a new order to her house in a hurry, having him stop at the bake shop on the way."

"I guessed that. But the way you played up Abbie Simons's meeting and got her—Millie, I mean—to thinking that Abbie was working off stale bread on her crowd because 'twas cheap. Ho, ho! Millie'll be telling that all over town."

"Presume likely she will. May get me into more trouble, perhaps. I never thought I should have to lie to keep trade."

"But you didn't lie, not once you never. All you said was that they wasn't all as particular as she was and that stale bread was cheaper and went just as far. She imgined all the rest, herself."

"Um-hm. Well, suppose I told you that Willie Snow might be stealing from us, what would you imagine? Maybe I didn't lie with my mouth, but I came awful nigh to doing it with my brains. Needn't be proud of me, Abner. I'm not proud of myself. Oh, well, I had to do it. Can't let our best customers get away from us, not in these days. . . . Mark's fault it was, too, so Willie says."

"Mark means well, Zenas. He's just kind of careless and in too much of a hurry, sometimes."

"Huh! Probably you could say that of a skunk."

"Mark's no skunk."

"I'd be the last one to say he was, wouldn't I?"

"Sartin you would. He's a grand young fellow. Remember, he isn't much more than a boy."

Zenas Bradshaw shrugged. "He's a man and he'll have to begin to act like one pretty soon," he said, as much to himself as to Mr. Hallett. "Either that or . . . Where in the world is he?"

A car drew to the curb and pulled up with a screaming of brakes. Mark Bradshaw ran up the store steps, flung open the door, and burst in. His handsome face was bisected by a broad grin.

"Hey, Grandfather," he shouted, "do you know what I did this forenoon? I took a plane off the ground, flew it for more than an hour, and nobody but myself laid a finger on the controls. Frank Seymour was with me, of course, but he didn't so much as give an order. I took off and I flew and I landed. *I* did. Do you know what that means? Means I can solo pretty soon, Seymour told me so, himself."

He was almost dancing with excitement. His grandfather sighed.

"Millie Fellowes all but stopped trading with us this morning because you were in too much of a hurry to put up her order as it should have been done. She was going to switch her trade to the chain store, and she would have told all hands at that big party that she had switched and why. It would have been repeated all over Harniss. Do you know what that would have meant to us—to Bradshaw's Store? Flying kites is fun, I don't doubt, but business is bread and butter. No, we won't talk about it now. Suppose you get to work instead."

Chapter 2

DURING the balance of that forenoon Zenas Bradshaw was busy. He consulted with Elsie Burgess concerning certain accounts which had, in his opinion, grown as large as they should be until some payment was made; chatted with and gave a small order to a "drummer" from a Boston firm who was showing samples of fishing tackle—for the store, as one of its sidelines, carried an assortment of lures, lines, reels and rods, and the striped-bass season was close at hand. He advised Abner Hallett as to the arrangement of one of the window displays, paid frequent visits to the back room to make sure that Willie Snow was getting his deliveries away promptly, and kept a general supervising eye on the store's activities.

He and Mark exchanged scarcely a dozen words before twelve, but Abner Hallett, who, as he would have said, knew the old man "like a book," noticed a certain abstraction, a troubled look in his employer's gaze when it turned toward his grandson. At least twice Abner was obliged to repeat a question in order to obtain an answer, and when this happened he noticed that Mr. Bradshaw was looking not at him, the questioner, but at Mark.

"Somethin' on the boss's mind," Abner told Miss Burgess, afterward. "'Tain't often you hear him say

'Hey? What's that?' when you speak to him. As a general thing he's got his answer ready afore you're finished askin'. That Millie Fellowes mix-up didn't set too well with him, I guess likely. All Mark's fault 'twas, too, and Zenas knows it. Mark's mind ain't on his job these days. It's over to that flyin' field, and he's there, himself, a good deal more than he'd ought to be. If he belonged to me, I'd—"

Elsie Burgess interrupted. "Oh, you'd do great things, I don't doubt," she broke in, tartly. "Mark is one of the most popular young fellows in this town. You can't expect him to keep his nose in a sugar barrel every minute."

"Be better in a barrel than pointin' up to the clouds —better for the store, anyway. And if he kept his head on the pillow nights instead of rubbin' it against some girl's cheek at dancin' parties 'twould help consider'ble. About the only time he takes a real interest in a customer is when she happens to be young and pretty. I notice there ain't many mistakes in the Thacher orders, not when it is Emmie Thacher that stops in to leave 'em. The sure way to make Mark hop to attention is to have that Thacher girl walk up to the counter. He can forget even his fool flyin' then."

Miss Burgess tossed her head. "He isn't any more attentive to her than he is to—well, to some of the rest of us," she declared. "Or he wouldn't be if she wasn't so silly about him. I saw her chasing him at the party last night. I declare I was almost ashamed of her, making him dance with her all the time. Some of the rest of us hardly got a chance."

Abner Hallett grunted. "So that's where he was," he

24

said. "Might have known it. Shufflin' his feet half the night and flappin' his wings half the day."

"Oh, rubbish! Why shouldn't he have a little fun at his age? We can't all behave like Methuselahs all the time—even if we do have to work in this ark."

Mr. Hallett grinned. "Little mixed on your Bible, ain't you, Elsie? 'Twas Noah skippered the Ark. Methuselah wasn't even a passenger, as I recollect."

"Well"—with sarcasm—"if you can't recollect I don't know who can. *I* wasn't on board, anyhow.... Oh, go away! I've got work to do."

It was the Bradshaw family custom for Zenas and his grandson to take the lunch hour by turns, one going home at noon on Monday, for example, while the other remained at the store, and reversing the order on Tuesday. It was Mark's early turn on this particular day, so he left promptly at twelve. He was back again at one, and Zenas, after a final tour of inspection of the premises, went out and walked toward the little house on Pond Road.

He walked briskly, for his age, and considering his slight lameness, very briskly. His step was firm and his shoulders squared. Acquaintances and friends of both sexes, natives and summer people alike, bowed to him, or exchanged a word of greeting with him as he passed. He turned in at the gate in the white picket fence and entered his home by the side door.

Mrs. Elizabeth Lemon, his housekeeper, called to him from the kitchen. "Sit right down, Zenas," she called. "I'll be right there."

Zenas Bradshaw tossed his hat in the general direction of the sofa in the sitting-room and went on into the dining-room. A comfortable room it was, sunny and bright, with one of its windows crowded with old-fashioned flowering plants, fuchsias, geraniums and begonias, in pots ranged on shelves or hanging in wire baskets. A plump and contented yellow-and-white cat was curled up asleep on the gay cushion of the Salem rocker, and the top of the sewing-machine by the other window was covered with a cloth with a design worked on it in cross-stitch. Over the sideboard hung an oil painting of the original Bradshaw's Store. It, the painting, was the work of a roving artist who had visited Harniss in 1848 and had been commissioned by Marcellus Bradshaw, the First—Zenas's grandfather—to do the job for ten dollars. He, the artist, was said to have admitted it to be the best thing he had ever done. A young friend of Mark's, a student in a Boston art school, to whom it was proudly shown by its present owner, declared soulfully that he wished he could have seen some of the others. Mark laughed, and his grandfather did not understand why.

Zenas Bradshaw liked that painting. He liked the windowful of plants and the cushioned rocker and the braided mats on the floor. He liked the whole room. It had always been like this, or almost like it, as long as he could remember. That was why, after his wife died, he selected Betsy Lemon as his housekeeper. Betsy was a second or third cousin of the Bradshaws, and he knew her tastes were as old-fashioned as his. She was the soul of neatness, a good cook and a hard worker. She had only one drawback, and that was, according to Zenas, her own fault.

"Why on earth she ever married Jake Lemon the Lord only knows," declared Zenas.

Mark, to whom this remark was made, suggested that

26

perhaps Jacob was the only one who ever proposed to her. "Probably it was Jake or nothing," surmised Mark.

"Humph! Then she'd have done better to stick to the nothing. What she got was considerable less."

Zenas pulled his chair up to the table and sat down. Betsy came in from the kitchen with a steaming dish of fish chowder and a cup of coffee. She placed them before her employer, went out, and returned with a plate of hot tea biscuit. "Cream-of-tartar biscuit" she would have called them, and so would Zenas. His mother had often made cream-of-tartar biscuit for him because he was so fond of them.

Mrs. Lemon, having finished serving for the time, wiped her hands on her apron and sat down in the Salem rocker. The yellow-and-white cat, in imminent danger of being crushed, gave vent to a smothered screech of agonized protest. Betsy jumped up and the cat bolted for the shelter of the dining-table, where it sat down to inspect damages.

Zenas Bradshaw laughed uproariously.

"Betsy," he said, "you'll wreck all the morals that cat's got, if you aren't careful. He's swearing yet."

Mrs. Lemon had not entirely recovered from the shock of her surprise. "I—I never!" she sputtered. "I never see such a critter for going to sleep anywheres and—and not giving a body warning. How did I know he was there?"

"He ought to have hung out a 'Don't disturb' sign same as they do in the hotels. Well, I guess he isn't hurt much, except in his feelings. All right, aren't you, Peter?"—stooping to peer under the cloth.

Betsy shook her head. "He may be all right, but how about me? When I felt that soft squashy thing under-

27

neath me I—I—well, I declare I thought I should die."

"So did he, I shouldn't wonder; sounded so. I wish I could swear like that, 'twould be a relief once in a while."

"You do well enough. What have you got to swear about?"

"Oh, this and that, now and again. Mark didn't keep your dinner waiting, did he?"

"No, he is almost always right on hand to the minute."

"Shouldn't wonder if he was—at his meals. Where's Jake?"

The housekeeper's back straightened. There was a distinct reproof in the tone of her reply.

"Jacob is out," she said, stiffly. "He had some business to attend to down street and he told me he wouldn't be home for dinner."

Zenas made no comment. Betsy's husband was the one point upon which he and his housekeeper disagreed. Jake Lemon had come to Harniss, in 1918, from Wapatomac, thirty miles up the Cape, and had, at first, occupied a small room at the Bayside Hotel. Betsy's mother was living then, and she and her daughter took a few boarders in their home on Clark Road. Lemon, after a few weeks at the hotel, moved to the Clark Road house and became star boarder there. He was, so he announced, temporarily disengaged, so far as active employment was concerned, and was in Harniss, looking about for a promising opening. He had been looking, unsuccessfully, ever since.

Betsy's mother died and Betsy carried on, earning a living as boarding-house keeper. When Mrs. Zenas Bradshaw died Zenas was obliged to look for some *one* to keep house for him and his young grandson. Betsy was a distant relative, and he knew her to be capable and a thoroughly good woman, one fit to assist in the bringing up of the boy. He sent for her and made his offer.

"You'll have a home of your own, or what amounts to that," he told her, "and it ought to be easier for you than taking boarders. You're the woman I want, as much for Mark's sake as anything, so . . . Eh? Why, what's the matter? Don't the wages suit you?"

Betsy seemed troubled and more than a little embarrassed. She reddened, hesitated, and fidgeted with her handkerchief.

"The wages are all right, Zenas," she stammered. "Fact is, they're more than you'd ought to pay me. It isn't that at all. You see—well, if you'd asked me only a month—yes, a fortni't ago, I'd have said yes and jumped at the chance. As it is, I—I, well, I can't do it, that's all."

Zenas Bradshaw stared. "Can't do it?" he repeated. "For the land sakes, why? You're all alone in the world, and, except for the boy, so am I. You can't be more than making both ends meet, from what I hear. I'll be at the store most of the daytimes, and Mark will be at school. Why can't you do it? What's stopping you?"

Her expression now was an odd mixture of bashfulness and—yes, pride.

"My husband is what's stopping me, Zenas," she confessed. "You see, I was married yesterday. I am Mrs. Jacob Lemon now. You're the first one to know it except us and the minister. Jacob and I haven't told a soul."

Zenas, when he could say anything, declared himself to be eternally condemned, or words to that effect.

Mrs. Lemon went on to explain. "It's real strange that you should say what you did just now—that about bein' all alone in the world. It's exactly what Mr. Lemon—Jacob, I mean—said to me when he—when we talked it over. He was all alone in the world and so was I, so why shouldn't we be alone together? If you know what I mean."

Mr. Bradshaw was not exactly sure what she meant, but he believed he knew what Jake Lemon had meant and had brought about. That plausible person had secured for himself three square meals a day, a comfortable lodging for the remainder of his life, and some one who would work hard enough to make these advantages a certainty. Zenas would have liked to tell the blushing bride exactly what kind of idiot she was. He did not, however. He requested a little time for consideration.

The following morning he made his amended offer. The Bradshaw house had an extension, an ell with the kitchen and washroom on the first floor and two bedrooms above.

"If you and Jake—"

Betsy interrupted. "I do wish you wouldn't call him that," she put in. "Jacob is a nice, respectable name. There is a Jacob in the Scripture, but there ain't any Jakes there, so far as I ever heard. Mr. Lemon don't like to be called Jake. He thinks it is kind of—well, low."

"Eh? Dear, dear! I'll try to remember. What I was going to say was that if you will come and housekeep for Mark and me, Betsy, you and your—er—Jacob can have those rooms upstairs in the ell for your own. I'll pay you what I said I would. Lemon won't get any wages, but he'll have a place to eat and sleep. Think it over."

Betsy, and presumably her husband, thought it over, and the offer was accepted. The Lemons moved into the ell and had lived there ever since. One of the two upper rooms they furnished as a sitting-room, the other as their bedroom. Betsy attended to the cooking and housework, but, except when her duties took her to the main body of the house, she and her husband kept pretty much to themselves in their own apartment. Zenas, in an early interview with Jacob Lemon, made that arrangement clear. He was diplomatic but firm.

"There'll be times when Mark and I won't want company," he said, "and when you and Betsy won't, either. So the two couples of us better eat separate and live that way. Nothing personal in this, Lemon, just common sense and comfort for all hands, that's all. Nothing like privacy when you want to be private, you'll agree to that."

Mr. Lemon, whatever his inward feelings may have been, expressed dignified approval of the plan. He was always dignified, always suave, always, as his wife said "soft spoken and genteel." He had been a school-teacher at one time, just when or where no one seemed to know, and his one idea in life appeared to be to get on with as little trouble for himself as possible. He rose late, strolled downtown in the morning, returning always in ample time for meals, read in the public library occasionally, or visited the pool and billiard room to watch the bowling matches in the evening—"I was something of an athlete myself in my young days." During the

31

summer months he was usually to be found at the little park by the shore where the summer visitors and motorists came to look off at the view of beach and ocean. There he made it a point to fall into conversation with strangers, volunteering information concerning points of interest, scenic and historical, in the town, and making himself generally agreeable. By these visitors he was regarded as a local oracle, a sort of middle-aged oldest inhabitant, so to speak. "Isn't he wonderful!" "Such a *gentleman!*" These were tributes paid him by maids and matrons among his listeners. They whispered to their masculine escorts: "George, do you think he would be insulted if you paid him a little something for all his trouble? We wouldn't hurt his feelings for the world."

Jacob invariably protested against accepting these offerings, but not strenuously enough to prevent their being thrust upon him.

"I bet you that loafer picks up as much as a couple of dollars in an afternoon," sniffed one disgusted native, who worked from seven in the morning to six at night for very little more than the sum named. "Don't it make you sick? Why, a feller can buy better lemons than him at Bradshaw's for a quarter a dozen."

The rating accorded him by the majority of the permanent population of Harniss was not high, but Miss Loretta Briggs, spinster, librarian in the Harniss public library, was sure he was a "real scholar," and the Reverend Mr. Eustis, the young, recently installed minister of the Methodist Church, found him a very interesting person. "He can talk on almost any subject," observed Mr. Eustis. "I was surprised."

"I'd have been more surprised if he hadn't," was

Zenas Bradshaw's comment when this statement was repeated to him.

As for Mrs. Lemon, she was, outwardly at least, very
proud of him. She hotly resented the slightest hint or
slur concerning her husband, waited upon him like a
slave, and was, or seemed to be, happy in her married
life. If Zenas had any doubts concerning this happiness
he had long ago learned not to express them to her.

Now, after his mistake in referring to Mr. Lemon as
"Jake," he did not mention him again. He ate his
chowder and biscuits and sipped his coffee, his thoughts
busy with the subject which had occupied them the
greater part of that forenoon, namely his grandson.
And, almost as if she were a mind-reader, Betsy's next
remark concerned that same young man.

"You know what I heard up at circle meetin' yesterday?" she asked. "No, course you don't, you wasn't
there. Well, I heard that John Thacher and his wife
didn't like it any too well the way our Mark and their
Emmie are goin' around together these days. Almost as
if they were keepin' company. Dora Smalley said she
got that pretty straight. Her husband is own cousin to
Sarah Ginn, and Sarah's sister Nellie waits on table for
the Thachers. Dora told me that Ike—that's her husband—told Sarah that Nellie heard John and his wife
talkin' about it at supper night before last. Emmie
wasn't there, so they could talk private as they wanted
to."

"Except for Nellie, I presume likely they could."
Zenas was not particularly interested. "Anything else
on the bill of fare, Betsy?"

Mrs. Lemon whisked out to the kitchen and came
back with a large triangle of apple pie. She removed

33

the chowder bowl and replaced it with the plate of pie. Zenas turned his attention to the latter. Betsy regarded him with impatient disapproval.

"My soul and body," she sniffed. "I don't believe you care one single bit. Or didn't you hear what I was sayin'?"

"Eh? Oh, sure, sure, I heard it. Any more coffee in that pot?"

She refilled his cup and returned to her chair. "Well, if you ain't interested, I am," she declared. "I told that Dora Smalley woman so, too. I said: 'Well, I want to know! And if our Mark and their Emily are runnin' around together, what of it?' That's what I said. 'If any Bradshaw ain't good enough for any Thacher then I'd like to know why.' Ever since John Thacher made money out of politics—and how he made it ain't for me to say, though there's plenty of 'em that do—ever since then he's been too big for his boots, and his wife is bigger. I told Dora, I said: 'Even if our Mark wanted to marry Emily,' says I—"

Zenas cut in on the flow. "Here, here!" he interrupted. "What's all this about marrying? Are you trying to tell me that Mark and the Thacher girl are fixing to get married?"

"I didn't say they was, did I? All I said was that even if Mark did want to marry her he had a right to. Nothin' out of the way with that, is there?"

"Not a thing. Nothing wrong with his wanting to get to the moon, either. And there's just about as much likelihood of his getting one want as the other. Either one of 'em would cost money, and Mark hasn't got any. Look here, Betsy, the last time you and I talked about the Thachers you were sure Emmie was setting her cap

34

for that young Davidson fellow, John's first wife's nephew, or whatever he is. He's down here from Boston pretty often nowadays: I thought, myself, he was the likely candidate."

"Zenas Bradshaw, how you do twist things around. I never told you Emily was settin' her cap for him. He's settin' his for her, I don't doubt that a minute, and John Thacher and his wife are helping him set it. They think he's well off and high up in society—his father's a judge or a senator or a policeman or somebody with a pull in politics. So—"

"There, there!" Zenas rose and pushed back his chair. "You better put the rest of the yarn on ice. I must get back to the store. Somebody in this family's got to work."

"Zenas Bradshaw, if that is a hint to me I want you to understand—"

"Shh! Heave to! Come up into the wind, Betsy. Anybody that hinted you wasn't a worker would be crazy. 'Twasn't you I had in mind. So long. See you at supper time. . . . Oh, hello, Jake! Thought you were downtown on business."

Mr. Lemon, who had entered the house by the side door, was in the sitting-room.

"Good afternoon, Zenas," he said, with dignity. "It is beginning to rain, and so, as I have a little cold, I put off my—er—appointment. Pet," addressing his wife, "I'm afraid I'm a little late for dinner. I hate to put you to extra trouble, but—"

Betsy did not let him finish. "My sakes," she protested, "if that was all the trouble I had I'd be a lucky woman. There's plenty of chowder left, and it won't take me but a jiffy to heat it up. Don't you think you'd

35

better change your shoes and stockin's? There's nothin' so bad for a cold as wet feet. You be doin' that, and I'll see to your dinner."

She hurried to the kitchen. Zenas Bradshaw picked up his hat and left the house. A heavy fog had drifted in from the sea, but there was no rain, as far as he could see. Probably Mr. Lemon had been hoping for an invitation to dinner downtown. Perhaps the Reverend Mr. Eustis had suggested such a possibility and had not carried out the suggestion. So Jacob, having been disappointed in that locality, had turned back home, knowing there would be no disappointment for him there. He certainly had that wife of his trotting to his whistle. And Betsy was nobody's fool, either, except when her precious Jacob was concerned. If she had heard another Harniss husband address his wife as "Pet," in the presence of a third party, her derisive comments would have been lengthy and caustic. But she did not resent Jake's calling her that. No, she seemed to like it.

Zenas shook his head. It was beyond his understanding. None of his business, however; he had troubles enough of his own just now.

At the store he found Abner Hallett rearranging the canned-goods shelves, making room for the new shipment which had just come in from the Boston wholesalers. Elsie Burgess was at her desk, but he did not see Mark anywhere.

And then he did see him. He was down at the farther end of the long right-hand counter, near the cheese and butter showcases. He was not alone. There was a girl with him, and they were deep in conversation. It, the conversation, was carried on in a low tone, and it

36

must have been engrossing, for neither of them paid the least attention to him as he walked in their direction.

It was the young woman who first noticed his approach. She turned and spoke.

"Oh, good afternoon, Mr. Bradshaw," she said. "It isn't a very nice day, is it?"

She seemed a little startled and embarrassed, so Zenas thought. Her eyes were reddened slightly, almost as if she had been crying. She had not, of course. What had Emily Thacher to cry about? As pretty as she was, perhaps the prettiest and most popular girl in Harniss, niece and adopted daughter of one of the town's most prominent and prosperous citizens, she could have no reason to cry. Probably he was mistaken; it was the wind and fog which had made her eyes look as they did. They were nice eyes, too. Zenas, old as he was, could still appreciate nice eyes, eyes that looked straight at a person, nothing shifty about them. Zenas Bradshaw liked Emily Thacher: a fine girl.

As to Betsy's intimation that Mark wanted to marry her, that was just "women's talk," nonsense, of course. He—Zenas—could think of no one he would prefer as a granddaughter-in-law, when the proper time came, but that time was not now, nor for a good many years from now. Mark must prove himself competent to take over and carry on the responsibilities of Bradshaw's Store before he could even dream of taking a wife. Well, the boy knew that, he must know it. He was headstrong and careless and—well, possibly a little selfish, but he wasn't a fool. Nothing for his grandfather to worry about along that line, at any rate.

He acknowledged Emily's greeting cheerfully and admitted that the weather was far from perfect. "What are you two looking so sober about?" he asked. "Nothing gone wrong up at your house, Emmie, I hope?"

"Oh, no, no"—hastily. "Everything is all right. I just stopped in a minute to—to—"

Mark finished the sentence for her.

"We were talking about the party last night," he said. "Had a good time, didn't we, Em?"

"Yes. A wonderful time. You are not sick, are you, Mr. Bradshaw?"

"Who? Me? I should say not. Can't spare the time to be sick. What in the world made you ask that?"

"Oh, nothing much. Uncle John said he saw you coming out of Doctor Stevens' office this morning, and I wondered why you were there, that's all."

Mark was surprised. "What were you doing at the doctor's, Grandfather?" he asked. "You didn't tell me you were going."

"Haven't had much chance to tell you anything so far to-day, as I recollect"—a little testily. "Anything special been going on here while I was at dinner? Willie been getting the orders out the way he should?"

"Why—why, yes, I guess so. Why shouldn't he?"

"That's what I asked myself when I found out about the stale bread. I asked him, too. Know what I mean, don't you?"

"What? Oh, you mean about Mrs. Fellowes's order. Abner told me about it. He says the old girl was red-hot but that you cooled her off like an east wind. Nice work, Grandfather. You ought to have been in the diplomatic service, and I always said so."

He should have been—his grandfather had expected him to be—embarrassed and troubled, yes, ashamed of

38

himself, but he showed no signs of either. He actually laughed, as if it were a joke. Yet he should realize that for Bradshaw's to lose one of its most profitable customers was anything but a joke.

Zenas Bradshaw's patience was wearing thin. He was on the point of expressing his feelings with considerable emphasis, but before he could do so there was an interruption. The front door opened and two men entered the store.

One was John Thacher, Emily's uncle—portly, well-dressed, a man of importance and quite aware of the fact. The other was a young fellow of Mark's age, or a year or two older, good-looking, blond, and carrying himself with a smart alertness. He was wearing the uniform of a lieutenant in the National Guard. It, the uniform, was obviously brand new, the cap worn a trifle to one side, the belt polished, the buttons shining like small sums. Zenas recognized him as Laurence Davidson, the relative of the first Mrs. John Thacher to whom Betsy had referred in their recent conversation. Zenas had met Laurie Davidson often before, but it was his first sight of that uniform. He heard Emily utter a smothered exclamation.

"Oh!" she exclaimed.

Zenas turned to look at her. She was shrinking back in the rear of the tall showcase, and the expression on her face had changed from embarrassment to trouble —almost, or so it seemed to him, to alarm. As for Mark, it was the uniform which had caught his attention. He was staring at it and its wearer and scowling as he stared. His fists were clenched and his lips shut tightly. He had been grinning the moment before; he was not grinning now.

39

Zenas couldn't understand it. "What's the matter, boy?" he asked. "You look as if you wanted to bite somebody. What ails you?"

Mark gulped, swallowed, and made an attempt to recover the grin. It was not a very successful attempt.

"Matter?" he repeated. "Why—why, nothing." Then, turning to Emily, "Where did *he* come from?" he whispered.

"I don't know. Aunt Etta didn't expect him for another week, I'm sure."

"Where did he get that rig? What is he wearing it for?"

"He belongs to the Boston Guards. I knew he did, but I can't see why he is in uniform now."

John Thacher was speaking to Abner Hallett, and Hallett was pointing to the trio by the butter and cheese case. Thacher and his young companion walked in that direction. Zenas greeted him with a "Hello, John." Emily stammered. "Oh, hello, Uncle John!" Mark did not speak.

John Thacher acknowledged the Bradshaw greeting with a curt nod. His attention was centered upon his niece.

"What are you doing here, Emmie?" he asked. "Your Aunt Etta and I couldn't imagine where you were. Laurie came unexpectedly and he wants to see you, of course. He can stay only a little while."

Emily and young Davidson shook hands. Zenas put in a word.

"You and my grandson know each other, Laurie, don't you?" he asked. "Why, of course you do. Maybe I ought not to call you by your first name, with those clothes on, though. What are you, on Fourth of July parade or something?"

Laurie Davidson laughed. He had a pleasant laugh and an easy confident manner.

"Not exactly that, sir," he said. "My company is being entertained up at Colonel Francis's country place in Wapatomac to-morrow and we are supposed to show up in full regalia. I came down a day ahead of time so as to get a few hours with Aunt Etta and Uncle John—and you, Emmie, of course. I am off again after breakfast."

Although it was his aunt and uncle whom he mentioned first, it was at Emily he looked—and smiled. John Thacher smiled, too, a knowing smile, an approving smile, or so it seemed to Mark Bradshaw, who, uncomfortably conscious that his white linen jacket was rather crumpled, thereby making it even more of a contrast to Davidson's beautifully fitted uniform coat, stood silent and glum in the background. Zenas noticed neither the smiles nor the contrast in apparel. He did, however, notice that neither of the young men had spoken to the other.

"Know each other, you two, don't you?" he said again, addressing Mark.

Mark's reply was brief. "Sure," he said, gruffly.

Davidson said, "Oh yes, we've met. How are you, Bradshaw?"

Emily, watching them both, seemed to feel the urge to say something.

"I—I'm sorry if I troubled Auntie and you, Uncle John," she stammered, hurriedly. "I—we weren't expecting Laurie so soon and I—I had nothing particular to do, so I went out for—for a walk."

John Thacher observed that it was a poor day to

41

choose for a walk. "The car is outside," he went on, "so I think you had better ride home. Good day, Zenas; I'll see you to-morrow at the Town Improvement meeting. Good day—er—Mark. Come, Emmie."

He led the way to the door. Davidson followed him. Emily lingered a moment. "Good-by, Mr. Bradshaw," she said. "Good-by, Mark. Oh, about this evening—I'm afraid—"

"I know. You'll be busy this evening. Good-by."

The Thachers and their guest went out of the store. Zenas chuckled. "Looks pretty smart in his soldier togs, doesn't he?" he said. "Fine feathers don't always make fine birds, as the saying is, but they help considerable, and that's a fact."

His grandson's speech was delivered almost like a bark.

"Grandfather," he demanded, savagely, "why do I have to wear this damned monkey coat here in the store? Makes me feel like a jackass."

Zenas was very much surprised. He had never before heard the lad swear. Zenas was no model of piety—he used a damn himself when occasion demanded—but, coming from Mark, this one was unexpected. Besides, what reason was there for all this heat?

"Eh? Why, what are you talking about?" he asked. "You agreed with me, when we talked it over a spell ago, that white coats on the clerks made the place look clean and more up to date. They are sort of expected, the regular run nowadays. All hands down at the chain store are wearing 'em. We can't have Bradshaw's playing second fiddle to that outfit, can we?"

Mark's reply was even more savage and unexpected than his first outburst. There was more profanity in it, too.

"Damn the chain store!" he snarled. "Yes, and damn Bradshaw's! I'm sick of them—both of them, if you want the truth."

His grandfather caught his breath. This was more than mere swearing, it was sacrilege.

"What's that you say?" he gasped. "You—you are cussing the store your great-grandfather started and that—that . . . O-oh, oh, *I* see," as the possible explanation crossed his mind. "Yes, yes, I see. It's those soldiers' duds that make you mad. Well, they are pretty, I own up, but they don't go with hard work, not our kind of hard work, son. Weighing out flour and measuring molasses don't call for brass buttons any more than they go with a brass band. No sir-ee, no uniform for the Bradshaws. You'll have to content yourself with the monkey coat, I guess likely."

Mark Bradshaw looked him straight in the eye. "I'll never content myelf with it," he declared. "As for the Bradshaws—well, so far as I can find out, the only Bradshaws who haven't worn a uniform at one time or another are just you—and I. My own father died in uniform."

"Eh? . . . Well, so he did, but that was war time. If—"

Mark did not wait to hear him through. "I'll wear one some day," he vowed, "and when I do it will be one worth wearing, not a dress-up, show-off, country-place chowder-party rig, either. . . . No, I won't listen. You can't make me listen. I've said what I meant and I shall keep on meaning it."

He pushed past his grandfather and started to walk away. Zenas looked after him.

"Boy," he said, to himself, "it *is* high time you and I had that talk."

43

Chapter 3

DURING supper that evening there was little conversation between the two Bradshaws. Zenas was waiting for the meal to end. The "talk" which he had determined must be no longer delayed necessitated a good deal of preliminary thinking on his part. He wanted to say just the right thing in just the right way. The frame of mind in which his grandson seemed to be at the moment, judged by the young fellow's outburst after the departure of the Thachers from the store that afternoon, was not one to combat with a club. Mark was angry, discontented, and inclined to be sullen. Zenas was sure of the reasons for this state of mind. Jealousy and envy were behind it, of course. Jealousy of young Davidson's favor with the Thacher family, John Thacher and his wife. Zenas was inclined to think that Emily's preference was for Mark rather than Laurie, but that meant little: the influence of her uncle and aunt was likely to count for more. The whole affair was, in Zenas's mind, inconsequential, not very important. Boy and girl stuff, he would have called it. He could remember being violently in love at least twice before he was Mark's age and recovering from each attack without so much as a scar. No, that didn't amount to much. Something might come of it, or it might not, but, at any rate, the outcome was a matter for the future, no present worry certainly—in spite of Betsy Lemon's hints and prophecies.

The envy was caused by the contrast between Davidson's glittering uniform and Mark's crumpled store jacket—"monkey coat," he had called it. More boy and girl stuff. Queer, what importance young folks attached to clothes. Laurie had looked grand and spick and span. Mark, in his own estimation, had looked—and, of course, felt—plebeian and shabby and humiliated. And the girl was there to note the contrast in apparel and self-assurance. Silly, almost funny—but not to Mark. Zenas was far too wise to laugh, but it was funny, just the same.

Mark, having finished his supper, went into the sitting-room. Zenas lingered a moment to light a cigar and then followed him. He was just in time to see his grandson, hat in hand, on the way to the outer door.

"Hello! Where are you bound?" he asked.

"Oh, I'm going out for a little while," was the absent-minded answer.

"Where to, especially?"

"Nowhere in particular, just down street, that's all."

"Why not stay home, for a change?"

"What for?"

"Well, for one reason, to keep me company. Maybe I'm lonesome. Don't seem to see much of you these days and nights."

"You see me all day long in the store."

"Not every day. Not this morning, for instance."

"Eh? This morning? Oh, that—well, yes, I was out a while this morning. Over at the flying field. Seymour said he would take me up with him and give me a chance to handle the plane. I did, too. Handled it as well as he could have done, Frank said so himself. . . . But I told you about that."

45

"So you did. Sit down a few minutes, son. I want to talk to you."

"Oh, not to-night, Grandfather. I don't feel like talking."

"Maybe so, but, you see, I do. Come back here and sit down."

"No. I'm going out."

Zenas looked at him. "Probably you didn't hear me plain," he said, slowly. "I said sit down."

It was an order this time, and Mark had been trained to obey orders. Zenas expected prompt, if reluctant, compliance. He was handed a very real surprise. Instead of returning to the sitting-room, Mark kept on through the hall, opened the outer door, and left the house, closing the door behind him.

The cigar fell from Zenas Bradshaw's lips to the floor, landing in the middle of the hooked rug which Great-grandmother Letitia Bradshaw had made with her own hands many years before. Zenas was unmindful of its fall. He continued to stare at the closed door until the smell of scorching wool reminded him of the need for action in an emergency. He bent, snatched up the cigar, and planted a number nine shoe on the smoldering rose in the rug. Then he thrust the cigar into his mouth once more and sat heavily down in the Salem rocker.

This was unprecedented, this was something entirely new. There had been evasions of his authority before, plenty of them, many differences of opinion, and some lengthy arguments and debates which had ended in obedience or, occasionally, in compromise. This, how-ever, was open, flat rebellion. This was ominous. Zenas had been amazed and shocked when Mark had pro-fanely condemned Bradshaw's that afternoon, after

46

Emily Thacher, her uncle, and their guest had left the store. But he had not taken the outburst too seriously. Now, however, he was wondering if he had taken it seriously enough. Perhaps—yes, it looked as if there was something real behind that damn.

Zenas Bradshaw, however, was no quitter. Opposition —and he had encountered plenty of it in his life—only made his chin squarer and his will to win stronger. In a way, this rebellion on his grandson's part might be a good thing. He had told himself that he and the young man should have their important understanding that very night. Now he *knew* they were going to have it, even if he, Zenas, was obliged to wait in that sitting-room until daybreak.

He found the *Weekly Item,* the Ostable *Banner's* successor, in its wrapper on the side table where Betsy had put it with the other non-business mail. There was a letter there addressed to Mark, and its address was—he noticed this particularly now—in feminine handwriting. He pushed it impatiently aside, tore open the *Item's* wrapper, and, cigar in mouth and newspaper in hand, went back to the rocker.

He finished the cigar and lit another. When the second one was smoked down to the last inch he waited a half-hour or so, then filled his pipe and puffed at that. He read the *Item* from its front page, "General News of the County," to its fourth page, "South Harniss Jottings."

It was twelve-thirty when the side door opened and Mark came in. Mark was a surprised young man when he saw his grandfather sitting in the Salem rocker.

"What are you doing up at this hour of the night?" he demanded.

47

Zenas looked at him, over his spectacles.

"Just what I've been doing since you went out," he replied, crisply. "Waiting."

"Waiting! Waiting for what?"

"Waiting for you to do what I told you to do four or five hours ago—that is, to sit down and listen.... No, you'll have your chance to talk when I've finished, but I'll speak my piece first. Sit down, boy."

Mark hesitated a moment, seemed about to speak, then to think better of it, shrugged, and sat. Zenas crossed his legs and spoke.

His was a fairly long preachment, although he used few unnecessary words. He began by giving a brief, condensed history of Bradshaw's Store, how the business was founded by the first Zenas, carried on by the first Marcellus, and how it had since been carried on by successive Zenases and Marcelluses to the present day.

"You know all this, boy," he said, "but I'm running over it again because I don't want you to forget what Bradshaw's Store means to us Bradshaws and how close it is tied up with me and you, as well as with all our folks who are dead and gone. It's been our living, the family living, for more than a hundred years. It has been my living since I was a young-one. It had been my main interest in life, and I looked forward to Zenas—your father, I mean—carrying it on when he got back from the war. Well, he didn't come back, of course, so I had to keep on with the carrying, looking forward to the time when you would be old enough to take over, and ease my shoulders a little mite."

He paused and knocked the ashes from his pipe into the saucer on the table beside him, and then continued.

"And so," he said, "that fetches me to what I've been

48

leading up to. You *are* old enough. You're twenty-one; it don't seem possible, but it's so. This age business"— he shifted uneasily in the rocker—"this business of getting old—er—older, is something we don't any of us really realize when it's happening, I mean. We keep on having birthdays, but we don't pay much attention to 'em until, first thing we know, something or somebody reminds us of how many we've had. The other day I happened to hear a young fellow in the post-office speak of me as 'old Zenas Bradshaw.' He didn't know I heard him, but I did. Lordy, yes, I heard him!"

He paused once more, then shook his head, as if to free it from the unpleasant recollection, and went on, more crisp and business-like this time.

"However," he said, "that's to one side. It is you I started to talk about. It's you—you and the store. Mark, you've been on my mind pretty steady for some time. I haven't spoke of it to you before, but it has seemed to me that, for a twenty-one-year-old man, and a Bradshaw, you aren't heart and soul in that store, the way you ought to be—the way you've got to be from now on."

He paused, waiting for Mark to say something in protest, make some comment, at least. Mark, however, said nothing. His grandfather drew a long breath and then added another sentence.

"This morning," he continued, "somebody else—an outsider—said the same thing about you to me."

Mark leaned forward. "Who?" he asked, sharply. "Who's been talking about me behind my back? . . . Was it John Thacher?"

"Eh? John Thacher! Why the devil should John Thacher talk to me about you? What on earth—"

49

"All right. I didn't know but—oh, never mind. It wasn't Thacher, then. Who was it?"

Zenas Bradshaw had no idea of telling any one, even his grandson, of the conversation with Doctor Stevens in the latter's office that morning. The doctor, he knew, would not tell, and he certainly would not. His answer to Mark's question was promptly evasive.

"It wasn't anybody with a grudge against you, you can take my word for that. And it wasn't your damning the store, as you did this afternoon, that set me to saying these things, either."

"I didn't really mean all that, Grandfather."

"Course you didn't, I don't doubt that. But, Mark, you have been—well, kind of loafing on the job, as you might say, for some time. You've been careless and letting your store work slip along any old how. Abner's noticed it, but he's your friend and he stands up for you. Elsie must notice it, but she's all for you, too. I must say"—with a one-sided grin—"you have the trick of making folks like you, boy, and that's a big help in anybody's life, it certain is. . . . However, that don't change the fact that you've got to settle down. You've got to quit staying up three-quarters of every night and chasing off to that flying field, or somewhere, every other day. You've got to—"

"Grandfather." Mark's interruption was quick and sharp.

Zenas was startled by its tone. "Eh?" he exclaimed. "Why—well, yes, what is it?"

"Grandfather, I'm glad you said that."

"Said what? I've been saying considerable many things, or I thought I had. Which one do you mean?"

"That about the flying field. Grandfather, that's what I want to do. It's what I'm going to do."

Zenas Bradshaw did not understand. "You mean you're going to keep on going over to that field, same as you've been doing?" he repeated, incredulously. "In spite of what I've been saying? Look here"—his indignation rising. "Do you think I've been sitting up here three-quarters of the night just for fun? Do you think I'm talking myself hoarse just for the pleasure of hearing myself? Do you think I'm fooling? Because if you do—"

"Oh, I don't—I don't! I know you're not fooling. I know the store means more to you than anything else in creation. Heavens and earth! I ought to know it, hadn't I? I've heard it ever since I was a kid. *I* know I was born to be a part of that store, just as much a part of it as the scales on the counter. Yes, and with just about as much to say as to what I want to be and do as those scales have."

"Now, see here, Mark—"

"No. I've started and now I'm going to get this off my chest. When I was a kid I just took it for granted, never thought much about it, but since I've grown up I've thought a lot more. Lately I've been thinking of mighty little else. Grandfather, I'm not going to spend my life in a grocery store. I'm going to fly."

Still Zenas did not understand. "Fly?" he repeated. "Well, you've been flying, haven't you? Flew this morning, you told me. All right, I'm not saying you shan't. I don't like the notion of your risking your neck up aloft there, but, after all, it's your own neck and you are old enough to be responsible for it, I suppose likely. If you want to risk it, in your spare time, I can't stop you. Don't know as I would so much as try, although it

51

seems a mighty silly risk, to my way of thinking. In your *spare* time, as I said before. But not in your working time—no sir! Your working time belongs to Bradshaw's Store. It belongs to it now, and it's always going to belong to it. And when you step off I hope there'll be a son of yours to pick up the load, same as I did, and my father did, and— What are you shaking your head like that for?"

Mark did not hesitate. "I'm shaking it because I don't agree with you. You're all wrong, Grandfather. I'm not going to belong to the store always. I don't really belong to it now, at least only part of me, and that part just because it is paying me wages. I'm not interested in it—not really."

Zenas Bradshaw sat back in the rocker so heavily that that ancient piece of furniture cracked in protest. "What!" he gasped. "Not interested in the store that— that your folks have—"

"Oh, don't say all that again! I am interested, I suppose, in a way, but not the way you are. I don't like the work and—well, I'm not going to stick at it forever. I'm not going to stay in Harniss forever, either."

"Harniss? Why, what's the matter with Harniss, for mercy's sake? It's as up and coming a town as there is in Ostable County. Why— See here, boy, you haven't been drinking, have you?"

"No. That is, unless you call one glass of beer drinking. I had that at the bowling alley, but that's all."

"Don't want to stick in Bradshaw's Store? What's the matter with you? Where's your ambition? Or haven't you got any?"

"Of course I have. That's just it. Maybe I'm too ambitious. Grandfather, let me do what I want to. I want to

52

fly, I tell you. I want to learn how to handle an airplane. I want to earn my pilot's license and get to be a regular airman. Frank Seymour says I'll make a good one."

Zenas thought he glimpsed the influence behind all this. Confound that Seymour fellow!

"Humph!" he grunted. "So Frank Seymour has been filling you full, has he? He better mind his own business." Then, choking back his anger, he went on in a milder tone.

"Now, now, Mark," he expostulated. "You are just letting your—your fancy run away with you. You haven't thought this thing through. You don't mean that you want to make a—a real steady job out of navigating one of those things. Course you don't. They are all right for playing around in, or carrying some mail maybe, or in wartime—"

Mark broke in eagerly. "There you are, Grandfather!" he exclaimed. "You've said it yourself. There is a war now."

"Eh? Why, yes, there's a war over across the ocean, but that's a long, long way from our side. You wasn't figuring to go over there and fight in your flying machine, was you? If the United States was in the war—but it isn't."

"Maybe it's going to be some day. Lots of people think it may be. Grandfather, this country has never been in a war without at least one of our family fighting. Every man Bradshaw from the beginning has been in the army or the navy when there was a war on. . . . That is—well, every one of them except—"

"Except me, you mean. That's true enough."

Mark's face was red. He had blundered and knew it. "That wasn't your fault, Grandfather," he hastened to explain. "You were going in. You would have enlisted somehow, in spite of your age—yes, and fought the Spaniards if you hadn't smashed your leg. Tell me, honestly: if this country did go to war you wouldn't stop my enlisting, would you?"

"No-o. No, I probably wouldn't. But there's time enough for that when the war gets here. Then it might be your duty to sign on. Just now your duty is alongside me in the store."

"But, don't you see? If I go to war I want to go as somebody worth-while. I want to know how to be some good to our side. If I am a trained air pilot—"

"Oh, bosh! Mark, what ails you is that fuss-and-feathers uniform young Davidson had on. That's what's throwing you off balance, that and the Thacher girl being on hand to look you both over."

This was a mistake. It was Mark's turn to straighten in his chair. The excited eagerness in his face changed to a different, not a less stubborn, but more sulky expression.

"All right," he muttered. "I knew there would be no use telling you. You wouldn't understand. I have told you, though, and you can't say I didn't."

Zenas had been holding a tight rein on his patience. Now that hold slipped.

"You are the one who doesn't understand, boy," he declared. "You don't understand that uniforms and airplanes and girls are pretty to look at, a whole lot prettier than ground coffee and corn meal and potatoes, but they don't pay the freight—and the potatoes and the rest of it do. You've got a living to earn, and your job is to buckle down and earn it. I need you in the store a darn sight more than Frank Seymour—yes, or Emmie Thacher

54

—needs you. And I'm telling—ordering you, if you must have it—to quit playing and go to work. There! That's the end. I'm going to bed."

It was not quite the end. Mark asked another question. "Why do you need me so much?" he demanded. "Abner is there, and he knows the business a whole lot better than I do. You could hire somebody to take my place as clerk."

"Certain I could. But who would I have to be the next owner of Bradshaw's Store and run it after I'm gone? I went to see Doctor Stevens this morning and he—"

He stopped short. His grandson waited a moment and then said: "Yes? Why did you go there? You told Emmie you weren't sick."

"Sick? Me? Not likely."

"Then why did you go to the doctor?"

"Eh? Why not? He and I are old chums. Good night."

"Good night, Grandfather."

Mark was regarding him thoughtfully as he moved toward the hall and stairs.

Zenas made no mention of the conversation when the pair met at the breakfast table next morning. It was Mark who referred to it, and then not until the meal was almost over.

"Grandfather," he said, slowly, "I've been thinking."

Zenas stirred his coffee. "Um-hm," he observed. "Well, a little thinking, once in a while, isn't bad exercise for anybody. Am I supposed to ask what you were thinking about?"

"I was thinking about you."

"Oh."

"Yes. I wish you weren't so stubborn."

"What? Stubborn? *Me?*"

55

"Yes, you. I wish you weren't because—because I can be pretty stubborn myself. I suppose it runs in the family."

This was a new idea. Zenas Bradshaw would never have considered himself a stubborn man. Determined— oh, yes. A little inclined to have his own opinions and stand for them, possibly. They were good opinions, or he wouldn't have them, of course, but he was always willing to listen to argument. He wasn't stubborn. To be stubborn meant—meant—well, he objected to the term.

"Humph!" he grunted. "So we are stubborn, we Bradshaws, are we? Never heard us called that before."

"I don't suppose you have. Grandfather, why won't you tell me what Doctor Stevens said to you when you went to see him yesterday? I have asked you two or three times."

Zenas hesitated. "It didn't amount to anything, any of it," he grumbled. "Not worth talking about."

"He didn't tell you that you had anything serious the matter with you, did he?"

"Eh?"—indignantly. "No, he didn't. Course he didn't."

"Well, I didn't know. You are older than you used to be, and—"

"Shut up! What kind of foolishness is this? Certain I'm older than I used to be; so is everybody, far as that goes. And none of 'em likes to be reminded of it, either. For heaven's sake talk about something else. . . . Come on. Time we were at the store."

He rose from the table. Mark followed his example, but more slowly.

"You kept saying—last night, I mean—that you needed me at the store. You don't really need me, you know. Ab Hallett is twice as good a store man as I am."

56

"Maybe he is now, but he wouldn't be if you put your mind to your job. And he isn't a Bradshaw. I was talking just for your own good, boy, yours and Bradshaw's Store's."

Mark drew a long breath. "All right," he said. "All right, I'll try—for a while."

Zenas let it go at that. The victory was his, and he could afford to be magnanimous. His grandson was sound enough, underneath. The young fellow had been thinking, he said so, and common sense had won out against frivolity and the playboy stuff, as it was bound to in a Bradshaw. The older man talked a good deal as they walked toward Main Street together. His talk was of town affairs and the weather and neighborhood matters; intimate and important topics he avoided carefully. Mark said scarcely a word.

During the following month Harniss moved on at its usual jog-trot pace, a pace that was slowing perceptibly as the summer season ended and the fall began. The hotel closed, and most of the boarding-houses followed suit. The cottages owned or rented by sojourners from the cities were, the majority of them, kept open, for September and October are, in Ostable County, two of the pleasantest months in the year.

At Bradshaw's Store Zenas thought he noticed a general speeding up of tempo and an increasing smoothness in the daily routine. Mark was, apparently, paying less attention to outside matters and more to business. The store, in accordance with the agreement among the town's shopkeepers, closed at noon on Wednesdays, and Mark spent that free afternoon at the flying field. His grandfather learned this from Abner Hallett or from post-office gossip; Mark never mentioned it himself, nor did Zenas question him. After all, it was a mistake to whip a willing horse, and so long as the "fool flying"— Zenas always thought of it as that—did not interfere with the welfare of Bradshaw's Store, he would not remonstrate. When, on those Wednesday afternoons, or on Sundays, an airplane whirred overhead, he shivered, thinking of whom it might be carrying and the catastrophic consequences of a possible crash, but he did not voice his forebodings to any one.

On one occasion, when John Thacher, at a meeting of the Improvement Society, made a rather disparaging remark concerning the "racket and nuisance of those confounded things," and the members, most of them, expressed agreement, as they usually did with Mr. Thacher's opinions, it was Zenas who defended the planes.

"We might as well get used to 'em, John," he said. "If what the newspapers and the radio are telling us is so we are liable to hear and see more of 'em rather than less. May possibly be that we'll be glad to know they're up there—always provided they're the right kind."

John Thacher snorted disdainfully.

"Good Lord, Zenas!" he exclaimed. "You don't think *we* are going to get into this war, do you?"

"No-o, don't know's I do, but you can't be sure. I recollect hearing my father tell how, when Abraham Lincoln was elected the first time, there was a lot of talk about war, but nobody around here really believed there would be one. The Government seems to think we'd better have an anchor to windward. It's spending money enough for training camps and the like of that."

58

Mr. Thacher expressed his opinion of the Administration and its extravagance. Incidentally, he prophesied its downfall in the November election.

"Of course," he added, cautiously, "I am in favor of putting our country in adequate shape for defense. In fact, I consider Camp Scott and similar enterprises necessary—er—evils, everything considered. Although"—with a dubious shake of the head—"why the Camp was located just where it is I confess I don't understand. Politics and graft, I suppose; the country is rotten with them."

Camp Scott was the huge military training establishment—it provided housing quarters for thirty thousand men, so it was said—nearing completion in the once-wooded area between Fairview and Wapatomac, fifty miles from Harniss. Carpenters, plumbers, and mechanics of all kinds, drawn from every community in the county and from as far as Boston in the other direction, were laboring there in night and day shifts. At least twenty Harniss men were employed there, and they returned home each Saturday with money in their pockets, for wages were high indeed.

There was some volunteering, also. And the papers were prophesying compulsory military service. The impromptu debating societies at the post-office and in the stores and the poolroom had heated sessions. The nearing of Election Day gave a political tinge to the arguments. John Thacher would never have called himself an Isolationist, but he waxed oratorical concerning the crime of sending our boys to fight other countries' battles abroad.

"Politics, the whole of it," he declared. "Politics and graft. Now, mind you, I am not saying—"

Betsy Lemon summed up his remarks in one of her own.

"He's always reminding you what he ain't saying," she observed, "but he keeps on saying it, just the same. Or the same as saying it. If I was to tell you that I wasn't exactly calling anybody—my husband, for instance—a liar, what would you think I was calling him?"

Zenas Bradshaw, to whom the question was put, answered absently. "You usually call him 'Lovey,' don't you?" he said. Betsy switched out of the room and slammed the door behind her.

Election Day came, and the Administration was retained in control of the nation. Political arguments and speeches ceased to fill the columns of the papers, and the war in Europe took up the space. In Harniss the last of the cottages closed and the town settled down to its winter routine. People began to talk of Thanksgiving and even of Christmas.

At Bradshaw's Store there was the usual falling off of business, a falling off which, because of the keen competition of the new chain store, was more noticeable than usual. The less well-to-do in the community could buy for cash a trifle cheaper at the chain store than at Bradshaw's, and the custom of those of them who could not, or did not, pay cash was a doubtful asset. If Zenas was worried he did not show it, and certainly never spoke of it. Bradshaw's had faced competition and hard times before and had come through the fight with colors flying. Whining did not help. Roll your sleeves higher and work harder, that was his remedy for such ailments.

He did not visit Doctor Stevens again, although the doctor dropped in on him occasionally. "I'm A1," was his invariable answer to the medical man's question.

60

"Quit asking me how I feel, Ben. I'm too busy to think about feelings. Sorry, but I can't spend my money on you these days. Run along and pester Millie Fellowes, why don't you? They tell me Millie run afoul of a skunk in her backyard a couple of weeks ago and hasn't been herself since. Don't know how the skunk is; haven't heard."

Emily Thacher visited the store almost daily, for she did most of the Thacher marketing. It was Mark who waited on her, as a usual thing, but Zenas made it a point to chat with her whenever he was disengaged. He liked the girl immensely. She was as sensible and straightforward as she was pretty. One day in mid-November he chanced to ask her if she had heard from or seen young Davidson recently.

"I haven't seen him for some time," she said. Mark was standing near, and Zenas noticed that he and Emily exchanged glances. Emily was very sober and quiet that day. Zenas remembered afterward that he had not seen her smile at all while she was in the store.

"What's this I hear about Laurie being up at Camp Scott?" he asked. "Seems to me somebody said he was a regular officer in the army up there now."

Emily nodded. "He is," she replied. "He has his commission as Lieutenant. It was given him last week."

"Humph! You don't say. That's on account of his Guard training, I presume likely. What does your Uncle John think of that? He's been kind of down on all this war training business, as I recollect. Seems to figure we ought to stop playing soldiers and attend to our own business."

Again there was that quick exchange of glances between the two young people. Mark looked as if he was about to speak, but Emily spoke first.

"Oh, Uncle has changed his mind about that," she said. "He says that, as long as we're going in for all this soldiery, we ought to turn out the best soldiers we can as quickly as we can. He would probably have objected if Laurence had volunteered as a—as a private, but since he is an officer—well, that is a different matter. Uncle John is pleased and Aunt Etta is delighted. She talks of practically nothing else."

There was a trace of bitterness in this statement, or so Zenas thought. He noticed that her foot was patting the floor as she voiced the last sentence.

"Um-hm," he observed. "I shouldn't wonder. Women do like to see their men folks dressed up and with handles to their names. It doesn't amount to much, really. About the biggest dumb-head this town ever turned out went up to Boston and got a job as door-opener at some theater show up there. You ought to have seen *his* uniform. Whew!" He laughed at the memory.

Emily did not laugh. "But, Mr. Bradshaw," she asked, earnestly, "if some one you knew, somebody you cared about the way—well, the way Aunt Etta and Uncle John care for Laurie, was to go into the service, you had rather see him go in as a trained officer than just volunteer as—as a private, wouldn't you?"

"Eh? Don't know as I would. My own boy—Mark's father—was a private when he enlisted in the last war. He was a sergeant, though, when—when he was killed over across."

"And you were proud of him, weren't you?"

"Why, certain sure I was proud of him. They gave him—a medal, or gave it to me and his mother after he

62

was dead. I've got it at home now, wouldn't sell it for a thousand dollars. Show it to you sometime."

"I've seen it."

"You have? When?"

Emily's cheeks reddened. "Oh, I happened to call at your house, and—and Mark showed it to me."

"Did, eh? Hm! He never told me you were there."

"Oh, I just happened by. But what I mean is—is that, in this war—the war we *may* be in—it is the trained man that seems to count. This is a mechanical war, that's what the papers call it, a mechanical war, and the soldier who is trained for some particular branch of service is worth ever so much more to his side than the one who isn't. And if he does train and gets to be a trained officer and—and to command other men, he ... Oh, I am just talking, I suppose. I must go, anyway."

She hurried to the door. Zenas watched her, with a pucker between his brows.

"Now what in the world was all that for?" he asked. "Seemed a little bit pleased, herself, about that Davidson fellow's getting his commission, wouldn't you think?"

Mark made no reply, and when his grandfather turned to look at him he was at the other end of the store.

Two days afterward Mark left on his trip to Boston. Zenas had intended going, for he was accustomed to make monthly trips to the city to look over stocks at the wholesalers' and to order supplies, but he had a slight cold, and his bad leg was troubling him more than usual. Nothing but a touch of rheumatism, of course; nevertheless the prospect of tramping the pavements and of the round of calls and business talks was not alluring.

"Why don't you let me go, Grandfather?" Mark suggested.

Zenas regarded him thoughtfully. "That's a notion," he said, slowly. "You might go, I suppose. There's nothing very important, nothing you couldn't do as well as me—if you'd set your mind to it. Yes, you could go, only—"

"Only what?"

"Only—well, nothing, I guess. You ought to know how to buy, as well as sell, that's a fact. If you want to take a shy at it, go ahead. I'll give you a note to Spencer, up at Colton, Howes, and Company, and to Barbour, and a couple of others. Go, if you want to. I'll stay home and take care of the store and my rheumatics, blast 'em!"

Mark regarded him oddly. "Look here, Grandfather," he asked. "You're all right, aren't you?"

"All right? What do you mean by that? Certain I'm all right. Why wouldn't I be?"

"I mean you're not sick—or—"

"For the Lord's sake stop telling me I'm sick! Who said I was? If Ben Stevens—"

He stopped short. His grandson did not seem satisfied.

"Yes?" he urged. "Go on. What about Doctor Stevens?"

"Nothing about him. He's pretty nigh as old as I am and thinks and talks twenty years older. Don't bother me now. Between having to listen to Betsy and her Jacob talking Hitler to death in the kitchen, and this pesky leg of mine, I'm fed up, as the boys say. Go to Boston. Only don't buy any lemons up there: there's enough of that kind of fruit right here on the premises already."

Mark left for the city the next morning. His grandfather expected him to return home the following afternoon, but he did not come. Nor did he on the day after that, nor the next. Zenas could not understand the delay. When, at noon of the fourth day, the bus which connected with the train at Ostable passed the door of Bradshaw's Store without stopping to deliver a passenger, he began to worry. He was worried when he went home for dinner, but when Mrs. Lemon declared that she didn't see where on earth Mark had got to, his reply to her remark was elaborately indifferent.

"He's got to Boston, I suppose likely," he observed. "And when he's got through with his jobs up there I shouldn't be surprised if he got here. I don't imagine he's been kidnapped, so I wouldn't begin to advertise for him in the papers, if I was you, Betsy."

Jacob Lemon, who happened to be passing through the dining-room, offered a suggestion.

"Time slides along a good deal faster in a big city than it does down here," he observed, with a condescending smile. "Especially for a young fellow Mark's age. There are—ahem—a good many things to keep him interested. I can remember—well, never mind. Don't let it fret you, Zenas."

"Thanks, I won't." Then, regarding Mr. Lemon with solemn admiration, he added: "I'll bet you were an up and coming lad in your day, Jake. No city slicker ever put anything over on you, eh?"

Jacob's self-satisfied smile broadened. His wife felt called upon for a word. "Jacob was always smart," she declared, proudly.

Zenas rose from the table. "Um-hm," he agreed. "Nobody ever sold *him* a gold brick—not for cash, anyhow."

He went out of the house. Betsy looked after him.

"Sometimes I've thought Zenas didn't appreciate you the way he'd ought to, Lovey," she said. "But maybe he's beginning to. What he said then sounded so, didn't it?"

She was perfectly sincere, but her husband seemed unappreciative. "Don't be a bigger fool than you can help," he snapped.

Mark came back late that evening, driving over from the Ostable station with a friend who was there with his car to meet an expected guest. The store was closed, so the car delivered him at the door of the Bradshaw home. His grandfather had finished supper and was in the sitting-room alone. No one would have guessed, from the tone of his greeting, that he had felt the slightest worry, or any relief when the young man entered.

"Hello," he said. "How are you, eh? Well, well! Glad to see you, boy. Had a good trip?"

"Yes. I ordered everything on your list and a few items on my own hook. I think you'll be satisfied, Grandfather. I hope you will."

"Sure—sure I will. You get your supper now, and we'll talk about it all later. Betsy'll have something for you, I know."

Mark put his bag in the hall, hung his hat and coat on the rack, and returned to the sitting-room.

"I don't want any supper," he said. "Had a couple of sandwiches and some coffee at the drug-store in Ostable. The train was late, and I had a big lunch before I left Boston. No, I don't want any more. Sit still, Grandfather, please. I—I've got something to tell you."

"Course you have. What kept you so long in Boston? I was expecting you two days ago."

"I know. I'm going to explain about that. First of all,

though, I want you to understand that I didn't neglect the buying and the other store business. I did it all—all I could do."

"You've said that once."

"I know I have. I spent my first day doing what you sent me there to do. Then, the next day—"

He hesitated. Plainly he was finding it hard to go on. Zenas Bradshaw's uneasiness was returning. The young fellow was troubled about something. He looked—he looked queer enough, and that was a fact.

Zenas leaned forward in his chair. "Next day?" he repeated. "What did you do the next day? What is all this, anyhow? Have you done something you're ashamed of?"

Somehow this seemed to be just the spur Mark needed. His answer was prompt this time, no hesitation at all.

"No," he declared, with decision. "I'm not ashamed of what I did. Why should I be? It is what I've wanted to do for ever so long. It is what I made up my mind to do months ago; only now I have done it, that's all. I've—Oh well, let me get it off my chest, then we'll both have our say afterwards. Grandfather—Grandfather— Gosh! this is even harder to tell than I knew it was going to be! Grandfather—"

"What the devil is all this? Stop stuttering! What have you done?"

"I have enlisted in the army as a flying cadet. I've passed my physical and mental examinations and been accepted. I have taken the oath. They let me have four days' leave to come here and tell you and then pack up and get ready. I am to report next Tuesday morning at the base and then I'll be sent somewhere—I don't know where—to a civilian flying school. After that—well, I don't know much of anything about after that. In the end, though, if I get through all right, I'll be a Second Lieutenant in the flying service of the United States Army.... There! I've told you and you can call me any-thing you care to. Perhaps I deserve it. In a way I suppose I do."

He stopped, his fingers tightly gripping the arms of his chair. He was, obviously, waiting for the explosion.

But there was no explosion. Zenas Bradshaw said not a word. He was looking at his grandson, but he was not aware of doing so. It was not Mark he saw. Instead, in his mind's eye, he was viewing the months and years ahead—many or few as it might be, in all likelihood not very many for him, certainly. He saw all his plans for the future of Bradshaw's Store, the plans with Mark as partner and eventual proprietor, utterly and completely smashed. He saw his hope of "taking it easy," in accord-ance with Doctor Stevens's insistent urging, thrown into the discard. He saw the business, founded by the first Zenas Bradshaw ever so long ago and carried on as a family tradition and worshiped as a family fetish ever since—he saw that business guided by a rapidly aging cripple, himself, for a time and then turned over to some one else, Abner Hallett, probably. And how far and to what end Abner, on his own hook, would carry any business was an uncertain question. He saw all this and much more. It was as if one of the bombs, which he read of daily in the papers as falling upon the English cities and towns, had been dropped upon all his hopes and schemes and dreams and blown them to bits. Noth-ing was left—nothing at all except a lonely old age and complete disillusionment.

Mark, watching him anxiously and waiting for him to speak, could wait no longer.

"Grandfather," he faltered, "I know this is pretty tough for you. I'm awfully sorry."

Zenas came out of his trance. He drew a long breath. "Sorry?" he repeated. "What for? That you enlisted?"

"No"—indignantly. "Of course I'm not sorry for that. If there was any question of my being sorry in that way I shouldn't have done it."

"So I judged. Then what are you sorry for?"

"Why, that—that I have to—to leave you and—and the store. I know what Bradshaw's means to you, and—"

"Humph!" Zenas Bradshaw rose and walked over to the side table where his tobacco tin stood. He opened the tin, took his pipe from his pocket, filled and lit it. The hand holding the match was shaking, and he turned his back upon Mark so that the tremble might not be noticed.

"Boy," he said, calmly, "Bradshaw's Store was running what you might call a considerable length of time before you went to work in it. I was running it then and I'm running it now. You've really done this thing, you say? Couldn't back out, even if you wanted to?"

"No. And I don't want to."

"I judged that, too. Then we won't waste time being sorry. You figure to be wearing a uniform some of these days, eh?"

"I certainly do."

"Yes, yes. Well, I hope, when you get it, it will take the shine off Laurie Davidson's. That will be something to look forward to, eh? . . . Well, what do you say we go to bed? You can tell me all the rest to-morrow morning."

69

Chapter 4

THE morning session was held, after breakfast, in Mark's own bedroom on the second floor of the Bradshaw home. Mark was eager to talk and would have told the exciting story of his Boston experiences as soon as his grandfather sat down at the table in the dining-room, but Zenas motioned for silence and, after Betsy went to the kitchen, explained why he did so.

"There'll be enough advertising of all this by and by," he said. "All Harniss will be chewing it over before the week is out. Of course I realize Uncle Sam can hardly wait to get his—what-d'ye-call-it?—flying service, rounded out and made perfect, but—well, how long has he resigned himself to do without you? How long can you stay here with us?"

That Mark recognized the sarcasm in the tone of the question was plain enough.

"They gave me four days' leave," he replied, curtly.

"I see. And this is the second day of the four. Um-hm. Then my advice would be to give the news to as few peo₁le as possible until you are on your way. No use to start the cackling until the egg is laid."

"But it is laid. I have passed the examinations and taken the oath. I told you that last night."

"I know; I haven't forgotten. Then let's put it that

the cackling better not begin until the pullet's off the nest. *You* won't have to hear it, anyway."

"Look here, Grandfather!"—hotly. "If you think I care what—"

"Shh! Shh! Course you don't. Neither do I, but seems to me it might be pleasanter for both of us, in the couple of days we'll have together, to spend the time talking over our own business instead of having to hear outsiders talk it over for us. . . . There, there! Here comes one of the advertisers. We'll finish this upstairs."

Betsy came in from the kitchen, and the rest of the meal was eaten almost in silence. Mrs. Lemon remarked upon the shortage of conversation, also upon the lack of appetite.

"I vow and declare!" she announced. "If you two ain't enough to discourage a body. Who do you think I made those popovers for? A—a bird couldn't stay alive on what you've et."

Mark had risen from his chair and was on his way to the door. Apparently he had not heard the housekeeper's complaint. Zenas Bradshaw also rose.

"Well, Betsy," he observed, soberly, "I don't know as I'd say that. 'Twould depend on what kind of a bird 'twas, seems to me. That and its digestion."

"Digestion! Why— Oh, if you ain't the most provokin'—"

But her employer was in the sitting-room and moving rapidly out of earshot. Mrs. Lemon snatched the plate containing the maligned popovers from the table and bore them to the kitchen where her husband was awaiting his breakfast. Jacob ate four. *His* appetite was normal.

In Mark's room, on the second floor at the head of

71

the stairs, grandfather and grandson talked for nearly an hour. Mark would have shut the door, but Zenas ordered it left open.

"I thought you didn't want any one to hear what we say," expostulated the young man.

Zenas nodded. "I don't," he replied. "With the door open we can hear them first and change the subject, that's all. Now heave ahead with your yarn."

It was an absorbing yarn. Omitting its beginning, which dealt with Mark's calls upon the wholesale grocery firms and details pertaining to the business of Bradshaw's Store, it went on to the other, and to both men just then, more important matters.

"As soon as I had done what you sent me to do, Grandfather," he said, "I started off on my own hook. You see"—he hesitated an instant and then hurried on. "You see, I knew where to go and—and all that before I left home. I had looked it all up and asked questions."

"Who did you ask 'em of? That fellow Seymour, I presume likely, eh?"

"Well—well, I did ask Frank some, yes. He helped me quite a lot. But don't you blame him, Grandfather. He's a fine chap."

"All right, all right. Never mind the references and testimonials, I'll take them for granted. Didn't cross your mind to ask me any of those questions, I suppose?"

"What would have been the use? In the first place you wouldn't know the answers, and, in the next, you would have tried to stop my doing what I had made up my mind to do. Come now, be honest. You would have done just that, wouldn't you?"

Zenas nodded. "Shouldn't wonder," he admitted dryly.

"Of course you would. And it would have ended in a row, with nothing changed but the feeling between you and me. I couldn't have that, Grandfather. So I planned to enlist first and argue afterwards."

"Umph! Well, you're going to be disappointed so far as my part of the arguing goes. No sense in telling a fellow not to fall in the well after he's in. Go on."

Mark had gone to the Boston recruiting office and made application for enlistment as a flying cadet in the Army Air Corps. He answered questions dealing with his age, general education, and the like. He answered those satisfactorily and was given printed forms to fill in, thereby making formal application for the opportunity to appear before the Examining Board at the city airport.

"They didn't tell me so," he added, "but I am sure my flying work with Seymour helped me in getting a prompt test. At any rate, I was notified, the very next day, to report to the President of the Board. You can bet I was on hand. That Board was a—a sort of—well, it was a pretty important-looking bunch for a young fellow to stand up before. Three flying officers and two medical officers. I found this out afterwards; they all looked alike to me then. Well—"

He had been given physical tests and then mental tests.

"The mental ones were the toughest. I knew I was in pretty good shape so far as the rest of my body went, but I wasn't so sure of what was inside my head. And I got through, Grandfather. By golly, I did—honest! I graded 110 out of a possible 150, they told me. Average 114. Not so darned worse, was it? Aren't you surprised? I tell you I was!"

He was glowing with excitement. His grandfather smiled faintly.

"You did pretty fair—for a Bradshaw outside the grocery business," was his comment. "Well?"

"Eh? Why—why, that's all. Then I was sworn in. Took the oath to stand by Uncle Sam through thick and thin. Then, after I told them about—about you, and the rest, they gave me my four days' leave. And here I am."

"Here you are—for a day and a half—yes." Zenas Bradshaw's right hand stroked his chin, and to his eyes came again the queer, lost look of the night before.

Mark, watching him, and, in a way, reading his thoughts, spoke quickly. "Grandfather, I—I—I know you think I haven't played square with you. I've told you why I kept all this to myself, all my plans, I mean. I had to. You understand, I had to. If—"

"Shh! I understand. Don't ask me that again. I understand you, and, when you get to be my age, maybe you'll understand—but that doesn't make any difference.... Getting back to you again, what do you do next?"

"I don't exactly know. When I report day after to-morrow I shall know more, I suppose. I shall be sent away somewhere, to what they call a Civilian Flying School, I believe. If I get along there all right, I shall be sent somewhere else, for more advanced training. Then, if I get by—if I do—I shall graduate and get my rank as Second Lieutenant, my wings and everything."

"Your wings?"

"I mean the silver badge they pin on you—on your uniform."

"Um-hm. How long will it take to measure up to that uniform—and the trimmings? Quite a while, I should guess likely."

74

"Only about thirty-five weeks, so they say."

"*Only* thirty-five! And after that?"

"Oh, then there is a lot more. All sorts of special training. They teach you real flying—war work, you know. Pursuit stuff or bombing practice—oh, about everything. Gosh, it ought to be fun!"

"Um—yes. Sounds like it. . . . Well, I don't know as there's much more to say. You'll have to do some picking over and packing, I suppose, and I must be on my way to the store. You're going to need a little money, I judge."

"No, not much. I've been saving for quite a while. And the Government provides almost everything."

"I've noticed that in the tax bills. . . . Well, are you coming along with me or not?"

"I'll come, I guess. Abner and Elsie would think it queer if I didn't. And I don't feel like explaining it all to them. They wouldn't keep it to themselves, I'll bet."

"Which is about what I said in the beginning. Have you—did you tell anybody of this enlisting notion of yours? Are all hands going to be as surprised as I was?"

Mark hesitated; he seemed a trifle confused. "Why—why, yes," he muttered. "I did tell one person—just one. But that person hasn't told any one else, I'm sure."

"I see. No, I don't imagine she would. And yet it might be good news in some quarters. Up at Camp Scott, for instance."

"See here, Grandfather, don't you get the idea that she is interested in that Davidson, because if you do you're away off. . . . And, anyway, how did you know it was Emmie I told?"

He asked the question seriously. Obviously he could not imagine how his grandfather had learned the identity of the "one person." Zenas regarded him almost with wonder.

"Boy," he said, gravely, "when I was a little shaver my mother took me to a Spiritualist camp-meeting a couple of times. One of the preachers there told Mother I had the right shaped head to be a—a clairvoyant. Every once in a while it comes across me how true that must be."

The remainder of the short leave passed all too quickly. Neither of the Bradshaws mentioned Mark's commitment to Uncle Sam's service, either at home or at the store, until the time of departure came. Abner Hallett and Miss Burgess noticed Mark's inattention to business and his frequent absences from duty and whispered comments to each other, but they did not venture to question Zenas or Mark himself. Willie Snow was the only one who hinted a complaint, and Zenas's reception of the hint was very unsatisfactory.

Willie was grumbling because of a mistake in putting up an order. "It wasn't my fault, none of it," he protested. " 'Twas Mark who sold the stuff, and he never put in any sugar at all. Instead of that he give me two quarts of vinegar to deliver. Old Lady Tibbets said that, knowin' me, if I'd have fetched flour she wouldn't have been so much surprised, but anybody whose judgment of sweet and sour was as far apart as that, and capped it off by deliverin' sugar in a jug, ought to see a doctor about his ears or his nose or his brains, or all of 'em together. I don't know nothin' about *her* nose and ears, but she's certainly got a tongue, that woman. Course I knew 'twas vinegar, I could smell it and hear it splash, but how did I know 'twasn't what she ordered? I'm ready to take blame when it belongs to me, Mr. Bradshaw, but I do wish you'd tell Mark to be more careful. It ain't fair to me, now is it?"

Zenas, whose attention had wandered long before the end of this plea for the defendant, said "Yes." Then, noting young Snow's expression, he said, "No." After which he walked away.

Willie carried his grievance to Abner Hallett. "He never paid no attention," he declared. "That's 'cause Mark done it. If it had been me 'twould have been different. I says to him, I says, 'I'm ready to take blame when it belongs to me—'"

But Mr. Hallett, being busy, was also inattentive. "Eh? What's that?" he broke in. "Don't bother me, Willie."

"Ain't goin' to bother you. I was just tellin' you what I said to the old man. I told him I was ready to take blame—"

"Yes, yes. That's fine, Willie. Take it any time you feel like it. Now run along. I've got things to see to."

Nevertheless, when Abner whispered to the bookkeeper that something was wrong with Zenas Bradshaw and that the something concerned Mark, Miss Burgess nodded agreement. "I've noticed it in a dozen ways," she declared. "And, whatever it is, it has to do with that Boston trip. Why, Mark has spent as much as half of this day away from the store and Mr. Bradshaw hasn't said 'Boo' to him. I do wonder what it can mean."

They were to find out, and that the very next afternoon. The train left Ostable at four-thirty, and at a quarter past three Mark drove up to the door of the store in his car. Zenas was with him. They came in together. It was Zenas who made the announcement. He beckoned to Hallett, and the latter came over to the bookkeeper's desk. There happened to be no customers in the store at the moment.

"Abner," said Zenas, "Mark here is saying good-by to you. He's leaving us for—for a while. You tell 'em, Mark. You've got about three minutes to do it in."

He walked away. Mark made his announcement as brief as possible. They both knew, he said, how interested he was in flying, and he had flown enough in the Seymour planes to convince himself that the interest was real and lasting, not merely transitory.

"So I have decided," he went on, "to make it my job. I have enlisted in the United States Army as a flying cadet. I have passed the tests, and I am starting in to-morrow morning up at Boston. In a way I am sorry to be leaving the store and you and Harniss, of course I am; but—well, I know I'm doing the right thing. I'll be seeing you both once in a while, I hope. For now, though, it is good-by and good luck."

He extended a hand to each of them. Miss Burgess limply shook the one offered her, but Abner Hallett was too greatly overcome to notice the other. His chin quivered with the effort to articulate.

"Why—why—what—what—" he stammered. "My Lord A'mighty! I— Does your grandfather—does Zenas—"

The bookkeeper came to his rescue. "Did Mr. Bradshaw know you were going to do this—before you did it, I mean?" she demanded.

"No, he didn't, but he understands why I did it. So will you, I hope, when you think it over. I don't believe I ever would have made a good storekeeper, but maybe I'll make a pretty fair flier. Grandfather under-

78

stands. And"—with a sudden gulp of emotion—"he's been a darned good sport about it. Say"—earnestly—"you'll look out for him, won't you? Don't let him overwork, or—"

Zenas Bradshaw called from the front of the store. "Time's up," he announced. Mark joined him, and they went out together. The car, with Mark at the wheel, drove off. Abner and Elsie hurried to the window to look after it. The bookkeeper spoke first.

"He is going to be a soldier," she said. "He is going to fly all the time. Oh, suppose he should have an accident and be killed! Or—my goodness, suppose we—the United States, I mean—really got into this awful war that's going on. Some folks seem to think we may. If anything happened to Mark I don't know what Mr. Bradshaw would do."

Abner Hallett snorted. "What's he going to do now, I'd say was the real question," he observed. "He's getting on in years, and this business here needs more attention than it ever has, with the chain-store competition and all. And that young cub clears out and leaves him like this! Leaves him flat without so much as a by-your-leave. And just because he—that Mark, I mean—had rather play flying foolishness than be doing worthwhile work. If you want to know what I think of it I think it's about as mean and selfish a trick as ever I saw played. And two-thirds of Harniss is going to think and say the same thing when they learn the news."

Which, coming from one who had shown no early signs of a talent for clairvoyance, was not a bad prophecy.

Elsie Burgess made one more remark before the pair turned away from the store window.

"I wonder how Emily Thacher will like her beau's running away from her?" she queried, a trifle maliciously. "Do you suppose he told her he was going? I'll bet he did."

Abner grunted. "John Thacher and his wife will like it, anyhow," he said. "From what I hear they've got their own plans for Emmie, and Bradshaw's Store isn't mixed up in 'em."

At the Ostable railway station the farewells were as brief as those in the store had been. During the drive over, neither of the Bradshaws had been talkative; both the old man and the young one had been busy with their thoughts, and, although those thoughts were vastly different in subject matter, each set was engrossing. Even on the station platform little was said. Your Down-Easter, although he talks fluently on casual matters, is curiously shy and reserved in emotional crises, and his dread of sentimentality is inborn. Mark, for at least the tenth time, cautioned his grandfather to be careful in driving the car back to Harniss.

"I shouldn't let you do it, Grandfather," he declared. "We ought to have brought Willie along."

Zenas was resentful. "And had to listen to his tongue-wagging all the way over and back? No, thank you. What's the matter with you, anyway, boy? I've driven an automobile ever since there was any made, pretty nigh. Had one of the first that was around in Harniss."

"I know, but you haven't driven one for almost six months, except little distances. Sixteen miles is quite a drive, at your age."

"At my age! The next fellow that says that to me will —well, I won't promise he may not die of old age some time or other, but I will say he'll have a spell of sickness right off. Don't you worry about my driving that car. And if you see in to-morrow's newspaper that I was hauled up for speeding don't let that fret you, either; I know Judge Ball pretty well. . . . Eh? Yes, there's the whistle. Good-by, boy."

"Good-by, Grandfather. Write to me, won't you?"

"I will. And, in between the letters you write to— other folks, you might drop me a line. I'll probably be pretty busy, but I promise you I'll find time to read it."

A handshake, a wave from the rear platform. The train disappeared around the curve. Zenas Bradshaw watched the last wisp of smoke drift away over the clump of pines. Then he turned slowly back to the automobile. There was so much more he wanted to say, so much more he probably should have said. Good-by! The meanest word in the language. Its time limit was so indefinite. In some cases it meant no more than "See you to-morrow." In others—

Simeon Baker, the Ostable station agent, an old friend, accosted him.

"Hello, Mr. Bradshaw. You're the one left behind, eh? Took it for granted 'twas you that was going and your grandson who was driving back home. That's the usual way you two work it, as I recollect."

"Yes, other way around this time."

"Um-hm. We all come to it, sooner or later. What is it they say? 'Youth will be served'—something like that. My wife's been at me for more'n a year to give up this job and let a younger man have it. May be good advice, but I haven't took it yet. Can't seem to resign myself to the notion, somehow. I've worked hard all my life. So have you, I guess likely."

"Yes."

"But now you are beginning to ease off. Is that it?"

Mr. Baker had not intended his remark as a joke; to his mind there was nothing funny in it. But Zenas Bradshaw appeared to find it so. He was smiling as he turned away.

"No, Sim," he said. "No, I wouldn't say that. Not exactly."

"Eh? Seeing the boy go, instead of you, I thought . . . Why, what do you mean? What would you say?"

The smile became a grim chuckle. "Nothing, Sim. I'll let the rest of 'em say it for me. I don't doubt they will. So long."

He climbed aboard the little car, settled himself behind the wheel, and pressed the starter with his foot. The automobile shot away from the platform and off down the road. Mr. Baker stared after it.

"Now what in time did he mean by that?" he soliloquized.

If he had visited Harniss on the afternoon of the following day he would have had his answer. All that Zenas had meant, and a good deal more, was being said by that time.

Chapter 5

ABNER HALLETT told it to his wife when he went home after the store closed. Mrs. Hallett told it to her next-door neighbor, Mrs. Frank Gould, within twenty minutes after her husband told her. Mrs. Gould told Frank, and he repeated it, with elaborations, at the poolroom on Main Street. From the poolroom it was carried to a dozen hands, and from those, the next morning, it spread like a brush fire in a high wind, meeting, as it traveled, the blazes started by Elsie Burgess and Willie Snow at their supper tables the previous evening.

Mark Bradshaw had cleared out. He had run off to Boston and joined the army. He had always been silly about flying, everybody knew that, and now the silliness had developed into a mania. If his grandfather had known about it beforehand and had been willing to let him go, that would have been one thing—silly enough then, although with at least the shadow of an excuse—but now, to clear out on his own hook and leave the old man this way! "I don't see how anybody with a decent bringing up could do such a thing...." "And when you think how much Zenas has done for that boy...." And so on, *ad infinitum*.

If the Bradshaws had not been the Bradshaws; if Bradshaw's Store had not been what it was, and what it had been for more than a hundred years; if Zenas had not carried his head high and always been as independent as the proverbial hog on ice; if Mark had not been so popular with the young crowd, permanent or transient; if every one had not known, taken for granted, that he was already "as good as a partner" in the family business—if these and so many more "ifs" had not been present to be reckoned with, the explosion would have aroused only minor echoes. A youth from one of the Fish Village families might have enlisted in the army, or shipped aboard a Chinese junk, and there would have been only a few casual comments and amused smiles. But Mark Bradshaw—Zenas Bradshaw's grandson, only heir and pampered and indulged pet— Whew!

This was 1940, remember. The presidential campaign had ended only a few weeks before, and the thunders of campaign oratory, promises to do and pledges not to do, were still echoing. America must prepare to defend herself against possible aggression—oh yes; but that there was any real likelihood of such aggression was an opinion held by a comparative few. We might conceivably be forced into war, but even if we were—a very remote chance—no expeditionary force of young Americans should again cross the ocean to fight Europe's battles for her, no sir! Sympathize with England in her brave struggle against the Tyrant? Why, of course; practically every one did that. Aid her in a material way? Certainly, so far as knitting and sewing and charitable work were concerned; "Bundles for Britain" societies were organized, or being organized, in most of Ostable County's towns. Do whatever we could to help the course of Democracy, but do it as an outsider aiding a friend in trouble, being careful not to get into that trouble ourselves. After all, it wasn't our war. Some politicians said that, either in print or orally, and the assertion was repeated by their followers.

As for Japan: practically no one, at that time, ever mentioned Japan, or thought of her, either—except as a small and remote group of islands inhabited by odd little yellow men. There had been a dreadful earthquake there at one time, and America had sent tons and tons of supplies and food and medicines to the sufferers. Some merchants in our cities had, in recent years, made good-sized profits by shipping scrap-iron and metal odds and ends to Tokyo. "The Japanese must all have gone into the junk business." Mr. John Thacher made that remark, jokingly, at the Harniss post-office one evening, and every hearer laughed.

So Mark Bradshaw's enlistment in the flying service of the United States Army at that time, when there was little patriotic call for his services—and particularly, the clandestine manner in which he had done it—set Harniss to exclaiming and wondering and criticizing.

The town talked and talked and talked.

Those first few days were hard ones for Zenas Bradshaw. He knew they would be and characteristically determined that no one else should learn from him, his speech or manner, how hard they were. His ordeal began at home the very evening after his return from the Ostable railway station. Before sitting down to supper he went out to the kitchen, where Betsy was preparing the meal. Her husband was sitting in the rocker by the window, reading the evening paper, the daily published in New Bedford, which had just been delivered at the door by carrier.

Betsy's round face was puffy about the eyelids. Mark,

just before he and his grandfather started for the store and Ostable, had sought her out and had said good-by.

"Pick your time when that Jake of hers isn't around," was Zenas's council. "Catch her when she's alone, and tell her then."

"Why? Jake will have to know it, like every one else."

"Certain he will, but she can tell him. If he is there you'll have to listen while he preaches what the papers call a farewell sermon over your remains. Personally I shouldn't care to go to my own funeral ahead of time. Anyhow, I'd want to pick my minister."

So Mark, waiting until Mr. Lemon had gone out, broke the news of his enlistment and immediate departure to the housekeeper, adding a brief explanation with the reasons for his action. He left her babbling incoherent "My souls" and "Oh, but I don't see why," and his good-by kiss was imprinted upon a damp cheek. Mark himself was not too composed as he shut the kitchen door. He was very fond of Betsy.

So Zenas, when he entered the kitchen after his return trip from Ostable, was prepared to meet wet weather, although he hoped sufficient time had elapsed for the worst of the storm to subside.

"Hello!" he hailed, cheerfully. "Kept supper waiting, have I? Sorry."

Mrs. Lemon had removed the lid from a kettle on the stove and was peering below it. Now she looked up at him through the steam. Jacob hastily dropped the evening paper between his chair and the wall. Zenas Bradshaw liked to be the first to read that paper after its delivery, and it was supposed to be placed unfolded beside his plate at the table.

"Hello!" hailed Zenas again. The kettle lid fell from

Betsy's hand to the floor. Mr. Lemon might have picked it up, but he did not. It was Zenas who did that.

"Oh!" exclaimed Betsy. Then in a kind of wail, "O-oh!"

"What's the trouble?" inquired Zenas. "Burn yourself?"

"Eh? Burn myself? Why—why, no, of course not."

"Good enough. Well, shall we eat?"

Betsy gasped. "Eat?" she repeated. "Eat! Why, yes, if—if you want to. How you can eat, though, after—after what's happened, I declare I don't know."

"Don't you? Well, you give me the wherewithal, as the fellow called it, and I'll show you. What do you mean—what's happened?"

"Zenas Bradshaw! When—when our Mark has gone—gone away..."

"There, there! Mark is all right. He's gone to do what he has wanted to do for a long time. No reason for us to stop eating on his account, Betsy. Told you why he went, didn't he?"

"He—he told me somethin', but I—I was too upset to understand it very well, I'm afraid. Oh, Zenas, what shall we do without him around? What will *you* do?"

Zenas Bradshaw's chin squared. "Do what the ship's cook did when there wasn't any butter aboard, get along without it. Come, come, Betsy, don't cry on the stove, you've just blacked it. Mark is happy and he would want the rest of us to be. Cheer up."

Betsy gulped back the tears and reached for the ladle and a soup plate. Her husband sighed heavily.

The sigh seemed to come as a relief to Zenas Bradshaw. He turned to look at the sigher.

87

"What's *your* ailment, Jacob?" he asked, solicitously. "Got a pain?"

Mr. Lemon shook his head. "I was thinking, that is all," he replied.

"Oh, I was afraid you might have read some bad news, or something. By the way, have you finished with that paper you've got on the floor there? Sure? Wouldn't hurry you for the world, you know."

Jacob snatched the paper from its impromptu hiding-place and handed it over without a word. Zenas took it, paused deliberately to smooth its rumpled pages, and went back to the dining-room.

While eating he told Betsy more of what Mark had told him: of the young man's experiences, his hopes and ambitions—always with sympathy and never with the slightest hint of criticism or blame. Mrs. Lemon heard it all and, when her employer finished, expressed her own mind with surprising candor.

"I don't care," she vowed. "You'll excuse him, of course, you would; but, just the same, I think his leavin' you all alone, with that whole store on your shoulders, is plain downright selfish. There!"

Zenas put down his coffee cup.

"Don't say that, Betsy," he ordered, sharply.

"It's what everybody else will say. You see if they don't."

"Maybe—but they won't say it to me but once. And I don't want to hear of it being said around here. That's an order, Betsy. You might pass it on to your—er—Lovey."

Betsy was no false prophet. Although no other person expressed his or her opinion to Zenas Bradshaw as frankly as she had done, he was obliged to listen to guarded innuendoes and expressions of sympathy which were harder to bear. He could order his housekeeper to be quiet, but he could not tell customers—good customers like Mrs. Amelia Fellowes, for example—to mind their own business.

Mrs. Fellowes, when she called at the store to leave her order, was *so* tenderly, sweetly solicitous. She did not tiptoe, exactly, as she followed Mr. Bradshaw about, but she walked as if she were a mourner in a house of death. Instead of the usual commanding shrillness, her voice was low and her manner aggravatingly gentle. When she left Bradshaw's, her shopping done, she whispered a word of comfort.

"We're all thinking about you, Zenas," she said, softly. "Everybody is so sorry for you. Any one who has lived as long as I—as you have—comes to realize that this world is full of disappointments. Bear up, you poor soul, bear up. Be patient."

Zenas breathed heavily. "Lord knows I'm trying to be," he declared, with emphasis.

After her departure Abner Hallett came over to speak to his employer. His reception by the latter surprised him. Zenas turned.

"Speak up," he ordered. "Say it out loud. And"—fiercely—"whatever else you do don't pat me. Not unless you want to be patted back. One of these days somebody is going to kill that woman, and folks will be subscribing to a monument."

Abner's expression of amazed uncomprehension was so ludicrous that even Zenas's irritation was vanquished by his sense of humor.

"Don't misunderstand me, Abner," he added. "The

monument won't be for Millie, it will be put up to the one that got rid of her."

Mr. John Thacher dropped in. He had heard the news, he said, and came seeking confirmation or denial. When smilingly assured of its truth he shook his head.

"I couldn't believe it," he said. "Youth is youth, of course, but youth in these days is—well, beyond me, I confess."

"You mean behind you, John, I shouldn't wonder," suggested Zenas. "You and I aren't exactly young—not any more. When you're twenty-one you know you've got wings and want to spread 'em. When you get further along all you can do is hope there's a set waiting for you at the next port."

John Thacher was not amused by the flippancy. Also it is possible that the reference to ages did not please him. Although he was ten years younger than Bradshaw, he was prominently mentioned as a likely candidate for nomination from the district to the State Senate, and the only important objection that had so far reached his ears was that he might be thought by the party leaders a little too old for the campaign. He did not smile.

"Zenas," he said, "this is not my affair, I know, but, in case I am asked, I should like to be able to answer definitely. After all, you and I are old friends. Did this grandson of yours—did Mark take this step on his own responsibility? Did he go into this—this flying outfit, whatever it is—with your consent and approval? I have heard that you knew nothing of it in advance, that he did it on his own.... You don't have to tell me unless you care to."

"That's so."

"Eh? What is so? What do you mean?"

"It is so that I don't have to tell you. I don't know that I *have* to tell anybody. I'd just as soon tell you, though, same as I'll tell all creation, if they're interested. It was Mark's idea, the whole of it. He is a man, and old enough to make his own decisions. He decided he had rather be a soldier—a flying soldier—than keep store here in Harniss. So he *is* a soldier. That's your answer, John."

Mr. Thacher was not quite satisfied with the answer, that was evident.

"I see," he said. "That was the story, but I couldn't swallow it. After all, he is a Bradshaw and—"

"And the Bradshaw men—all but one of 'em, anyhow—have been soldiers for a part of their lives. Some of 'em have been darned good soldiers. Mark's father for one."

"That is true, of course. But they were real soldiers, soldiers who volunteered to fight for their country. There is no war now, not on this side of the water, thank God."

"Amen."

"And there won't be, if the sane people of the United States have anything to say about it."

"They'll be the ones to say it, if it has to be said, I guess likely. . . . Anything else you want to ask me, John?"

"No-o. I— Confound it, Zenas, what about yourself? You and the store?"

"What about me and the store?"

"Why—why, we all knew Mark was your right-hand man and that you were breaking him in to handle the business after—well, after—"

He hesitated momentarily. Zenas offered a suggestion. "After I'm dead, you mean?"

Mr. Thacher hastened to deny having had any such shocking idea. "Oh, no, no," he protested. "Nothing like that. You'll live for a good many years yet. Dear me, yes; to be sure you will. My thought was—" He lowered his voice and bent nearer to his listener's ear. "This again is not in the least my affair, Zenas, but it occurred to me to wonder how much longer you may think it worth while to carry on here alone. If you should decide to—well, to retire some of these days, to sell out the business—"

Again he paused, and again Zenas helped him over the hurdle.

"Um-hm?" he grunted. "If I should decide to sell out —then what?"

"Why, from some things I have heard, in certain quarters, it might not be impossible to find a buyer. If you cared to let me know—er—in advance, I *might* be able to put you on the track of one. Nothing to do with me, personally, of course, but I hear things occasionally and I am passing this on to you, as one friend to another."

He straightened, drew back, and looked intently at Bradshaw. If he expected to learn from the latter's expression whether his friendly tip was welcome or otherwise, he must have been disappointed. Zenas's countenance was about as expressionless as the wall behind him. John Thacher tried again.

"You understand, Zenas?" he asked.

"Eh? Oh, certain, I understand. Much obliged, John."

"You're very welcome. We can have another talk later on, if you are interested."

"Um-hm. Why not?—when I am. So long, John. My regards to your wife and Emmie."

He escorted Mr. Thacher to the door and watched him walk importantly down the platform steps. Zenas stroked his chin for a moment and then beckoned to Abner Hallett.

"Abner," he asked, "are any Harniss folks financially concerned in that chain store up yonder? Any of 'em hold stock in it, as you ever heard?"

Hallett thought it over. "No," he replied, "not as I know of. It's a Boston concern, the main company, so they say. Why?"

"Nothing. . . . Ab, you're a friend of mine, aren't you?"

"What? Why, course I be. What in the world—"

"Shh! You don't come around and tell me you are, though."

"Tell you! Why would I tell you? You know it."

"Yes. Well, don't tell me. When you do I'll begin to get suspicious. . . . Hello, Ben Stevens! What are you doing in here? We're all out of castor oil, but I can let you have plenty of kerosene."

Doctor Stevens seldom visited Bradshaw's. He was on his professional rounds this time but had stopped for a moment.

"Come out back here, Zenas," he ordered.

He led the way to the shipping-room at the rear. Zenas followed him. The doctor turned.

"I want to talk to you, Zenas," he announced.

"To me—or with me?"

"Mostly 'to' this time. I've just heard the news."

"About Mark, you mean? You're late for the broadcast. Radio out of commission, or what?"

93

"Be still! Blast you, you know why I'm here. Is it true that he has gone, quit you for good?"

"He thinks it's for good. Maybe it is for his good, anyhow."

"Stop fooling, will you! What are you going to do without him?"

"*Do* without him. And keep on doing."

"Keep on working in this store every day, from morning to night? Haven't I been trying to make you realize—"

"Shh! Turn back your volume control, Ben. Don't holler. Elsie and Abner will think there is a fight out here."

"I'm not sure there won't be. I'm mad, mad clear through. You can't do this thing, Zenas. You aren't well enough to do it. I'm telling you that as a—"

"Shh—shh—shh!"—hastily. "Don't say you're telling me as a friend. One dose of that in a forenoon is plenty. Come, come, Ben! Let me tell you, for a change. Mark has quit on me—yes. He thinks he's right, and it may turn out that, for him, he is."

"For him? How about you?"

"I don't know. All I know is that *I* shan't quit, nor Bradshaw's Store won't quit—not so long as there's a Bradshaw left to run it." He paused, and grinned. "Talking big, you think? Well, I am. As I recollect, you didn't find anything wrong with my talking machinery, so I can afford to strain it."

Doctor Stevens gave it up, for the time.

"I ought to tell you to go to the devil," he declared, disgustedly, "but I don't want you to go to him, that's the trouble. I'm going to worry you from this day on.

94

I'm coming down to your house this evening, as a beginning."

"Fine! Come right along. I've got a new box of cigars, and, judging by the sample I've tried, they need a doctor. Come on, Ben; be mighty glad to see you."

Doctor Stevens came, smoked one of the cigars, and talked a great deal. When he left, it was with the feeling that most of his talk had been wasted. Zenas Bradshaw had patiently listened, had kept his temper even when the physician had been close to losing his, had promised to be careful of his health—"Careful as a working man can be, Ben"—and had, in fact, agreed with almost everything his friend said. On only two points had they disagreed, but there the disagreement was absolute: that Zenas should give up active participation in the daily work at the store, and concerning Mark's selfishness in leaving him as he had.

"Let Hallett run the place for you," counseled Stevens. "Go in there for an hour or so once a day, if you want to, and keep a general eye on things, but don't get there at eight every morning and wait on customers, bargain with drummers, and superintend putting up orders until it's time for you to help put up the shutters at night. Abner has been with you for goodness knows how long. He ought to be able to run things by this time."

Zenas nodded. "I see. And what will I be doing while he is running 'em? Spend my time wondering how the job's done?"

"No. Forget it all—and rest. That's what you need more than anything else—rest. If you would go away, on a cruise or a trip somewhere, it would please me more than anything. But I suppose you won't."

95

"You're right, Ben."

"Eh? What! You mean you'll go?"

"No, no. I meant you were right when you supposed I wouldn't. Bradshaw's Store without a Bradshaw in it wouldn't know itself. And without that store I wouldn't know *my*self. So we'll stick together long as we can. I've told you that at least once before, to-day, and twice ought to be enough. . . . How about another cigar? You lived through that one."

He would listen to no criticism of his grandson. "Mark picked his new job," he said, with decision. "I didn't pick it for him. I am wishing him all the luck in the world."

The doctor snorted. "By the Lord Harry!" he ejaculated. "I can't get you at all, Zenas. You sound as if you were standing up for him. You don't have to pretend to me, you know. Why not say what you feel? It won't go any farther."

Zenas Bradshaw tossed the stump of his cigar into the coal hod and picked up his pipe from the table.

"Ben," he said, with deliberate earnestness, "I *am* standing up for the boy. I'm going to keep on standing up for him. You can let that go just as far as it will. Don't hold it back on any account."

It went, from one end of Harniss to the other, was town talk for a week or less, and then faded out to be replaced by other items of gossip. Bradshaw's Store was minus one of its Bradshaws, but the other was in daily superintendence there, and, in a little while, customers ceased to do more than casually inquire as to the news from Mark.

There was little news. Mark wrote every week, to say that he was well and was working and studying hard.

A paragraph in one of his letters was unintentionally informing.

"I did think I knew something about flying," he wrote, "but so far these people don't seem to care to find out that I do. I am treated like all the others, greenhorns or not. I study, work, and drill, drill, drill in between times. I get up when they turn us out—and that's early—eat when I'm ordered to, and go to bed when I'm ordered to. And that's early, too, believe me, Grandfather! No time to see the sights, and, as a matter of fact, I am generally too tired to care about seeing them, anyhow."

Zenas Bradshaw's eyes twinkled when he read that. Must be something of a change from the young fellow's Harniss round of parties and dances and automobile trips. Good thing, too. Zenas had been an easy disciplinarian—too easy. Hen with one chicken stuff. Well, from what he had read, and the cartoons he had seen in the papers, the average drill sergeant was likely to be a tough old bird and his brood a large one. His chickens scratched when he cackled; they did not cackle back.

How about girls? Letters to grandparents were not intimate confessions, generally speaking, but it was odd that not once did Mark, in his writing, mention Emily Thacher's name or so much as inquire concerning her. Odd? Or wasn't it? Probably the latter. No doubt he was receiving first-hand information from that quarter.

Zenas saw Emily occasionally, and, although she seemed interested when he spoke of getting a letter from Mark, she was never unduly so. Zenas took it for granted that she had already heard all that he could tell her. Either that, or—

He did not like to consider the alternative. Laurie Davidson, handsomely spick and span in his uniform, had visited Harniss twice since Mark's departure. He and Emily had been seen together in public places. Nothing in that, either, for Mr. and Mrs. Thacher had been with them, but Harniss spoke of it and smiled. Zenas Bradshaw liked Emily. She was a nice girl, a sensible girl. He did not dislike Lieutenant Davidson, but—oh, well, that was Mark's trouble, if it was a trouble—not his.

Only once did Emily, in her chats with Zenas at the store, touch on a personal note, and then the personality was Zenas's, not his grandson's. Emily, after she had left the family order and had turned to go, turned back to ask concerning his—Zenas's—health.

Zenas declared he was fine, first-rate, didn't know as he had ever been better. Emily was regarding him intently.

"Are you sure?" she asked. "That is really true, Mr. Bradshaw?"

"Eh? True? Why, certain it is. Don't you believe me? I 'most generally tell the truth—unless I'm selling something, and even then, every now and again."

Emily smiled, but she seemed, he thought, still a little doubtful.

"I believe you, of course," she said. "Only I thought you looked a little—a little tired. You mustn't work too hard, you know."

"I shan't."

"I'm afraid you are. Why haven't you hired another clerk in—in Mark's place?"

"Eh? Oh, for a couple of reasons. One is that I haven't decided I really want anybody and the other that I

haven't so far located anybody I'd want if I did. . . .
Sounds kind of mixed up, that does, don't it?" he added,
chuckling.

She laughed, too, but the tone of her next speech
was grave enough.

"Please don't," she urged.

"Don't what? Get mixed up?"

"No, no. Don't work too hard and don't get over-
tired. I feel—well, almost responsible for you, you
know."

"You? Responsible for me? Much obliged, but why?"

"Oh, I don't know. Silly of me, isn't it?"

Zenas decided that this conversation strengthened his
surmise that she and his grandson corresponded regularly. Mark, no doubt, had asked her to check up on
his grandfather's health. Some gratification in the
thought: it would seem to prove that, even amid the
excitement of his new job, Mark had not lost all interest in the old man.

Mark came home at Christmas. His was a very short
leave: he arrived on Christmas Eve and left the following afternoon. He declared that home looked "mighty
good" to him, greeted Betsy with enthusiasm, and vowed
that the supper she had ready for him was the first meal
"with a taste to it" he had eaten in a month. Betsy was
alarmed.

"My heavens and earth!" she exclaimed. "Don't they
give you enough to eat up there?"

"Enough? Yes, indeed, and not bad, either. They
don't flavor it right, that's all. No Harniss sand in *their*
spinach, no *sir!*"

Mrs. Lemon's face flushed. "Sand!" she repeated indignantly. "I don't believe it. How can you talk so,

Mark Bradshaw! I washed every single bit of that spinach just as careful. And"—as a triumphant clincher—"it wasn't spinach anyhow, it was cauliflower."

Zenas cut in to explain that the sand was not to be taken literally. "He means your cooking tastes like home and the other doesn't, that's all," he explained.

"But 'sand' was what he said. And, so far as that goes, there isn't any sand in this house anywhere. No, and there won't be so long as I am able to sweep."

Mark looked well, very well, so his grandfather thought. Perhaps it was Zenas's imagination, but it seemed to him that the young man's shoulders were squarer, his back a bit straighter, and his eyes brighter than when he went away. This early-to-bed and early-to-rise routine had done him no harm, at least.

The after-supper chat in the sitting-room lasted about an hour. Zenas asked a good many questions, all of which were answered freely and frankly, so far as the questioner could judge. Mark questioned, too, mainly about how things were going at the store, about his grandfather's activities, and, once, why in the world no one had been hired to take his own place as clerk.

"I understand you haven't so much as taken any one on trial," he said. "Why haven't you, Grandfather?"

Zenas stroked his chin. "How do you know I haven't?" he asked. "I never wrote you a word about that, did I?"

Mark was slightly embarrassed. "Why—why, no, I don't think you did. I—I just took it for granted, I guess. But you ought to: you must."

"Um-hm. So I've been told. . . . There, there, don't look at that clock again, you make me fidgety. Go along out, if you want to. I'll 'most likely be in bed when you come back, but I'll see you in the morning."

Christmas Day was altogether too short. Betsy's dinner was a triumph and duly appreciated. Zenas would again have driven the car to Ostable and returned, but Mark had already provided for transportation.

"It is too long a drive for you to tackle, Grandfather," he said. "I saw Willie Snow when I was out last evening and arranged for him to do the driving."

Zenas Bradshaw thumped the table. "You did, eh?" he protested. "Well, how long since I had to have somebody else do my arranging for me? Next thing I know you and that Thacher girl will be hiring a trained nurse to sit and hold my hand. I might have known when she —Emmie, I mean—was telling me the other day how tired I looked that she would send the word to you. Tired! Good Lord! If anything makes me tired it's that sort of drivel.... Oh, all right, all right, have it your own way. Only you tell that Willie if he brings our car back with a dent in the fender I'll show him that I'm the freshest tired man in this county."

Which was a glorious declaration of independence, brought a laugh from Mark, and helped to make the handshake and good-by a trifle less uncomfortable for both Bradshaws. And yet, as Zenas turned back to the sitting-room after the handshake, the room looked so empty, so dreary, and Betsy, in the doorway of the dining-room, wiping her eyes with the corner of the table cloth she was folding, was no burst of sunshine.

Zenas gritted his teeth. Just what sarcastic blast might have come from behind those teeth is an unanswered question. Mrs. Lemon's woe would have probably changed to shocked indignation if it had been delivered in her direction. It was not, however. Her husband, strutting in from the kitchen, replete with turkey and mince pie and radiating self-satisfaction, was a heaven-sent target. And the target itself invited the shot.

"Well, Zenas," philosophized Jacob, with irritating complacency, "our young soldier boy has left us again. Here to-day and gone to-morrow, as the saying is. Life is like that, and we have to make the best of it."

Betsy said she guessed likely that was so, only she sometimes wondered why it always had to be the good things that went. Zenas Bradshaw saw his chance and took it.

"Not always, Betsy," he protested. "You're one of the good things, and you stick around pretty regular. You figure she's a good thing, don't you, Jacob?" he asked solemnly, turning to Mr. Lemon.

Betsy beamed, but there was a hint of suspicion in her husband's eye as he regarded his questioner. He hesitated.

Zenas did not wait for a reply. "I'll bet you do," he observed, and left them. He was in a happier frame of mind when he reached his own room at the head of the stairs. Jake Lemon, although always a pest, was a help occasionally. It took a pretty strong poke to penetrate his hard shell, but, when the jab did get through, it was fun to watch him squirm. Big, blown-up loafer! If it wasn't for Betsy . . .

But Betsy was always to be considered.

January came, bringing 1941 with it. January passed, and February came in. Mark, to judge by his letters, was doing well at his work, although always fearful that he might not pass certain tests and examinations which were just ahead and which he dreaded. "They are weeding us out all the time," he wrote. "A dozen fellows have been dropped already. I am doing my best to hang on, but I don't know, I can't tell. I thought I knew a lot about engines and planes when I came here. Well, I didn't."

Then came a short but joyful note. He had passed, and with a good average, too. Next he was to go to what they called a Basic School, somewhere in the South, he had not been told just where. He came down to Harniss for another brief leave. Then he was off again, and his next letter was postmarked from a town in Alabama.

"It is warmer here," he wrote, "but they don't give us time to look at the thermometer. It is work, work, work, and plug, plug, plug, all the time. I thought the discipline at the other places was strict enough, but this is tougher. I get cramps in my arm from saluting."

Zenas Bradshaw chuckled when he read that. He had noticed a different attitude toward his elders on the part of his grandson during the latter's recent visit. Several times Mark had used a "sir" when addressing him. So far as he himself was concerned, Zenas cared nothing about the "sirs," but they were illuminating. He could not remember the boy addressing even the minister as "sir" when he had been a resident of Harniss. Polite enough—oh, yes, but it had been politeness without trimmings.

Chapter 6

A T Bradshaw's Store, business was going on as usual. Or, if not quite as usual, going on pretty well. The competition from the chain store was making itself felt even among some of Bradshaw's regular customers. Zenas sold goods at not more than a fair profit, but the chain system, buying, as its city purchasing agents did, in larger quantities, could afford to shade prices at its branches, a cent or two here and there. Zenas Bradshaw could not meet these prices and did not try. "Handle the best stuff I can buy," he explained, "and sell it for as little more as I can afford to. That's what Bradshaw's has done since it started, and that's what it will do till it finishes—or until I finish, anyhow."

"Let them go or stay," he told Abner Hallett. "That's up to them. If they don't know by this time that Bradshaw's prices are fair, quality and service considered, then they never will know. If they tell you they can buy cheaper somewhere else just say you're sorry but you can't do any better. Don't cut a cent. Go or stay, that's their affair."

And, which was somewhat surprising, the majority stayed. Some did not, however, and, in consequence, profits were smaller and the necessity of considering even small economies greater.

It was principally for this reason that Zenas Bradshaw

had hired no one to take Mark's place. "Of course," he told Hallett, "if I could hire just the right sort of young fellow I should do it, but so far I haven't been able to sight that one. Meanwhile, you and I will have to work a little harder, that's all. My father used to tell me that hard work never hurt anybody."

Abner repeated this remark to Elsie Burgess and shook his head as he did so. She shook hers also.

"It's hurting him," she whispered. "He looks awful tired these days, I think."

Hallett thought so, too. Then, to change the subject, he asked if she had attended the Improvement Society meeting at the town hall the evening before.

"They tell me there was quite a hot time up there," he said. "That Boston fellow the Bundles for Britain crowd brought down was called on to say something, and he told the meeting that we Americans must stiffen our backbones and be ready to fight any minute. According to him, we were just as good as in this war already."

Miss Burgess nodded. "That's what he said," she agreed. "And Mr. Thacher jumped up and said he couldn't sit still and listen to such nonsense. That certain politicians in prominent places—that's what he said, 'in prominent places,' and everybody knew what that meant—were trying to drag our country into war was plain enough, but that the common-sense people of the United States would let themselves be dragged in he didn't believe for a minute. The Boston man came right back at him, and they had it hot and heavy. What do you think, Abner? Will we go to war, or not?"

Hallett was non-committal, as he usually was on any controversial subject.

105

"Why, maybe yes, maybe no," was his cautious reply. "If any one of those Hitler folks should pitch into us we'd have to go, naturally. Couldn't sit still and let 'em kick us around. But which one of 'em is going to be fool enough to give that first kick? That's the question, as I look at it. They've got fight enough on their hands already."

"That's just exactly what Mr. Thacher said. 'A man who has got his head in a hornets' nest doesn't knock over a bee-hive on purpose,' he told the Boston fellow. You should have heard the crowd laugh. John Thacher is awful smart."

"The old man," whispered Abner, with a jerk of the head at Zenas Bradshaw, "got mixed up in it a little, didn't he? I heard he did."

The bookkeeper, after a cautious look in the same direction, nodded. "Um-hm," she whispered in reply. "After the Boston man and Mr. Thacher got through, somebody—Frank Holden, 'twas—got up. 'I'm sure we've all been interested,' he said, 'but I, for one, would like to hear opinions from more of our Harniss citizens. Mr Bradshaw,' looking right at Zenas, who was sitting across the aisle from him. 'Mr. Bradshaw, you've always lived right here in town, you're one of our businessmen, and, more than that, you've sent your grandson off into the army. He's learning how to fly, we know, and how to fight, if necessary, we take for granted. Do you think he's liable to have to fight? What's your opinion about our getting into this war? Do *you* think we'll get into it—or that we ought to get into it?'

"There was a kind of rustle all over the hall, all hands leaning forward to look at Zenas. Frank Holden is one of John Thacher's right-hand men in County politics—you know that, Abner. And Frank was one of the town folks who had the most to say about Mark's selfishness in leaving his grandfather the way he did and in criticizing Zenas for taking Mark's leaving so calm and matter-of-fact. You notice the way he put his question, too: 'You've sent your grandson'—that's what I mean. Now nobody really thinks—"

Mr. Hallett interrupted. "Yes, yes, sure," he broke in impatiently. "I know Frank Holden. His son is clerkin' in the chain store, too: don't forget that. Go on, Elsie. Hurry up! Zenas got back at him, they say. How?"

Miss Burgess looked doubtful. "I don't know as you'd call it getting back at him, really," she admitted. "I hoped he'd tell him to mind his own business, but he didn't. He got up, slow and deliberate, and, provoked as he must have been, he didn't show it. He was smiling and pleasant as could be.

"'Well, Mr. Holden—and gentlemen,' says he. Oh, I hope some of the rest noticed that he stopped just a second after the 'Holden' and before he went on to the 'gentlemen.' 'Perhaps,' he said, 'I'd better say in the beginning that I don't like war any better than John Thacher or Frank Holden does. No sane person can like it and be sane. And Frank is wrong when he says I sent my grandson into the army. I didn't send him anywhere—except to Boston. What he did after he got there he did on his own responsibility. I've told that to anybody who has asked me, and now I say it again here. So much for that. But—'

"He stopped and looked around: still good-natured and smiling, he was. 'But,' he went on, 'now that he has done it I'll say that, on the whole, I'm rather glad he did. I don't know whether we'll get into this war or not.

I don't believe anybody, even the folks in Washington, know that. But we may have to get into it, and if we do ... well, let me tell you a story, one that my grandfather—some of you will remember him, I guess—used to tell about Jerry Kelly, who lived down in the village in the old days. Jerry and his wife didn't get along very well, and once she had him arrested for assault. They got him into court over in Ostable, and after the witnesses for the prosecution had been heard, old Judge Staples, who was holding session, asked Jerry if he had anything to say for himself."

" ' "Well, Your Honor," says Jerry, "it was this way. The old gal," ' meaning his wife, ' "had got in the habit, when she got a little mite out of sorts, or was playful, as you might say, of firing the lids of the cookstove at me. I had to learn to ward off them lids with my hands, or whatever I happened to have in 'em, or get dented. Well, this time, after I'd warded off the two front lids and she was reaching for the back ones, I jumped in under her arm and—and argued with her with my clam hoe. All that dodging I'd done afore was only practice, you mind, Judge, but it come in darned handy, when things got serious." '

"Everybody in the hall laughed, of course, and Zenas laughed too. 'I guess that is about my answer to you, Holden,' he said. 'A little practice may turn out to be a handy thing when, or if, things get serious.' "

Abner Hallett chuckled. "Sounds like him," he admitted. "But it wasn't really an answer, now was it? Didn't change any opinions, I wouldn't think. Nor make him any new friends, either."

Elsie Burgess sighed. "When you see Zenas Bradshaw knuckling under so as to make friends you will see a

Bible miracle," she declared, and added, "But I do wish he wouldn't get himself so tired."

Zenas never would have admitted getting or feeling tired—to others, that is. There were times, however, as the hard winter crawled by and the days lengthened to spring, when he was forced to admit it to himself. He was thinner, by five pounds, than he had been in the fall, and his color was not good and his appetite uncertain. Several times, either while busy in the store or at home in the evening, he had experienced odd, un-uncomfortable seizures of giddiness. They did not last long, or seem to leave any serious aftermath, but they were distinctly unpleasant. On one occasion, when he was alone in the sitting-room and that sitting-room had tipped to an angle of forty-five degrees, while he clung to the arms of his chair, the perspiration spouting from every pore in his body, he had been on the point of summoning Betsy. The attack passed, however, and the sitting-room slowly sank back to its normal level, so he mopped his dripping forehead and called no one. It didn't mean anything, he told himself; something he had eaten, probably. He must be more careful. At his age a man couldn't eat anything at any time, and next to nothing part of the time, and get away with it as he could when he was twenty. He must—

Here, here! This wouldn't do. This was the same sort of fool stuff that Ben Stevens was forever preaching to him. He swore at himself for thinking such thoughts. He wasn't sick—nor so old that he could not take a man's trick at the wheel. He couldn't afford to be, with Bradshaw's Store on his hands.

In his letters to Mark he always declared himself to be "feeling fine."

One cloudy afternoon in April he left the store an hour later than usual and started for home and supper. The store had closed at its customary closing time, but Zenas had remained, after Hallett and the bookkeeper left, to look over the bills on his desk. The bills were not unduly large: he could and would pay them when due, but May was almost here, summer cottages would soon be opened, and he must stock up and prepare for summer custom. He would have to go to Boston in a week's time; he ought to go now. The trip looked like a hard job; no reason why it should, but somehow it did. He used to enjoy those trips, meeting old friends in the city, lunching with them, smoking and eating more than he ought to, perhaps going to the theater occasionally. It used to be fun, and he looked forward to it. He did not look forward to it now. He dreaded it.

There was no Mark to go in his place. He might send Hallett, but Abner lacked "savvy." He was all right in the store, but his judgment in buying goods, anything but staples, that is, was not likely to be too good. No, he could not send Abner. He must go himself.

All right, he would. He would start, not the next day, but the day after that.

At the corner of Main Street and the Pond Road some one called his name. He turned and saw Mrs. Thacher, John Thacher's wife, crossing the street in his direction.

Henrietta Thacher—her friends called her "Etta"—was a large woman, distinctly of the dowager type. Roman nose, determined chin, and a pair of keen, if slightly short-sighted, eyes behind rimless eyeglasses. The glasses were attached to her ample bosom by a fine gold chain. "I know it is old-fashioned nowadays to wear glasses on a chain," she sometimes condescended to explain, "but I do it because I like it. All old-fashioned manners and customs are not bad, by any means."

Her listeners invariably agreed with this statement. It was good diplomacy to agree with Mrs. Thacher, as it was with her husband, although the story, whispered about town, was that even the masterful John usually agreed with his wife at the end of one of their family debates, and that it had been she who made the decision leading him to consider favorably the prospective senatorial candidacy.

Having attracted Zenas Bradshaw's attention, she swept across the road like a ferry-boat crossing a channel. Elmer Cowen's sixteen-year-old son, at the wheel of the Cowen "Chevy," jammed his foot down on the brake lever to give her room. It was only the second time he had been permitted to drive the car, and if, as his indulgent but fearful mother had prophesied, he was certain to run down half a dozen folks before he got through learning, he was determined that Mrs. John Thacher should not be first of the six.

The lady was a trifle out of breath when she reached her objective, but her dignity was unimpaired.

"Oh, Mr. Bradshaw," she panted. "It is you, isn't it! I thought it was, but I wasn't quite sure."

Zenas smiled. "You can be sure now, Etta," he told her. "I haven't been anybody else since I can remember. How do you do? How are they all up at your house?"

Mrs. Thacher said they were well. "Excuse my stopping you right in the street this way, but I haven't seen you for a long time—to talk with, I mean—and when I happened to see you here, and alone . . . You *are* alone, aren't you?"

"Yes. Or I was up to a minute ago."

"What? Oh, I see what you mean." She laughed. "You do love to have your joke, Mr. Bradshaw–Zenas, I should say. I don't know why I am so formal. Old friends as we are shouldn't be formal, of all things."

"Don't see why they should, that's a fact."

"Yes, of course. Certainly. No, they shouldn't."

She seemed a bit confused, not exactly sure of herself, a most unusual condition for her to be in. Bradshaw turned to look at her.

"What is it, Etta?" he asked. "Something on your mind?"

"Oh no"–hastily. "Nothing at all, nothing of importance, that is. Zenas, the other evening, at the Improvement Society meeting, you said something–or John said you did; I wasn't there, you know, I had one of my dreadful headaches, so . . . Well, at any rate, John, when he came home, told me that in the course of your remarks–"

"Remarks? Oh, you mean when I answered Frank Holden? I wouldn't call what I said 'remarks,' exactly. I didn't make a speech, just answered Frank's question, that's all."

"I know. Well, Mr. Thacher–John, I mean–said that you said, or as much as said–perhaps you didn't exactly say it, but you implied it, he thought–that your grandson had gone into the army to–to stay. That you never expected him to come back here to Harniss–to live, I mean. Is that really true? I can hardly believe it."

Zenas Bradshaw shrugged. "Whether it is true or not

I didn't say it, or imply it either. John was mistaken. Didn't hear me very plain, maybe."

"Oh. . . . Oh, then it isn't true. He is coming back?"

"He'll come back every once in a while, I hope. Whether he'll come here again to live is—well, that, I suppose likely, we might call uncertain."

"I see. I see. What does he say, himself? In his letters, I mean? Does he like army life? Does he think there is a—what we might call a future in it for him?"

Zenas stroked his chin. "There's some kind of future in 'most everything, Etta. Mark seems to like his work, so far anyhow. It is hard work, but he likes it, I judge."

What was all this, anyhow? What was the woman fishing for? He was not greatly interested, whatever it was. He wanted to go home—and rest. Mrs. Thacher still lingered.

"I have always heard," she said, "that army life was very hard and uncertain, particularly for a married man. No one can tell where he may be stationed, what part of the world he may be sent. That must be dreadful for his wife, I should think, shouldn't you?"

A light began to dawn upon Zenas's understanding. Not a very clear light as yet, but a glimmer, nevertheless.

"Never thought much about it," he observed. "No reason to. Mark isn't married."

"Of course he isn't. Nor even engaged. I'm sure you are thankful for that, Mr. Bradshaw—Zenas, I mean. I should be, if I were in your place. Of course, if he were in the service only temporarily, just for the time, as Laurie is, it would be different. Laurie—Laurie Davidson I am talking about now—is in the army and enjoying it, too, but some of these days he will give up his

113

commission and go back to the career that is waiting for him. His people will be happy when he does, I know."

The light was still dim, shrouded in a fog of words—carefully chosen words, Zenas was inclined to think. He decided to attempt clearing it a bit.

"The Davidson boy?" he suggested. "Is he planning to get married?"

Henrietta did not giggle, of course, but her little laugh was as near a giggle as a Thacher laugh could be.

"Oh, not planning exactly," she confided. "No, I mustn't go so far as to say that. But—well, he is interested along that line, very much interested, that John and I know. . . . This is between ourselves, Zenas. You won't repeat it, will you?"

Zenas made no promise. "Is the other party interested, too?" he asked.

"We think so. They see each other often and are very happy together. Very happy indeed. We expect—Mr. Thacher and I expect—to hear of an important announcement before long. . . . There! I mustn't say any more: I'm afraid I have said too much already. I haven't mentioned names—both names, now have I?"

"No."

"You must wonder why I have told you all this. Well, I just had to tell some one, and—and your family and ours have always been so intimate. Give our love to your grandson when you write him. Good-by, Zenas. Do come and see us some evening. Thank you so much for listening so patiently."

She swept majestically away. Zenas Bradshaw gazed after her.

"Now why on earth?" he soliloquized aloud. Then he moved on, thinking about that "why." The idea, or the hope, was, so far as he could surmise, that when he, Zenas, wrote to Mark, he would repeat in the letter those parts of Mrs. Thacher's conversation dealing with Laurie Davidson and Emily Thacher. How often they saw each other, how happy they were together, and about the "announcement" which, according to Etta, was expected to be made at any moment. The lady had asked him not to repeat those confidences, it was true, but if she did not want him to repeat them, and in the right quarter, why did she stop him on the street to impart them?

No, no, she meant them to be repeated. She wanted Mark to know of the "happiness" and the expected announcement. The knowledge was intended as a warning to Mark that his own cause was hopeless, and therefore he might as well keep off the grass, so far as the Thacher niece was concerned. An obvious move, clumsy and rather raw, very raw indeed to be made by as smart a woman as Mrs. John Thacher was supposed to be.

Why did she make it? She and John must be worried. That they had picked young Davidson as the ideal husband for their niece all Harniss knew. There was no secret about that.

Hm-m. It looked almost as if their match-making arrangement was not progressing as smoothly toward the desired end as they hoped and expected it would. There was a rock in the channel somewhere. Possibly Etta had discovered that Emily and Mark were corresponding. Perhaps Mrs. Thacher had found and even read one or two of Mark's letters. Or, perhaps, Emily had grown tired of being pushed around, had put her foot down and refused to be pushed any farther. Must be something, something important, or Henrietta Thacher would never have played such a silly, transparent trick.

All that stuff about "having to tell some one" and "your family and ours were always so intimate." Bosh! Fiddlesticks! Etta would have to use better bait than that, if she expected Zenas Bradshaw to bite.

Write Mark what she had said? Not a word of it. Zenas had no intention of aiding in the "pushing around." Mark and Emily and Davidson could manage their own business. That the Emily-Mark mutual attraction was likely to lead to marriage sometime or other was not a matter for immediate consideration. Mark, certainly, was in no financial condition to dream of taking a wife, was not likely to be for a long time. When, or if, he was, Zenas could think of no one he would prefer to Emmie Thacher, but much could happen to young people's love affairs in a year or two or three. Where would he—Zenas Bradshaw—be in three years? In Bradshaw's Store, he hoped; but—

"Oh, go on home, you fool! You haven't had your supper, that's what ails you."

He went home, found that the supper in reality did not taste as good as it had in anticipation, ate little, and went to bed almost immediately afterward.

He was even later in leaving the store the following evening and quite as low in spirits. The projected trip to Boston looked just as laborious a chore as it had looked when he first decided he must make it. He would not start to-morrow; no, he would put it off for another couple of days, might feel more "up to it" then. He plodded on for a hundred yards or so, then realized how slowly he was moving, straightened his back, lifted his chin, and walked faster, much faster.

A Harniss citizen, one of its fishing fraternity, watching from the window of the post-office, commented as he passed.

"Look at the old boy go," he exclaimed. "Limps it off as if he was fifty, instead of God knows how old. Ain't changed a mite in the last ten years, seems so. That's the way to discourage the undertaker. Hope I'm as peppy as that when I get to be his age."

Zenas Bradshaw himself did not realize how fast he was "limping it off" until he had left Main Street and was well on his way down the Pond Road, his home around the next corner and only a short distance ahead. Then he was reminded of his pace, a most unpleasant reminder. Pond Road suddenly decided to be a level byway no longer. It tilted to the right, then to the left, like a ship in a heavy sea, and continued to heave and tilt and rock, varying the rocking occasionally by whirling in great circles.

Zenas recognized the symptoms: he had experienced them before, although never as severely as this. There was a rail fence bordering the narrow sidewalk just here, and he clutched at it. Clutched and held on desperately. Great waves of nausea swept over him; perspiration streamed from his every pore. He clung to that fence rail as the woman clung to the "Rock of Ages" in the picture on his sitting-room wall at home.

That was his last clear recollection for a time. There were others, but they were foggy and disconnected. Some one was speaking to him, bending over him, asking what was the matter. He declared that nothing was the matter and tried to prove it by letting go of the fence. This was a mistake, for his next realization was that he was on the ground. How he got there he couldn't be sure, but there he was.

And there he remained for a while, long or short he had no idea. Then the agitation of all creation became a little less violent, the dizzy swoops into the depths and the rocketing shoots toward the skies not quite as turbulent and the intervals between them longer. He felt better, yes, he did. Not good—oh, no, anything but good, but better. He fought to raise himself on one elbow, and succeeded. Some one, in an agitated voice, bade him lie still.

"*Please* lie still, Mr. Bradshaw. You musn't try to move. There, there! Wait! Wait just a minute!"

Zenas opened his eyes and made the pleasing discovery that he could see. He could not see plainly, for the world about him was still in commotion, like a sea after a heavy blow. The chop was going down, but a ground swell remained. One arm and hand supported him, and he raised the other hand to his dripping forehead.

"Whew!" he gasped. "Whew!"

"Hush! You musn't talk. You feel better now, don't you? Say you do."

"Eh? Sure I'll say it. Why wouldn't I? What in the devil am I lying down for, anyway? Not in bed, am I? If I am, somebody has put a brick in the mattress. . . . Whew! . . . Let me up, I'm all right now."

"No, no, you musn't move yet. Oh, *please!*"

Zenas made another effort, this time to sit up, and again he succeeded.

"Humph!" he grunted. Then, increasingly conscious of his surroundings, he asked another question.

"Who are you?" he asked. "Eh? Why it's Emmie, isn't it?"

That is who it was, or seemed to be. Emily Thacher, of all people. Two Thachers in the Pond Road in two successive evenings. When Tod McCue, the blackest of Harniss's black sheep, was carried out of his barber shop and incarcerated in the town lock-up, Tod had expressed satisfaction with the procedure. "Don't give a darn where you're luggin' me," he declared, "so long as it's where I can't keep on seein' things. They chase me, them cussed things do." Adding, in an agonized screech: "There's one of 'em now!" Tod, or so he subsequently said, had been chased by many "things," some with twenty legs and some with none. And now Zenas Bradshaw was being chased by Thachers. He was "seeing Thachers." It was funny. He began to laugh, weakly.

Emily Thacher did not laugh. She looked as if she were going to cry. This would not do. Zenas stopped laughing.

"All right, all right, Emmie," he said, his voice, like the rest of him, stronger as the last whiff of giddiness faded. "Scared you, I expect, didn't I? It's nothing. Help me up. . . . You *are* Emmie, aren't you?"

"Of course I am. No, you mustn't get up. You must lie where you are till I run to your house and get some one to help me with you. I'll be right back. I shan't be gone a minute."

Zenas was on his knees now. "No, no!" he ordered. "Don't do any such thing. I'm all right, I tell you. . . . Just a jiffy, till I get my underpinning steadier. . . . What are you doing down here, anyway? Past eight o'clock, isn't it? Must be."

"I came to see— I was on my way— Oh, I'll tell you that some other time. I am going to get somebody to help you now."

She had gone. The only way of stopping her would have been by main strength, and Zenas Bradshaw un-

119

willingly realized that he had very little strength, main or subsidiary. He sank back into a sitting position and swore at himself and the world in general.

Emily's minute was not more than three. When she came running back, Betsy Lemon was lumbering behind her, and—Zenas's worst forebodings were realized —Jacob Lemon was behind his wife.

Betsy was short of breath and wasting the little she had left in ejaculations and lamentations. Her husband was dignified and full of suggestions put in the form of orders. Betsy and Emily got Zenas Bradshaw to his feet and supported him during the short walk to the house. Jacob followed, as rear marshal of the parade.

Among them all the protesting Bradshaw was helped up to his bedroom and forced to lie down on the bed. He was too exhausted to put up more than the feeblest resistance, even when Betsy removed his coat, vest, collar, tie, and shoes and then retired to the hall while Mr. Lemon remained to divest the patient of his trousers.

This was too much. Zenas sat up in bed. "Let go of me, you Jake," he commanded. "When I can't take off my own pants I'll be too far gone to wear any. . . . Don't touch me, I tell you!"

He took them off himself. "You can hang 'em up, Jake, if you want to," he panted. "Sure it won't be too much work for you? Wouldn't want you to strain yourself, you know."

He lay down, breathing heavily. "Where's Emmie?" he asked, after a moment.

"She has gone. She said to tell you she would call tomorrow to find out how you were."

"But I want to see her."

"Perhaps you can to-morrow, if the doctor thinks you are well enough to see anybody."

"The doctor? What doctor?"

"Doctor Stevens, of course. Emmie has 'phoned him to come right away."

Zenas Bradshaw writhed. "The doctor!" he groaned. "That blasted Ben Stevens! How he will crow over me! And try to keep me in this blasted bed for a week. Well, he'll have a sweet time doing it! What did you have to drag *him* into it for? Doctor! Oh, my Lord A'mighty!"

It was the final straw.

Chapter 7

DOCTOR STEVENS wasted no time. Emily's telephone message caught him at his home, just as he was about to start on his evening round of professional calls, and he came in a hurry. Mr. and Mrs. Lemon met him at the door and had much to say. Betsy said the most, but her remarks were exclamatory and not too coherent. Stevens gathered she was sure her employer was about to die and that, generally speaking, the wonder was he had not died before this.

"With all he's been through!" she wailed. "Mark—his own grandson, as you might say—"

Her husband interrupted. "There, there, my dear," he put in. "Never mind, never mind."

Betsy, her train of thought off the track, seemed to be not quite sure where the track was.

"Eh?" she gasped, in bewilderment. "What did you say, Jacob? Never mind—er—somethin', was it?"

"I said never mind all that. The doctor knows Mark is Zenas's grandson, you don't have to tell him."

"But—but I wasn't tellin' him. I was just sayin' that—that— Oh dear me. I don't know what I was sayin'! You and him and this, and—and everything comin' on me so sudden I—I'm all scattered 'round."

Doctor Stevens left Mr. Lemon to pick up the pieces. He pushed past the pair unceremoniously and hurried to Zenas's bedroom. He found the patient in much better condition than the Lemons' doleful diagnosis had led him to expect. Zenas's greeting lacked enthusiasm.

"Ugh!" he grunted. "There you are, eh? See here, Ben, if you say 'I told you so' just once, I'll climb out of this bed and heave you out of the window."

Stevens' only reply was a grin. Paying no attention to sputtered expostulations, he proceeded to feel his friend's pulse, apply the stethoscope to his chest, and, finally, thrust a clinical thermometer between his lips.

"There!" he said. "That will keep you quiet for a couple of minutes, anyway. Here, here! Don't you dare bite that thing: thermometers cost money."

Zenas did keep quiet until the instrument was removed. He even waited an instant while the doctor held it to the light, but when Stevens laid it on the table without speaking, his impatience boiled over.

"Well? Well? What of it? Say something. What's the answer?" he demanded.

"Oh, about a hundred and ten."

"You're a liar, and you know it. Bet you a dollar it's normal. Now, come."

"You lose. Now I'm going to take your blood pressure."

Zenas endured the procedure. When it was over he again demanded results. This time the doctor obliged.

"You're a lucky man," he said. "Your pulse is weak and your blood pressure is away down, but you are lucky just the same. You're not dead, for one thing."

"Huh! If I was dead the other things wouldn't count much. And if I was, you'd be the unlucky one, for you couldn't be running up a bill on me. Come on now,

Ben. I can get up to-morrow morning, can't I? I've got to."

"You can not. I want you to stay in that bed for a week, at least. You are in better shape than I was afraid you'd be, but you need rest, absolute rest.... Shh! This is serious. I'm not talking for the fun of it. Listen!"

He spoke earnestly and at some length. Zenas Bradshaw heard him to the end.

"And that's that," concluded Doctor Stevens. "Oh, I know it's tough on you, Zenas, but, in a way, it's your own fault. I warned you—"

"Be still! ... A week, eh? Won't be any longer than that? You're not letting me down easy? When the week's up you won't tell me you meant to say a month?"

"No, probably not—if you behave yourself."

"Got to behave, haven't I? ... All right. ... Say, Ben, do one thing for me on the way home, will you? Stop at the Hallett place and tell Abner I want to see him here first thing in the morning. Oh, yes, and one thing more. When you go through the kitchen send Betsy in to me."

Stevens chuckled. "How about her husband?" he asked, innocently.

Zenas sniffed. "You said my—what-d'ye-call-it—blood pressure was down, didn't you? Um-hm. Well, if you want to see it go up just head that Jake this way. I'll be seeing you again before long, I suppose, eh?"

"You will. Why?"

"Because you need the money, maybe: that's the only reason I can think of. Oh, all right, Ben, don't get mad. I'm just sore at all creation. Much obliged to you. Good night."

The doctor delivered the message to Mr. Hallett,

and Abner called upon his employer before eight the following morning. Of the two, Hallett was by far the more shaken and nervous. In all the years of his connection with Bradshaw's Store this was the first time there had been no Bradshaw to call upon in case of emergency. Doctor Stevens had taken pains to impress upon Abner the necessity of not troubling Zenas with business matters. "Just tell him you'll attend to everything and that everything will be all right," he had ordered. "If he asks how things are going tell him they couldn't go better."

"But—but suppose something turns up?"

"Turn it down again. Don't worry him about it, anyway. I have ordered him to rest, and I want his mind to rest as well as his body. He has got to take it easy; he must. So far as the store is concerned, it is up to you to see that he does. Understand?"

Mr. Hallett understood and did his best to appear calmly confident and cheerfully optimistic.

"Oh, sure! Certain!" he told his employer. "With Elsie and Willie to help I can run her just like clockwork. Why, I've been in that store for—for I don't know how many years."

Zenas nodded. "I know," he agreed. "So you have."

He might have added: "But I have been there with you." As to Abner's ability to manage the everyday routine of Bradshaw's business he had no doubts. It was the unexpected happenings, the little disagreements with fussy customers like Mrs. Fellowes; the running short of important items of stock; the getting orders out promptly; the watching for and attending to the hundred and one trifles which came under the head of what he would have called "keeping a general eye on things

125

in general." Here was where his confidence in the Hallett capability was not entirely whole-hearted. Abner would try hard, he would do his best: this was by no means the first time his employer had left him in charge for a few days. Abner would get along all right: why not?

Only—Bradshaw's Store was without a Bradshaw and would be without one for a week at least. Something like this he had realized as a possibility, one increasingly likely to happen as the years moved by. He had faced its likelihood and had, or thought he had, provided against it. He had been training his grandson, bringing him up in the Bradshaw tradition, to take over in the Bradshaw way. And now Mark . . .

But that milk was spilled months ago. One thing was certain: he—Zenas Bradshaw—would stay in that bed and that room for not more than a week, in spite of Doctor Stevens's "at least." Why the devil did Ben have to put that "at least" in? What did he mean by it? If he thought . . .

Abner Hallett broke in on those gloomy musings to ask if there were any other orders. Zenas stared at him.

"Any others?" he repeated. "Haven't given you any yet. Now, you listen."

Abner listened and promised faithful and vigilant performance.

"And if anything should bother you, you are to come here to me with it right off."

This being precisely what he had promised the doctor he would not do, Mr. Hallett pretended not to hear. He mumbled that it was high time he was at the store and hurried out. Zenas called after him, but the call was not heard, either.

Late in the afternoon another visitor came. Mrs. Lemon entered the sickroom to make the announcement.

"I don't suppose," she began, "that you want to see anybody, do you? The doctor said you didn't."

"What the blazes does he know about it?"

"Well, he said you wasn't to, anyhow. Anybody but Abner, that is. I was tellin' Jacob—"

"Hold on? Does Jake want to see me?"

"No."

"Fine! Motion carried unanimously!"

"Eh? I don't know as I just understand?"

"Nothing, nothing."

"Well, anyhow, I told her you didn't want to see folks, so—"

"Shh! You told—who is 'her'?"

"Why, Emily Thacher. She's come to ask how you are. She's goin' now, though."

"She is not. Send her up this minute."

"But—but, Zenas, you don't look—er—very pretty. You're in bed."

"Think I'd look prettier if I got up? Send her along, I tell you. I want to talk to her."

"But the doctor—"

"Damn the doctor!"

Betsy uttered a shocked protest and departed. A minute later there was a knock on the bedroom door.

"Come in, come in, Emmie," ordered Zenas. "What are you waiting for? Well, you look as fine as a fiddle, anyhow. Glad of the chance to thank you for helping lug me home last night. First time I ever was in that condition, as I recollect. Ought to swear off drinking altogether, I suppose. Well, maybe I will."

Emily shook her head at him. "I can hardly believe it," she declared, with a sigh of relief. "I was almost afraid to come here this afternoon. I didn't know what I might hear, and I dreaded to ask Mrs. Lemon how you were. When she told me you were ever so much better I—"

She paused momentarily and Zenas broke in. "Said I was better, did she?" he observed. "Well, that's considerable, coming from Betsy. Every time she tiptoes into this room she looks as if she was fetching lilies. What else did she tell you about me—anything?"

Emily smiled. "She said you must be better. Nobody who was really sick could be as cranky as you were."

Zenas laughed, and she laughed with him.

"Now that I have seen with my own eyes that you are better I must go," she added. "I am supposed to be uptown on an errand for Aunt Etta."

"Eh? Go! Why you've just got here. Sit down, sit down. I want to talk with you."

She hesitated; then, declaring that she really must not stay more than a minute or two, she took the rocker by the window. Zenas Bradshaw regarded her with satisfied approval.

"I vow it is a comfort to see somebody that doesn't look like a sprinkling can," he told her. "Betsy is one of the best-hearted women that ever lived, but she's as full of water as a sponge. She cried last night because I was so sick, and this morning she told me she was crying because I'm so well."

Emily said she was sure that Mrs. Lemon must be a good nurse. "She certainly means to be. She thinks the world of you, Mr. Bradshaw."

"I know. Oh, she's a good nurse enough. She is a little

too much of a wet nurse to suit me, that's all. Did you tell your aunt and uncle how you picked me out of the gutter last evening?"

"No. I didn't. I—I was afraid . . . well, I thought they might not understand. Understand why I was down here on the Pond Road, I mean."

Zenas did not ask why she was there. He waited, and after a moment, she went on.

"You see," she said, "I came because—well, because I wanted to see you, Mr. Bradshaw. To see you and talk with you. I had meant to come to the house here, but—but I lost my courage, I guess. I was turning back, giving up for the time, when I saw you. And then it all happened."

"I see. Well, you're here now, and so am I—and I'm liable to stay, worse luck. If you feel like talking I feel like listening."

"But I mustn't talk now. Betsy says the doctor left strict orders that you must not be worried by any one about anything."

"He did, eh? Well, he has worried me more than anything else so far, so suppose we leave him out of it. It was Mark you wanted to talk to me about, wasn't it?"

Her astonishment was so apparent that he grinned broadly. "There, there," he said. "Don't look as if I'd just taken the rabbit out of the hat; there's no miracle about it."

"But how did you know? How could you know?"

He shook his head solemnly. "It is wonderful how smart I am, I give in," he admitted. "Trouble is that every time I face a looking-glass it kind of shocks me to see how little of the smartness shows. Maybe I didn't know exactly, but I could guess. What other subject

129

would you and I be likely to have in common? Important subject, I mean. Mark is important enough to me,
and—well, I have had a suspicion he was important to
you, had it for quite a while. Let's say you and he are
important to each other. That's so, isn't it?"

She looked at him steadily without speaking. Then
her answer was brief and unequivocal.

"Yes."

He nodded. "All right," he told her. "Engaged, are
you?"

"Yes. . . . Do you mind?"

"Not a bit. I don't imagine it would make much difference if I did, but I don't. Fact is, I think he's a lucky
young fellow. Have you told your aunt and uncle yet?"

"I—we—haven't told any one. Perhaps I shouldn't
have told you now, if you hadn't asked. Not that I am
ashamed of it"—proudly. "It is only—"

"I know. There's no use advertising your own business until the firm is ready to put up its sign. Something
like that?"

"Just that. Mark and I decided not to announce our
engagement until—well, at least until he has finished his
training and has his commission. Then—well, we haven't
planned beyond that."

"I see. Good judgment, seems to me. . . . And this was
what you wanted to talk to me about?"

"Why—why, partly. I just had to talk with some one,
some one that—that I felt would be on our side. At
home—oh, I can't tell you how hard it is for me at home.
Uncle John and Aunt Etta are—well, they—"

"Never mind. I understand. Worry you, do they?"

"Yes. You see, they are determined—well, they have
other plans for me. There is—there is something . . ."

Again she hesitated, and again he helped her on. "Something named Davidson, I shouldn't wonder?"

"Why—why, yes. You know that, too?"

"Just more guessing. Putting two and two together, as you might say. Maybe a little more than that. Your Aunt Etta and I had a little talk the other afternoon."

Emily leaned back in the rocker. "Oh!" she gasped. "What did she say?"

"Not much of anything. It was what she didn't say that started me thinking."

He told her of his wayside chat with Mrs. Thacher. His listener's cheeks were very red when he finished.

"Oh, it isn't true!" she declared, vehemently. "There isn't going to be any 'announcement,' not the kind she hinted at, anyway. I am *not* going to marry Laurie. I have never thought of such a thing, never really considered it, I mean. How could she tell you that!"

"Maybe she hoped I might pass the notion along when I wrote—er—south. That is the only reason I can think of. If I wrote Mark that you and Davidson were—well, like that, it might head him off, if you see what I mean."

Her eyes were flashing now, and her lips set. "It won't," she said. "And when I get home I shall tell her and Uncle John why—just why."

"Shouldn't if I were you. Not yet, anyhow. . . . Oh, now, wait a jiffy: let me say a word."

He went on to explain. An open break between the girl and the older Thachers would help no one and make it doubly hard for her.

"As long as you and Mark have your own understanding and trust each other, as you do, that's all that really counts. If you and your aunt and uncle have a real row,

131

nobody knows what may come of it. It might get out—
such things do—and be talked about all over town. You
wouldn't like that. It might get to Mark's ears, and—
well, there is no knowing what he might do. He's young
and middling hot-headed, and if he knew you were
being made miserable he ... Look here, Emmie, you
haven't written him just how tough they were making
it for you, have you?"

"No. I was afraid if I did he might—might—"

"Might drop everything, training and his chance for
a commission and all, and come straight up here. I
don't know as he wouldn't; don't know that I wouldn't
if I were in his place. You wouldn't want him to do
that?"

"Oh, no, no!"

"Course you wouldn't; neither would I. Fact is"—
with a one-sided smile—"I am a little set on his making
good down there. The job he picked out wasn't the
one I had picked out for him, not by a long shot, it
wasn't. But, he picked it out and—well," with a snap of
his jaws, "I want him to go through with it, if only to
wipe away some of the pitying grins I've had to pretend
not to notice, and shut off some of the mean little hints
and back-handed sympathy I've had to listen to since
he went away. . . . But that's only a side reason; it doesn't
count. I don't count, either. You and Mark and what
you make of your lives do count."

He had been speaking rapidly and with emphasis.
Now his voice dropped, and, looking absently past her,
he added, almost as if he had forgotten she was there:
"As things are now I guess likely it is about all that
does count."

She waited for him to continue, but he did not, so

she spoke. "Then you think I should keep on—at home, I mean—just as I have been doing? Say nothing to Aunt Etta or Uncle John—or Laurie—about Mark and me?"

"Eh? What's that? . . . Why, yes, I do, for a spell anyway. If you can stand it, that is. Mark will be coming home again some of these days—he's hoping for another leave, or whatever they call it. When he comes, or if he comes, you and he can talk it out between you. If you need a referee or umpire or something—well, I'm always around, you know. And just now, while I'm in sick bay, if you get too hot under the collar and need a place to blow off steam in, this room is as good as any. I'll blow off some of my own at the same time. . . . Now who in thunder is that?"

It was Doctor Stevens who had knocked, and now he entered. "I looked in again to see if you were lonesome, Zenas," he said. "I take it you're not. Humph! Having good-looking girls come to see you must do you good. All right, only don't overdo it. Rest is what you need. Seems to me I've told you that—well, perhaps once before."

"Once! If you've told it only once then this place has got a better echo in it than the Mammoth Cave. Between you and Betsy my head has been ringing with it all morning. . . . Don't go, Emmie; I'm going to need a friend in a minute or so. I can see it in this fellow's eye."

Emily, however, declared that she must go: she had stayed too long already. "I will come again to-morrow, though," she added. "That is, if Doctor Stevens thinks my calls won't do you any harm."

The doctor was emphatically sure that they would have the opposite effect. After she had gone, however,

133

and after Stevens left, Zenas Bradshaw realized that he was tired. When Mr. and Mrs. Lemon peeped in at the door almost immediately afterwards his eyes were closed.

"He's asleep already, I bet you," whispered Betsy to her husband.

"Put five on that for me, will you," said a drowsy voice from the bed. Then, with unmistakable emphasis, it added "Good night."

Emily Thacher did call the next forenoon and the forenoon after that. In fact, she called daily throughout the week. Zenas looked forward to those calls as the bright spots in dreary days. He was slowly gaining strength, but as the week drew to its close it was evident, even to him, that he would not be able to leave the house and take up his duties at the store for a while longer. How much longer, Stevens refused to commit himself.

"Not for five more days, at least," he said. "You are doing first-rate. Be quiet and be thankful."

"You be thankful if I have money enough left to pay your bill. Stop in at the store and tell Abner I want him. Say, have you ordered him not to talk business with me? All I can get out of him is that things are going so smooth that he has to put on skates to keep up with 'em."

"Well, what's the matter with that?"

"Nothing, except that they never went that way when I was around. When it's too slippery, folks sometimes fall down. Oh, Lord, I've got to get out of here! I ought to have gone up to Boston a fortnit ago."

"Send Hallett. He ought to know how to attend to such things."

"Ought to—maybe he does, but there's a devil of a

134

lot of difference between knowing and doing. Abner is as honest and willing a man as ever lived, and when I'm on hand to nudge his elbow he steers pretty straight. He's never had to set his own course, though. Besides, with Mark gone and me laid up, the store is too short-handed as it is. If he goes, even for a day or two, the customers will have to wait on themselves."

He had spoken to Abner about the possibility of hiring another clerk. Hallett agreed that one was needed, but it was very hard to find the right man. Even then, in the early summer of 1941, the Government's first great effort for national training and defense was under way, and there were calls for workers of all descriptions. Men whose experience as carpenters had been limited to building chicken coops and repairing fences were leaving Harniss for Camp Scott and similar establishments, where they were being paid fabulous wages for, so local gossip reported, "lugging a chisel in one hand and a saw in the other and looking busy." The opportunity of standing behind a counter and selling groceries, at a wage distinctly not large, did not tempt the young and able-bodied.

One middle-aged citizen had been hired on trial, but Abner reported the trial as unsatisfactory, and he had been dropped. "I've got my eye on a couple more," said Mr. Hallett. "One of 'em—Elmer Bailey, 'tis—has rheumatism pretty bad, but he's thinking about the job."

"For heaven's sakes don't let him think too much or he'll have something worse than rheumatism. Elmer Bailey—thinking! What does he do it with?"

The almost daily talks with Emily Thacher were Zenas's oases in the desert. Emily, after that first confession concerning the state of affairs at home, never again referred to her own troubles. Things were better, she invariably replied to his questions, and just as invariably changed the subject. Zenas asked her if her aunt and uncle knew that she came to see him.

"I have never told them," she said. "Uncle John is knee-deep in politics just now, and Aunt Etta is head of the committee to raise money for the church. They are too busy to bother about me."

"How about young Davidson? He get around once in a while?"

"He was here day before yesterday, but only for a few hours. He is busy, too—at the camp, I mean."

Zenas thought it over and spoke what was on his mind.

"John and Etta will find out you're coming here," he said. "They are bound to. Betsy won't tell, she's got my orders not to, but I wouldn't trust Jake. He'd let the cat out of the bag any time, if there was a dollar bill tied to the gathering string. Suppose they do find out, what will you tell 'em?"

"Why, the truth, of course. That I like you and enjoy coming to see you. I shall tell them no more than that. They may—I suppose they will—suspect something else, but they won't learn it from me."

"Fine!"—with emphatic approval. "If they make any objections send 'em to me. The way your aunt rubbed against my leg and purred the other afternoon, she can't scratch—much. Not on such short notice."

A little later in the conversation Emily made a surprising suggestion. She prefaced it with an announcement.

"I am going to Boston day after to-morrow," she said.

"I shall stay three days with a friend in Somerville. She has been writing me to come, and Aunt Etta is willing I should. I mean to do a little shopping, but I shall have ever so much spare time on my hands. I was wondering if—"

"Yes. If what?"

"Well, Mr. Bradshaw—oh, I suppose this is presuming or—or something like it, but I—well, you have been troubled, I know, about a Boston trip you had intended to make. You told me you supposed you would have to send Mr. Hallett, but you didn't see how he could be spared from the store. Of course I don't know exactly what you wanted to do in the city, but if it was just—er—business errands, seeing certain people, or things like that, I wondered if I couldn't do it for you. You could tell me what you wanted to tell them—the most important part of it—and I could explain why you couldn't come yourself. Then, when you are well enough to go, you could—you could straighten out any mistakes I may make."

She paused. Zenas Bradshaw said not a word. His expression was, principally, astonishment. She glanced at him and then hurried on.

"Oh, probably I couldn't do anything, really," she said. "But if I could help I should love to. I shall have lots of time and—and, honest, I wish you would let me try. You could tell me just what you wanted done, and I could make notes of what you told me. Maybe—"

Zenas lifted his hand. "Wait!" he broke in. "Hm-m! ... Well, I declare! ... I declare I don't know but— And it would keep Abner at home where he's needed. ... Let me think."

He was silent for a rather lengthy interval. Then he nodded.

"You mean this, Emmie?" he asked. "You wouldn't mind?"

"Mind? Why, I've told you. I'd love to do it. Probably I wouldn't be of much use, but—"

"Shh! . . . Hm-m! Emmie, you won't go until day after to-morrow, you say? And you could come here and see me to-morrow forenoon?"

"Yes. Certainly."

"Fine. I'll think it over, all of it. And, if I make up my mind to take up your offer, I'll have a couple of letters for you to give to men I've dealt with for years. They know me, and I know their advice is worth a lot and that they can be trusted to be as square with anybody I send to 'em as with me. No need for me to say that I'm more obliged than I can put into words or that nobody can realize more than I that I haven't any right to ask it."

"You didn't ask, you know."

"Eh? Ye-es, I suppose that's true. Glad I can credit myself with even that much self-respect. Oh, Lord! Here comes my jailer, so you'll have to run along, I guess likely. See you to-morrow. I'll have a yes or no for you then."

The jailer, of course, was Mrs. Lemon, and Emily took the hint and departed. She was on hand early the following forenoon, however, and found Zenas awaiting her, his mind made up and three penciled notes hidden under his pillow.

"Yes," he told her, "I'm going to let you do it, and the Almighty forgive me for saying so. Here are those introducing letters I said I'd give you. I hope the ones they are written to can read 'em. Between scribbling them here in this bed and having to shove them out of sight every time Betsy showed up, I imagine they look more like Chinese laundry tickets than they do like United States language. Now, if your patience holds out, I want to give you a few sailing directions, as you might say."

The directions were simple, and to Emily, although she was careful not to say so, they seemed a trifle superfluous, but Zenas evidently considered them very important, and she listened carefully.

They shook hands. "No need to say you'd better not mention any of this to anybody?"

"Of course not. It is to be just another one of our secrets, yours and mine, Mr. Bradshaw."

He did worry a little, however. The rest of that second week in bed seemed longer than the ten days which had preceded it. His directions had been specific enough, but there were certain matters which could only be decided there in Boston, on the spot, and Emily would have to make those decisions, using her own judgment. He had thought of having her telegraph him if she faced a really important question, but a telegram, in Harniss, was by no means a secret communication. It would be delivered there to his house, and Betsy—or, worse still, Jacob—would receive it from the messenger. Betsy, if it was handed to her, would ask a hundred questions; she would tell Jacob surely, and the doctor probably. Jake would talk: he would want to know the whys and wherefores, and, if the information his curiosity craved was not given him at home, he would seek it in other places. The Thachers might hear of it. . . . Oh, no, no!

He, Zenas, could do nothing but trust to luck—and Emily—and wait.

After all, he reflected, this whole affair was not so dreadfully important. Regular old woman, he was getting to be. Whatever mistakes the girl might make could not be past correcting: he tried to console himself with that thought.

A letter from Mark, which arrived on the second day, was a distinct help. Mark was getting on well, studying hard, trying hard, and was by turns optimistic and discouraged.

"A month more and I shall know for sure," he wrote. "It will be a tough one, but, if I keep on as well as I've been doing, I'll pass, get my commission and wings, and be able to flap those wings and crow. And I *hope* they will give me a short leave and let me come home for a week or so. The old town will look good to me, I tell you, Grandfather."

Not a word about Emily Thacher. Mark was getting that information from headquarters, of course. And no mention of the "engagement," either. Probably Emily had not had time to write Mark that she had told their secret. "Keeping it from the old man," soliloquized Zenas. "Wonder what else he is keeping? None of my business, I presume likely. I just can't realize that boy is a man."

The last sentence was spoken aloud. Betsy, who was setting the room to rights, wanted to know what he was talking about. He looked at her over his spectacles.

"I was talking to myself," he told her. "When a fellow does that it's a sign of something, isn't it?"

"My grandmother used to say it was a sign the one who did it was either rich or crazy."

"Um-hm. Couldn't be both, at the same time, eh? How about Nebuchadnezzar? He was a king, as I recollect, and they caught him out in the yard eating grass."

Betsy thought that over. *"He* was crazy, that's sure," she admitted. "The Bible says so. And I suppose he was rich. Kings always are."

"Not all of 'em, nowadays, according to the papers. Maybe the grass needed cutting, anyway. Which reminds me of our own yard. Has that been cut lately?"

Mrs. Lemon smiled proudly. "Jacob cut it—some of it—yesterday. If the lawn mower hadn't been so dull he'd have cut it all, he said so."

Zenas Bradshaw whistled. "Jake cut it?" he repeated. "Well, well!" Then, innocently: "Haven't caught *him* talking to himself, have you, Betsy?"

Emily returned home by the late train on Saturday evening. Sunday morning she attended church with her aunt and uncle, but that afternoon she made her anxiously awaited call at the Bradshaw home.

And her report was surprisingly satisfactory. She had seen the Boston wholesalers listed by Zenas Bradshaw, had delivered his letters of introduction and had, according to her story, been graciously and cordially received.

"They were very nice, every one," she confided. "In fact"—with a laugh—"one of them asked me to lunch with him. He said he always asked you, Mr. Bradshaw, and you always accepted, so he didn't see why I shouldn't."

Zenas grinned. "Did you?" he asked.

"No-o, but I said I was awfully sorry not to. . . . Oh, it's all right; he was an old man, past fifty, I'm sure."

"Um-hm," dryly. "Right on the edge of the grave, as you might say. Well, go on."

She had ordered the various items on the list Zenas had given her, had made arrangements for further relays to be shipped later on, had discussed prices and the business outlook in general, had listened to advice, and, in every case, had been asked for and had supplied information as to the Bradshaw health.

"They knew about Mark's going away, of course," she went on, "and they had heard, too, that you hadn't been quite as well as usual this spring. No, I don't know who told them."

Zenas could guess. Traveling salesmen from the city firms called at the store, and some of them were young.

"Humph!" he grunted. "Confound that Elsie! She's a good girl, but she does like to go to the movies—with the right company. Look here, you didn't tell them I was sick, did you—real sick, I mean?"

"Oh, no, no! I just said what you wrote in your letters, that you were very busy and couldn't leave and that that was why I came. They all like you, Mr. Bradshaw. They do, honestly: it wasn't make-believe. They like you very much."

"Yes? Well, I've paid them a considerable amount of cash in my time. Liking folks that hand you money isn't a hard habit to get into. . . . There's something else on your mind, young woman. Now what is it?"

Emily flushed. "Am I as easy to see through as that?" she exclaimed. "You are right, though, Mr. Bradshaw, there is. I did a few things on my own responsibility. They are all subject to your approval, though, and if you don't approve I warned every one concerned that

you, or I, would telegraph or 'phone and the—er—
arrangements would be off—canceled, you know. They
agreed to that."

In her conversations with the representatives of the
Boston firms she had gathered that certain staples, those
in everyday demand in communities like Harniss, as
almost everywhere in the country, were likely to advance in price. The possibility of our becoming involved
in the European war was even then growing more and
more of a probability. Opinion was still divided, of
course, but the majority, she found, were inclined to
think involvement likely. The prices of the staples mentioned had already advanced to some extent and, as the
European war continued, whether the United States became an active participant or not, would certainly jump
much higher. Now, therefore, was the time to buy, to
lay in a reserve stock.

"That is what they all thought, I am sure," Emily
continued, "and one of them—that nice old Mr. Barbour, it was—said so in so many words. I looked around,
went into other places than those you sent me to, and
asked questions, how prices were with them—all that
sort of thing. It wasn't my affair, I had no authority
from you to do anything of the kind, but Mr. Barbour's
firm happened to have supplies of those things on hand
and so—and so—well, here is what I did."

She handed him a memorandum, a list of certain
goods she had ordered in the name of Bradshaw's, subject to its owner's approval. They were to be shipped
and paid for, not immediately or all at the same time,
but in instalments at intervals during the coming summer and fall. Zenas Bradshaw took the list from her
with barely concealed trepidation, scanned it slowly and

with great care, not merely once but twice. Then he looked up from it and at her.

"Well?" she asked, hesitatingly. "Is it *all* wrong? Was I *very* silly—and—and fresh?"

He drew a long breath, a breath that ended in a slow whistle.

"Fresh?" he repeated. "Not the way you mean it, no. If fresh means that you've put some new thinking into the Bradshaw business, and just about where it needed it, I'll say yes. Tell me, did you pick this stuff out yourself, or did Barbour do it for you?"

"Both, I guess. He suggested a number of other things, but I wasn't so sure about them. Of course"— hastily—"I am not really sure about these, either; but I—well, I took the chance."

"Um. So you did. Are you one of those critters that read folks' minds, young woman?"

She laughed. "If I am I don't know it."

"You'd make a good job of it, anyhow. To tell you the truth, I have had the notion of doing some buying along these lines for some time. It was one of the things I meant to look into when I went to Boston. I didn't mention it to you when you went because—well, because, to keep on with the truth-telling, I was—er—you hadn't had any experience and—oh, Lord"—impatiently—"why can't I say what I want to?"

"Never mind. You haven't answered me. Did I do right? I know I took a great deal on myself, but—"

"Hush!"—thumping the bedclothes which covered his knee. "Right? You did righter than I could have done it myself. And you did it now, instead of the two or three weeks from now when Ben Stevens might possibly let me go. You've saved me time and money, do

144

you realize that? . . . See here, Emily Thacher, you're a business woman. When you want a job in Bradshaw's Store there's one waiting for you."

"Splendid. I may remind you of that some day."

"You won't have to do it but once."

Chapter 8

THE next morning when Doctor Stevens called, he was astonished to find his patient no longer in bed but sitting in an upholstered arm-chair by the window. The chair, a big one, had been a part of the living-room furnishing, and to see it there, on the second floor, was almost as surprising as to see Zenas Bradshaw occupying it.

The doctor had entered the house without knocking, and Mrs. Lemon, who had heard the stairs creak, rushed up after him, arriving in the sick-room just at his heels. Between righteous indignation and alarm she was sputteringly hysterical. "What the devil—?" demanded Stevens.

Betsy burst forth. "That's just what I said," she vowed. "Those very words. I—eh? No, I don't mean that; I *hope* I don't use that kind of talk. Oh, dear, there I go again! Of course I'm not criticizin' *you* for saying it, Doctor, but—well"—defiantly—"it's what I meant, anyhow. When I came into this room an hour or so ago, and he told me he was going to get up, and stay up, I—I—"

"All for your sake, Ben," observed Zenas, cheerfully. "Last time you came you told me your back was hurting you, so I figured to fix things so you wouldn't have to stoop over. Didn't want you to put that back into my

146

bill along with the rest. How do I look folded in the middle? Feel better than I did stretched out, I'll tell you that."

Stevens did not answer. He felt the Bradshaw pulse and applied the stethoscope to the Bradshaw chest. Betsy watched in agonized anxiety. Zenas winked at her over the doctor's shoulder.

"Well, what's the news over the telephone?" he inquired. "What you might call getting an inside tip, eh?"

Doctor Stevens straightened, the tube of the stethoscope dangling from his hand.

"Confound you, Zenas!" he exclaimed. "What do you mean by doing this without orders from me? Don't you realize—"

"Shh! I asked you one first. I'm better than I've been for a fortnit, and you know it. Why don't you say so?"

His friend frowned, then shrugged, and finally gave in.

"I've got to say so," he admitted, with a reluctant smile. "But, all the same—"

"Never mind the buts. Who do you suppose lugged this chair upstairs for me? Betsy's own particular Jacob, that's who. I gave orders, and he did the work. I don't know whether he enjoyed his half of the exercise or not, but my half did me good. Now don't you tell me to get into bed again, because you'll be wasting your breath."

Doctor Stevens gave no such command. He yielded to the inevitable. Zenas remained in the chair all that forenoon and an hour in the evening. The following day he lengthened his stay. The day after that he did not go to bed at all until after supper. By the end of the week he was walking about the room and, a few morn-

147

ings later, was helped into the Ford and paid the first visit he had made to the store since his illness began.

Stevens shook his head but could not deny that his patient seemed to be in remarkably good condition, everything considered.

Betsy was happy but puzzled. "You picked up so all of a sudden," she told her employer. "That day when Emmie Thacher came to see you was the start of it, after she got back from visitin' up to Boston, I mean. I told her so, I said to her: 'I declare, Emmie,' I said, 'seems as if you've done him more good than the doctor.'"

Zenas's nod was emphatic. "She has," he agreed. "Her running in once in a while just about set me on my feet. That"—with a twinkle—"and one other thing."

"What was the other thing?" asked Betsy, innocently.

"Watching your Jacob lug that chair upstairs. If I could have seen him mowing the lawn I'd have been well a week sooner.... There, there, don't get mad. I only said it to make you ruffle up, old girl. And I'm much obliged to both of you, that's a fact."

Mrs. Lemon was mollified but not entirely freed from suspicion. She sighed. "Oh, I know you don't appreciate my husband. Never mind"—with a satisfied smile. "There's others that do. One in particular."

"Who's that?"

"Never mind"—mysteriously. "You'll find out one of these days, and so will other folks. Jacob is goin' to surprise this town before very long; you'll see."

Zenas Bradshaw muttered an absent-minded "I bet you," and paid no further attention to the prophecy at the time.

He found matters at the store in fairly good condition. With the summer season close upon them, it was absolutely necessary that another clerk be hired, and he finally located a middle-aged citizen named Eli Gammon who had had some experience in a small dry-goods shop in Bayport and who consented to give Bradshaw's a try. Zenas's estimate of his ability was summed up in his announcement to Abner Hallett.

"Eli's no seven days' wonder," he told Hallett, "but he ought to be able to wait on customers. You and I will have to keep an eye on him first along and see that he doesn't try to measure flour by the yard, but he'll be better than nobody."

Abner snorted. "Just about," he growled, but he offered no strong objection. As a matter of fact Mr. Gammon did very well. He was a good-natured, obliging man, and people liked him.

Competition from the chain store was keener than ever. Bradshaw's felt it more and more as the weeks passed. Abner and Miss Burgess noticed the falling off in trade and discussed it between themselves. They never mentioned it to Zenas Bradshaw, however, nor he to them. His health seemed to be no worse than it had been before his recent breakdown, and he had had no more attacks of giddiness. He was busy from morning to night and, outwardly at least, was in good spirits. If he worried he never did so publicly.

The news from Europe grew constantly more alarming, and the differences of opinion as to whether or not the United States would or should join forces with Great Britain more sharply marked. Congress was in controversy over this bill and that, vast sums were appropriated for defense projects, for armament manufacture, for ships, for planes. The expenditures, com-

149

pared with those which came later, were to seem almost trivial, but they did not seem so then. And the local Isolationists, although comparatively few in number, were outspoken and emphatic in protest.

"I do not," thundered the Honorable John Thacher, at a meeting in a neighboring town, "I do not object to judicious spending for defense of our own home front, nor for that of our possessions about the globe. What I do most strenuously protest against is the squandering of our national wealth and our personal savings in so-called loans to foreign powers who are using us as cat's-paws, as instruments to further their own ends. Shall we play their game for them? Shall the minds of our youth be insidiously inflamed with the spirit of war? War!"—with lofty derision. "Fellow citizens, you— I—all of us—are ready to fight if attacked, but who—I appeal to your common sense when I ask it—which of the war leaders over yonder will ever be mad enough to attack this free land of ours? I ask that question, and I pause for a reply."

He got no reply, of course. There was much applause. Nevertheless, on street corners, in post-offices and shops, in sewing meetings, in halls following lodge sessions, wherever men and women paused to chat, the question of war or peace for our country was debated, and there was far less emphatic head-shaking than there had been. To the thinkers, most of them, the feeling that, regardless of personal beliefs and oracular outpourings like Mr. Thacher's, war was almost an inevitability was growing steadily. Nazi armies were marching into Russia. Few thought opposition to their advance would amount to much or be prolonged. "Hitler will go through 'em like a fish knife through cod liver," prophesied Frank Holden. The majority agreed that he was right.

In Bradshaw's Store there was little discussion of the war. Mark's desertion of his grandfather was an old story now, and besides, by this time several other Harniss youths had enlisted in the army or navy, and more were contemplating doing so. This does not mean that Mark was forgiven by those who had condemned him. By them, and they were a majority, he was still considered an ungrateful renegade who would rather play soldier than work. He had ceased to be the topic of interest, that was all, and now, therefore, he was no longer talked about.

Zenas did not speak of him, except in answers to questions, and when he was asked how his grandson was getting on at his new job, he replied: "All right, from what I hear," and left the question to infer whatever he or she wished. Only with Emily Thacher did he exchange confidences. Although he saw her not as frequently as during his illness, he saw her every few days, usually at the store.

Once his curiosity led him to ask: "Do your Aunt Etta and Uncle John know you came to see me so regular when I was laid up?" he inquired.

"Yes," she said. "I told them. Of course they had heard that I was the one who found you that afternoon —at the beginning, I mean."

"Um-hm. Well, naturally they understood you would be interested in how I was getting on."

She said "Yes," but that was all. Obviously she did not wish to talk about it, so he asked no more.

Lieutenant Davidson's week-end visits to Harniss were frequent. He was very handsome and soldierly in

151

his uniform. Occasionally he accompanied Emily when she came to the store on household errands. There were no confidences exchanged with Zenas Bradshaw at those times. Davidson was chatty and cheerful enough, but the girl, or so Zenas imagined, was sober and troubled. The cause, he felt, was obvious. Betrothed to one man and being obliged to accept the attentions of his rival without open objection must be pretty difficult. However, this was the young people's problem, not Zenas's. They must work it out themselves.

Two happenings worth recording took place in early June. One, a conversation with John Thacher, occurred at the store late one afternoon just as Zenas was preparing to go home. Abner Hallett, Gammon, and Miss Burgess had already gone, and Zenas was alone. He had lingered to look over his bank-book and the unpaid bills in the file. Neither was a particularly encouraging occupation. He was still solvent, and there was small danger of his becoming anything else, but business was not too good, no doubt of that. For the hundredth time he caught himself wishing that Mark were there to talk it all over with him. The business needed young blood. It needed some one who was active, whose friends and acquaintances were of the coming generation, not the going. That confounded seventieth birthday of his was no longer something to be looked for with a spy-glass; it was in plain sight and almost close aboard.

It was then that John Thacher opened the street door and entered. Zenas Bradshaw awoke from his gloomy musings and saw him. The visitor spoke first.

"Good afternoon, Zenas," he hailed, graciously: John Thacher could no more have dropped the hint of gracious condescension from his manner and speech than he could, or would, have dropped his upper denture. "Good afternoon. Perhaps I should say 'good evening.' You are sticking to business late, aren't you?"

Zenas smiled and came out from behind the book-keeper's desk. "If you want to have any business at all you've got to stick to it these days," he observed. "How are you, John? Haven't seen you, to talk to, for some time."

John Thacher remarked that he happened to be passing and saw, through the window, that Zenas was in the store and, apparently, alone.

"So I dropped in to say hello," he added. "How is everything with you?"

"Oh, ranging from so-so to middling. All well at your house?"

Yes, all was serene in the Thacher domicile. Its owner added a flattering comment on the weather. Zenas Bradshaw agreed that the weather was quite satisfactory. In his opinion the Honorable John was sparring for an opening. That the purpose of his call was merely casually social Zenas did not believe for a moment. John Thacher usually had a reason for whatever he did.

There was a little more sparring. Mr Thacher offered a cigar. Zenas refused it, with the excuse that it was too close to supper-time. Thacher lit his own cigar and blew a smoke ring; he did that deliberately and well, too. After watching the ring float away and disintegrate, he turned suddenly to ask a question.

"Zenas," he said, bluntly, "why the devil do you do all this?"

Zenas looked incomprehension. "Do what?" he inquired.

"Why, this sort of thing. Get down to this store at

153

eight o'clock every morning except Sunday; stay here till bedtime almost; work and fret yourself sick? Oh, don't tell me you're not sick. Perhaps you are not now, but you have been, and we have all been very much alarmed about you."

"Have you so? Much obliged, but you needn't have been. Nothing much to be scared about."

"Nonsense!"—with good-humored impatience. "Of course there was. Even Doctor Stevens worried about you; he told me so."

"Did, eh? He never told me."

"He wouldn't be likely to. My niece, Emily, was very much frightened. As she was the person who was on the spot when you—er—collapsed, she, naturally, felt almost responsible."

"For what? She was responsible for lifting me out of the—what did you call it?—collapse, not pushing me into it. I might have been in a good deal worse one if she hadn't been on hand."

"I know, but she was very anxious about you. She insisted on keeping almost a daily watch on you until you were up again. Mrs. Thacher and I would have called, but she kept us posted on your progress."

"So she did. I shan't forget it."

"She was glad to do it. And, of course, Etta and I were glad to have her. But that is water over the dam now. When I looked in here a few minutes ago and saw you at that desk, at this time in the evening, I—I give you my word I just had to come in and talk to you. What do you do it for?"

Zenas Bradshaw shrugged. "Oh, partly for money, but more because I like it. What do you want me to do? Sit at home and put my feet up?"

"At your age you ought to be doing just that.... Oh, I know you don't like to have it said, but it is the truth. Come, come, why not be sensible? Perhaps you need the money—so does almost everybody—but there are easier and safer ways of getting it than this—er—slavery."

"That so? What, for instance?"

"Let some one else do it. Hang it all, Zenas, why don't you sell out while you can? Sell out and retire."

Zenas turned to look at him, then turned to look out of the window at Main Street, still bright in the sunset light. "What does that mean?" he inquired, with a smile. "You wasn't figuring to make me an offer, was you, John? You aren't thinking of signing off law and politics to take up measuring out groceries, not to mention hay, grain, and feed? Shouldn't hardly think so. You've done fairly well at your own jobs, or so I've always understood."

He chuckled as he said it. John Thacher smiled. "Well, no, not exactly," he admitted. "I don't expect to take up a new—er—profession at—at—"

"At your age, as you said to me just now. Didn't think you did. But you sound almost as if you had a likely buyer in your mind. Who is it?"

Thacher hastened to protest. "Oh, no, no!" he exclaimed. "Nothing as definite as that. It is only that—well, I have been given to understand—it has come to my ears that—er—certain people might—I say *might*—be interested enough to buy out Bradshaw's, even pay an adequate price for the store, stock, good will, and all the rest of it, if they knew it could be bought. You may remember my hinting something like this to you before."

"I do. But I don't recollect your telling me who the people are. And so I ask you again: who are they?"

155

"That I am not at liberty to tell you. Of course, it is not my business, but—"

He was not permitted to finish the sentence. Zenas Bradshaw broke in at the middle of it.

"I remember you said that before, too," he interrupted. "I'm not just sure what I said then, but this is what I say now: it isn't your business, nor anybody else's outside of the Bradshaw family. And"—with unmistakable deliberation and emphasis—"it isn't going to be while I'm alive. After I'm dead—well, I'm not dead yet, by a darned sight."

He paused, and then, the slow smile returning to his face, he added: "Sound as if I was a little hot under the collar, don't I? Well, maybe I am, but that's no excuse for boiling over. Thank you, John, for all your good intentions and interest and so on, but I won't sell Bradshaw's. And I won't quit running it, either—until I have to."

He expected his caller, if not to take offense at this plain speaking, at least to show some symptoms of ruffled dignity. It was not often that John Thacher condescended to offer friendly counsel gratis. Legal advice, yes, but that—or so common report whispered—was very adequately taken care of in the bill for professional services rendered. Zenas had stated his mind without reserve, and if the Honorable John had stalked out, with a straight back and a heightened color, he would not have been greatly surprised. Zenas had no wish to offend, but he did intend to make himself understood. Having done just that, he could only wait and see what happened.

And nothing happened. Nothing at all. The Thacher

back did stiffen just a bit, perhaps, and the Thacher neck above the immaculate collar reddened ever so little. But even this may have been only in the Bradshaw imagination, and there certainly were no signs of active resentment. Nor was there a prompt departure. In fact, Mr. Thacher, although he did turn toward the street door, seemed almost reluctant to leave. When he spoke it was with a tolerant smile.

"All right, Zenas, all right. I can understand how you feel. No doubt I should feel the same way if I were in your place. Bradshaw's is a—sort of a Harniss institution, I know that, and no one could feel worse than I to see it drop out. But—well, it is my experience that dropping softly is a whole lot pleasanter than falling hard. This isn't the world your father and mine lived in, and conditions for all us—er—survivals are changing. Your friends don't want to see you kill yourself. We want you to stick around for a good while yet. I believe—well, I happen to know that there is a chance for you to get rid of this particular care"—with a gesture indicating the store and its contents—"at a—or I shouldn't wonder—a fairly adequate figure. If I were you I should do it.... There"—with a shrug. "I have said more than I came to say. Now you can tell me to go to—er—the hot place. Good evening, Zenas."

He took another step toward the door, but still he lingered. Zenas Bradshaw's eyes narrowed as they watched.

"No use my telling you to go there, John," he observed. "I wouldn't anyhow, and from what I hear, that place is crowded as it is. Only, since we're speaking right out in meeting, suppose I do some of the catechizing.

You won't tell me who the folks are that are willing to take that chance you mention, of buying me out, I mean?"

"No-o. I can't do that. The matter is—well, confidential. It—er—happened to come to my ears, as I said. I believe it to be genuine. I am practically sure you could sell if you cared to, that's all."

"Um-hm. You do sound pretty sure, that's a fact. Look here, John: these folks you talk about haven't delegated you to talk turkey for them, have they? You aren't acting as their agent, are you?"

There was no doubt of the resentment now. The door latch clicked sharply as the caller's thumb snapped down upon it.

"Certainly not," sputtered John Thacher. "I—I must confess I don't like— Good day."

"Wait a jiffy."

But Mr. Thacher did not wait. He went out. Zenas Bradshaw, looking after him, pulled thoughtfully at his upper lip. He had not been diplomatic, that he realized. It might have been better to wait. To wait and, perhaps, learn more about this around-the-corner game and what—or who—was behind it. Whoever they might be, this was their second approach, and each time it was John Thacher who did the approaching. Thacher had denied that he, himself, was the principal. He had just as hotly denied that he was that principal's duly appointed agent. Nevertheless...

Zenas, tugging at his lip, admitted that he might have been a little hasty. He had offended one who had come to him as a friend. That did not amount to much; that the Honorable John's professed friendship for him was deep he doubted. That it was disinterested he doubted even more. They had differed too often and on too many points for that to be considered a possibility. John Thacher had an ax to grind, and, if it was not his own ax, then he was turning the grindstone for some one else and would be duly recompensed for the turning. Recompensed in one way or another.

Nevertheless, it might have been better to profess interest and listen longer. Oh, well, it was done now, for better or worse. He was no diplomat, never had been. And, at least, he had made his position clear. Bradshaw's Store and the Bradshaw business were not for sale. Thacher and those behind him—the chain store group or whoever—could put that statement in their pipes and smoke it.

He squared his shoulders and turned back to the heap of bills on his desk.

Dear, dear! How he missed Mark. Missed him quite as much now as when he first went away.

The second worth-recording incident had nothing to do with Bradshaw's Store or, directly, with any Bradshaw. It was Mrs. Lemon who imparted the news to her employer, and although that news was surprising enough, to Zenas, thinking it over afterwards, even more surprising was the fact that Betsy had managed to keep it to herself as long as she had.

She had been in a curiously excited, almost exalted, state, for some time. Zenas, although he had quite enough of real importance to occupy his mind, could not help noticing his housekeeper's absent-mindedness, her fits of alternate elation and depression, and the fact that the excellence of her cooking varied with these moods. He did not complain; his own mind, just now, was not concerned with what he ate, and if the biscuits were heavy or the clam fritters too greasy he took them as they came and said nothing.

One day, however, as he sat down to his lonely noon meal and filled his cup from the coffee-pot, he stared at the result of the pouring and rang the hand bell. Betsy hurried in from the kitchen. She was in one of her "up" moods that forenoon. Zenas looked her over. Her round cheeks were very red, her eyes were shining, and her fingers, as they played with the bowknot of her apron strings, were trembling. Her voice, too, when she addressed him, had a quaver in it.

"Eh?" she queried. "Yes. What is it?"

Zenas Bradshaw slowly shook his head.

"Betsy," he observed, gravely, "you shouldn't let yourself sit on the front of the stove so long. You ought to move yourself back when you begin to bubble."

Mrs. Lemon, naturally, made nothing of this. She stared and gasped.

"What kind of talk—" she expostulated. Mr. Bradshaw went solemnly on.

"It would be an awful thing if you boiled dry," he continued. "I've seen many a good kettle ruined that way."

"What *are* you sayin'? I never—"

"All right, all right. Let's change the subject. Did the doctor tell you coffee was bad for me?"

"What? No, course he didn't. Seems to me he said that you mustn't have too much of it, if it was too strong."

"Um-hm. He'd be a happy man if he could see my ration of it this noon. Look here."

He handed her the half-filled cup. She stared at it

unbelievingly. "Why! Why!" she gasped. "There's—there's no coffee in it. It's nothin' but hot water."

"That's what it looked like to me."

The housekeeper snatched the pot from the table and turned back the lid.

"My soul!" she exclaimed. "Why, I—I believe I forgot to put the coffee in. I never done such a thing before in my life."

She was on her way to the kitchen, but Zenas called her back.

"Never mind the coffee," he ordered. "Come back here and sit down. What's it all about, Betsy? Better tell me, hadn't you?"

Betsy hesitated, stammered, and swallowed several times. She did not sit, but she did remain where she was, the steaming coffee-pot in a shaky hand. Zenas Bradshaw chuckled.

"The verdict is guilty," he said, "but with recommendations for mercy. What's going on, Betsy? Now, now, don't say 'Nothing,' or I'll call for the extreme penalty. You've been working up a fever for a week or more. I've noticed it. One time I think you're in bad trouble, the next I judge you must have assurance of full salvation or something. This is one of your 'Glory hallelujah' days: I saw that soon as I came in the door. Course you don't *have* to tell me anything— Hi! Look out! You'll scald yourself—or me."

He sprang from his chair and seized the coffee-pot just as it was about to slip to the floor. He placed it carefully on the table.

"When I was a little shaver," he commented, "I had to take a hot bath in the kitchen every Saturday night, but I never took one in the dining-room, as I recollect.

161

. . . Well, Betsy, what do you say? Is Jake coming down with the smallpox or have you been left a million? Which one is it? If you hold it in much longer you'll blow up."

The housekeeper gazed at him almost in awe.

"How did you know it was Jacob?" she demanded. "Nobody could have told you, because nobody knows it yet—nobody but him and me and—and her."

Zenas selected the most important pronoun from the assortment offered.

"Her?" he repeated. "Who is 'her'?"

"Why, Mrs. Bodley. She wouldn't tell, I'm sure she wouldn't. She was the one that said we wasn't to tell nobody until the arrangements were made."

"Mrs. Bodley, eh? Humph! Arrangements, you said. Well, that might mean something to somebody, but it doesn't to me. Mrs. Bodley? You mean that woman down at the hotel?"

"Yes"—excitedly. "Yes, of course. Mrs. Carleton Bodley, the—the awful rich one, the millionaire one. You've seen her, Zenas. She's the one that—that—"

"Shh! Hm-m . . ." reflectively. "Yes, I know who you mean. Widow of somebody or other, isn't she?"

"Yes. Oh, yes! Why, her husband was president of an —an oil company. No, come to think of it, I guess it wasn't oil. Seems as if it was somethin' to drink."

"Beer?"

"No!"—with scornful derision. "I should hope not! My Jacob wouldn't have anything to do with a—a beer woman, no matter how much money she had. It was somethin' like—like—oh, why can't I think of it? You see the signs up everywhere. Gin—seems to me there is a gin in it."

"So? Well, that ought to make it popular. What has Jake got to do with—"

"Wait! Why can't I get that name? *I* know!"—triumphantly. "It isn't gin, it is vin—no vite, that's it. Mr. Bodley was head of the Vito Pep Company. And Vito Pep is sold everywhere, all over the world, so Jacob says. All over the world! Just think of that."

"I will, if you'll give me the chance. Wait a minute before you say any more, let me get my bearings. Mrs. Bodley—yes, yes. Tall woman, broad in the beam, wears eye-glasses. Down at the Inn last summer for a month and came early this year. Widow—yes, yes. Well, she looks like one—or a monument. Humph! Seems to me I did hear she and Jake were pretty chummy. I didn't pay much attention, though. She and he going to get married?"

"What? Why, he is married. Don't be so—"

"All right, all right.... Well, are you going to tell me?"

"I—I don't know as I ought to tell you. It's such a secret."

"All right. Then I'll have to keep on guessing. They can't get married, so—"

"Be still! . . . Yes, I will tell you. Everybody will know it pretty soon, anyway."

She burst in a freshet of words, a freshet that had evidently been backing up behind the dam of enforced secrecy for days and days. Now that the dam had gone the words spurted. The outpouring was so torrential, with fresh jets of enthusiasm shooting out in the middle of every other sentence, that Zenas Bradshaw found it hard to keep his understanding above water. He was patiently long-suffering, however, only diving into the

163

flood to ask an occasional question, and, at last, he had strained the facts from the mess of drifting verbiage.

They were interesting facts, too. And totally unexpected, so far as he was concerned. He remembered having heard chuckles and facetious remarks to the effect that Jake Lemon, in his capacity as tourist guide and oracle at the park by the shore, had apparently found a "soft thing" in the wealthy Mrs. Bodley. Some of those remarks returned to his mind. "He's got her on the string. She's down there about every other day, listening to Jake tellin' how Harniss was first settled and who settled it and how much better job they'd have done if he'd been on hand to help 'em, all that regular line of his, and they say she just eats it up." ... "I bet you! And pays full price for every meal, too." ... "Why, my wife swears she see 'em out ridin' together t'other day. In that big car of hers, they was, with the Bodley chauffeur man, cap and brass buttons and all, up in front, and Mrs. Bodley and Jake on the back seat, lookin' grand as Hitler and his wife out for an airin'. Haw, haw! Shows what a slick tongue'll do, don't it? The rest of us have to get along with a Model T, or hoof it, but not Jake Lemon, no sir! ... Well, she may be rich now, but you give Jake time and—"

And so on. Zenas had heard those things, but, as he would have said, they went in at one ear and out of the other. If they meant anything it was that the smooth Mr. Lemon had struck pay dirt for a time. But, according to Betsy's story, there was much more than that. Mrs. Carleton Bodley, it seemed, was an ardent lover of antiques. Whether the love was a recent seizure or a disease of long development seemed uncertain, but, according to Betsy, the emotion was deep and ardent. And

164

in Jacob Lemon she had, apparently, found a kindred soul. Jacob—this, also, was news—loved antiques, had always loved them, had had long experience with them and possessed a discerning and judgmatical eye. Under his guidance Mrs. Bodley had "antiqued" in Harniss and vicinity. And now—this was the amazing outcome, and Betsy swore it to be true—Mrs. Bodley had decided to open an antique shop of her own in Harniss, "just as a—well, hobby, shall we say," and Mr. Lemon was to be its resident manager, director, salesman, and purchasing agent.

"The store is all picked out," gushed Betsy. "They signed the what-do-you-call it—the lease this very mornin'. They won't call it a store, though. Jacob says they don't call that kind of store a store any more. It's a 'shoppe,' that's what it is. Only when you say it you don't say 'shoppy,' you say 'shop,' just as if there wasn't an 'e' on the end of it. You know what I mean: like the Crescent Gift Shoppe over to Bayport, or the Sea Gull Shoppe and Tea Room at South Ostable, or—"

"Yes. Certain. Sure. I get you. The lease is signed, you say. Where is this—er—shoppy shop shoppe going to be?"

Mrs. Lemon's ample chest swelled with importance.

"Right here on Main Street," she announced. "Right in sight of Bradshaw's, it is, only across the road. It's that place where Nathan Beams used to have his barber shop. You know it, Zenas. Of course"—rather reluctantly —"it isn't awful big, but it is pretty good-size—too big for a barber shop, that's why Nathan moved out—and they're goin' to fix it all up—"

"Who is? Jake?"

"No. I do wish you'd say Jacob. It sounds so much more important."

"Couldn't sound more important than Jacob does—is, I should say. Go on."

The shoppe was to be renovated, repainted, and decorated. It was to have bay windows, "the old-fashioned kind, with little tiny panes, and shelves to show the pitchers and vases and things," and the street door was to have bull's-eye glass panels: "Jacob says he knows where he can buy some lovely old bull's-eye glass ones, the kind that are so thick and—so—bubbly you can't hardly see through 'em. He is to buy whatever he thinks is correct and in keepin'. Mrs. Bodley says it's very important to keep everything in keepin'. And—"

The rhapsody continued. Zenas Bradshaw learned that the shoppe was not to open for business immediately. Repairs and alterations would take some time, and the purchase of stock even longer. It was possible that the establishment might not be ready until the following spring. Meanwhile, and after Mrs. Bodley's departure for her city home, Mr. Lemon was to superintend and use his judgment. "Mrs. Bodley told him she knew she could depend on his judgment for everything, making the place look in keepin' and to pick up nice bits here and there—museum pieces especially. That's what Jacob always calls the kind of antiques he likes, museum pieces."

Zenas was a half-hour late in getting back to Bradshaw's that afternoon. Betsy's last words to him at the door were that he was to be sure and not tell any one one single bit of all this because it was a dead secret. He promised, reflecting that, if what he had just heard

166

was true, or only partially true, the secret would be dead but a very short time. This was Harniss.

His judgment was soon verified. The next day the news began to spread. Jacob Lemon, himself, when questioned, did not deny the story: in fact, he amplified it. Mrs. Carleton Bodley, when the local correspondent of the New Bedford paper called on her at the Inn for an interview, confirmed it.

"Mr. Lemon," she was quoted as saying, "is an exceptional man. One of the most gifted and generally well-informed men I have ever met. I soon discovered that he and I shared a love for rare old things. I have always wished that I might own an antique shop—not"—with an amused smile—"for the profit to be gained but because of the enjoyment I knew I should find in it. The difficulty was to find exactly the right person to conduct it. In Mr. Lemon I have found just that person."

The paper's representative gathered that the lady considered Jacob Lemon's talents to have been wasted in Harniss and that the new antique shoppe was to be opened principally to permit those talents to develop and blossom. Financial return was a secondary consideration.

A traveling salesman from one of the Boston firms was in Bradshaw's, and, when he heard of the Bodley-Lemon venture, he nodded knowingly.

"Mrs. Carleton Bodley," he said. "Of course. Her name gets into the paper every month or so. She is always breaking out with some new stunt or other. She is a great person for taking up with what she calls 'protégés.' One time it is a fellow who plays the piano, she

167

is going to make another Paderewski out of him. Next time it's an artist. Now it's an antique dealer, eh? Well, well!"

Zenas Bradshaw grinned. "Being what you call a protégé sounds like a made-to-order job for Jake Lemon," he observed.

The salesman chuckled. "Maybe," he commented. "Only—well, being protégé of a weather-vane isn't exactly what I should call paid-up life insurance."

Zenas was called away then, and the conversation ended.

So, in due course, the carpenters came to what had been Nathan Beams's barber shop, and work began. Townspeople watched them take out the windows to make room for the old-fashioned ones with the little panes, and Mr. Jacob Lemon superintended their labors and offered suggestions and rode in the Bodley limousine behind the brass-buttoned chauffeur and was very busy and important indeed. And, at home in the Bradshaw dining-room, his wife expatiated upon his importance to her employer and shone in an aura of reflected glory.

Letters from Mark came with fair regularity. Sometimes they radiated optimism and sometimes dripped doubt and gloom. Still, on the whole, Zenas gathered that his grandson, although working hard, was reasonably hopeful. The final test, when he was to learn whether he had earned his commission and his wings, was only a short time ahead.

Trade at Bradshaw's picked up a bit as the summer season neared its peak, but it was not as brisk as in previous years. War was more than ever the absorbing topic in the papers and in local conversation, and Congress was voting this and that and still debating heatedly the question of this country's attitude toward the struggle. A western senator of fame as an Isolationist spoke at a meeting in Ostable, and he was introduced by the Honorable John Thacher.

Zenas saw Emily more or less frequently, but they had few intimate conversations. When he mentioned something which Mark had written him she was interested, but he could see that it was old news to her. He judged that her letters from the southern training camp were quite as informing as his and probably very much more frequent. She looked, it seemed to him, troubled about something. She did not say so, and he asked no questions. Lieutenant Davidson's name she did not mention, nor did he.

Another event of local interest happened about this time. Frank Seymour, Mark's friend, the amateur aviator, sold his flying field to the Government. It, the field, was to be enlarged and made a part of the coast defense plan, so it was said. The report was that Seymour got a big price for it. He resigned from Ex-Senator Buck's employ but remained in Harniss to help with the work at the field. Later, he told intimate friends, he was to be given a commission in the country's air service.

The first week in August was the critical week for Mark Bradshaw. On Thursday of that week Zenas received a short letter. The fatal day was the following Tuesday. Two days later a boy came into the store with a telegram.

"Got those wings, Grandfather. Going to see you soon, I hope. Everything grand, swell and A1. Shake.

Mark."

Two days later came another.

"Coming home for a ten-day leave. Be there Monday. Am I sorry? What do you think?"

Zenas met the train at Ostable. The sun-burned young man in the new uniform with the shining insignia on his breast jumped from the car step before the train had stopped moving and rushed across the platform. They shook hands.

"Gosh!" exclaimed Marcellus Bradshaw, Third.

"Amen!" devoutly agreed Zenas Bradshaw, Second.

Chapter 9

MARK was a very happy young man. His grandfather was a very happy old one. Betsy, when she met them at the door of the Bradshaw home, declared she was so glad she didn't know whether to laugh or cry, and, to prove it, she did a little of both. Even Mr. Jacob Lemon momentarily deigned to forget his responsibilities and importance as manager, purchasing agent, and construction superintendent of "Ye Genuine Antique Shoppe" and shook the hand of the newly fledged Lieutenant and expressed himself as very glad to see the latter.

"You look very fine in your new uniform," he added. "Becoming, very becoming."

Zenas Bradshaw, watching the ceremony, chuckled inwardly. He seemed to detect a note of repressed envy in the Lemon comment. If there could be a flaw in Jacob's self-satisfaction and pride in his new position, it might very likely be that the latter did not necessitate wearing a uniform. Brass buttons and shoulder straps—or, better still, epaulettes—would have been the crowning touch on the day when "Ye Genuine Antique Shoppe" opened its doors.

Mark had told much during the drive home from Ostable station. After supper he told more. He had passed his examination with high marks. The graduating exercises, with the presentation of insignia and the formal induction into the armed service of the United States, had been impressive.

"I kept wishing you were there, Grandfather. But you couldn't leave the store, of course. I knew that."

It was the first time Mark had mentioned the store since he stepped from the train. Zenas, to whom Bradshaw's was the second most important item in the world's inventory—the person who had hitherto neglected to mention it being the first—noticed the omission but found it excusable. One could hardly expect a young chap who had worked as hard as Mark had done to attain a desired end and had finally attained it, to think of much else—yet. Flour, feed, and groceries were everyday and dull: they did not glitter romantically as those wings did.

So Zenas Bradshaw merely agreed that he could not leave the store, even to see the precious wings pinned on his grandson's breast. "Wish I could have, though," he added.

"I'll bet you do! Some of the fellows flunked. Gee, I was sorry for them! They'll have another try, most of them, but—"

He was off again. After another session of rhapsody, he did, however, come back to Bradshaw's. "Everything going all right, I hear," he said casually. "Gammon's doing pretty well, eh? You told—I mean you wrote that he was."

"Yes, he'll do. Getting better right along."

"That's fine. Well, Grandfather, at least you haven't been giving us any more scares—like the one when you keeled over out here in the road, I mean. I tell you, honest, I was on the point of dropping everything, ex-

172

ams and all, and heading north. But, almost as soon as I got the news, they said you were better."

"Emily kept you posted, of course. I knew she would."

"Why—er—yes, she did. Say, Grandfather"—with some embarrassment—"she—she wrote me she had told you how things were with us?"

"You two being engaged, you mean? Yes, she told me."

"You were surprised, I'll bet."

There was no hint of sarcasm in this speech: it was honestly uttered. The boy actually believed that the announcement had come as a complete surprise. Zenas, who had wondered whether or not he was expected to laugh, saw at once that the laugh would have been a bad mistake.

"Knocked right off my feet," he agreed, gravely. "Congratulations, boy. You've got a grand girl."

"I'll say I have. Glad you don't mind. I sort of guessed you wouldn't."

"You're a good guesser. You're itching to go and see her this minute, of course. Run right along, why don't you?"

"Well—er—if—say, I hate to leave you so soon. But—well, you know how it is."

"I can recollect how it used to be. There, there, clear out. . . . Oh, you might give her my love, too—if you can find any room for it."

A moment later the outer door closed. Zenas Bradshaw sighed. As Mark had said, he knew how it was. And, yes—it was scarcely a comforting reflection but it was a true one—this was how it was likely to be. He reached for the cigar box and the newspaper.

173

He was in bed and asleep long before Mark came home and away to the store before the young man awoke. Mark came to the store, himself, later in the forenoon, however, and he and Abner Hallett and Miss Burgess and Willie Snow exchanged greetings and handshakes and, in the case of the masculines, slaps on the back. The new uniform and the wings were inspected and talked about and unanimously approved. Elsie Burgess's inspection was the most careful and her approval most enthusiastically expressed.

"I will say this much," she announced, with emphasis. "Army clothes do set a person off and make him look— oh, what do I want to say?—distinguished. I always thought that Laurie Davidson looked swell in his uniform, but I honestly think you look better. Don't you agree with me, Mr. Bradshaw?"

Zenas, who was standing near-by, nodded. "Sure thing," he agreed. "Finest looking soldier in the family just now. Of course, when I get my own rig on he may have to— Oh well, we'll let him shine while he can."

Elsie tittered. "Your rig?" she repeated. "Are you going to enlist, too, Mr. Bradshaw? What are you going to be—a captain or something?"

"Me? Nothing so low as that. I'm going to get elected Major General of Supplies. Then, when the Army folks need a quarter pound of saleratus, I can hand it to 'em in style."

The bookkeeper and Mr. Hallett thought this a wonderful joke and laughed uproariously. Mark did not laugh, however: if he heard the witticism he ignored it. His grandfather, turning to look at him, noticed a pucker between his brows and a glint in his eye which was obviously not a merry one. He took little part in the chatter which followed and, a minute or two later, walked away. Zenas took a step in his direction and then turned back. Something was wrong, that was plain. And yet, so far as he, Zenas, could remember, nothing had been said to displease his grandson.

Nothing except the bookkeeper's reference to young Davidson. Humph! Yes, it might be. Davidson was out of the running, so far as Emily Thacher was concerned, but he, probably, did not know it. And John Thacher and his wife did not know it, either. And Emily might have told Mark of the very trying position she was in, there, at home. She had told him—Zenas—that she said nothing about it in her letters, but now that she and Mark were together, she might.

By this time, Zenas, too, was frowning. He was realizing that things could not go on as they were much longer. There would have to be a showdown, the cards would have to be laid on the table some day. And when they were—then there would be real trouble. Neither Thacher, John or Etta, was used to being thwarted. Each of them was strong-willed, obstinate, and persevering. Emily, too, had a will of her own. She was grateful to her aunt and uncle for all they had done for her, she was fond of them, but gratitude and affection were not enough to force her into a marriage with one man when she loved another. Not Emmie Thacher, no sir-ee!

So, when the showdown came it would mean—what? Open war, or something like it. Half the world was already at war and the other half on the ragged edge of hostilities. If a private war between the Bradshaw and Thacher families was to be added, as a side-show to the main circus, it would be, to Zenas's mind, a most undesirable complication. He must find some excuse and opportunity to talk the matter over with Mark, drop a few judicious hints, and make the boy realize that, for Emmie's own sake, tact and diplomacy were still necessary. The young people were in no position financially to consider immediate marriage, so the crisis must be delayed for a time longer.

Possibly young Davidson might be transferred to some other post much more distant than Camp Scott. That ought to help.

At supper that evening Zenas led the conversation around to the fringe of the subject concerning which the judicious hints were to be dropped.

"Emmie was glad to see you last night, I shouldn't wonder," he observed.

"Yes."

"Looking pretty well, she is, don't you think?"

"Yes."

Short answers. Not too encouraging a beginning. Nevertheless, Zenas persevered.

"See John and Etta when you called?" he asked.

"Yes."

"What did they have to say about your new rig, the wings, and all the rest of it?"

"Not a great deal."

A moment of silence. And again it was the senior Bradshaw who broke it. "I see," he said, goodnaturedly. "That's that. . . . Well, what *do* you want to talk about? The weather, or how the hens are laying? Something like that?"

Mark picked up a teaspoon, twisted it between his fingers, and then threw it down with a petulant clatter.

"Who the devil do they think they are?" he growled, savagely.

"They? What they?"

"Old Thacher and his wife. Why, darn it all, Grandfather, when I called there last evening they treated me as if I was a—a peddler, or something."

"Humph! If you had been a peddler they wouldn't have let you in. Etta's down on peddlers."

"She is down on me, so far as that goes. It was the maid who opened the door, and she acted as if she had made a mistake. Emily came then, and she really let me in. And when the Thachers, the old ones, I mean, showed up and saw who I was, they—well, I wish you could have seen the expression on Mrs. Thacher's face."

"Didn't look happy, eh?"

"Happy! She looked as if she would like to bite me. At first, that is; she thawed out a little afterwards, and so did he, but there was plenty of frost, even at that. When Emily called their attention to my wings, Mrs. Thacher said, 'Oh, yes, quite pretty.' Not what you would call enthusiasm, I'll say."

"Not like three cheers and a tiger—no. Oh, well, I suppose you know the reason?"

"I didn't—then, but I could guess. I do know now. Emily met me this forenoon and she told me. Davidson, of course, blast him! Emily says it has been going on all summer: they've got it all fixed that she is to marry him, and they never let her forget it."

"Well, well, I shouldn't let it worry you. He won't get her."

"You bet your life he won't! But to think of all she has had to put up with. And she wrote me scarcely a word about it. Said she wasn't going to trouble me. Trouble! By the Lord, if she *had* written, I—"

He stopped short. His grandfather helped him along. "Suppose she had," he suggested. "What could you have done?"

"Done? . . . Oh, I don't know. I'd have done something, though, even if I had to quit and come up here, myself."

"That wouldn't have been too good for her, and just about ruination for you. It would have meant wiping out all the hard work and study you've put in and set you back to the beginning. Mark, you take my advice and let Emmie Thacher handle matters here at home for the present. She's a mighty smart girl; she can look out for herself."

This, the first of the "hints," was not too graciously received. Mark grumbled something under his breath, and then turned upon the hinter.

"She says she told you all that was going on," he declared. "And you didn't tip me off, either. Why didn't you?"

"Just the same reason she didn't. That it would take your mind off more important things."

The word was badly chosen. The tone in which it was repeated proved that. "Important! If you think having her badgered and nagged from morning till night isn't important, then you and I differ, that's all."

"There, there, boy! Smooth your feathers. What I mean is that your army job is a good deal more important just now than anything else can be, important for you and her both. And an open row here at home won't help anybody—except maybe the gossip swappers in Harniss. What a gay time *they* would have."

"Who cares a damn about them?"

"Why, I do, for one. Maybe Emmie does, for another. You would be out of it, down south or somewhere, but she would have to stay here and take it."

This bit of common sense seemed to make an impression. Mark thought it over. He was still far from complacent, however.

"H'mph!" he grunted. "I suppose you are right there. I tell you this much, though: she shan't be driven to marrying him or any other stuffed shirt that John Thacher and his wife pick out for her. Who do they think they are, I ask you?"

"I know—that's what you asked me to start with. I imagine they think they are themselves—and are pretty well satisfied with their thoughts. But their niece thinks for herself, and you know what she thinks. So you ought to be satisfied, too, seems to me."

Mark Bradshaw relapsed into another interval of moody silence. Then he rose from his chair.

"I'm going out, Grandfather," he announced. "See you later."

"All right. I'll be here to be seen. And, Mark—"

"Yes?"

"Don't think I'm butting in on your affairs. Maybe I'm just—or almost—as much interested in having those affairs turn out right as you are."

"I know, I know. Sorry I've been so grouchy to-night. Couldn't help it, I'm mad clean through. As for this particular affair turning out all right—well, it will. I'll make it. There is one way that—"

He did not finish the sentence, and when Zenas called after him there was no acknowledgment of the call. The door slammed.

179

Zenas reflected that he had done his duty: he had dropped the precious hints. How judiciously they had been dropped or whether good would result from the dropping were questions for time to answer. The trouble with that was that young people were so impatient where time was concerned. For them a thing must be done immediately; whereas an elderly person, possessed of a fair share of sense born of experience, had learned the value of waiting.

A satisfactory reflection of itself, but provocative of another, namely: that the said elderly person, having spent practically all his or her life in learning how to wait, had little or no time left in which to do it.

Like fussing with a broken umbrella on a wet morning. By the time you had it fixed the shower was over.

Mark's leave ended altogether too soon for him, for Emily, and for Zenas. One morning, in the latter third of the brief vacation, the young man, at breakfast time, asked permission to borrow the Bradshaw car. His reasons for the loan seemed to be rather vague.

"Just want to drive around a little," he said. "May go as far as Bayport, or somewhere. Do you realize I have scarcely been off the Harniss main road since I came?"

"That's true enough. Only, when you first got back here, I seem to recollect your saying you never wanted to be anywhere else. . . . Oh, all right, all right. Course you can take the car. Have a good time—both of you."

Mark, who had put down his coffee cup and had risen, turned and stared. His expression was an odd one. He looked fixedly at his grandfather.

"Both of us," he repeated, slowly. "Who—what do

you mean by that? I didn't say any one was going with me, did I?"

"No, I'm just practising my mind-reading. Getting good at it, too, don't you think?"

Zenas laughed as he said it, and after a moment Mark laughed, too.

"You may be right, at that," he admitted. "I don't know for certain that you are—yet; but you might be, if I'm lucky."

"And that's just possible, I suppose. . . . Eh? Yes? Something else you wanted to say, was there?"

Apparently there was. Mark hesitated. Then he asked what, to his grandfather, was a quite unexpected question.

"How is the store doing—in a business way, I mean? Profits about the same as usual?"

"Couldn't hardly expect 'em to be, times like these. Manage to keep afloat, that's about all. . . . Why?"

"Oh—nothing. I just wondered. You haven't said much about it."

"Probably not." Then, dryly: "Neither have you, so far as that goes."

"Haven't I? I meant to. People pay their bills on time, don't they?"

"Some of 'em do. Those bills aren't as big as they used to be and there aren't quite as many of them, that's the main difference."

"I see."

Another pause.

Zenas waited for the next question. This might be the moment he had hoped for, the opportunity to talk over the affairs of Bradshaw's Store with the only other Bradshaw, to whom that store and its business were, or should be, of personal consequence. He had led up to the subject several times, but hitherto Mark had not shown a real interest. Zenas, although disappointed, had not resented this lack of concern. He understood. Mark's success in winning his commission and, above all, his—and Emily's—troubles with the Thacher family had monopolized the young fellow's thoughts. Bradshaw's, to him, was a settled and established fact: it had always prospered and, to his mind, always would. That was the reason, of course.

Now, however, it was Mark himself who had broached the subject. He had not forgotten, after all. Good! First rate! Now Zenas could say a few of the things he had been wanting to say, might even ask for counsel on one or two points which had kept him awake when he should have been sleeping. Not that Mark's advice on business matters was likely to be good for much, but at least it would do no harm, and might direct Zenas's own ideas to new paths leading out of the tangle.

So Zenas Bradshaw waited for Mark Bradshaw's next question, but Mark's next remark was not a question at all.

"Well," he observed, cheerfully, "so long as the old bank account is all right the concern needn't worry, I'd say. We always kept a good-sized balance in the Harniss National, I remember. I'll bet you haven't let that slip, Grandfather. I know you."

Zenas grunted. "It has slipped more than I wish it had," he admitted. "There's a shot still left in the locker, of course, and so long as it can stay there I shan't take down the sign."

"Yes"—with a grin. "Not much danger of that, I

guess. . . . You may not be feeling exactly—well, flush, perhaps, but I'll bet—"

"Flush!" The interruption was sudden and sharp. Some of the distressful thoughts which had filled Zenas Bradshaw's brain for days and nights were spoken aloud. They burst forth of themselves.

"Flush!" he blurted. "Boy, you don't know what you are talking about. Let me tell you there are times when I'm ready to thank the Lord on my knees that I, and the string of Bradshaws afore me, had sense enough to put a few thousand to one side in what my dad used to call the 'hard luck fund.' Something to have as an anchor to windward when the ship was running close to the rocks. If it wasn't for that I— Here! What's the matter? Have I scared you? I didn't mean to. We aren't sunk yet, not by a darned sight."

The grim emphasis with which the first part of this declaration was uttered appeared to have taken Mark very much aback. He was not grinning, now. Instead, he was very sober indeed.

"You—you mean that?" he faltered. "You mean that—that you are—are hard up? Really hard up? That Bradshaw's is—"

"There, there! I don't mean that we're flat broke. And I don't mean that we can't pay our debts. I do mean that we are where every cent counts and I have to be careful. You see, Mark—"

But Mark was not waiting to hear the rest. He had picked up his hat and was already in the living-room on his way to the front door.

His grandfather shouted. "Here! Hold on! What's your rush?" he called.

Mark did not turn back. He muttered something

183

about it being later than he thought, and added: "Much obliged for the car. I'll take good care of it."

Zenas Bradshaw hurried to the living-room window to look after him. Now what on earth was all that about? Why the sudden interest in the store's welfare and the quite as sudden ending of that interest and the conversation? He, Zenas, had been pretty emphatic in his statement concerning the necessity of counting the pennies and being careful, but he had not exaggerated the situation. It was the first time he had said anything of the kind to his grandson—or any one else, for that matter—and he had not meant to say it now. It might be that the boy detected, or thought he did, a reproof in the outburst, thought that his grandfather was still nursing a grudge against him for deserting Bradshaw's and going off on his own. If that was the difficulty it must be cleared away, and should be. No ill-feeling in the Bradshaw family: that family was too small for misunderstandings. Especially now, when its youngest member might soon be—goodness knew where.

So Zenas took pains to be especially cordial and cheerful when the pair next met. Mark did not return from his outing in the car until supper time, and he went out again soon afterward. To his grandfather's inquiry as to where he had been and what sort of a time he had had, he replied, "Oh, over to Bayport and around" and that he had had a good time. He volunteered no particulars and Zenas asked for none. Mark seemed preoccupied, so Zenas thought, and alternately in high spirits or depressed and silent. Whether or not Emily Thacher had been with him on the drive he did not say, and that, too, Zenas did not ask.

During the course of the conversation Zenas hap-

184

pened to inquire if Mark had heard from his friend and first instructor in aviation, Frank Seymour. Seymour, since contracting to sell his flying field to the Government, had been in Harniss but once and then only for a day or two.

"Nigh as I can find out, hardly anybody saw him while he was here this time," Zenas went on. "When he first went away the story was that he expected to get a commission as an Army or Navy flier, but I haven't heard of his telling anybody that he'd got it. Has he, do you know?"

He looked up to find Mark regarding him with an odd expression.

"That's funny," was the young man's comment.

"Eh? What's funny about it? You and he were such chums, I thought maybe he'd written you, or something."

"Well, he has, as a matter of fact. The funny part was that you should ask me about him now. I was thinking about him myself, you see. . . . Yes, I got a letter from him a while ago. He didn't get the commission. Something wrong with his age—or health—so the doctors said."

"Hum! Too bad. Where is he now?"

"In Connecticut. Bridgeport, I believe."

Before his grandfather could ask more Mark hurried on.

"Frank thinks we will be in the war sure, and inside of a year," he added. "I wonder if he's right. It hardly seems possible—a real war."

"Guess likely it will be real enough, if it comes; doesn't seem to be much make-believe over there on the other side of the big pond. And the way the Washington folks are spending money, building every sort of killing machine and getting ready to repel boarders, looks as if they expected a fight. And the draft doesn't sound like peace. Do you realize how many young chaps you used to know have been taken already?"

"I know, but that is for defense, in case the Hitler gang should attack us. A great many people think they never will be foolish enough to do that. According to Emily, her uncle is perfectly sure they won't."

"I'll bet he is! John Thacher is sure about a whole lot of things, always has been ever since I can remember. His opinion swings on a greased joint, like a weather-vane; when the wind shifts he can switch from due west to due east without a squeak. If we do go to war—say, on Tuesday—by Wednesday morning John's nose will point in the direction the blow comes from, see if it doesn't. Yes, and if you dare tell him it used to point exactly opposite, he'll prove that the trouble was with your eyesight, you haven't been looking at him right. John Thacher is a smart politician."

Zenas concluded this estimate of the Honorable John with a chuckle. Mark's smile was a faint one: if he had listened it was absent-mindedly.

"Well," he observed, "I wish I knew."

"Whether we'll be in the war or not? So do a whole lot of us, far as that goes."

"You think we will, don't you, Grandfather?"

Zenas nodded. "Yes," he said. "I do."

Mark seemed about to say something else, to be, or so his grandfather imagined, considering how to say it. If so, he changed his mind. He said nothing more, and the talk ended.

"There's something on your mind, boy," said Zenas

to himself. "Most likely it will come out by-and-by. Hope so, anyway."

It did not, however, and two days later, the leave was over. There was another drive to the Ostable station, another handshake and good-by, and once more Zenas Bradshaw was left alone on the platform to watch the last car of the train disappear around the curve. He felt lonelier than ever as he turned back to the automobile. Why did the happy times in a man's life have to be so short and the intervals between them so long? You didn't notice the difference as keenly when you were young, but you did later on.

His old acquaintance, the station agent, wandered over to chat.

"Just another one of them good-bys, eh?" he observed. "Ain't much fun, be they?"

"Not much, no."

"Um-hm. I'm seein' a good many of 'em these days. Three of our young fellows went off to one of them army or navy camps this week. Makes you kind of wonder how many of 'em will come back—to stay for good, I mean, don't it?"

"Eh? . . . Oh yes, yes; that's right, it does."

"Um-hm. Lots of queer stuff in the newspapers mornin's. My wife is scairt to death over it; she more'n half expects to be blown out of bed by a bombshell some night. I tell her there's no sense settin' up and waitin' for it. Might as well sleep while we can, eh?"

"Yes"—absently.

"That's what I say. That grandson of yours gets over to our town kind of often, don't he? Three times in a week or so."

"Yes. . . . No. What do you mean—three times? How do you figure that?"

"Easy enough. Once when he came on the train. Once, just now, when he went off again. And last Wednesday, when him and his girl—I suppose likely she was his, 'twas a girl, anyhow—was down street in that same car of yours. I see 'em, myself. Along about noon time 'twas, when I was goin' home to dinner. I didn't know the girl, but I knew Mark right off and hollered to him, I did, but he never heard me. Had somebody better-lookin' to listen to, I guess likely. Ho, ho!"

Zenas Bradshaw rubbed his chin. Wednesday—that was when Mark had borrowed the car for the day. He had, in answer to his grandfather's question, said something about having been as far as Bayport, but nothing about Ostable. Ostable was more than twice the distance from Harniss. Not that that would have made any difference to Zenas—the length of the ride, that is—but why had Mark and Emily—she was the girl, of course—gone away over there? And why had Mark said nothing about their having done so?

Oh, no particular reason, probably. They were so wrapped up in their own personal affairs and so absorbed in each other that they may not have realized or cared where they were going. It was their affair, anyway, and what difference did it make? None, of course, so forget it.

Matters in the Bradshaw household settled back into the old routine. For Zenas that routine varied, on each work day, very little. Breakfast, the store, home for the noon meal, the store again, home for supper, the newspaper and a cigar, and then to bed. His health continued to be fairly good, and there were no more of the

188

disturbing attacks of giddiness. Doctor Ben Stevens kept a careful watch over him, dropping in every day or two, ostensibly to gossip, but really, as Zenas well knew, to check up on the patient.

"Getting sick of seeing me, aren't you?" asked the doctor.

"Not a bit, Ben. So long as you don't see me sick, I'm satisfied. Say, if you are looking for a likely patient why don't you keep a weather eye on Jake Lemon? Jake's head is swelled so nowadays that his neck is liable to snap under the weight of it."

"When is that antique shop—excuse me, 'shop-pe'— going to open?"

"Give it up. I ask Jake that every once in a while, and he doesn't like it. He's never quite certain whether or not I'm having fun with him, and the notion lets a little air out of the balloon, as you might say. Not much, nor for long, but some. He'd like to tell me it is none of my business, but he doesn't quite dare. Near as I can find out the place will open when the Bodley woman gets through spending money for stuff to stock it up with. When that will be only Lemon and she and the powers above—naming 'em in the order of their importance—know."

Mrs. Bodley and Jacob were together daily. The Bodley car rolled from one end of the county to the other, and little homes along the back roads received unexpected visitors who, after perfunctory apologies, asked permission to look about a bit, explaining that—to quote Mr. Lemon—they had heard rumors of an "interesting chair," or a piece of glass, which might possibly be "Old Sandwich." "Of no value to you, of course, but we make a—er—hobby of such things, you understand."

The owners of the "interesting chair" and the old glass understood surprisingly well, even if they did not admit it. It was by no means the first time that searchers for antiques had called, although the majority had not declared the purpose of their visit as openly. These householders were not altogether ignorant of the chair's value: in fact, most of them had an exaggerated estimate of that value. Also, they had heard of other visits paid by the Bodley-Lemon combination and were ready when their own turn came.

Consequently, these calls were altogether too likely to slip from the high esthetic plane upon which they began and degenerate into bargaining matches. Some of those matches ended with the Bodley chauffeur tenderly bearing the purchased article out to the car, but others—far too many of them—concluded with Mr. Lemon's haughty and empty-handed departure, with Mrs. Bodley's disgusted exclamation of "Ridiculous!" and "I never heard of anything so ignorantly outrageous!" as an accompaniment. She did not trouble to lower her voice when making these comments, and they were heard and noted for repetition in the neighborhood.

By the end of the month it was plain that "Ye Genuine Antique Shoppe" would not be sufficiently stocked with museum pieces to open for business that season. The Inn closed early in September, and Mrs. Bodley returned to her city home, leaving Jacob Lemon in charge of the Harniss venture. He was to continue searching until spring for treasures worthy of the Shoppe's high standard, and, some time in June, the opening would take place.

"She has left it all to my husband," Betsy Lemon

told Zenas Bradshaw proudly. "He is to hunt for the—what-do-you-call-'em—pieces, and buy 'em just as he sees fit. Mrs. Bodley won't have to do one thing about it."

"Except pay the bills," suggested Zenas.

"Eh? Why, of course. You wouldn't expect Jacob to do that, would you?"

"Not for a minute"—promptly.

"Of course not. But it's a great compliment to him, ain't it? Her trusting him so absolutely, his judgment and everything, I mean."

"It is. Something ought to be said about *her* judgment, too, I should say. Well, Betsy, you'll probably see a little more of your husband, now that his other girl's run away for a spell. That ought to be a comfort. Weren't getting jealous, were you?"

The last sentence was accompanied by a chuckle, but Betsy did not, apparently, see the joke. Instead of smiling, she sighed.

"No-o," she said, solemnly. "No, I wasn't jealous, not really. Only—"

Zenas turned to look at her. "Only what?" he demanded in incredulous amazement. "You don't mean—"

"Well, I am foolish, sort of, I know. But—but—well, he was with her so much, about all of every day lately, and a good many evenings, and he talked about her so much, and I couldn't help hearin' so many of the grand things she said about him. . . . Oh, why"—with sudden exasperation—"do folks that you always figured were your friends like to come runnin' to you with—with things that they know perfectly well will stir you up? I declare I got so sick of hearin' how somebody or other saw her and my Jacob together at this place and that, and how close together their heads were. 'She was whisperin' right in his ear, Betsy,' and all such stuff. Oh, I know they just say it to tease me, but—well, I'm glad she's gone, if only to stop that kind of talk for a spell."

Her employer wanted to laugh, but he restrained the impulse.

"Wouldn't let it bother you, Betsy," was his advice. "One of those heads is a good way from here now, so your nosy friends won't see *that* again—until next summer, anyhow."

Betsy did not appear to find too much solace in this statement.

"Humph!" she snapped, "if they don't see that they'll find somethin' else just as provokin'. Now it's letters. Up to the post-office yesterday that Clark girl, the one who hands out mail, was all of a giggle when she passed me ours. 'Two more Boston letters, Mrs. Lemon,' says she, 'and both of 'em for your husband. Somebody up there must miss him awfully, to write so often.' Both of those letters were from Mrs. Bodley, and Ann Clark knew it, the fresh thing!"

"Trouble is that your husband is altogether too fascinating, Betsy. The woman can't let him alone."

"Stuff and rubbish! Now don't *you* start being funny, Zenas Bradshaw. Those letters were nothin' but business ones, about antiques and such. I knew that and so did that Clark one, but she had to be saucy just the same. I'm gettin' tired of it, and I told Jacob so."

"You did, eh? Well, well! What did he say?"

"Nothin'. Except to tell me not to talk when he was writin'. Yes, and he was writin' to her that very minute. I saw the name on the envelop."

Zenas was amused by this exhibition of wifely resentment, but he forgot it by the time he reached the store. The Lemons, even the pompous Jacob, were crowded from his thoughts by the pressure of business and other matters, personal or public. This was the fall of 1941, and the papers were shouting the news of the slowing down of the Nazi drive toward Moscow and of the President's calls for more and larger appropriations for national defense, and they were head-lining the debates in Congress. They gave much space to the speeches of Senator This and Congressman That, as the arguments for and against Isolationism waxed hot.

In Harniss, as in all towns in the country, more and more young men were called into service. The local detachment of the Coast Guard, from a comparatively small body manning the two stations four miles apart on the beach, had grown to three times its ordinary number. Uniforms, of one kind or another, were frequently seen along Main Street. A number of the older men who had been working at odd jobs, lawn-mowing, painting, shingling, or gardening, suddenly discovered that they were carpenters and left town for Camp Scott or some other of the Government projects, where, so the story went, they readily found work at more than twice the wages they had ever before been paid. The problem of finding some one to do this or that little household repair began to be troublesome.

Mark's letters to his grandfather came at irregular intervals. He, Mark, was busier than ever. He had been shifted to a training base in another southern state, where he was being taught what he called "advance work." And from this station he was ordered to another.

"This is the real thing, Grandfather," he wrote. "Pursuit School, they call it. They are pushing us along fast now, I tell you. I truly believe I may see some real fighting and before very long, too. The fellows here are hoping that we will be in the big fuss by spring. That's something to look forward to, eh? I'll say it is! If I can get an Interceptor Command, be boss of my own plane in a scrap, that's all I ask. They are teaching us tactical flying, close formation stuff, and gunnery. That looks like business, doesn't it?"

Zenas Bradshaw was obliged to admit that it did. And day by day it looked increasingly that way. It was true that certain men of country-wide notoriety still wrote and orated violently against war, that largely attended public meetings were held in the cities to protest against involvement, and that, in Harniss, the Honorable John Thacher and his lessening group of followers still criticized and protested and sneered at the Administration's policy. Nevertheless, confidence in the maintenance of peace was waning fast.

Even Japan was beginning to be mentioned as another possible source of trouble, although comparatively little attention was paid to that. What could Japan do, even if she wanted to? She had her hands full with China, as it was. The Japs, as a menace, were a joke: for particulars listen to Mr. Thacher and his satellites.

Zenas saw little of Emily Thacher. They met occasionally at the store, but there they had no opportunity for lengthy talks together. On the few occasions when they were alone for a minute or two they exchanged information concerning Mark, but Zenas could tell her nothing along that line which she did not know already, and, if she knew more, she never mentioned it.

That her position in the Thacher home was as uncomfortable as ever he inferred from her manner more than from her words. He came to the conclusion that she did not like to talk about it, and so he, too, dropped the subject.

In late November came a short note from Mark. "I am getting on tip-top. I can handle a fighter plane as well, and almost as easily, as I used to handle that old car of ours, Grandfather. Training now is fun. I can shoot pretty straight, too, if I do say it. There are stories that a bunch of us may be sent out of the country pretty soon. Nobody knows where, except the chiefs, of course, but that's the rumor. I'll let you know as soon as I know, myself. Maybe they'll let me have another leave before I go—if I go. I shall try to work it that way, if I can."

There was a brief postscript. "Say, Grandfather, if I *should* be ordered away, and can't get home beforehand, keep what you would call a weather eye on Emily for me, will you? I shall count on that."

Thanksgiving was a lonely day for Zenas, and he spent more than half of it in the office at the store. Elsie Burgess was a satisfactory bookkeeper, but the opportunity to go through the books and check up on the unpaid accounts without her company was welcome. Business these days was not as flourishing as it had been in other years, even in this, the off season, but it was not too bad, everything considered. He, Zenas, was obliged to be careful with his buying. The necessity which he had mentioned to Mark, that of counting the cents, was always there. He wondered how the chain-store people were making out, and wondered, too, if Mark would get the leave he hoped to get. If he should—if he could be home at Christmas time. . . . Probably that was too much to expect.

And then, on a Sunday early in December, as Zenas, lounging in his favorite rocking chair in the sitting-room of the Pond Road house, was considering whether or not to go down to the store for another glance at those books, Betsy Lemon came rushing in from the kitchen. Jacob was at her heels.

"Oh!" she gasped. "Oh, Zenas! We just heard—Jacob and me just heard— Oh, it can't be so! But they say it *is* so. It came over the radio. I was listenin' to—to that about—oh, you know, about that man that's always tryin' to—to hang pictures or lay carpet and—and falls down and smashes it up. You know, that funny one—"

Zenas raised his hand. "Easy, Betsy, easy," he cautioned. "Whoever he is, he *must* be funny if he falls down when he's laying carpet. Easier to fall up from that job, I should say. Little mite mixed, aren't you? What is all this?"

It was Jacob who answered. The radio had broken in upon the adventures of the carpet layer to give the news of the surprise attack upon Pearl Harbor.

"That's what it said," blurted Mr. Lemon, in conclusion. "But—but I don't believe it."

Zenas Bradshaw rose from the rocker. "Neither will John Thacher," was his impulsive comment. "And I don't know as I—"

He did not finish the sentence. The thought struck him like a blow. Suppose it was true! And Mark—

"Where are you goin'?" demanded Betsy, as he pushed by her.

"To that radio," sharply. "Where have you got the darned thing?"

196

Chapter 10

JACOB LEMON'S "I don't believe it," as uttered by him when he came into the Bradshaw sitting-room following that first radio announcement, was but a fore-runner, or an echo, of thousands of similar expressions all over the country. The incredulous ones did not be-lieve it then, but within a very short time they were forced to believe it. The United States, which no foreign power would ever have the effrontery to attack, had been attacked. Pearl Harbor, the Navy's great base in the Pacific, had been bombed and our fighting ships destroyed, our sailors and soldiers killed, our sea power temporarily crippled, our security challenged.

And by the Japanese, those little yellow men at whose "ridiculous blusterings" the Honorable John Thacher, his leaders and followers, had so contemptuously scoffed. All America rocked from the treacherous blow and then clenched its fists and vowed vengeance.

The Honorable John, when the word reached him, at first expressed incredulity, then amazement, then right-eous and fiery indignation. True to Zenas Bradshaw's prophecy, the weather-vane swung from due west to due east and by noon of December eighth was pointing as directly to conflict as it had hitherto pointed to peace. And this, to quote Zenas once more, "without a squeak." To a daring individual who, at the post-office, presumed to suggest that it looked as if the folks at Washington were right after all, Mr. Thacher retorted that, so far from being right, they were, as always, inexcusably wrong. "If they had been right this outrage would never have happened," he thundered. "We have poured out millions and millions for defense, your money and my money. What has become of that money? Where is the defense we paid for? I ask you that, James Cahoon!"

Mr. Cahoon was not ready with a satisfactory answer and was, therefore, squelched.

Zenas Bradshaw's first sensations were, like those of all his fellow Americans, amazement, shock, and then a furious desire to fight. He sat up far into the night listening for the last scrap of news the radio could give him and went to bed to toss and tumble and wish, even more than he had wished it at any previous time, that he was a young man instead of an old one. His grandson was young, however. Mark was going to see the real fighting he had been hoping for. Mark was lucky.

The newspapers next day were filled with the story. Not the whole story, of course—months were to pass before that was given to the public—but enough to show that the disaster was serious indeed. Betsy, as she served her employer's breakfast, was in a curious state of mind. Her ideas of just what had happened seemed to be a trifle vague, but that it meant battle, murder, and sudden death she was acutely aware. Pearl Harbor was, to her, but a name, but that "those awful Japan critters" had killed she did not know how many of our people and that they must be stopped before they killed more she was loquaciously certain. She expatiated on the subject each time she came into the dining-room. Zenas, when she paused for breath, said yes or no automatically, quite as often in the wrong place as in the right.

"Jacob says we've all got to go to war now," was one of her excited declarations. "Yes, sir, that's what he says."

Zenas stirred his coffee. "Is he going?" he inquired.

"Who? Jacob? Of course not. He's too old.... Not"—hastily—"that he's an old man, because he isn't. It's only that it is the real young ones the Government wants. He says if it wasn't for that he would enlist in a minute. That's the only thing that stops him."

"I bet you it is! Tough luck for the country. Hand me the sugar, will you, Betsy."

Betsy pushed the sugar bowl in his direction. "He's kind of worried, Jacob is," she went on.

"So? Didn't know he ever worried, except about his meals."

"Oh!"—in exasperation—"I wish you wouldn't keep sayin' those things. If I thought you meant 'em I'd be *so* cross. He is worried about his business, that's what troubles him."

"Business?"—innocently. "What business?"

"Oh, stop it! You know what I mean. His new shop, of course."

"Tut, tut, Betsy! Musn't leave off the tag that way. It's a shop-pe, not just a plain shop."

"Well, what of it? It's the same thing."

"I wouldn't say so. There's liable to be considerable difference in the prices charged.... Yes, I will have another muffin, even if you don't press me. You're a good cook, Betsy. Why don't you start a bake-shop-pe? You'd do well."

Mrs. Lemon ignored this frivolity. She filled the muffin want and then rattled on.

"Jacob says he's kind of fearful that, if this war keeps on until spring, folks may not be quite as much interested in antiques as they are now. He thinks all the fightin' and soldierin' may sort of take their minds off."

"Dear me! Now I *know* war is what Sherman said it was. Yes, I shouldn't wonder if a good many minds were taken off, as you call it. I shouldn't wonder at all."

He sipped his coffee absently. The housekeeper bubbled over once more.

"We was talkin' about Mark, Jacob and I was," she observed. "Jacob says Mark'll have to go to fightin' right off. Do you think he will?"

"Presume likely," curtly. "That's the job they hired him for, isn't it?"

A moment of reflection. Then a long sigh.

"Why, I suppose 'tis, in a way," agreed Betsy. "It's kind of—of awful, though, to hear you call killin' folks a job, as if it was keepin' store, or somethin'. Somehow I never really thought of his goin' soldierin' that way. I always kind of figured his doin' it was a sort—of— oh, I don't know—play—game—hobby, like Mrs. Bodley's fussin' with antiques. He'd do it for a while, until the newness wore off and he got tired of it, and then, of course, he would come back to Bradshaw's, where he belonged. That's what I thought."

Zenas did not answer. Betsy went on.

"Oh, dear," she groaned. "Suppose—why, Zenas, suppose he—suppose—er—somethin' happened to him? Suppose he never came back? What would *you* do? You are —I mean you ain't as young as you used to be. If anything happened to Mark what would become of the store? There's always been a Bradshaw in Bradshaw's Store. Have you thought of that?"

Zenas put down his empty cup and pushed back his chair. "Why, yes, Betsy," he replied, solemnly. "Now that you mention it, seems to me I have thought of it – once or twice."

At the store, conversation centered on only one topic. Abner Hallett and Elsie Burgess and Mr. Gammon and Willie Snow discussed it among themselves and with customers. It was on the lips of every man and woman who entered the front door. Even before he or she inquired a price or gave an order there was a preface dealing with the war which had been thrust upon us. But, even so, there was comparatively little realization of the great fact or what it was to mean to America or to the speakers as individual Americans. We were going to fight—oh, yes. We must fight now. We were going to wipe "those sneaking Japs" off the face of the earth. "When we get going we'll clean 'em up with one hand."

Just as simple as that.

It was a hard day for Zenas Bradshaw. Almost every person who accosted him had something to say about Mark. "That grandson of yours is going to see some hot work, after all, eh, Zenas?" "Bet you Mark is some excited this morning, eh, Zenas?" "Haven't heard from the boy yet? No, of course you haven't."

Zenas said as little as possible. His replies to those questions were monosyllabic. Only in the case of Mrs. Abigail Simons did his tactful reticence slip.

Mrs. Simon's temper was ruffled. She was in an awkward position. She had been a devoted follower of John Thacher in his opposition to our participation in the war and had echoed his scornful sneers at the ridiculous idea of an attack upon our land and flag. Now that the attack was a reality, those sneers, like chickens, were

201

coming home to roost, and they were by no means welcome prodigals. To eat her own words and pretend to enjoy the taste was something Abigail had never learned to do gracefully. She spluttered recriminations against the enemy abroad, but she could not forbear tossing a brickbat in the direction of former opponents here at home.

"Well," she declared, "they've got the war they've been pushing us into, and spending our money on, and all that. Now I hope they are satisfied."

Zenas, to whom this remark was addressed, asked if she had given her order yet.

"No, I haven't," she snapped. "I'm so upset by this dreadful news I haven't thought about housekeeping at all, scarcely. Oh, dear! Isn't it awful? Our fine young fellows having to go off goodness knows where to be killed and our cities and towns being bombed to pieces. It isn't Christian, it's just heathen."

Zenas stroked his lip. " 'Why do the heathen rage?' " he quoted. "What can I do for you, Abbie? Got some especially good turnips; Solon Bearse brought 'em in this morning from his own field."

Abigail ignored the turnips. "Well," she observed, "I am glad I did my best to keep us out of the wicked mess. *My* conscience is clear, anyhow. *I* haven't any son to see marched off to his death.... Dear me, perhaps I shouldn't have said that—to you, Zenas."

"Why not?"

"Why—why, because everybody knows how much you think of Mark. And now—"

"Wouldn't be likely to think any the less of him now, would I?"

"No, no, of course not. Only I'm so sorry for you. If anything should happen—"

It was at this point that Zenas Bradshaw ceased to be the polite storekeeper and spoke what was in his heart.

"You needn't be sorry," he broke in. "Mark is where he ought to be and I'm glad of it."

Mrs. Simons gasped. "Glad!" she repeated, incredulously. "Glad?"

"Yes, glad. Damned glad!... Abner, wait on Mrs. Simons, will you? I'm busy."

Before nightfall most of Harniss had heard how Zenas Bradshaw told Abbie Simons he was damned glad his grandson was where he might be killed at any time. Also how the insulted Abigail had marched right out of Bradshaw's Store and would never darken the Bradshaw portals again.

If the lady whose sensibilities were thus outraged could have heard some of the comments with which the story was received she would have been greatly surprised. The drift of local feeling had been changing direction for months, and Pearl Harbor turned the drift into a rush. John Thacher was by no means the only easy-swinging weather-vane in town, and Mrs. Simons was not overpopular throughout the community. The tale, exaggerated and embroidered by its many repetitions, was chuckled over in quarters where its heroine would have expected it to arouse sympathetic indignation.

As one listener put it: "Served her right. Wish I could have been there to see her face when Zenas handed her that damn.... Don't know as I blame him for telling her off. It's a good joke. Only"—as an afterthought—"it has cost Bradshaw's a good customer, and I can't help wondering if Zenas can afford to be that extravagant. Judging from what I hear—"

Others had heard the same thing. It seemed certain that the business of the chain store was growing. That meant new customers, of course. Where did those customers come from? There could be but one answer: they had formerly traded at Bradshaw's.

If Zenas Bradshaw regretted his extravagance in the matter of Mrs. Simons, no one ever heard him admit it. To those who jokingly twitted him on the affair he good-naturedly agreed that maybe he had got a little peppery. He did not say too peppery, however, nor did he offer any excuses. "Independent as a hog on ice": that was the ancient simile so often used when his name was mentioned.

He anxiously waited word from Mark, but it was not until ten days after the fateful seventh of December that that word came. By that time the United States was formally at war, not only with Japan, but with all the Axis nations. The word was but a brief telegram. "I am off, do not know where. Will write as soon as I do know. Love. Mark."

Zenas read the telegram and absently told the boy who brought it that there was no answer. He was tempted to ask the messenger if there had been telegrams for others—Emily Thacher, for instance. He did not ask, however. Emily would make it a point to see him, he knew. Perhaps her message had been longer and more explicit than his. Perhaps Mark had found time to write her, even though he had not yet written his grandfather.

Zenas tucked the telegram into his pocketbook for rereading later on.

The pocketbook was crowded with papers and letters, the letter from Edmund Taylor among them. This, the Taylor letter, had been a pleasant surprise when it came, a fortnight before the Pearl Harbor outbreak, and important, too, in a way. He had noticed the post-mark, a resort city in the south, and wondered, as he tore open the envelop, who the writer could be.

He had not seen nor previously heard from Edmund Taylor for years. They became acquainted there in Harniss in the days before the motor launch superseded the catboat when Zenas, in the bluefishing season or during the shorebird shooting in the fall, could afford to take an occasional day away from the store and sail his own boat to Twelve Mile Point for a trolling cruise through the tide rips or a gunning tramp along the beaches.

Taylor was then a guest at Mrs. Seth Frazier's boarding house on Dock Road. He, Taylor, was a well-to-do bachelor, retired from business, who had come to Harniss for rest and sport. The acquaintanceship, which begun casually enough, developed into friendship. Zenas Bradshaw and Taylor went on many fishing and shooting trips together. Sometimes Mark, then a boy, accompanied the two men. Taylor spent two seasons in Harniss and then went abroad for a year or two. Zenas and he exchanged letters for a time and then the correspondence lapsed.

And, oddly enough, it was because of Mark that Taylor now wrote. He, Taylor, so the letter said, was spending his winters in the far south. "The confounded doctors are responsible. If I had my way I would be up there sitting in a duck blind with you. I suppose you are shooting as straight as you ever did. I can't picture you as getting old and worn out like the rest of us. I am more or less of a ruin nowadays. The mountains in the summer and down here in the winter, that is my schedule, worse luck."

The resort where Edmund Taylor was spending this particular winter happened to be within a few miles of the airport where Mark was getting his "advanced training." Taylor had visited the port as a guest of one of the commanding officers. As he was leaving the camp, after luncheon, a young second lieutenant came up and introduced himself as Mark Bradshaw, of Harniss.

"I must look younger than I thought I did," wrote Taylor, "for he recognized me and called me by name. I should never have known him, of course, for he was a ten-year-old kid when he used to sail with you and me in your catboat. I was delighted to meet him again, and he told me all about you and my other acquaintances up there in Harniss. I have seen quite a lot of him since, have taken him to hotel parties and to dinner several times. I shall keep an eye on him and do what I can to keep him happy, partly for your sake, of course, but quite as much for his own. He is a fine young chap, Bradshaw, and you should be proud of him, as you probably are. His superiors speak highly of him and say he is bound to do well in the service. The only odd thing about him is that he doesn't seem to be interested in girls. I have taken pains to see that he made the acquaintance of some rather nice specimens—an old boy's judgment, of course, but my eyesight is still fair and they looked good to me—but he shows no signs of caring to follow them up. A stronger attraction somewhere in your neighborhood, I imagine. At any rate, meeting and coming to know him is the spur responsible for my writing you. Be a good fellow and drop me a line when you can. Those two seasons with you in your town were about the most enjoyable I ever spent and I mean to get there again, provided this heart of mine, which my doctor keeps using as a text for his sermons, behaves as it should."

Zenas's reply to this letter was a prompt one, but Taylor had not, as yet, acknowledged it. Mark in his brief notes had not mentioned meeting Mr. Taylor, and Zenas, in one of his chance conversations with Emily, asked the latter if his grandson had written her of the meeting. She replied that she believed he had said something about running across an old pal of Grandfather's but gave no particulars. When she next wrote she would ask him about it, she said.

The fateful telegram drove all this from Zenas Bradshaw's mind. Just now the news that Mark was "off"— off somewhere, to wear his new uniform into battle, to fight, to risk his life—was all that mattered. Zenas, when he put that telegram into his pocketbook, gave a quick glance about him, at Elsie Burgess behind her desk, at Abner Hallett serving a customer, at Eli Gammon rearranging a shelf of canned goods. They were not watching him, and he was glad of it. He ducked to look at the reflection of his face in a showcase mirror. He was pale, just as he knew he must be. He walked briskly into the back room to rub his cheeks with the towel hanging by the hand basin. No one should see that pallor, if he could help it; no one should know that his knees had bent under him when he read those few words. This was exactly what he had been expecting, wasn't it? Precisely what he knew must surely happen and at any time? He had told Abbie Simons he was damned glad Mark was where he was. Yes, and he *was* glad. Only—

Never mind. It was his private property, that "only." Inside of a few hours he would have to hear a dozen "I told you so's." Across how many supper tables would the question be tossed: "Wonder how Zenas Bradshaw feels now?" They could answer that question themselves, they would get no help from him. They should never know how he felt: they would have to be content with seeing how he looked and acted, and they would get no satisfaction there, either.

Emily came to the Bradshaw house that evening. Zenas, feeling almost sure that she would come, had been watching from the window, and he opened the door before she could knock. He ushered her into the sitting-room. She could stay only a minute or two, she told him, from which he inferred that her aunt and uncle were unaware of her intended call. She, too, had had a wire from Mark. It was almost, word for word, a replica of that sent to Zenas.

"He did say, though, that he had written me," she added.

"Had written, or was going to when he could?" was Zenas's question.

"That he had written already." Then, noticing his expression, she went on hurriedly. "Oh, of course I shall tell you what he wrote as soon as I get the letter. He would want me to do that, I know."

She did not say she would show him the letter itself, and Zenas Bradshaw noted the omission. Naturally she would not do that, but once more he felt, and was ashamed to feel, a twinge of jealousy. When a fellow writes to his girl he says things meant for her eye alone, of course he does. Don't be a fool, old man, don't be a fool. Take care that Emily never suspects that jealousy.

"What are you thinking, Mr. Bradshaw?" Emily asked.

"Eh? . . . Oh, I don't know. Nothing in particular, I guess likely."

She laid a hand on his arm. "This is very hard for you, I know," she said, gently.

"Hard for both of us, I shouldn't wonder. No harder, though, than it is for a good many thousand other folks and will be for thousands more in the next few years, if that's any comfort—which it isn't. And being sorry for yourself—out loud, anyway—only makes other people stop being sorry for you. . . . There"—with a smile and a shrug—"having got rid of that, we'll get down to business, as the fellow who asked the blessing at the Odd Fellows' annual dinner said after his Amen. . . . Do your Uncle John and Aunt Etta know you got that telegram from Mark?"

"Yes. The boy brought it to our house when I was out, and Aunt Etta opened and read it."

"Did, eh? That was helpful of her."

"She said she thought if it was bad news she could break it to me gently."

"I see. Um. Was she—er—gentle when she saw who it was from?"

"Why, yes, she was, really. She surprised me. I rather think—yes, I do think that she and Uncle John were pleased, on the whole."

"Pleased? Oh, yes, yes, I see. Pleased to learn that Mark was going where he would be out of the way— way out of the way, for a while, anyhow."

"Yes. That was it, I suppose. They have been especially nice to me since. Uncle John told me that Mark was doing his duty as an American."

"You don't say! That sounds like what you might call a change of heart. How about young Davidson? When is he starting for the front?"

"I don't know.... I mustn't stay any longer, Mr. Bradshaw. Good night. You won't worry too much, will you? I shall try hard not to."

"That's right. Mighty glad you came in. When that letter you spoke of comes you'll tell me what it says, maybe. Most of it, I mean."

"I certainly will."

The letter came two days later. Emily, true to her promise, called at the store to report its arrival. Mark had written her, she said, little more than he had wired. He was well and very much excited. That he and his squadron were to leave the following day for parts unknown was a certainty: his commanding officer had told them so. As soon as he learned what or where those parts were he would write again, to her and to his grandfather.

"He did say," she added, "that we must not expect him to be very specific about things like that, for the report was that all letters would be censored. I suppose that means they will be read by—by other people, doesn't it?"

"Read and more or less chopped to pieces. That's what those censor fellows do, I understand. It's what they're hired for, so we can't blame 'em."

"Of course not." She paused momentarily, as if she were considering. Then she said: "He did say one more thing that I don't understand. He said he—"

Another pause. "Yes? What was it?" Zenas prompted.

210

As she still hesitated, he added: "Don't feel you've got to tell me, because you haven't, you know. Keeping things to yourself is a pretty good rule, generally speaking. If I had stuck to it I'd have considerable more money and a lot less trouble."

She smiled. "I think I won't repeat it now," she decided. "He might not want me to, and, anyway, I don't know what it means. But your mentioning trouble reminds me of something else he said. He said if *I* got into any real trouble to go straight to you."

Zenas was pleased. "Did he? Well, well! That's all right with me. Course I hope it won't be necessary, but, if it ever is, try it and we'll see how it works. Good night again. Take good care of yourself and come 'round this way often as you can."

He did not see her again for more than a week and then only at the store, where anything more than a brief interview was impossible. There were no more letters or telegrams from Mark, and Zenas tried his best to forget his worries and speculations concerning his grandson's whereabouts by working harder and figuring closer even than he had hitherto done. War talk and war meetings and war activities of all sorts were engrossing the town's attention, and they were already having their effect upon business. Bradshaw's suffered, perhaps, no more than other local shops, but the Christmas trade was not quite as good as it had been in other years. Supplies were harder to get, and, although no one foresaw the many rationings and bans upon this and that which were to come, there were difficulties and shortages.

The fishermen were making money, as were the few mechanics, electricians, carpenters, and laborers left in

Harniss. Those latter were elderly men, often slow and unsatisfactory, but becoming more and more independent and "choosy" as to where, when, and for whom they worked. Already there were but few of the younger men left. The draft or the tempting wages offered by great factories and shipyards had taken them away, and now the middle-aged group was leaving.

Gammon, the latest addition to the Bradshaw staff, came down with the disease early in January. Looking rather sheepish, but with his jaw set determinedly, Mr. Gammon led his employer to one side, just before closing time, and broke the news of his seizure.

"Mr. Bradshaw," he began, shifting nervously from one foot to the other, "I've got something to tell you."

Zenas looked at him over his spectacles. "That so?" he observed. "Well, I've got something to tell you, too. Willie says you made two mistakes in one order to-day. Don't you think that's kind of bad arithmetic, Eli? Two never went into one when I was at school."

Gammon shifted from right foot to left. He had spent hours planning just how to break his news to the man who hired him, and he did not intend to be diverted by errors in arithmetic.

"Zenas—Mr. Bradshaw, I mean," he went on, "what would you say if I told you I knew where I could earn thirty-five dollars a week? A *week*, mind you!"

Zenas pushed the spectacles up into place. He began to suspect what was coming.

"Did you say 'earn' or 'get'?" he inquired.

"Eh? Why, I said 'earn,' but that means 'get.' Same thing, ain't it?"

"Not necessarily—in some cases. So you know where you can get thirty-five a week, do you, Eli?"

Mr. Gammon nodded solemnly. "Yes, sir, I do," he affirmed. "I had that offer made to me no longer ago than yesterday afternoon. And what do you suppose I said to the folks that made it?"

"Don't know, but my guess would be that you said 'Yes.' Either that or 'When do I start? Well, when do you?"

Gammon gulped. He had been prepared to face protests and, possibly, reproaches; perhaps to be reminded that, prior to his employment in Bradshaw's Store, he had been out of a job for several months. To have his statement received in this matter-of-fact way was surprising and not too flattering to his pride.

"Why—why, I—I was figurin' on givin' you a week's notice, Mr. Bradshaw," he stammered. "I don't like to leave you, honest I don't. I hate to quit like this."

"Um-hm. But you're going to?"

"Eh? . . . Why, yes, looks as if I'd have to. That is— er—unless you feel you want to—to—"

"I don't. Well, that's all, isn't it, Eli?"

"Why—why, yes, I suppose likely 'tis. Only—"

"Sounds about all to me. Good luck to you."

He walked away. Mr. Gammon gazed after him, open-mouthed. At the end of his week he left Bradshaw's to take up his new duties.

Abner Hallett was close to despair. "What on earth are we goin' to do without him, Zenas?" he demanded.

"Do just that, unless or until we can find somebody else. Eli isn't such a terrible loss. Did first rate for the first few months after he came here, but he's been loafing on the job more or less ever since. You've been complaining about him, yourself."

"I know. But—but—oh," disgustedly, "it's all the

fault of them darned Nasties—them and them Japs. I wish to the Lord they was all dead, every last one of 'em."

"Carried, unanimous. Trouble is, they aren't—yet. Willie Snow told me the other day that his brother had been turned down by the Camp Scott employment people on account of his bad leg. Tell Willie to ask him to come and talk with me, will you?"

Mr. Hallett snorted. "Jeff Snow!" he exclaimed. "The last job he had was with the W.P.A., leanin' on a shovel. Story is that he leaned on it so hard the handle broke and that's what lamed him.... Oh, all right, all right. I'll get word to him. But think of it! Bradshaw's comin' to the point where it has to go out and haul in the lame and the halt and the blind, like it tells about in the Bible."

Jeff Snow was hired and put to work. Abner declared him to be about as much bother as he was help, which was a slight exaggeration. "I'll say one thing for him," added Mr. Hallett, "he's got a grand sense of time. Don't need any clock to tell him when it's noon—nor suppertime, either. His leg may be out of whack, but his stomach ticks regular as a pendulum."

Eli Gammon's desertion was a nuisance, but Elsie Burgess's announcement that she, too, was leaving Bradshaw's threatened, when it came, to be a major disaster. Miss Burgess had kept the store's books for a long time, and when she informed her employer that she had been offered and had accepted a position in Boston, at nearly twice her present salary, Zenas was staggered.

"I—I feel dreadful about it," confessed Elsie, who was

almost in tears. "I feel as if I was doing a perfectly awful thing. But it is so much money and—oh dear!"

Zenas patted her shoulder. "There, there, Elsie," he said. "Nothing to cry about. But we are going to miss you and that's a fact. I wish I could tell you that we'd meet the raise if you would stay, but—well, I'm afraid we can't do that."

Elsie was horrified by the suggestion. "Of course you can't," she declared. "I wouldn't let you, anyway. You couldn't afford it. Don't you suppose I know?"

And then she added sadly: "But you will have to get somebody to keep the books, and where you are going to find that somebody I don't see. Nobody is out of work nowadays, nobody that is good for anything, I mean."

Zenas Bradshaw pulled at his upper lip. " 'To him that hath shall be given,' " he quoted, dryly. "Maybe I need an extra job to keep me out of mischief. Looks as if I'd got one, anyway."

"You mean you'll do it yourself? Why, you can't, Mr. Bradshaw! You're doing ever so much more than you ought to, already. I heard Doctor Stevens tell you so, only the other day."

"Well, if you heard that you must have heard what I told him. Don't have me on your mind, Elsie; I'll get along somehow. And don't tell Ab Hallett you're leaving until just before you go. He'll howl loud enough when his tail is really caught in the door: I don't want to have to hear him yelping ahead of time."

Get along somehow. Perhaps, but how? Zenas lay awake at night trying to find an answer to that question, but found none. Competent bookkeepers were scarce in normal times; just now times were distinctly not

215

normal, and, as Miss Burgess had said, nobody in Harniss who could work was out of work. Nor was Bradshaw's in a position to bid high for an accountant. Zenas Bradshaw asked guarded questions here and there but was given no encouraging answers. He considered advertising in the paper, although that, too, was little more than a forlorn hope.

But an answer did come and from an absolutely unexpected quarter. Elsie Burgess's two weeks' notice was almost at an end. The coming Saturday night was to be her last in the employ of Bradshaw's. True to her promise, she had not told Mr. Hallett, but she had dropped a hint or two among her closest friends, and rumors were spreading. Those rumors had reached Abner's ears, and he was already "yelping," although not in his employer's presence. Broaching the subject in guarded fashion he had been peremptorily ordered to keep still.

"But they are sayin'—"

"Let 'em, you don't have to say it. This isn't a garage: you are selling groceries, not pumping 'free air.' "

So Abner's reply to the rumor carriers was that he "didn't know nothing about it." His facial expression, however, was that of a mourner at a funeral, and from it the inquisitive ones deduced all that was necessary.

Thursday evening Zenas was alone in his sitting-room, smoking and, as usual, doing a great deal of thinking. The Lemons, Betsy and her Jacob, had gone out to attend a meeting of the Town Defense Committee. Betsy was not a member of that Committee, but her husband was. He spent his days, most of them, in the search for antiques for the "Shoppe," or in writing long letters to his patron, Mrs. Bodley. That temperamental lady, from having been a professed pacifist, had swung to the opposite extreme and was now subscribing patroness or honorary vice-president of this and that society for women's aid in the active prosecution of the war. Letters signed by her were printed in metropolitan dailies, and her photograph, showing her as presiding officer, introducing some distinguished female orator from the Dutch East Indies or Timbuctoo, adorned the society pages.

Jacob Lemon, the born diplomat, took his cue from these reports of his good angel's activities. He, too, decided that the country needed his services. Through the influence of the Honorable John Thacher he became a local Air Raid Warden, and no one was more alert than he to detect a spark of light beneath the drawn window-shades of his neighbor on blackout nights. His voice was raised wherever discussion of ways and means to beat the Axis went on, and several times excerpts from his speeches found space in the New Bedford paper's local jottings. Whenever this happened, the excerpts were carefully clipped by Mrs. Lemon, and by her mailed to Mrs. Bodley.

"Shouldn't think you would be the one to keep reminding that woman of your husband, Betsy," commented Zenas. "Thought you were a little bit worried because they were writing each other so often. As I recollect, you told me it was getting to be town talk and you didn't like it."

Betsy colored and seemed embarrassed.

"Did I?" she asked. "Well, yes, I don't know but I did. You said it was silly of me and I suppose 'twas. Anyhow"—she could not entirely repress the note of satisfaction in her voice—"she don't write him nigh as often as she did."

"Don't, eh?"

"No, she don't." Then, as if fearful of being considered disloyal, she went on: "Jacob understands why, though. It is because she's so busy doin' her patriot work up there. There's been considerable printed about her; maybe you've noticed it, Zenas. It must take up an awful lot of her time."

"I should think likely."

"Yes. Well, Jacob, he feels sure she'll be pleased to know about how patriotic he is right here to home. That's why he has me send her the newspaper pieces. He writes her about his antiquin' and the Shoppe and all that, but he *couldn't* send her those clippin's about himself. 'Twould look as if he was braggin'."

"Um-hm. I see. I hadn't thought of that. Jake Lemon would be the last person to brag about himself."

The look Betsy gave him was not entirely free from suspicion.

"If I could be sure—" she began.

"Sure of what?"

"Why, whether you mean what it sounds like or are just pokin' fun."

"Tut, tut, tut! I meant what I said then all right. Your Jacob *would* be the last person to brag about himself.... And the first, too, I shouldn't wonder.... There! Now you're mad again. You've got an awful quick temper, Betsy."

Zenas Bradshaw, alone that Thursday evening, puffed at his cigar, thought until he forgot to puff, and then, the dead cigar between his lips, went on thinking. There was a knock at the front door which he did not hear. The knock was repeated, louder this time. He put the

218

evil-smelling stub in the ash-tray on the table and walked to the hall. Opening the door and peering out into the dark, he could see that the person standing there was a woman, but for an instant he did not recognize her. She spoke first.

"Oh, Mr. Bradshaw," she exclaimed, "I am so glad you are here. I was afraid you might be out. May I come in?"

"Eh? Why—well, if you can't I don't know who can. Glad to see you, Emily."

She followed him into the sitting-room. He pushed forward a chair.

"Sit down, sit down," he urged. Then, voicing the explanation that was in his mind, he added: "Heard from Mark, I suppose, eh? That's fine. Now sit down and tell me all about it."

She did not take the proffered chair, but remained standing. He turned to look at her and saw her face. His own expression changed.

"What is it?" he demanded sharply. "Not bad news? Mark isn't—isn't—"

She interrupted. "No. Oh, no," she said. "It isn't that at all. I haven't heard from him. It is something else. Mr. Bradshaw, I—I came to tell you that—that I am going away."

"Going away?" He did not understand. "Going away?" he said again. "Going—where? What do you mean? . . . Here, let me look at you."

He lifted his hand to her chin and turned her face to the light. "Hm-m," he mused. "Not too good, whatever it is. No, no"—noticing her glance in the direction of the kitchen—"that's all right, nobody can hear us. They have gone out, both of 'em. Now sit right down

219

in that chair. Yes, I want you to. That's right, that's better. Now then."

She sank into the chair. He sat in the rocker facing her. As she still hesitated he tried again.

"Go on, Emmie," he ordered. "What is the trouble? Tell me all about it, that's the girl."

She tried to smile, but the attempt was not a complete success. "I know I am behaving like a coward," she faltered. "I *am* a coward, I suppose. I came here to tell you, but—but it isn't easy to tell. And I had to tell somebody. I—you see—Mr. Bradshaw, could you lend me some money? Not a great deal—just a little? Could you? I mean, will you?"

His answer was reassuringly prompt.

"Certain sure. Of course. How much do you want?"

"I don't know, exactly. Enough to pay my fare to Boston and—well, I suppose enough for me to live on for a week or two, until I can find some sort of position—some sort of work. I'll pay you just as soon as I can, although it may have to be a little at a time."

"There, there! You're going to Boston, you say? And to look for work? Well, from all I hear there is work enough to be had nowadays. Only—"

She raised her hand. "You must think I have gone crazy," she broke in. "You look as if you did. I should have explained first and asked afterwards, of course. Mr. Bradshaw, I have had a—a dreadful quarrel with Uncle John and Aunt Etta. They are very angry with me. They said things that I can't and won't forget—ever. And I'm afraid I said some almost as bad to them. At any rate, I shall never go back to live with them, even if they want me to—which I am sure they don't. It isn't altogether a surprise, I have seen it coming for a good

220

while. Only I kept hoping it might not have to come, at least not yet. You see—"

She paused. Zenas Bradshaw helped her along. "Young Davidson, eh?" he suggested. "Yes, yes. I've been afraid the squalls in those latitudes might get to be a hurricane some day. Things you've told me, yourself, you know."

"Yes, but I have never told you half of it. I never told any one, not even Mark, until—until he was here, on his last leave—before we were in the war, I mean. They didn't give me any rest. They were bound—my uncle and aunt—that I should marry Laurie. They kept hinting at it—oh, more than hinting, taking it as a settled thing, you know. Mr. Davidson, Laurie's father, has a lot of political influence, and Uncle John is planning to run for the State Senate in the fall. Laurie expects to be sent away with his regiment at almost any time, and he was down here for the weekend, and he asked me again, and—"

Once more she hesitated, and once more Zenas helped her to continue.

"And you said no again, I judge," he observed. "Well, I've heard folks talk about the fellow who wouldn't take no for an answer as if that was something to praise him for. It depends, I'd say, on what he was asking. Did Davidson swallow his no this time—and keep it down? Did he believe you meant it?"

"I really think he did. At any rate, he went back to Camp Scott sooner than he had planned. And then Aunt Etta and Uncle John began to say—to say those things I told you they said. They called me ungrateful and selfish and spoke of all they had done for me, and what they did for my father after Mother died, and how

221

I had taken it all for granted, as if it was no more than they should do, and—and they were so hateful—and bitter—that I began to say things on my own account. . . . Oh, I don't want to talk about it! I won't."

"Don't blame you. Sounds as if there had been talk enough already. And it ended just that way, eh?"

"It ended when I told them—told them the truth."

"I see. You mean—"

"I mean that I told them that, if there were no other reasons—and there were plenty—I could not marry Laurie because I was married already. You see, Mr. Bradshaw"—she was obviously bracing herself for the disclosure—"you see, Mark and I were married, by the Congregational minister in Ostable, when we went over there in your car that day in August. We agreed not to tell any one, not even you, for the present, but now— now I have told. And you may tell any one you like. I am not ashamed of it."

She leaned forward in her chair and looked Zenas straight in the face, her cheeks flushed and her eyes ablaze. Zenas said nothing whatever. After a moment she spoke again.

"Well?" she said. "I have surprised you, of course. Whatever else you expected to hear, it wasn't that, I know."

Zenas Bradshaw slowly shook his head. "No-o," he admitted. "You are right—it wasn't."

Her foot tapped the floor. "And now you're going to say something else. Very well, say it. I am ready."

Zenas tugged at his lip. "Give me a little time to get my bearings," he suggested. "I haven't quite come to yet."

Chapter 11

"A ND now," said Zenas Bradshaw, a few minutes later, "suppose you tell me a little more about it. You had me on my beam ends first off, but I'm more or less on an even keel now. Go ahead."

"But I have told you about my quarrel with Uncle John and Aunt Etta."

"I know, I know. Yes, you told me that. Tell me more about you and Mark getting married. I am—well"— dryly—"interested in that, too."

"Very well. It was that day in August when he borrowed your car. He—I— Oh, this is so *hard* to tell!"

"Needn't be. I take it you told Mark what you had to bear at home and he vowed you shouldn't bear it any longer, that there was one way to stop it for good and all. Something like that, I presume likely, eh?"

"Why, yes. That is almost exactly what he said. How did you know? He didn't tell you: of course he didn't."

"He told me nothing"—rather grimly. "If he had, I— well, I might have given both of you some advice. Probably wouldn't have done much good. You are both young, and if there is one thing young folks have no patience with, it is patience. I recollect he dropped one or two hints in his talks with me, but I wasn't smart enough to pick 'em up. Never mind that. He said to you: 'We'll get married now—before I go back to Camp.'

And you said no at first and then yes. About like that, wasn't it? . . . But here"—as the thought came to him—"no, it couldn't have been sudden as all that. The law in this state—"

She did not let him go on.

"I know, I know," she broke in, hurriedly. "It couldn't have been—and wasn't, really. You see, Mr. Bradshaw, it wasn't so very sudden after all. Oh, our actually deciding to get married then, right away, was sudden enough; but we, Mark and I, had talked about the situation at home, my home—the situation with my aunt and uncle and Laurie—we had talked about that when he was in Harniss before, not on this August leave, but the other. We were engaged, you know, and—and—"

"Yes, yes. All right, I understand. He didn't like the idea of Davidson's being right here, on deck, while he was a thousand miles or so away. Natural enough, I guess. Can't hardly blame him for that. Wanted to marry you then, maybe?"

"I think he would have if I had been willing. I wasn't. I hated—and I still hate—all this secrecy and hiding, as if our marriage was something wicked and disgraceful. I *couldn't* marry him then, for his sake. Nothing, certainly nothing for which I was responsible, must be permitted to interfere with his future, getting his commission—all that. So I wouldn't listen. And in my letters I tried to make him think everything was all right here. But when he came to see me, in August, that first evening, he saw for himself. After that I *had* to tell him. So then—"

She hesitated. Zenas Bradshaw nodded. "I see," he observed. "Plain enough. After that your no wasn't quite

224

as—er—rock-ribbed as it had been. Mark kind of took charge, as you might say."

"Yes. Mr. Somers, the town clerk, is a good friend of Mark's, and he promised to keep the news of issuing the —the license from getting out—as well as he could, that is."

"He did it pretty well, I judge. How, I don't know, but he must have."

"Yes. And—and Doctor Stevens—"

"Eh? So Ben was in the know, too, was he? Why, the tight-mouthed old scamp! Hm-m. Another vote of thanks this family owes him. . . . Well, well! And then came the actual marrying. That was in Ostable, you say?"

"Yes. Even when we started in the car that day I didn't realize why Mark insisted on going to Ostable. He had planned it all but told me only just before we got to the minister's house. . . . There, that is the whole story. I—I — Oh, I suppose it was a dreadful thing to do—in a way."

"There, there! It isn't a crime they hang you for. After it was done you decided to keep the news of it to yourselves a while longer, eh?"

"Yes. Perhaps that was cowardly of us, I'm not sure. It was the easiest way and we took it, that's all. We were married. No one could undo that, at least."

"Hm-m. I have heard of its being undone, in considerable many cases, especially nowadays. But that doesn't apply here, I judge."

She straightened in her chair. "Do you *want* it undone?" she demanded.

"No, no. I'm satisfied. In fact I am pretty well contented. Maybe it would have been better for all hands if it had been done out in the open and less around the

225

corner, but that's a question nobody can answer now. You two made up your minds not to tell anybody, you say. Go on from there."

"That's all. Mark felt that he could leave me, for, as he said, Laurie Davidson's guns were spiked. We would wait until he was in the Air Force—Mark, I mean—as an officer, and then we could announce our marriage and I could join him, wherever he was stationed. Then came the war—and now this."

She paused, and then added: "I wish we had told you. You have been so—so understanding and so kind. Mark might have told you, I think, but I wouldn't let him. I knew what a miserable scene there would be with my people, and—I'm sorry, Mr. Bradshaw. It was my fault, most of it."

The tears came to her eyes.

Zenas hastily cleared his throat. "Bosh! Nonsense!" he remonstrated. "No more your fault than his; not so much, probably.... Hum—ha—well, that's that. Now let's move on to what comes next. You have told John and Etta that you had married Mark. They understand that it is something done, not just planning to be done?"

Emily's lips tightened. "They do, indeed," she said, shortly.

"Um-hm. And that you have left them for good, won't live with them any longer?"

"If they don't it is not my fault. Judging from the things they said they are perfectly satisfied to have it that way."

"I know, but sometimes folks say things when they are red-hot and change their minds after they cool off."

"My mind isn't going to change, even if theirs do. Mr. Bradshaw, if you think—"

226

"Wait a minute. Maybe I'll think faster if I set my own course. We'll call that part of it settled: you and they are through. Now what's this about your going to Boston?"

This, plainly, was not as clearly settled. Emily had a friend in Boston, a girl she had formerly known and liked in Harniss and with whom she had kept up a regular and intimate correspondence. This girl had been urging Emily to make her a visit, and Emily had planned to do so at some time during the winter.

"May"—the friend's name was May Foster—"has a very good position as secretary in a law office, and she wrote me, only a little while ago, that if I ever should think of leaving home and—well, earning my own living, she was almost sure she could find some sort of place for me. She says so many girls and women have given up the work they have been doing and have gone to Washington—in the Government offices, you know— that competent typists and secretaries and bookkeepers are in demand. She says—"

"Just a second. How did she come to think you might possibly want to earn your own living? Know about you and Mark, does she?"

"She doesn't know we are married. She does know that we are—are fond of each other. And she knows that I haven't been happy at home."

"I see. . . . Hm-m! . . . Typewriting and secretary work, eh? You don't know typing or shorthand, do you?"

"No, but I could learn. If I could get some sort of office work to do in the daytime, I could study in the evenings. I am pretty good at figures, or I used to be in school, and I think I could manage simple bookkeeping. You see—"

"Hold on!" The interruption was sharp this time. Zenas Bradshaw seemed to have been struck by a brand-new and intriguing idea. He motioned her to silence. His brows puckered and he pulled at his lip. Emily waited for him to speak. After an interval he did so.

"Hm-m!" he grunted, musingly. "Hm-m. . . . I wonder. It might . . ."

She was watching him intently. "What is it, Mr. Bradshaw?" she asked.

"Eh? Oh, nothing, nothing. I am thinking, that's all. I always act funny when I think, not used to it, probably. . . . Hm-m. . . . Look here, Emmie: are you dead set on running away from Harniss?"

"Running away? I am not running from anything—or anybody. Why should I?"

"Shh! I just asked. Ought to have known better."

"Yes, you should. I told you I was not ashamed of what I have done."

"Ought to have known that, too—and did, as a matter of fact. . . . All right, then we'll put it this way. Suppose I told you you needn't go to Boston to find a job. Suppose I said I knew of a place for you right here in this town. Nothing grand, or highfaluting, and the wages just fair, but the work's something I am practically sure you can do—with, maybe, a little overseeing, at the start. Suppose I could get that sort of job for you, would you consider taking up with the offer?"

She did not answer immediately. Then, slowly, she shook her head.

Zenas was greatly disappointed, his face showed it. "You wouldn't, eh?" he said. "I don't know as I'm surprised. Of course I understand why you might rather go somewhere else. There's bound to be a lot of talk, and things said. I can't blame you for wanting to get clear of it all."

"It isn't that: I said I wasn't running away. It is only that—well, I don't know what you are hinting at, Mr. Bradshaw. I don't want to have a pretended position found for me—just a make-believe. I won't have you feel you must help me out of charity, because I am the wife of your grandson. I did ask to borrow money, a little money, from you, but—"

"*Charity!*" The interruption was almost a shout. Zenas thumped the arms of the rocking chair with his fist. "Charity!" he repeated. "Good Lord above! If there is any charity in this notion of mine I'm the one that's asking for it, not you. If you've got the spunk to stick right here in Harniss and keep books for Bradshaw's Store you'll be helping me a darned sight more than I help you. I say *if* you will. I haven't got the nerve to ask you. I won't ask you. I'll just tell you that Elsie Burgess is walking out on us in a couple of days and I'm at my wits' end to know how to get somebody in her place. There! That's the living truth. Now you do just what seems right to you, and for you, and leave the charity out of it. Charity! Good Lord!"

This outburst left no doubt of his sincerity. That Emily was greatly surprised was evident. Zenas waited for her to speak, but she said nothing. It was he who broke the silence.

"Well," he observed, with a sigh, "that's that, then. Boston it's going to be, eh? All right. Now, how much money do you need? Hundred dollars be enough, to begin with, think?"

229

If she heard the question she did not answer it.

"Mr. Bradshaw," she asked, "do you really believe I could do it?"

"Do? Eh? Do what?"

"Keep your books well enough to be a help to you? I am not a good bookkeeper—at least, I don't think I am. I haven't had any experience. I could try, of course, and perhaps, after a while—"

"Wait! What's that? You mean you are willing to try?"

"Yes. If you are willing to have me. If you will be perfectly honest and promise to tell me if I am a failure. I may be, you know."

Zenas Bradshaw's chest rose and fell with a long breath. "Whew!" he exclaimed. "What is it the Moody and Sankey hymn used to say? 'Light in the darkness, sailor, day is at hand.' That's the first streak of sunshine I've sighted in a fortnit. Can you come to work Monday morning?"

"I could come now, so far as that goes. But—oh, we can't hurry it this way: I mustn't let you. Don't you see? There are so many things to be settled."

"Eh? Settled? Oh, you mean your wages. Well, I'll pay you what I paid Elsie, to start with."

"No, no, no! Never mind the wages. If I could I shouldn't let you pay me anything—at least until we were both satisfied that I could do the work. But I shall have to have a little money, I'm afraid, even if I don't go to Boston—if I stay here in Harniss. I must find a place to room and board, and that will cost something. If I knew where Mark was—but I don't."

"Hush! What are you talking about? Room and board! So far as the room goes, there is Mark's own

230

room upstairs here, and I don't know who's got a better right to it than his wife. And board—well, Betsy's cooking isn't so bad. That husband of hers kind of takes away a person's appetite, but you won't have to see him at mealtimes. . . . Now, for mercy sakes, stop arguing, You'll live right here in this house, certain sure you will."

Again it was evident that Emily was confronted with a hitherto undreamed-of idea and that it was both alluring and troubling. She considered it carefully.

"Mr. Bradshaw," she asked, "are you sure you would like that? Do you think it would be a wise arrangement, everything considered? I am not likely to be very popular in Harniss when all I have told you is made public. Aunt Etta and Uncle John will be furious, and people always listen to what they say. So long as I am on my own, Mark and I will be the only ones blamed and criticized, but if I go to work for you and live here with you, everybody will think you helped to plan it all from the beginning."

Zenas Bradshaw's big fist struck the chair arm another blow. "Stop it!" he commanded. "Stop that arguing, I tell you! You're going to work in Bradshaw's Store and live right here in Bradshaw's house. If that's what you meant by settling, then the settling is done. Yes, sir—done! Understand?"

He paused and then added with a quiet chuckle: "Maybe you think I'm ordering you around as if you belonged to me. Well, you do, in a way. Next Monday morning I'm going to be your boss—and I'm your grand father-in-law already. There are two settled facts that you mustn't forget, young woman."

Emily's eyes were wet, but she smiled.

"I never shall forget them," she said, simply. "Thank you—Grandfather."

And so, on Monday morning, residents of Harniss who visited Bradshaw's Store saw Mrs. Marcellus Bradshaw at the desk in the bookkeeper's enclosure, where Elsie Burgess had been installed for so long. To a few the sight of her at that desk was a great surprise, but to the majority it was no surprise at all: in fact, many of them dropped in at the store for the definite purpose of seeing her there, to make sure that the story which had been circulating through the town was true. Some of them remembered to address her as Mrs. Bradshaw and ventured to offer congratulations, but more merely bowed and said: "Morning, Emily." Mrs. John Thacher, in answer to cautiously worded questions of intimate friends, spoke freely of the runaway marriage and, in certain instances, permitted her feelings concerning it to become known. In response to expressions of sympathy she remained outwardly calm, although the ornament in her new hat quivered with the effort.

Mrs. Abigail Simons patted the Thacher gloved hand. "I know exactly how you must feel, Etta, dear," said Mrs. Simons. "You and John have brought up that girl as if she was your own, and we all know how you had planned for her. To have her marry that—er—person, and in this underhand way, is *such* a disappointment for you both. And to have her leave your beautiful home— you don't mind my calling it beautiful, do you, dear? That's just what it is, you know. To have her walk right out of that lovely place and all the luxury and—and comforts you've given her, and go and keep books in a store, is—well, I declare it is almost humiliating, it is so.

232

Everybody is talking about it, and we are all *so* sorry for you."

Mrs. Thacher was game, there is that to be said for her. She was quite aware of the fact that every one was talking, and the sugar-coated malice in her dear friend Abigail's dose of condolence was bitter to swallow. She did swallow it, however—swallowed it and even smiled faintly.

"John and I are not the ones to be sorry for, Abigail," she said. "We have done our duty by the girl and have no reason to reproach ourselves. We can only hope she may be happy, that's all. . . . Oh, how do you do, Mr. Bodfish? Yes, I am very well, thank you."

But, on another occasion, when Zenas Bradshaw's name was mentioned, she was not quite so stoical.

"He is behind it all," she declared, venomously. "John thinks so, and I am sure of it. He put them up to it, just out of spite. John says that, in town-meeting or other public places, he always takes the opposite side— oh, not openly: he is too clever for that—but asking troublesome questions and smiling in that provoking, sarcastic way of his. I'm sure, if we could know the whole truth, we should find out that it was his plan from the beginning. Jealousy, of course. Well, it won't help him any. He will pay for it, and in more ways than one. Just wait and see."

Her husband, when in conversation with the average fellow townsman, or townswoman, was more circumspect. "A disappointment—oh yes, but life is full of disappointments. Certainly we shall miss Emily: we do miss her very much."

The listener—in this particular case the Thacher clergyman—gathered that the Honorable John, al-

233

though his feelings were deeply wounded, forgave those who had wronged him and bore no grudge. Which was another of the reverend gentleman's mistakes.

If he could have listened in at a brief interview between John Thacher and Zenas Bradshaw, realization of the mistake would have been forced upon him.

There were no listeners, however. The two men met at the corner of Main Street and the Pond Road one evening about ten o'clock. Zenas had gone back to the store after supper, to write a few business letters, and was now on his way home again. Thacher had attended a committee meeting and was walking toward his own house.

Because of the war regulations the street light at the corner was heavily shaded, and the pair did not recognize each other until they were almost face to face. Then Zenas said, "Evening, John," and passed on.

Thacher did not return the greeting. An instant later, however, he spoke sharply.

"Bradshaw," he hailed.

Zenas turned. "Yes?" he said.

"Come here."

It was not an invitation but a command. Zenas hesitated momentarily. He was tempted to suggest that the distance between Thacher and himself was no greater than that between himself and Thacher. He did not, however. He walked leisurely back to where the other man was standing.

"Zenas Bradshaw," said John Thacher, "I've been waiting for a chance to see you alone."

The tone of this speech was ominous. It suggested that the speaker was suppressing his emotions by main strength. Zenas was quite aware of the tone and its implications, but his reply was calmly matter-of-fact.

"That so?" he observed. "Well, you could see me plainer in a better light, but here I am, anyhow. What did you want to see me about?"

"I wanted to tell you what I think of you. You are an ungrateful, underhanded, double-crossing sneak. And if you think you are going to get away with it without a comeback you were never more wrong in all your life. That's all."

He turned on his heel and moved away. He had taken but one step when a hand was laid on his shoulder.

"Hold on a minute. . . . Yes, I said 'Hold on,' but I'll say 'Stop,' if you like that better. . . . Yes, stop!"

Mr. Thacher stopped. The hand which had been on his shoulder had now shifted to the collar of his coat. It was a good coat, and the grip was dangerously firm. Its wearer whirled about.

"Take your hands off me," he ordered, furiously. "I've said all I intended to say. You understood it."

"There was one word I didn't understand—that was 'ungrateful.' Suppose you tell me just how and when and why I've been ungrateful to you. Yes, and for what?"

"Let go of me, I tell you! I know, and the whole town knows, that you are responsible for maneuvering my niece into marrying that tin soldier grandson of yours."

"Steady! Wait a minute!"

"Wait be hanged! She was sneaking around to see you months ago: of course we knew that. The three of you have had your heads together from the beginning. You

235

knew—and so did that cub of yours—that Emmie was a good catch."

"Shh! You are—but never mind: stick to the text. 'Ungrateful' was the word I asked about."

"You knew, both of you Bradshaws, what that girl was to her aunt and me: how we educated her, indulged her—yes, and planned for her future. Why, we have always treated her as if she was our own daughter."

"As to that—oh well, let it go. I don't doubt you treated her as if she was your daughter, or that you would have treated a daughter the same way. Your daughter—if you had one—might not have had a mind of her own and Emily has, that's the difference, or one of the differences. But that's off the subject: that isn't the text I'm asking you to stick to. Just how have I been ungrateful to you? And what should I be grateful to you for? Come on now: I want to know."

John Thacher was not at a loss for a reply, exactly. His experience as a political speaker had taught him to be ready with a retort when a heckler asked an inconvenient question. He had been a little reckless in this case and, in the white heat and fury of his denunciation, a trifle careless in his choice of words. His hesitation was, however, but momentary.

"Bradshaw!" he orated, crushingly. "For more years than it is worth while to count we Thachers have made it our rule to patronize and stand by local—er—institutions. Sometimes—yes, often—we have done this at considerable sacrifice to ourselves. My father—yes, and his father—bought the family—er—household supplies at Bradshaw's Store. There have been times when our support of your business has cost us money, when we knew perfectly well that—"

Zenas's patience slipped its tether. "Oh, for heaven's sakes get down from the platform!" he broke in. "Cut out the Fourth of July stuff and talk plain English. Thachers have traded at Bradshaw's for sixty-odd years, I know that. And they have never been cheated or over-charged or short-weighed once in the whole sixty. I know that, too—and so do you. Cost you money? Certain sure it has. But you have always got the worth of that money, every last cent of it. Don't deny that, do you?"

Mr. Thacher did not deny it—directly. "So far as I know—" he began.

Zenas did not let him finish. " 'So far as you know,' " he repeated. "You know all the way. Fair and square buy and sell, that's what it has been always. Where does the gratitude come in on that—for either side? Are we Bradshaws supposed to get down on our knees and say, 'Thank you for condescending to buy your salt and sugar at our store?' Why should we? To a Thacher, any more than to any other customer?"

The Honorable John dodged this one.

"We won't discuss it," he announced, with dignity. "You know perfectly well—"

"I know that you and Etta are sore because Emily had grit enough to pick out a husband for herself instead of letting you do the picking for her. You and she had a row over that and she walked out. She had nowhere in particular to go so I took her in. She had no money of her own and was going to Boston to hunt a job. I needed a bookkeeper and I offered the place to her. I didn't know that she and Mark were married until she told me, and that was after she had told your wife and you. That's the truth, believe it or not. I'm not apologizing for any of it, understand: I'm just telling you."

Mr. Thacher snorted and once more turned to go. Again he was detained.

"You don't believe it, eh?" queried Zenas. "Well, I didn't expect you would, and that doesn't much matter, either way. But here is the one important thing: I don't want to hear of your going around talking about sacrificing your own interests to support my business. My business is Bradshaw's Store, and when that can't support itself without sacrificing anybody's interest but its own it will put up its shutters. Talk about me, if you get fun out of it, but let Bradshaw's alone.... Good night."

John Thacher saw an opportunity here, and he did not let it slip. "*I* shall let it alone, you may be sure of that," he retorted, with emphasis. "And, unless I am very much mistaken, others will do the same thing. A good many others!"

Having fired this parting shot, he started off. Zenas Bradshaw looked after him, shrugged, and walked in the opposite direction.

Zenas, when he entered his living-room, found Emily sitting up for him. She asked if he had got through with the letters. He said he had. He did not tell her of his meeting with her uncle, did not mention it, then or later. It would only trouble her, and nothing she could do or say would change the situation. No one could change it. It had existed before he and Thacher had their frank exchange, and that exchange had merely brought it into the open. John Thacher and his wife had never been close friends with the Bradshaws, but, at least, they had not been avowed enemies. Now they

238

were enemies, avowed and vindictive. The "private war," the "sideshow to the main circus," which he had dreaded and hoped might be avoided, or at least deferred, was on.

He told Emily that he was sleepy, and went to his room, but his gloomy reflections accompanied him and got into bed with him. If the young people had only waited a little longer. If they had consulted him.

But no, they had not consulted any one but themselves. The blow-up was bound to come, sooner or later, but if it had come when his hands were not quite as full, when business conditions were easier, when he was feeling less tired...

Oh, rot! Fooling himself again, he was. Would he never learn to face facts? Tired? Certainly he was tired! A man seventy years old was bound to be tired. Yes, and to grow more tired instead of less, as the days slid by. "Slid" was the word for it, too. That is what days and weeks and months and years did now—they slid, flew, like a young-one's sled down an icy hill. True, he could not yet actually see the bottom of that hill, but, in the natural course of things, it could not be so very far ahead. It might, as like as not, be just around the next curve. The end, not only of himself, Zenas Bradshaw, but of Bradshaw's Store. If Mark—

There he was! Going over all that again! If he could, he would not bring Mark back home, to stay, would he? No, certainly he would not. Mark was where he ought to be, fighting for the country whose free institutions had given all the Bradshaws their chance. The country that had afforded them the privileges of good schools, the opportunity to earn a comfortable competence, to live well, to make names for themselves as good citizens, respected and independent, asking undue favors of nobody. Worth fighting for, this United States of America—yes, indeed it was. Mark was doing the right thing. He was lucky to be young and able to do it.

But as for his own luck—what about that? He was the only Harniss born-and-bred Bradshaw since before the Revolutionary War who had not done some fighting for the country. That confounded leg of his had kept him out of the war with Spain, had knocked him out just as he was about to enlist. Since then his only son had gone away to fight and die in France, and now his son's son had gone—somewhere—while he himself could do nothing but stay at home. Stay at home and keep store. And how much longer he could do even that was a question.

He did not often permit himself to go into this black mood. This night, however, the blackness lasted. He could not shake it off. It was not until three o'clock in the morning that he made his resolution, the resolution that he swore not to break, whether alone or in company, as long as he lived—no matter how long or short a time that might be. Oddly enough, what caused him to make it was a rhyme that came into his head, a jingle that he remembered his father reciting to him when he, Zenas, a small boy, had rebelled against his daily chore of filling the woodbox.

"If I could pick my earthly lot
    I wouldn't be a worm,
To burrow in a garden plot
    And squirm and squirm and squirm.
But yet, I'll say this for that worm:
    No matter how he feels,

He does his job—which is to squirm—
And squirms—but never squeals."

Zenas Bradshaw laughed aloud when the memory of that rhyme came to him. Somehow or other, that bit of foolishness was just the reminder that he needed. He had been "squealing," not aloud, it's true, but squealing, nevertheless. Staying at home and selling groceries might be—and compared to flying a warplane or shooting Nazis and Japs, it probably was—a sort of worm's job, but it was *his* job, his earthly lot, and he would do it as well as he could and as long as he could. And, no matter how difficult the squirming might be, he would not squeal again, not even to himself.

He fell asleep with that resolution firm in his mind, and at six-thirty, his usual rising hour, it was still there. With it, rising with him and with the sun, was a new feeling, not of hope exactly, nor of contentment or satisfaction, but a mixture of all three. He was an old man, certain sure he was, but there had to be old men in the world to take their turn at the grindstone when the young fellows let go of the handle. He could still grind, thank the Lord, and maybe grinding was, in its humble way, as necessary as fighting. And as for a fight, he was in for one, wasn't he? He would have fighting enough of its kind.

"They haven't licked us yet, old boy," he said aloud to his reflection in the shaving mirror. "We Bradshaws are still squirming."

He was almost happy in the prospect. Emily noticed the change when he joined her at the breakfast table.

"Why, Grandfather," was her comment, "you look fit this morning. You must have had a good night."

He chuckled. "Had a devil of a night," he confessed. "The first part of it, anyhow. Then I got busy and cast him out. Want to know how to cast out devils, Betsy?"

Mrs. Lemon stared at him. "You say the most outlandish things," she declared. "What *are* you talkin' about this time?"

"About casting out devils—blue ones. I'll give you the receipt. Take a worm."

The housekeeper lifted her hands and let them drop in a gesture of hopeless disgust.

"Just as crazy as a—as a bedbug!" she vowed. "Just stark loony, that's what he is."

Zenas shook his head. "Don't know much about the critter you mention, Betsy," he told her, "but there's nothing crazy about a worm. He has a job to do and does it.... Come on, Emily. It's time you and I were doing ours."

That job grew no easier. That the private war was on and the enemy attacking was plain almost from the first. His attacks were not made openly but were more in the nature of a siege. Little straws moved here and there, indicating the direction of the wind. Since Pearl Harbor, criticism of Mark Bradshaw in Harniss had practically died away. So many of the town's young men had gone to enter the army or navy that sneering references to "playing soldiers" were now rare and likely to be risky. On one occasion, a good-for-nothing member of the fishing contingent who had spoken disparagingly of certain governmental rules concerning the color his boat must be painted and those responsible for the ruling, was removed to the Denboro hospital, suffering from "contusions." Just who was responsible for the infliction of the contusions no one seemed to know. Even the sufferer himself prudently refused to make charges.

Yes, Mark Bradshaw had, for some time, ceased to be the Harniss "bad boy." He was no longer in the spotlight.

Now, however, he stepped back into it again. There was a sharp revival of the sneers and criticisms. He had married John Thacher's niece, not in an honest, open and aboveboard fashion, but in the secret, sly, utterly selfish way characteristic of him. The Thachers had done everything for that girl, and look how she had repaid their indulgence! "Never so much as told 'em she was goin' to be married; no, nor even told 'em she *was* married until months afterwards." Her fault, a lot of it, certainly, but more the fault of that young Bradshaw scamp. "Look how he treated Zenas!"

All this and very much more. It came to Zenas Bradshaw's ears, of course. He was conscious that he himself was on many Harniss family griddles, suspected of having known of the marriage before it took place, and, very likely, of planning, aiding, and abetting it.

"He knows the Thachers have got money and nobody to leave it to but that Emily. Trust a Bradshaw to know how to get the Bradshaw bread buttered."

"Took her right into his house to live, he did. Never waited to ask John and Etta whether they wanted her there or not. Yes, and gave her a job in his own store. Wanted her where he could keep an eye on her, I guess. Doesn't mean for a good thing to get away from him."

All Harniss did not say or think these things, not

even the larger part of its people, certainly not the most sensible and level-headed part, but the Thachers' following was still numerous and their influence strong. Even the local correspondent of the paper, evidently feeling that the community's reigning sensation could not be ignored, was circumspect in his—or her—reference to it.

"The marriage of Miss Emily Thacher, niece of the Honorable and Mrs. John Thacher of this town, is an event causing much interest and surprise in our midst. The bridegroom is Second Lieutenant Marcellus Bradshaw, grandson of Mr. Zenas Bradshaw, the well-known proprietor of Bradshaw's Store on Main Street. According to popular report, the couple were wed in August of last year by the Reverend Miles Coburn, at that time pastor of the Congregational Church in Ostable. Announcement of the marriage has only recently been made, however. Lieutenant Bradshaw is in the Army Air Service, absent on active duty with his squadron. Neither his wife nor his grandfather have heard from him for some time. Your correspondent wishes to congratulate Lieutenant Bradshaw upon his fortunate choice of a wife."

It was noted by many—Zenas and Emily among them —that no congratulations were handed Mrs. Marcellus Bradshaw upon her choice of a husband.

There was another paragraph in the paper's "Harniss Jottings."

"Mrs. Marcellus Bradshaw, formerly Miss Emily Thacher, has taken over Miss Elsie Burgess's duties as bookkeeper in Bradshaw's Store. When Miss Burgess announced her intention of leaving Bradshaw's where she has been employed for several years, to accept a similar,

244

but more responsible position in a Boston establishment, there was considerable speculation as to who would take her place. Mrs. Marcellus Bradshaw's selection was, naturally, a great surprise to all. She no longer resides with her uncle and aunt at the Thacher residence but is living at the Bradshaw house on the Pond Road."

Zenas Bradshaw read this, of course, but he did not refer to it in conversation with his new granddaughter until she herself spoke of it.

"It looks as if I had surprised this town in several ways," she said, smiling, as she put aside the paper. "Well, *I* am not surprised—at that."

Zenas shook his head. "I hope you noticed that you are living in a house now, instead of a residence," he observed. "You seem to be standing the come-down pretty well, judging by your looks."

Her smile broadened. "I am happier than I have been for a long, long while," she told him. "If I—if we—could only hear from Mark, and know that he is all right, I should be perfectly happy."

That was the principal drawback to complete happiness in the Bradshaw home. No word had come from Mark since the telegram that he was "off," he knew not where. The most likely guess was that he was somewhere on the other side of the Pacific, for the papers reported our marines and some of our air forces as in action with the Japanese in that region. But the Pacific is a big ocean and its other side a long way off. Week after week passed and the mails brought no letters from the absent one, and, although Zenas never, and Emily very seldom, mentioned that this fact caused them the least worry, the worry was there and constantly growing. Their duties at the store occupied their minds on weekdays, but the evenings were long and Sundays interminable.

Other occupants of the Pond Road house were not as reticent. Betsy Lemon would have been voluble on the subject, and was until her employer, as he might have said, put on the muffler.

Emily was in her own room on the second floor one evening, and Betsy caught Zenas alone in the sitting-room. He had taken a half-dozen letters from his pocket and was looking them over when she came in. Her curiosity could not be restrained.

"Ain't a letter from Mark there, is there?" she asked, eagerly.

Zenas glanced up at her over his spectacles.

"No," he replied, absently. One of the letters was from a firm in Boston with whom Bradshaw's had done business for many years, and its contents troubled him somewhat.

Betsy sniffed. "Didn't suppose likely there was," she observed, with sarcasm. "And Emmie ain't heard a word, either. I must say, for anybody that's just married and gone off and left his new wife all alone, he's the poorest letter writer ever I heard of."

Zenas Bradshaw put the letter he had been reading back into its envelop and returned it and the others to his pocket. He looked at his housekeeper.

"Have you been bothering Emily about her not hearing from Mark?" he asked.

"Eh? Botherin' her? No, course I haven't. I just ask her once in a while, that's all. Why wouldn't I?"

"Why should you?"

"Because I'd like to know, of course. Anybody would.

246

Far as that goes"—a little tartly—"everybody is. They keep askin' me about it, too. Only this forenoon Huldy Sparrow says to me, 'Any news from that Mark of yours yet?' And when I told her no, not as I'd heard of, she says: 'Um! Well, they say no news is good news, and maybe that's right—in some cases.' Yes, that's what she said, those very words. Course I don't pay attention to Huldy Sparrow. She's been down on us ever since you made her husband pay that store bill he owed so long, but all the same—"

Zenas interrupted. "That'll do, Betsy," he broke in, with decision. "I don't want to hear what the Sparrow woman said to you or what you said to her. And I don't want you asking Emily every few minutes whether or not she's heard from Mark. When she does hear she'll tell me and I'll tell you—probably. Up to that time you let her alone and keep still about the family affairs."

Mrs. Lemon stared at him. "Well!" she gasped. "I never did! I don't believe I ever was talked to like that before in all my life! I must say—"

Again Zenas interrupted. "No, you mustn't," he told her. "Saying is the one thing I don't want you to do. When the Sparrows and the other—er—birds say it, you just remember what the tintype man used to tell the folks who were having their pictures taken: 'To get the best results keep your mouth closed, smile and look pleasant.' If I know Hulda," he added, with a grin, "your saying nothing will make her a good deal madder than if you talked. Which ought to comfort you. I know it would me."

When Betsy repeated the "order" to her husband, the latter's dignity, much inflated in those days, swelled almost to the bursting point.

"Did Zenas Bradshaw say those things to you?" he demanded, hotly. "And you let him?"

"Why now, Jacob, he didn't mean nothin' out of the way. He don't like Huldy Sparrow any more'n I do."

"And you stood there like a—a sheep and took it. Well, I won't."

"Jacob," in alarm. "Jacob, where are you goin'?"

"I am going to tell that Bradshaw man where he gets off."

She tried to detain him, but he shook his arm free and marched into the sitting-room. Zenas was still seated in his favorite rocker. He had again taken the Boston firm's letter from his pocket and was rereading it. He did not look happy. Jacob cleared his throat.

"Zenas," he began.

Zenas looked up. "Eh? Oh, hello!"

"Zenas, I—I've just been told something and—and I want to know if it's true."

There was not quite as much bluster in his tone as there had been when he stalked from the kitchen, but there was still a little and Zenas Bradshaw noticed it. His eyes narrowed a trifle behind his spectacles.

"Well, Jake," he said, mildly, "maybe I can tell you more about that when I know what 'twas you heard."

"I—heard—I've been given to understand that—that you told my wife to shut her mouth. Is that so?"

Zenas shook his head. "No," he said.

"Oh! . . . Well, well, I—I'm glad to hear you say so. I—"

"Wait a minute. I told her to keep her mouth closed when people ask her about things that aren't any of their business. Any objection to that?"

"Why—why—er—no, but—"

248

"I didn't tell her to shut up, not in the way you put it. I don't do that very often, and then only when I mean it. I can, though: I haven't forgot how."

He rose, very deliberately, to his feet. "Want to hear how I say it, Jake?" he asked. "If that's what you want I'd hate to disappoint you."

He paused, awaiting a reply. Mr. Lemon's gaze met his, then faltered and strayed toward the door. He muttered something to the effect that all he wanted was to make sure that his wife had not been insulted. As long as the matter had been explained he was satisfied. His hand was on the knob by that time.

Zenas laughed aloud. "Betsy and I understand each other, Jake," he said. "You tell her I said so. As for you and me—well, any little misunderstandings we happen to have can be cleared up just the way this one was. No trouble at all—to me, anyhow."

He was chuckling as he went to his room. The expression on Jacob's face when he, Zenas, got up from his chair had been funny. Looked as if he expected to be punched, he did. "Wonder what Doctor Ben Stevens would say if I told him I was figuring on starting a rough-and-tumble at my age and in the shape I'm in." Not that there had been any danger of a fight: Jake Lemon was not the fighting kind. Oh, well, much as he despised the fellow, there was some advantage in having him around—he did occasionally distract a person's thoughts from real troubles.

The distraction was of short duration, however. The troubles were too real and too many. The letter from the Boston firm was but one. Never before, in the course of Bradshaw's business dealings with this company, had there been any mention of time of payment for goods ordered. Bradshaw's had always paid its bills with reasonable promptness, sometimes in thirty days, but occasionally a month or so later, according to the amount of ready money on hand or the promptness of payment by its own good customers, whose family names had been on its books, some of them, for three generations. The Boston firm understood this. They knew their money was perfectly safe.

And now, in this letter, it was suggested that payments be made within, or under, the thirty-day limit. Reasons were given, of course. The war, scarcity of commodities, difficulty with collections in general, all that. True, no doubt; nevertheless, no firm had ever before written Bradshaw's Store exactly that kind of letter. For this particular firm to do it was—well, it was, to say the least, strange.

Rationing, "points," and all the multitudinous restrictions and rules which were, later on, to drive the small businessman to the verge of nervous prostration, were only beginning to be talked about, were not foreseen as actualities by the average person. Zenas Bradshaw could not understand why this letter had been written to him. Then he remembered that there had been changes in the personnel of this Boston company; he had heard of them but had hitherto given them little attention. The older members, men with whom his father and he had dealt, were dead or had retired, and new blood had come in. He made some inquiries of a friend of his who was a traveling salesman for another Boston house.

Only one of the particulars given him by this man appeared to have any bearing on the question of the letter, and that one seemed far-fetched indeed. One of the new members of the Boston firm was named Philips. A young man, so the salesman said, but, according to report, holding an important and influential position in the management.

"Young Philips is no heavy-weight, himself, but his old man has a barrel of money and the boy married the Davidson girl, and the Davidsons are bankers, with another barrel of their own. There's a Davidson son, too, but he's in the army, I believe."

Zenas Bradshaw's hand moved upward. Its fingers tugged at his lip. "Hm-m," he observed, thoughtfully. "That army—er—son's name doesn't happen to be Laurie—er—Laurence, does it?"

"Why, yes, I think it is. Laurence Davidson, that's right. Why? That mean anything to you?"

Zenas said no, he guessed not, but he wondered how much it might mean. John Thacher and Laurie Davidson's father were close friends and associates in politics. Could it be possible that the Thacher-Davidson determination to get square with any one bearing the Bradshaw name was responsible for—

He could scarcely believe it. It was not much of itself —the letter, that is. And it seemed so cheap, so picayune a move for people of the Davidson rating. And yet it might be . . . it might be.

The surmise was strengthened within the next two weeks. Two other firms, with whom Bradshaw's had dealt for long, wrote similar politely phrased hints that prompter payments would be considered a favor. Zenas was forced to believe that rumors were afloat concerning the Bradshaw credit. He answered those letters and asked direct questions, but he received no satisfaction. The replies were always courteous, usually even genially good-humored, but in no case was he assured, as he and his father had so often been assured, that the credit period of Bradshaw's Store was practically unlimited. He remembered the phrasing of one of those old assurances. "Buy all you need and pay when it is convenient. Bradshaw's is the least of our troubles. We are satisfied if you are."

Nothing like that nowadays. All right, he would show them. Every bill should be now, and was, paid within the thirty-day limit; sometimes sooner, with the cash discount carefully deducted. As long as there was anything to pay with, Bradshaw's would pay its debts.

Meanwhile the siege was on in Harniss. The Thacher family account was definitely closed, which was to have been expected. But there were others, and hitherto profitable ones, which either were closed altogether or shrank to half their usual weekly footings. The falling-off of trade was not yet calamitous, but it was worrisome, very. And the supply of ready and available money was diminishing. Zenas might be careful to pay his bills in thirty days, but not all his customers were so minded. They had been accustomed to paying "every little while," and they continued to pay that way.

Zenas told no one of his anxieties and apprehensions, least of all Emily. She was, for a green hand, doing a first-rate job as bookkeeper, and that was a great relief. She must have noticed—of course she did notice—the slackening of custom, but she did not speak of it. And, although still no word came from Mark, she did not whine about that, either.

And, at last, word did come. Merely a few words in a censored cable despatch. No hint of where it came from, nothing but a date and a few words.

"All right and safe so far. Also busy. Write me often. One of your letters received. Keep them coming. Hope you got mine. Love to both of you."

That was all, but it was wonderful. So one of their letters, at least, sent as directed to a Government forwarding address, had reached Lieutenant Marcellus Bradshaw, with his squadron away "over there"—wherever over there might be. And Mark was well and safe, thank the Lord. Great news! Glorious news! Zenas and Emily read the cable separately and together, over and over. Betsy read it and exclaimed and hallelujahed. She read it to her husband, who condescended to express pleasure.

The message was delivered early in the evening, and the following morning, when Zenas and his new bookkeeper walked to the store together, the sun was shining, and, for them at least, this war-torn world was a brighter place than it had been for a long time. As they passed the door of the Surfside Rest, Mrs. Joanna Coles' little inn and eating-house on Main Street, some one tapped on the window. They both heard the tap and turned to look. A hand moved between the ruffled curtains behind the panes.

"What's all that?" asked Zenas. "Somebody beckoning, isn't it?"

"Yes, I think so. I can't see who it is."

"Humph! Looks like a man's hand. Is it me he wants, or you?"

"Probably you. Another salesman, perhaps. Most of them stay at the Rest, when they are in town."

"Shouldn't wonder if you're right. Well, he may want to see me, but I don't hanker to see him. Seen all the drummers I care to see for a year. . . . Oh, well, all right, all right. Can't get rid of this one till I do see him, I presume likely. It won't take me long, Emmie. You go on to the store."

They parted, and Zenas walked across the street and up the short walk to the Surfside Rest's front door. The door opened just as he reached it, and the man who had opened it extended a hand.

"How are you, Mr. Bradshaw?" he cried, heartily. "Mighty glad to see you again. Come in."

Zenas stared in astonishment. "Well, well, well!" he exclaimed, clasping the proffered hand. "Surprises will never cease and then some, as the fellow said! Fine to set eyes on you once more, Frank, it is so."

The man was Frank Seymour, former owner of the Harniss flying field, Mark Bradshaw's first instructor in aviation, and, while both were Harniss residents, his most intimate friend.

Chapter 12

ZENAS BRADSHAW again expressed his pleasure at meeting Seymour and added that he was not expecting him in Harniss.

"Hadn't any idea in what part of the world you might be by this time, Frank. Heard yarns about your being in this place or that, but nobody seemed to know anything definite. Good to look at you, though. How you making out?"

"Oh, so-so. They tell me you are all right again. That's fine. What do you hear from Mark?"

"It's only this minute, as you might say, that we've heard at all."

He told of the cable despatch. "Not much, but it's a whole lot better than nothing. The Rest folks have told you about him and Emily getting married? That must have surprised you some."

Seymour said yes, but rather absently, or so Zenas imagined. He seemed to be much more interested in the cable message.

"Mark didn't give you any idea where he was, you say?" he inquired.

"Not a hint. Under orders not to, I guess probably. Said he'd written, but we haven't got the letter yet.... But there, don't let's stand talking here. Come on over to the store. Emily will be glad to see you, too."

Frank Seymour shook his head. "I've got to talk with you alone for a few minutes, Zenas," he said. "Can you come up to my room, where nobody can hear us and we won't be interrupted?"

Zenas looked at him. What in the world might this mean? What could Frank Seymour have to say to him which necessitated such privacy and freedom from interruption? And the man was very serious about it, too.

"Why, yes," he replied, "I suppose I can, if you say so. I ought to be at the store, but Emmie's there and she'll handle things till I come. Say"—with a confidential wink —"that girl can handle pretty nigh anything in the business way. She's got a head on her, Frank. Mark is one lucky fellow, and I'm beginning to think I'm another. She is just about the prescription us Bradshaws needed, looks to me."

Seymour did not appear greatly interested in this statement, either.

"Sure, sure," he agreed, hastily. "Don't doubt it at all. Now will you come on up, Zenas? First room to the left, top of the stairs."

He led the way, and Zenas Bradshaw, beginning to be vaguely troubled, followed. The room was of the usual small country hotel variety—pine furniture, bed, dresser, washstand, small table and two chairs. Seymour pushed forward one of the latter, and Zenas, tossing his hat on the bed, sat down. Then Seymour made another odd move: he locked the door, before seating himself in the remaining chair.

"Nobody's likely to come," he said, "but I don't want them to try. And we'll keep our voices down, too."

Zenas's vague premonition of trouble was becoming more definite and alarming.

"Look here, Frank," he broke in, "what is all this? Anything the matter?"

Frank Seymour motioned for quiet. "Shh!" he cautioned. "I wouldn't have this heard for a good deal. And"—with emphasis—"I'm a lot more sure you wouldn't. Zenas, I came back to Harniss on purpose to see you, and I give you my word I didn't want to come —not for the reason that sent me here. If I could have seen any way of getting out of the jam I'm in—but I couldn't. And I can't. That's the truth, and I want you to believe it."

Zenas Bradshaw nodded but said nothing. He waited for what was coming, his mind busy with disquieting guesses as to what that might be. A request for a loan? He would hate to say no to his grandson's best friend, but a loan of any considerable amount was out of the question just now. To his relief, Seymour's next speech seemed to have nothing to do with that or with any other of the Bradshaw guesses.

"Zenas," he asked, abruptly, "did you ever sell anything to the Government?"

"Eh? Why, no, not as I recollect. Why?"

"Just wondered if you had, that's all. If you had, and especially now, in these war times, you might understand a little clearer about this jam I'm in. I turned my flying field over to the Government, months and months ago. You know that, of course."

"Certain. Understand you got a good fair price for it, too."

Frank Seymour grunted. "You better have your understanding overhauled. I haven't got a cent for it."

"What! Why, I—"

"There, there, let me tell you. I *thought* I was going

257

to get a good price. Not exactly the figure I named, I didn't hardly expect that, but the Government folks made their offer and I wouldn't accept it, so appraisers representing both sides were to be appointed—were appointed, so my lawyer tells me—and a compromise price, fair to both sides, was to be agreed on. That"—with a sarcastic laugh—"is the joker in the pack—that 'was.' Near as I can find out it isn't any closer to being an 'is' than at the beginning."

"Why—I don't understand. Couldn't they agree?"

"They might agree in ten minutes if they ever got together and set their minds to it. Perhaps they will some day, but I'm likely to die of old age in the poor house before that. This Government of ours is a big concern, busy with big things. I'm just one everyday citizen, and my concerns are pretty small—except to me. Those appraisers met once, I believe, and are going to meet again, if something more important doesn't interfere. Put off, put off, put off, and red tape, red tape, red tape, forever and ever, amen. Oh"—impatiently—"I know, I know. The United States doesn't cheat people. It pays its debts and will pay this one, when it knows how much it is and, after that, when it gets around to it. Meanwhile, I'm getting poorer every minute. I've got to have money now, that's all there is to it."

So the first guess was the correct one. It *was* a request for a loan which had brought Frank Seymour back to Harniss and to him, Zenas Bradshaw. Dear, dear, this was going to be mighty unpleasant.

"But—but," he stammered, "I—I don't see . . . Why, Frank, they've got your field, the Government folks, I mean. They've had a big gang working on it, making it twice as big. It—it's theirs."

Seymour's laugh was short and grim. "You bet they've got it," he agreed. "And they'll keep it. And after I'm dead and gone, my heirs—whoever they may be—will be paid for it, even with interest added, perhaps. The trouble is—"

He stopped. Bradshaw, with a vague hope of heading off, or at least deferring, the crisis he dreaded, changed the subject. "You are in the flying service yourself, aren't you, Frank?" he queried. "Last I heard you were going to have a commission."

Frank Seymour frowned. The tone of his reply was gruff. "That's something I don't like to talk about," he said. "I was promised a commission, and I would have had it, too, long before this. Everything was all right until—well, until I took my physical examination. Then the blasted doctors wouldn't pass me. They said I had valvular trouble, bad heart, rot like that. I told them— Oh well, forget it. I would if I could."

"But what did you do? What are you doing?"

The frown deepened. "I was sore. The whole business was silly—more red tape. I could have had some sort of job, I guess, but I was mad and walked out on them. A mistake, maybe, but when you've been fit as a fiddle all your life, and know you are fit, to have a couple of doctor squirts tell you— Oh, never mind. You wouldn't know how I felt, of course."

"Maybe I would"—dryly. "Shouldn't be surprised if I did. What did you do next? When you walked out where did you walk to?"

"Oh, a friend of mine in Bridgeport had a garage and automobile machine-shop that was doing well. He was getting older, and the affair was bigger than he

259

liked to swing alone any longer. After going into the proposition pretty carefully I bought a partnership with him. It looked promising enough then. Who could have seen how things were going in the automobile game? I couldn't, for one."

He paused, no doubt expecting Zenas to make some comment. None was forthcoming, however. The Bradshaw expression was not as gloomy as his own. Zenas, tugging at his lip, was thinking. A few years ago, in the days when Bradshaw's Store was on what the boys called "Easy Street," when he, himself, was younger and stronger, when business was good and there were none of the thousand and one complications hampering him and it as now, then, if as honest and straight a fellow as Frank Seymour had come to him asking for temporary financial help, that help would, in one way or another, have been forthcoming—to a reasonable extent, that is. He had loaned other good men money and had, in most cases, been repaid. But now—why, well, it was out of the question. He must say no, which, in this case, would not be easy. And to write to Mark that he had said it would be harder still.

Seymour went on. "This has been a devil of a year. To begin with, my pal, this partner of mine, dropped dead in the shop. He left a wife and four kids, two of them in school and the two older boys in the service— like Mark, God knows where. She, the mother, I mean, hasn't got anything but the house they live in, a little insurance money, and her husband's share in the garage business. That business was prospering when I went into it; now it has gone to pot, most of it. Every cent I had put by has gone with it. If I can sell out, I shall, and get a defense job somewhere. But I can't just shut up the place and leave that widow and the girls flat. See that, Zenas, don't you?"

"Eh? Yes, sure, I see how you feel."

"I knew you would. Well, I've been a long while getting around to what brought me to you, but I'm there now. I am fighting along, trying to sell, but not having any luck so far, and I need every penny that is owed me to keep my head above water...." He drew a long breath and added: "I feel as if I were going back on one of my best friends, and I know I'm breaking the promise I gave him to keep my mouth shut about this. He is where I can't get at him, and I don't see how he himself could help me, anyhow. So—well, here we are."

He took a billfold from his pocket and from it drew an oblong slip of paper. Zenas Bradshaw gazed at him and it uncomprehendingly.

"What—" he began, but stopped short, staring at the paper which had been thrust into his hand.

It bore a date in August of the preceding year and was a note for $1,500, payable on demand to Frank Seymour. The handwriting was as familiar to Zenas as his own. The signer of the note was Marcellus Bradshaw.

Mechanically he turned it over. There was no endorsement on the back. He reversed it once more and sat gazing at the handwriting and the signature. Mark's own, no question about that. Seymour laid a hand on his shoulder.

"Surprised you, have I?" he queried. "Mark didn't write you about it before he left? That's queer. When he came to me there in Bridgeport, he told me he hadn't told you beforehand, nor Emily, nor anybody; but, by now, I—thought—"

Zenas broke in. "Wait. Hold on," he ordered. "I

don't understand. I—I— Came to you in—in Bridgeport, you say? When did he ever come to Bridgeport? How did he get there?"

"Wait. I'll tell you all about it. He stopped off in Bridgeport after he was here, that last time. He didn't stay but an hour or two, was on his way back to camp. I didn't know he was coming: I don't think he knew it, himself, ahead of time. This was something he had thought up after he left you and his brand-new wife. They had just been married, he told me about that, but said it was a dead secret."

He went on with the story. Zenas Bradshaw listened, hearing what was said, but not once interrupting or questioning. He was in a sort of daze, through which the one indisputable fact loomed like a promontory in a fog. His grandson had borrowed fifteen hundred dollars of a friend—one whose friendship was real enough to grant the loan of such a sum merely on his, Mark's, unbacked note of hand, a simple promise to pay. And Mark, in his letters home, had not mentioned having done such a thing. It was— And why—*why?*

Seymour was explaining that why, partially, at least. Mark, having told of the secret marriage, explained the reason which had impelled it. He told of Emily's unhappiness at home, of her and his conviction that she simply could not live with her uncle and aunt much longer. The break was inevitable, as she saw it, and when it came she was seriously considering going away, to Boston probably, to seek a position of some sort and earn her own living.

Mark, of course, disliked the thought of his wife's being driven to this extremity, but, as things were, he conceded that there seemed to be no alternative. After he left Harniss, however, and when he was alone on the train, he fell to thinking and planning and considering, and his doubts and anxieties deepened. Emily had no very definite place to go and no position in sight. It might take some time for her to find one. Meanwhile, she would have practically no money of her own, nothing to live on. So—

"So he came begging to you!" Zenas Bradshaw almost shouted it. "Why in the devil didn't he come to me? To *me*, I ask you?"

"Shh! Not so loud. He said he didn't go to you because—well, for one reason, you didn't know about the marriage: Emily and he had agreed nobody should know about it until they were ready to make the news public. And, for another—well, he said you hadn't been feeling too fit."

"Oh, be hanged! He just came to you and you let him have fifteen hundred right off the reel, without any security. My Lord above! Fifteen hundred *dollars!* What on earth did he want all that for?"

According to Seymour, Mark had intended to put the money aside, deposit it somewhere in safekeeping, as a reserve fund for his wife in case of her necessity. He was not going to use any of it himself, he declared: it was just what he had called it, a reserve fund for Emily. He had his commission, and expected soon to be stationed somewhere more or less permanently. Then— well, then it might be possible for his wife to join him, after which the fifteen hundred would be repaid to Seymour and everything would be lovely. The outbreak of war, however, had knocked all that in the head, just as it had knocked the business of the Bridgeport auto-repair shop.

"He didn't say so," Frank Seymour added, "but I got the notion that there might be the prospect of a baby sometime or other. There sometimes is, you know, with young married folks."

Zenas made no comment. He would have known, before this, if there had been any expectancy of that kind. He dismissed the suggestion as not worth a denial. But there was so much he did not, could not, understand.

"He was borrowing all this for—for Emily, you say?" he queried. "For her to keep as a—what-did-you-call-it?— reserve fund? But he didn't tell her he was going to?"

"He had told nobody when he left me. He didn't exactly say so, but I gathered he felt she wouldn't have wanted him to do it."

"I'll say she wouldn't. She would have no more let him take on a debt like that for her sake, than—than— Oh, never mind that. What I can't get is your letting him have it this way. No security—nothing. Just handing it over as if it was a nickel for a bag of peanuts."

Frank Seymour flushed.

"Mark is about as close a friend as I have," he declared, crisply. "And square and straight, all through. If I needed money and he had it, I should have gone to him, just as he came to me. He is a Harniss Bradshaw, and I never saw nor heard of a crooked one. I was pretty much on top of the world just then, or thought I was. Single, nobody dependent on me, and cash in the bank. I had sold my field at a profit to the United States Government for a good lot of money. I expected to get that money any day. I was flush, or, as I say, I thought I was. Yes. I did let the boy have his fifteen hundred. I'd do it again, under the same conditions. There's your answer to that."

He shrugged and then added grimly, "I never expected to have to bother you, or anybody else about it. I could have waited till Mark paid me, a little at a time, or any way that suited him. And he would have done just that, I'd bet on it.... The trouble is that—well, as I told you, I am in a jam and I *can't* wait. That's why I'm here. I thought you could take the matter up with Emily, and maybe she would let me have that money, or as much of it as she has left. Mark would want her to, I know."

Zenas appeared to be scrutinizing a figure in the worn rug on the floor. Now he looked up.

"She hasn't got it," he said. "She never has had it."

"*What!*"

"I say she hasn't got it and never has had it. More than that, I am dead certain sure she doesn't know even yet that Mark borrowed it."

Seymour's face expressed blank astonishment.

"Why, that's nonsense," he protested, incredulously. "Mark borrowed it for her, not for himself. He must have sent it to her—have written her about it, anyhow—before he left this country."

"Well, he hasn't. I'll stake my last shirt on that."

"I can't— Look here, are you sure? Maybe she hasn't told you because he asked her not to. How do you know?"

"There, there: I know enough. Why, when she came to me, telling me she and Mark were married, she told me she had scarcely a cent of her own and asked me if I could lend her just enough to get her to Boston and keep her there while she was hunting a job. If she had fifteen hundred tucked away she wouldn't have done that. Not that girl, no, sir!"

Seymour rose to his feet. He walked to the window and back, muttering to himself. "This is—this is crazy," he vowed. "I don't get it at all. I gave the boy my check, and that check, with Mark's endorsement on it, came back to me from the bank with my other canceled checks, long ago. I've got it somewhere, I suppose. Oh, he got the money, all right; but—but if what you are telling me is true—"

"It is."

"I know, I know. But, hang it, he couldn't have spent it all. At least, if he did—"

Zenas Bradshaw interrupted. "Said he wasn't going to spend any of it, didn't he? . . . Um-hm. Well, then he didn't."

Seymour nodded. "So I'd say," he agreed. "Mark was reckless sometimes, liked to take chances when he was flying and all that. When he set out to do a thing he would do it, make or break. His getting married the way he did, slap-dash, without taking time to figure where he might be sent, or how he was going to support a wife—well, that would be like him: it didn't surprise me too much. But I never knew him to play a dirty trick or to lie to me. And to ask me a favor like this, with nothing but a lie behind it—no."

Zenas was silent.

Seymour stopped his pacing and turned. "You believe what I've told you, don't you?" he demanded, shortly. "You don't think *I* am lying?"

"Eh? Oh, no. Mark borrowed the money, I don't doubt that. This thing"—indicating the note—"is proof enough, even if I wanted more than your word—which I don't. He borrowed it, but—" He did not finish the sentence.

Frank Seymour nodded. "I know," he said. "You are stumped, just as I am. He borrowed it, but, if he didn't spend it and didn't send it to his wife, or even so much as tell her about it, what *did* he do with it? What became of it? Where is it?"

Zenas slowly shook his head. "God knows," he said, wearily. "If I knew where he was I should ask him, of course. I might try sending a cable, care of the Army, or the U. S. Air Service: that's how Emmie and I sent our letters, and he got them—he said he did. But sending a cable or writing and getting an answer—well, it will take time, how long I'm sure I don't know. I'll do it right off, of course. But—"

Once more he left a sentence unfinished. He was sitting there, pulling his lip, his gaze again fixed upon the figure in the shabby rug between his feet. Even Frank Seymour, his mind filled with his own trouble, noticed how old and tired he looked, much older and more weary than when they entered that room. And he had been ill not so long before. The younger man's conscience should have been clean enough: he, certainly, was blameless in the affair. As a matter of fact, he was the victim, and it was he who would suffer most. Nevertheless . . .

He walked to the window once more and stood there, his back to Zenas Bradshaw. He spoke, without turning.

"Oh, well," he said, after a moment. "You'll do what you can, I'm sure of that. Sorry I bothered you with it. I took for granted— But there is no use going through that again. I won't keep you any longer, Zenas. Much obliged. When you hear from Mark, or if you do, you can let me know." He crossed to the door and turned the key.

Zenas was on his feet now. He spoke.

"Hold on. Wait a minute," he ordered. "What are you going to do about that—that jam you say you are in? How are you going to get out of it?"

"Don't know. Sell the shop and what's left of the business for what I can get, I suppose."

"How about your partner's widow and those children? What's going to happen to them?"

"They can have whatever I get: I'll get along somehow. I'm moderately healthy, even if the army doctors don't think so. And Mark will pay up some day—if he lives. . . . Good-by, Zenas."

He had opened the door, but Zenas Bradshaw did not go. He remained where he was and asked another question.

"Come on the train, did you?" he queried.

"No. Drove through in my car. That is"—with a shrug —"it's my car now. It probably won't be much longer."

"Don't have to start back right off this minute, do you?"

"Why—no, if there's any point in waiting."

"Might be. You be in this room at—well, say about noon. You'll see me again then, or hear from me, anyhow."

He went out without another word. Seymour, from the window, watched him cross the road and enter Bradshaw's Store. The sudden termination of the interview, and particularly the manner and parting speech of his visitor, astonished and puzzled him. The old man had not wasted much sympathy, certainly. Had not so much as expressed regret that his grandson had been the cause of his, Seymour's, present trouble, or a part of it, nor offered apologies for Mark's neglect. That did not square with what he had previously known of Zenas Brawshaw, nor with the latter's reputation in Harniss.

And yet Zenas had been hard hit by what he had just heard, no doubt of that. He looked—well, he looked badly shaken, and as he climbed the steps to the store platform he stumbled, Seymour had noticed that. And, for some reason or other, he was coming back at noon. Why? What good would that do?

Oh, well, might as well wait and see. It would be a long wait, a long forenoon, but he, Seymour, would spend it where he was. He had many acquaintances in the town, but he did not care to meet them now, to have them tell him he was looking well and ask him joking questions about why he was not in uniform or whether he had bought a yacht with the money he had been paid for the airfield. No doubt Harniss gossip was rating him a millionaire by this time. He did not want to meet those people: he did not want to meet anybody.

He lit a pipe and sat down in the chair Bradshaw had just vacated, his back to the window. After a time he took a notebook and pencil from his pocket and began jotting down columns of figures. It was a disheartening occupation, and he soon gave it up. Every fifteen minutes or so he looked at his watch.

At a quarter to twelve there was a knock at the door. He rose wearily. Here was Zenas. Now there would be another painful session. Nothing helpful would come of it, of course. He wished he had told the old fellow that he could not wait.

It was not Zenas, however, who had knocked. Instead, it was Willie Snow, driver of the Bradshaw delivery truck. Willie's freckled face was bisected with a broad grin.

"Well, I declare!" he exclaimed. "It *is* you, Mr. Seymour, ain't it? When the boss—Mr. Bradshaw, I mean—told me I'd find you over here to the Rest I couldn't hardly believe him. Glad to see you back in Harniss, Mr. Seymour. Didn't nobody know you was comin', did they? Goin' to give us all a surprise, eh?"

Seymour said he guessed that was about it. He noticed that young Snow had an envelop in his hand.

"That for me?" he inquired.

"Why—why, yes. Zenas—the boss, I mean—said I was to fetch it to you. Said I was to wait for an answer back, he did. How's things up in the sky these days, Mr. Seymour? Flyin' for the army, same as our Mark, ain't you? That's what I heard."

His questions were not answered. Frank Seymour ignored them altogether. He held out his hand for the envelop, and Willie, evidently disappointed in the lack of sociability on the part of the returned celebrity, gave it to him. Seymour walked over to the window, and there, with his back to the messenger—another disappointment for the latter, who had been wondering why Zenas Bradshaw was writing to a man only across the road, instead of coming himself—tore it open and stood there looking at the enclosure, or enclosures.

He stood there for several minutes. The envelop fell from his fingers to the floor, but he did not pick it up. Why didn't he say something? Willie ventured a reminder.

"Everything's all right, ain't it, Mr. Seymour?" he ventured.

"Eh? Yes." Then, turning suddenly. "What do you mean—all right? . . . He didn't— No, course he didn't. . . . Well, I *will* be darned!"

"What did you say, Mr. Seymour?"

"Oh, nothing, nothing." He crossed to the small desk in the corner, rummaged in its drawer, and took from it one of the Seaside Rest's own envelops, not too clean. Then, from the bed, where it had lain since Zenas Bradshaw's departure, he picked up an oblong bit of paper—there was writing on it, Willie's sharp eyes glimpsed that fact—folded the paper, and placed it in the Seaside Rest envelop, which he sealed carefully. He took up the hotel pen, dipped it in the hotel inkwell, and attempted to write. As the pen was rusty and there was no ink in the well, the attempt was a failure.

Willie Snow chuckled. "Some rig-out, that is, I'd say," he observed. "Can't make much headway with a busted pen and no ink, can you? I'll tell the world you can't! Like to use my fountain pen, would you, Mr. Seymour?"

"What? . . . Yes, much obliged."

"All right. Now—" His hand made a move toward a pocket, but stopped in mid-air. "Pshaw!" he exclaimed. "I ain't got it on me. It's in my vest over to the store. Want I should run acrost and get it for you? Just as soon as not."

"No. Never mind. This will do." With his pencil he wrote "Mr. Zenas Bradshaw" on the envelop. "Give this to your boss," he said. "And be careful, don't lose it."

The Snow pride was hurt. "I ain't in the habit of losin' things," announced Willie, with dignity.

"Fine. And here's something to tell Mr. Bradshaw. Tell him I said 'Thanks' and that I would write him and say a lot more as soon as I get back to—as soon as I get home. Got that straight, have you?"

"Sure. Why wouldn't I have it?"

"Don't know. Now take this, for yourself, along with it. Much obliged, Willie. So long."

Willie Snow found himself outside, in the hall. The "this" for himself was a dollar bill.

Willie said "Gosh!" He reflected that it must be great to be rich. With the dollar in one hand and the addressed envelop in the other, he descended the stairs and, crossing the road, delivered the envelop to his employer. The latter tore it open, looked carefully at the slip of paper within it, and put both envelop and enclosure into his pocketbook. He said not a word. Willie told Abner Hallett about the affair afterward.

"What in thunder do you suppose *that* was all about, Ab?" he queried. "Kind of funny-actin', both of 'em, seemed to me. Somethin' to do with Mark, I shouldn't wonder: that's all I can figure out."

Mr. Hallett, evidently, was not sufficiently interested to figure. He brusquely ordered his young associate to stop talking and get back on his job.

Late that afternoon Frank Seymour, at the wheel of his car, pulled up at a filling-station on the highway between Saybrook and New Haven, to purchase a few gallons of gasoline. While the station attendant was busy at the pump Seymour took the opportunity to read the note which young Snow had brought him at the Seaside Rest. He had read it before, but now he read it again.

DEAR FRANK:

Guess you must have thought I walked out on you kind of sudden this morning. Well, I did, but I wanted to think over and consider what you told me, and I could do that better alone. I have come to the conclusion that this business is, as you might say, a sort of family affair and that it would be easier for me to handle it inside the family than for you to do it from the outside. So, as you will see by the enclosed, I am taking it over and you won't have to bother. Just send that note thing of Mark's back by Willie and oblige

Yours truly,

ZENAS BRADSHAW

P.S. There ought to be some interest added on, I know, but you did not say how much, so you can send me a memo of it later. I am almighty sorry you have had all this worry and trouble. Hope the worst of your jam is over. If you get time, write me a line by-and-by telling me how things go with you and what your plans are. See you again some day, I hope.

Z. B.

The "enclosed" was Zenas Bradshaw's personal check for fifteen hundred dollars.

The station attendant came around to the front of the car.

"Tank's full up," he announced. "Nothing else you wanted?"

"What? . . . No, that's all."

"All set, eh?"

Frank Seymour heard, but his answer was an odd one. It seemed to be addressed to himself more than to the gas salesman.

"Yes," he said, slowly, "it looks as if I was, for just now, anyhow. Only—"

"Yes?"

Seymour came out of his trance. "Not a thing," he said, hastily. "On my way . . . Oh," reaching into his change pocket, "of course! How much do I owe you?"

Chapter 13

ZENAS, when he entered the store after his interview with Seymour in the room at the Surfside
Rest, was fighting hard to show no signs of the shock
he had received. His first spur-of-the-moment idea had
been to go home, to his own room in the house on Pond
Road, where he could be alone and think without interruption. The idea lasted but a moment. It would not
do, it would not do at all, Emily was expecting him at
the store. He had told her he would join her there as
soon as he could get rid of the man, presumably a salesman, who had beckoned at the window. He had been
absent almost an hour, and she must be wondering what
had detained him. Very likely she might be watching,
and if she saw him turn away and go in the opposite
direction, she would not understand, might fear he was
ill, might imagine almost anything.

Abner Hallett would be expecting him, too. Abner
always had a dozen questions to ask concerning what
had better be done about this or that, little matters of
store routine. That was Abner's greatest drawback: he
never acted on his own initiative when he could find
some one else to take the responsibility. A good man,
honest as the day was long, and a hard worker, but a
born subordinate, an executive only when circumstances
forced him to be. Emily would have told Abner that he,

274

Zenas, was on the way, so Abner would wait, as usual, for orders. No, the store it would have to be, so to the store Zenas went.

Emily had been watching, as he surmised, and she came out from behind her desk to meet him.

"What is it, Grandfather?" she asked, anxiously. "Are you all right?"

Zenas did his best to appear surprised at the question.

"Eh?" he queried. "Why, certain I'm all right. Why not?"

"Well, I thought— When you came up the steps I noticed—"

"Oh, yes, yes. You saw me trip. That's my feet, Emmie. When they first measured me for feet they gave me oversize, and I've had trouble steering 'em ever since. No, no, I'm all right. Where's Ab?"

"In the back room. Who was the man at the Rest, Grandfather? He kept you a long time."

"You'll be surprised when I tell you. Last person I expected to see in these latitudes. It was Frank Seymour."

Her surprise was obvious enough.

"Frank Seymour!" she repeated. "Why, what is he doing here? I supposed he was in the army somewhere— Mark said he hoped to be."

"I know. Everybody supposed the same thing, but he isn't. Army doctors turned him down account of his heart, so he says. . . . Oh"—with a glance toward the back room—"I wouldn't mention his being here, if I were you, Emily. He doesn't won't folks to know, kind of sensitive about the heart business, I presume likely. He is just here overnight. Going this afternoon."

"But isn't he coming in to see me? He knows that Mark and I are married, doesn't he?"

"Oh, sure, sure he knows."

"He must"—a trifle bitterly. "He couldn't be in Harniss ten minutes without being told that." Then, eagerly, "Has he heard from Mark?"

"Not a word. . . . That—well—er—that was part of what he wanted to see me about. Wanted to know what I'd heard from the boy. . . . Abner's out yonder, you said? Hi, Ab!"

He hurried to the back room. Emily looked after him, her brows wrinkled in puzzled speculation. His explanation was satisfactory as far as it went, but it had not gone very far. She still could not understand why Frank Seymour should not wish the people of Harniss to know of his presence in town. And why was he so carefully keeping away from her? Mark had been, perhaps, his most intimate friend, certainly one of the most intimate. Frank knew of the marriage—Zenas had said that he did. She herself had, so far as she knew, never done or said anything to cause resentment on his part. And she was Mark's wife.

Yes, whatever was wrong with Zenas Bradshaw—and, in spite of his protestations, she was sure there was something wrong—must, in some way, be connected with Frank Seymour. And therefore, although she could not imagine how, the probability was that Mark was concerned in it, too. It was a distinctly unpleasant surmise.

Nothing Zenas did or said, however, during the remainder of the forenoon gave her any hint of explanation. He was actively busy, giving orders to Hallett, supervising Willie Snow's delivery baskets, waiting on and chatting with customers. Shortly after eleven he came to the desk and asked her if she would mind going home for an early luncheon that day.

"I know it is my turn," he said, "but I've got a dozen or so odds and ends to see to here."

It had become an understood custom that both Emily and he should not be absent from the store at the same time. Only on Sundays were they together at the noon meal. On weekdays one went home to lunch early and the other did not go until after his return. It happened to be Zenas's turn to "feed early," as he called it, on this particular day, but she told him that she did not mind going first, and went immediately.

As she walked toward the Pond Road house, her new home—and it had come, by this time, to seem very much like home—her vague disquiet accompanied her: she could not shake it off. As she reached the corner she saw a dignified figure approaching from the other direction. She spoke.

"Good morning, Uncle John," she said.

Mr. Thacher's nod was hardly perceptible.

"Morning," he said, stiffly, and went his way.

Emily sighed. Oh, well, if that was the way he and Aunt Etta wanted it, that was the way it would have to be. For herself, or for Mark, she would have minded little, but she was quite aware of the difference the Thacher enmity had made, and was making, to Bradshaw's Store and its owner. Fine, brave old Grandfather Bradshaw! It was hard to think that she was at least halfway responsible for making his struggle more difficult. Her conscience troubled her always, but if she dared to mention her feeling of guilt he would not listen. "Bosh! Nonsense! Don't be silly, girl. Got by long odds the best part of the Thacher family on my side, haven't I? Mark and I won out on that deal. You bet *we* are satisfied. Of course, if you are sorry for yourself—"

There was only one answer to that, and so the subject was changed. She had given up trying. And yet, although she was not allowed to speak, she thought much. And now here was another puzzling and disturbing thought. What was this mysterious business of Frank Seymour's and what had it to do with the Bradshaw family?

If she could have watched—secretly, of course—Zenas Bradshaw's behavior after her departure from the store she would have been still more disturbed and puzzled. At twenty minutes to twelve Zenas entered the tiny office enclosure at the rear of the bookkeeper's desk, opened the little old-fashioned safe with "Bradshaw's" painted on its door, and from a locked drawer in that safe took out a checkbook. It was not the store checkbook, but one much smaller, and the checks in it were to be drawn, not upon the Harniss National Bank, where Bradshaw's kept its account, but upon the Ostable Savings and Trust Company in Ostable. It was Zenas Bradshaw's private checkbook, and the account was his own personal account. For many years he had kept money on deposit there, as a savings fund to be augmented when profits were larger than usual and to be drawn upon only when he bought an occasional bond for investment or purchased something which was not in any way concerned with the store or its business.

As a young man he had opened that account, and it was his father who had suggested his doing so.

"The saving habit is a good one for any young fellow to get into," his father told him. "Put your spare cash
278

into a savings bank, and you think twice afore you take it out again. Best kind of umbrella I know for that rainy day we hear so much about. And, if I was you, I'd put it somewhere out of town, instead of here in Harniss. For one reason it won't be so easy for you to get at when you feel extravagant, and, for another, you'll be the only one in this neighborhood that knows about it."

There had been times when this Ostable "rainy day" fund totaled several thousand dollars and the bonds in the Bradshaw deposit box several thousand more. Now it was not so. The bonds went first. The depression of the early thirties and the slump in the market value of all securities, good or bad, took these down with the rest. A number of Bradshaw's longest and supposedly safest customers among the Harniss summer colony coasted from affluence to bankruptcy during those depressed years, and Zenas, disgusted, like so many other small investors, with what he called "paper savings," sold his bonds for a fraction of what he paid for them and put the money into the depleted working capital of the store. The "rainy day" fund, however, he did not touch. The Ostable Savings and Trust Company stood firm while other financial institutions were crashing, and he was certain it would continue to stand. The money he intrusted to its keeping was safe. A comforting thought, that. He did not withdraw any of it and, from time to time, added a little.

He had added nothing for more than a year now. On the contrary, within the six months just past, he had twice made small withdrawals. The thirty-day credit limit established by the city wholesalers made it necessary for him to have money to keep Bradshaw's credit good. The Harniss account must not be permitted to be-

279

come too low. John Thacher was an influential member of the bank's board of directors, and the Honorable John would be only too glad to see Bradshaw's balance shrink. So, although the withdrawal of each dollar was, to him, as painful as the extraction of a tooth, he had drawn upon the Ostable fund.

And now that source of supply was drying up. To pay fifteen hundred dollars to Frank Seymour would leave but a few hundred in his "rainy day" reserve. Why, therefore, did he pay it? Seymour could not expect him to pay. Mark was of age, had been when the debt was contracted. There was no obligation on him, Zenas Bradshaw, no legal obligation at all.

True enough, but what of it? That did not alter the fact that Mark had borrowed money of a friend, and now that friend was, himself, in pressing need of money. Something Seymour had said to him, Zenas, could not be shaken off or forgotten.

"Mark is about as close a friend as I have. And square and straight all through. . . . He is a Harniss Bradshaw, and I never heard of a crooked one."

Neither had any one else. No Harniss Bradshaw had ever been crooked. There was no use fooling himself with excuses about legality. This was a Bradshaw debt, a Bradshaw obligation, and he, Zenas Bradshaw, must pay it. Afterwards, repayment might—might, possibly— be made to him. The explanation—but that, too, must come afterwards. He could not afford that fifteen hundred dollars, the Lord knew that was true enough, but neither could he afford— No, of course he couldn't.

During that forenoon, after he left the Surfside Rest, while he was giving orders to Hallett, or serving customers, the resolution had been strengthening in the back of his mind. Now he drew the check on the Ostable Savings and Trust Company, wrote his short letter to Seymour, enclosed the check and letter in an envelop, carefully sealed the letter, and sent it by Willie Snow across the street. When Willie came back bearing the return envelop, he made sure that the demand note Mark had given Seymour was within and then put note and envelop into his wallet and the wallet into his pocket. Young Snow was watching and loaded with questions.

"Say, Mr. Bradshaw, did you know that Frank Seymour was coming back to Harniss? Know it ahead of time, I mean? I never. I was some surprised when I see him, you bet."

Zenas nodded absently. "There are lots of surprising things in this world, Willie," he said. "Sometime, maybe, when you and I have nothing else to do, we'll talk about 'em. Just now, though, you'd better run along and see to your orders."

That evening, in the sitting-room after supper, there was a certain atmosphere of constraint between Emily and himself. It was Emily who brought Seymour's name into the conversation. She had been waiting for Zenas to do so, but he had not once referred to the man. She had dropped several hints, and, although they were plain enough, Zenas had not picked them up. He talked about the war, the weather, and matters connected with the store, but he would not talk about Frank Seymour.

At last, those subjects being pretty well exhausted, she took up the sock she was knitting for the local branch of the Red Cross, and Zenas unfolded the Boston newspaper. The needles clicked and the paper rustled. After a few minutes the clicking ceased.

"Grandfather," said Emily.

He looked at her around the edge of the paper.

"Eh? Did you say something?" he asked.

"I said 'Grandfather,' but now I am going to say more. Why haven't you told me what Frank Seymour is doing here in Harniss?"

"Er—what's that? Why, I did tell you, didn't I? He—er—he just came back here on a little matter of business. He isn't here now: went away again early this afternoon. Or I suppose likely he did—he said he was going to."

"He did go. Willie told me he saw him drive off in his car. What sort of business was it that brought him to Harniss? It couldn't be about the flying field. He sold that to the Government long ago."

Zenas thought he saw a way out. He told her what Seymour had told him, of the sale of the field and that he had, so far, not been paid. He went on to tell of Frank's Bridgeport venture, of the death of his partner, of the falling off of trade. He made a long, rambling story of it, and Emily more than suspected that the rambling was intentional. She did not wait for the end.

"But why did he want to see you?" she asked. "You could not help him get his money from the Government. At least, I don't see how you could."

"Oh, no, no. He didn't expect me to. He just—well, I imagine he wanted to see what the army folks had done to the field: that is likely enough."

"I think, if I were he, and considering how I had been treated, I shouldn't much care what they had done. And that doesn't answer my question. What did he want to see you about?"

"Why—why—well, he and Mark were such chums, as

282

you might say, and I am Mark's grandfather. Naturally, he'd want to see me, wouldn't he?"

"Well, I am Mark's wife, and it is plain that he didn't want to see *me*."

"Now—now, Emmie—"

"Now, Grandfather. Tell me the truth. Did Frank Seymour want to borrow money from you?"

The paper crackled as Zenas dropped it into his lap.

"Borrow money from me?" he repeated. "From *me?* Good Lord, no! What would he want to do that for? What on earth put that in your head?"

"Well, it was the only reason I could imagine. I couldn't imagine any until you told me just now of his not being paid for the field and how bad his Bridgeport business had become. Then I thought—but, of course, it was silly of me."

Zenas chuckled and did his best to make the chuckle sound unforced. "Borrowing money from me just now would be considerable like trying to scratch water from the bottom of a dry well with a rake. No, no, he wasn't trying to borrow anything."

She looked at him for a long moment without speaking. Then she said: "No, that wasn't it; I can see that it wasn't.... Never mind. We won't talk about it any more."

"Now, Emmie, don't you get to thinking foolish things."

"I'm not going to think, I am going to knit. If I don't get ahead faster than I have been doing the war will be over before these socks are finished. Read your paper, I won't bother you again."

So she knit, and he read or pretended to do so. Occasionally he ventured to peep at her around the edge of the paper, and on two of these occasions he caught her looking at him with, or so he imagined, that same questioning glint in her eye. A little after nine he announced that he was going to "turn in," said good night, and went to his room. There, with the door carefully shut, he sat down to write a long letter to Mark. In it he told of Seymour's coming to Harniss, his reason for coming, and that he, Zenas, had "taken over" the fifteen-hundred-dollar note.

"I am not going to blow you up for doing what you did," he wrote. "You had a reason, of course, or thought you had. Frank said you told him it was some notion having to do with Emily, but that she did not know about it and it must be kept secret from her and from me, too. Well, unless I am clear off soundings, she does not know it yet, and that means, of course, that you never sent the fifteen hundred to her. What did you do with it? You would not be likely to take all that with you in your pants pocket, I should imagine. Considering that I, instead of Frank Seymour, hold that note of yours now, I guess you will agree that I am entitled to an explanation. I am not mad at you, don't get the idea that I am, but I do expect you to tell me the whole thing, all the whys and wherefores, no matter what is behind them."

He began another sentence here, then scratched it out, and began again as follows:

"That last line may kind of read as if I figured you had got mixed up in something underhand or crooked. I don't. Only for the Lord sakes, boy, why didn't you come to a Bradshaw instead of an outsider? I have never given you any reason to be scared of me, as I know of. Now write me and write the whole of it. Emmie shan't see what you write if you say you still don't want her to. And she shan't know about the fifteen hundred, either. I have fixed that so she won't."

He dropped the letter in the slot at the post-office next morning, noting, as he turned away, that Emily was waiting to post one of her own. Neither asked to whom the other had written: that was taken for granted. Zenas reflected that she would have been surprised if she had read his letter to her husband. He, too, would have been surprised had he read one section of hers. She told of Frank Seymour's return to Harniss and his brief stay. Also of her not being able to understand why he carefully kept out of every one's way except Zenas Bradshaw's.

"He called Grandfather over to the Rest," she wrote, "and kept him there more than an hour. I tried to find out what they talked about, but Grandfather dodged every one of my questions. He declares it was nothing important, but I think it was, for he came back looking very much upset and, I am sure, greatly troubled. He is still troubled, I am certain of that, too. Mark, dear, can you think of any possible private business Frank Seymour could have with Grandfather? *I* can't, yet, but I shall keep on trying to find out. No matter what he writes you and what he tells me, or others, he is not too well and he has more than enough on his mind as it is. Business at the store is not too good, and the Government regulations and restrictions on what can be sold, how much or how little, are more and more confusing and contradictory every day. We order this or that and then are told that we can't have it, probably won't have any more of it 'for the duration'—and of course no one knows how long that will be. But I shouldn't be worrying you with this, and I know it. Our little bothers and nuisances count for nothing. We are all right, truly we are. If only I could know each morning when I wake that *you* were safe and well I should be completely happy. And so would Grandfather. My dearest love to you—"

The remainder of the letter had nothing to do with Bradshaw's business or Frank Seymour.

In spite of her reassuring assertion that she and Zenas Bradshaw were "all right," Emily, as the days passed, was less and less certain of that statement's truth. Zenas neither looked nor acted all right. He made a grand show of cheerfulness and optimism and would not listen to any hints or suggestions from her that he must not work so hard or that his occasional intervals of brooding and absent-minded silence were due to anything more than the usual worries attendant upon what he called "keeping store."

"When you have been at it as long as I have, Emmie," he explained, "you get to look as if you were lugging the world on your shoulders, like that fellow—Geography—no, what's-his-name—Atlas—they used to have pictures of in the patent-medicine almanacs. Looking that way is part of the job. If you look too contented your customers get the notion that you're rich and that they needn't be in any hurry about paying their bills."

"Some of them seem to have that idea already," she observed. "Three of our biggest accounts have run for months. Don't you think I might stir them up a little?"

He tugged at his lip. "It's the Holworthy family and the Colvins and the Saybrooks you mean 'specially, I suppose," he said. "They've traded with us since they first took to coming to Harniss summers, and that was twenty years or more ago. They'll pay when they get around to it, same as they always do. Grocery bills don't mean much to them, just chicken feed. They'll settle up at the end of the season. Better let 'em alone."

She found it hard to keep her patience. "Well, I wish the Boston people we buy from would be as easy-going," she said, shortly. "They don't let *us* alone. We have to pay cash, or what amounts to that."

"I know. They can afford to. We have to buy from them. The Holworthys and the rest don't have to buy from us. There's always the chain store for them to go to."

"Yes, but they would pay cash at the chain store. The chain-store people don't run any charge accounts."

"I know, but Bradshaw's has always done the other thing. If we should put up a sign saying we sold only for cash down, what do you suppose would happen?"

She shook her head. There were times when she wondered what was going to happen, even as it was.

"I'm afraid you are old-fashioned, Grandfather," she observed.

"Shouldn't wonder. The 'old' part is right, anyhow. . . . No, no," hastily, "I don't mean that. I'm not old, can't afford to be. When I get really old I am going to retire. Heard me say that before, haven't you?"

"Yes, I have heard you *say* it."

"Oh, it's a fact, has been for the last dozen years. What is that word that's been printed a couple of thousand times? 'A man is as old as he feels,' that's it. Well, this morning I feel about twenty-five—make it twenty-six. I set up until 'most ten o'clock last night and that's aged me some. I'll have to be careful."

He chuckled and walked away. Emily, watching him,

saw him stagger momentarily, then catch at the counter edge, steady himself, and go on. Again she shook her head. Doctor Stevens had dropped in at the store the previous afternoon, and he had voiced her own thought.

"I don't like it," said Doctor Ben. "I don't like it at all. He has been pretty well, surprisingly well, but now he looks as if he were slipping again. He must give himself a rest. He must. I wish you would make him see it: he won't listen to me. If Mark were only here! Heard from him, have you?"

As a matter of fact, they had. The letters which Mark, in his cable despatch, had mentioned as having written finally arrived. Dated two months before, the envelops soiled and plastered with censors' stickers, they drifted in at last. From what part of the world they came was not disclosed, that they could only guess, but the length of time taken in transit and a paragraph in Zenas's letter, in which Mark said something about never expecting to be "away down here in this side of the earth," gave a hint.

"Hm-m," mused Zenas, as he read this paragraph aloud. " 'Away down here.' That does sound like t'other side of the Pacific, same as you and I thought. Australia, or that neighborhood, probably."

Emily nodded. "And he writes of the 'long voyage' as if it was very long. He doesn't say that he has been in any battles."

"Pretty certain he hadn't when he wrote that. Most of it written aboard ship, I don't doubt. Says he feels fine. That's comforting, anyhow."

"Yes, and he said the same thing in his cable. Oh, dear, it is such a long, long way off."

"Not nigh as long as it was in the old square-rigger

days. My wife's uncle made two voyages to Sydney, and I recollect his talking as if it was half-way to the moon. Now those Clipper fliers make it in ten days, or some such matter. Amazing, I do declare!"

He read all of his letter to Emily, and she read a part of hers to him. The letters were a help to both of them. The newspapers, with their brief communiqués and rumors, were not as helpful. Things were going to happen away down on that other side: might be happening now, or even have happened already—a probability neither of them mentioned.

The time had come when Zenas Bradshaw felt he ought to take a trip to Boston, but on the day before the one set for his departure he had another slight attack of vertigo, similar to that which put him out of commission the year before. It was not severe and lasted only a short time, but it was sufficiently alarming to cause Doctor Stevens to vow that he should not go.

"If I can't keep you any other way I'll have the blacksmith rivet an anchor on your off hind leg," declared Stevens. Zenas demanded to be told where the doctor thought he was likely to locate a blacksmith. "The last one in Ostable County starved to death five years ago," he added. "Just after the last horse died of old age, that was. I've got to go, Ben, I tell you."

He did not go, however; Emily went, instead. She was absent only a day and a half. Her report, when she returned, was not as discouraging as Zenas had feared it might be. Oh, yes, supplies could still be bought, in limited quantities and subject to a still more limited selection, but she had done pretty well, everything considered, so she said. Every one had been very kind and pleasant.

Zenas sniffed. "I bet they were!" he declared. "Anybody that wasn't pleasant to you would be a hundred years old—or blind. The young fellows—those from twenty to fifty, say—were especially kind, I suppose likely."

Emily laughed. "No more so than the older ones. I am surprised at you, Mr. Bradshaw. What sort of granddaughter-in law do you think you have, I want to know?"

Zenas's answer was prompt.

"The number one sample from the top of the box," he declared. "Where I would be without you I swear I don't know."

She wrinkled her nose at him. "It is too bad that soft soap has gone out of fashion," she said. "You handle it so beautifully. And, while we are handling it, suppose you try to imagine where I should be if it weren't for you. . . . There, that's enough about soap: I didn't order much of that in Boston, anyway. Now let me tell you just what I did buy."

There were some things she was careful not to tell him. Of those the most important and, to her mind, the most disturbing, was the changed attitude toward Bradshaw's and its custom that she noticed, or was almost sure she noticed, in certain of the wholesale houses she visited. The people were very polite and agreeable— oh, yes, but it seemed to her that they were by no means as eager to recommend purchases as on her previous visit and in several instances had even suggested cutting down the quantities ordered. The excuse was always the same, shortage of stock on hand and the increasing difficulty of obtaining fresh supplies. It was a plausible excuse and would have been perfectly believable were it not so promptly offered and, so she thought, too politely overemphasized.

In one establishment, that of which Zenas Bradshaw's friend Barbour had formerly been the head, she ventured to bring up the subject of a longer term of credit for the store. She quoted what Zenas had told her so recently about the necessity of not offending good customers of long standing by asking them to pay by the month.

"It would not do," she said. "You can see that it wouldn't. It would make it so much easier for us if you could allow us—well, perhaps, sixty days. I remember your Mr. Barbour's telling me, when I was here before, that he counted Grandfather as a personal friend and that Bradshaw's could buy as much or as little as it saw fit at any time and pay for it at any time, too. That is exactly what he said—at any time. That doesn't sound like your 'thirty-day' letter at all. Now does it?"

The salesman—he was a young man—explained that there had been some changes in the firm. Mr. Barbour had retired as president, although he still kept an interest in the concern, and Mr. Philips, who was now what he called "active manager," had his own ideas about things. "More up to date, I suppose you might call it," he added. "I'll speak to Mr. Philips and see what he says. Glad to, of course."

Philips? The name sounded familiar to Emily. Then she remembered.

"That isn't the Mr. Philips who married into the Davidson family?" she asked.

"Oh, yes—yes, it is. Mr. Philips is the Davidson son-in-law."

If he had said son-in-law of Saint Peter he could not have spoken more reverently. Emily went away with a brand-new and disquieting suspicion. She was ashamed of it. It was so small, so mean, so picayune. Decent people did not bear grudges or, at any rate, would not stoop to get even in such a way. It was true that her uncle and Davidson, Senior, were political associates and that Laurie had been—well, spiteful enough at their last meeting. And he did not then know of her marriage to Mark. Nevertheless—oh, it could not be! To try and ruin an old man just because— She would not believe it.

When she called again, later that afternoon, the young salesman informed her that he had spoken to Mr. Philips and the latter had declared it quite impossible to extend the Bradshaw credit limitation. "An ironclad rule, Mr. Philips said it was. He told me to tell you that he imagined you would not find our firm alone in insisting upon it. Mr. Philips is an officer of the Wholesalers' Association, and he naturally knows the feeling in the trade."

Emily's suspicion was very close to a certainty now. The Thachers and Davidsons were out to break Bradshaw's and punish Zenas Bradshaw. And all because of her. She was now a Bradshaw, but she had been a Thacher, a Thacher who had dared to reject a Davidson. That, as they undoubtedly rated it, was high treason, *lése majesté,* not very far below sacrilege.

She wondered if Zenas guessed or suspected. It was possible: he was not easy to fool. Well, he should never guess that she knew. Knowing, he would realize how she must feel about it all and be sorry for her. For her, not for himself. If he was ever sorry for himself he never permitted any one else to suspect it. She, certainly, was not sorry for herself. She was indignant, however: indignant, resentful, and very angry.

She realized fully that Bradshaw's and Mark, her husband, were Zenas Bradshaw's two outstanding interests in life. Almost his only interests now. They were what made him wish to keep on living—and fighting. The battles overseas were not the only ones. There were others, ever so many of them, going on here at home and in England, all over the world. In little towns like Harniss, men and women, people like Zenas Bradshaw, who had, as she knew he had, been looking forward to comfortable, easy-going old age, had seen their sons and grandsons off to war and were carrying on without a whimper, doing their humble part in preserving the liberty and independence which had always been theirs and which they meant should be passed on to their descendants. They were soldiers, too, but they did not get into the newspapers.

In the mail one morning she saw a letter addressed to her grandfather and marked "Personal." The postmark, she noticed, was Bridgeport, Connecticut. Zenas opened the envelop, read the letter, and put it in his pocket. He did not read it to her, nor did he speak of it afterward. Bridgeport, of course, meant Frank Seymour. Zenas had told her Frank was living there.

A sequel, this might be, to the errand, whatever it was, which had brought Seymour to Harniss and which was, in some way, connected with one or both of the Bradshaws. Mysterious business, certainly, and secret. It was not her affair, that was obvious, but was it Mark's? She wondered.

For, in her letter from Mark, in the portion which she had not read to Zenas, was another mystery, or a hint of one.

Mark had written: "In your letters, at least in the

293

only two that have reached me so far, you have not said anything about hearing from Mr. Edmund Taylor. I thought he would write you long before this. I told him not to do anything about it until he heard from me, and when our orders came and I knew we were almost surely going into active service, he had left my neighborhood. I sent him a note asking him please to get in touch with you and ask what you wanted him to do. He was mighty kind to take the responsibility and trouble, a grand man. I liked him a lot and he seemed to like me. Now that I know you are with Grandfather at home and at the store there is a tremendous load off my mind. No one else must know one word of this. Especially—well, you know who I mean. Don't show him this letter. He would never forgive me for not coming to him, and that I simply would not do. If you have not heard from Taylor—but of course you have by this time. Anyhow, I have written him again. All this is pretty indefinite, I realize that, but our letters are read and censored, and a fellow's private affairs are his own, some of them, at least, even in wartime. Please let me hear about this right away. Mr. Taylor is square as a brick, I know, but your not mentioning his name bothers me."

Indefinite? That term was no exaggeration. What was it all about? Who was Mr. Edmund Taylor? Mark was certain she had heard from him, but she had never heard *of* him until now. Who was he? And where was he? Mark had not given the man's address.

And what was it that Taylor was to get in touch with her about? In her letter to her husband, written that evening, she asked all this and a good deal more.

Chapter 14

"YE Genuine Antique Shoppe," the Bodley-Lemon storehouse of treasures for the discriminating collector and connoisseur, had not yet opened for business. The small-paned front windows of the two-roomed white building on Main Street, a short distance from Bradshaw's Store, displayed shelves loaded with colored bottles, jugs, and vases, interspersed with specimens labeled "Choice Lacy Sandwich." Between those shelves, passers-by might catch glimpses of chairs, tables, and dressers, in various stages of decrepitude, arranged on the floor behind. The front door, with the antique brass knocker in the shape of a flying eagle, was, however, still tightly locked.

As the summer season had now really begun and the Harniss inns and boarding-houses were filling with vacationists, this inhospitable attitude of Ye Genuine Antique Shoppe caused remark. The articles displayed were, presumably, for sale, so why was no one permitted to enter and buy—or, at least, inspect? The summer visitors asked this question more or less casually, but the year-round residents, who had been greatly interested in the venture, were pressingly curious and more specific. Mrs. Carleton Bodley—Christian name Luella—the Commander-in-Chief, was not in Harniss and—or so it was reported—was not likely to be for the duration of the war, being actively engaged elsewhere, but Jacob Lemon, so recently her companion and confidant, was, or was supposed to be, the officer in charge of local operations, and it was to him that the questioners turned. The average Harniss man or woman would not have presumed to question Mrs. Bodley, but they did not hesitate to catechize Jacob.

Some of the questions bordered on the flippant.

"Eh, Jake, when you going to start up your shop-py? Them cripples you've got in there will fall apart if you let 'em set much longer."

"That doesn't worry Jake any. Most of 'em were falling apart long before he got hold of 'em. Does an accident policy go with any chairs you sell, Jake?"

"Sell? How can he sell what he can't get at? Have you lost the key to the place, Jake? Or wouldn't Luella Bodley trust you with one? How about that?"

These were some of the irreverent jibes Mr. Lemon was forced to hear. He bore them with fortitude, even smiled, although the smiles were somewhat mechanical.

"We'll open up when we are ready," he told the cross-questioners. "Mrs. Bodley and I know what we are doing. She wants to be here at the opening, and I'd like for her to be. Just now she is busy with other things, like everybody else—everybody who amounts to much, that is. Maybe you fellows haven't noticed, but we've got a war on our hands."

The individual to whom this particular retort was addressed confessed that he had "pretty nigh forgot" the war. "I understood that you and John Thacher were handlin' it, so why should *I* worry?" he added.

Jacob ignored the sarcasm. "You needn't worry about the Shoppe, either," he proclaimed. "As for the—er—

goods in it, well"—crushingly—"they are old already and a few more weeks won't make them any younger. Antiques don't have to be new to be good—like fish."

As his tormentor was a fish-peddler with whom Mrs. Lemon had recently held controversy concerning the freshness of his wares, Jacob walked away feeling pretty well satisfied with himself. His self-satisfaction did not long endure, however. He knew, only too well, that he would have to listen to more questions and suffer similar irritating proddings before the day was gone, perhaps even at the next corner. Except among the vacationists and the more recent additions to the summer cottage colony, Jacob Lemon was not popular. The Thacher following used him, when it suited their purpose to do so, but even they were inclined to condescend and patronize. They nodded to him, but they seldom shook hands with him. Jacob accepted this attitude with outward serenity, even with smiles, but he did not like it.

His patroness, Mrs. Bodley, while she ordered him about, had, nevertheless, treated him as a person of importance. She consulted him, even asked his advice, and often took that advice. There had been times when he had ventured to tell *her* what should be done—and she had done it, too. That was something like, that was as it should be. For a time, after her departure from Harniss, she had written to him frequently, always replied to his letters, and her interest in Ye Genuine Antique Shoppe had shown, financially at least, no sign of abating. Jacob, on his own, bought choice pieces at prices of his own fixing, sent the bills to her, and she paid them without a protest. She appreciated him; she rated him at his real value. Things were moving wonderfully well. Jacob began to dream—peculiar dreams, impossible of fulfilment, probably—but, as dreams, very pleasant indeed.

And then the confounded war had to come and upset everything. Mrs. Bodley, in her more recent and much shorter letters, scarcely mentioned the Shoppe. When he risked calling it to her attention she wrote that she had other matters on her mind: "Matters of great importance to our country and its brave soldiers. I must leave the Shoppe to you for the present," she wrote. "Buy what you think advisable—in reason, that is—and keep them carefully until the time comes to put them on public view. Invitations to the opening must be sent to a select list, of course, and I shall hope to be in Harniss on the day set, but when that day is to be I can not yet tell you. I am very glad to learn that you, too, are doing your part in the defense of our nation. I am sure your duties as Air Warden must be very interesting. Don't hesitate to write me concerning them."

Jacob had definitely not hesitated to do that very thing. He had no intention of permitting even the temporary erasure of his name from the Bodley memory tablet. Taking his cue from the lady's letter, he wrote her frequently, saying very little about the Shoppe, but discoursing expansively upon the importance of the labors of the Harniss Defense Board and his own part therein. And Betsy dutifully forwarded the newspaper clippings.

Betsy was an obedient helpmeet, but even she had the bad habit of asking inconvenient questions. Repeated snubbings should have put her in her place, but the provoking fact remained that she did not always stay in it.

"But when *are* you goin' to open up, Jacob?" she pleaded, one evening. "Folks keep askin' me, and I don't know what to tell 'em. With all them expensive things you've bought, I should think—"

Mr. Lemon interrupted. "How do you know how expensive they are?" he demanded. "You haven't had to pay for them."

Betsy sighed. "If the stories I hear about what they cost are true I couldn't pay for 'em if I wanted to. And you couldn't neither, Jacob; of course you couldn't. If it wasn't for that Bodley woman's money—"

"Look here!" sharply. "How many times must I tell you not to call her 'that Bodley woman'?"

"Oh, well, I forgot. I'm sorry. But I don't see anything wrong—"

"Never mind what you don't see. You call her 'Mrs. Bodley.' "

"Oh dear, I wish you wouldn't get so cross. I was only goin' to say that I didn't see any harm in callin' a woman a woman—when she *is* a woman, I mean."

"Humph! Well, Luella is a woman, all right. She's a darned fine woman. I never met a finer one. She and I understand each other, so you don't have to fret—about the Shoppe or anything else."

Betsy, a clipping in one hand and an envelop in the other, turned to look at him.

"So you call her 'Luella,' " she said, slowly. "Does she call you 'Jacob'?"

Her husband grinned. It was a pleasant relief to torment instead of being tormented. "Never you mind that," he retorted. "What we call each other is our own business."

He walked away, chuckling. His wife's expression, as

299

she slowly put the clipping into the envelop, was, for her, a peculiar one.

The other occupants of the house on Pond Road scarcely mentioned the delay in opening Ye Genuine Antique Shoppe. Zenas Bradshaw's mind was too full of his own cares and worries to think of it, and Emily was not interested. She had grown fond of Betsy, but she did not like Mr. Lemon. She did not like his ridiculous pomposity and the manner in which he bullied his self-sacrificing and adoring wife.

"He makes me furious," she confided to Zenas on one occasion. "Nothing she does suits him, and she tries so hard. She trots at his heels like a dog. If I were a dog I would bite him."

Zenas sniffed. "Once in a while you hear of a dog going mad," he observed. "Betsy won't even *get* mad—except once in a while, at a fish-peddler or somebody that doesn't count. Where that husband of hers is concerned she isn't even a dog, she's just a rabbit. Too bad, but I don't know what you and I can do about it."

Emily reluctantly agreed that they could do nothing about it. "When he goes out on one of his Air Warden inspection evenings," she went on, "she always waits up for him until he comes in, no matter how late it is. And then it is she who has to get up early and cook breakfast, while he lies in bed. I sometimes wonder if he really does all the patrolling and watching for lights that he pretends. I can hardly believe he tramps up and down the back roads and lanes as he says he does. That sounds like work—and work does not sound like Jacob Lemon."

Zenas nodded. "I know," he said, "but, from what I hear, he is pretty keen on his light-spotting job. The summer folks tell me he watches their water-front windows like a cat watching a mouse-hole. The only fault I've ever heard from any of them was that he is a little too Lord-Almightyish in his way of telling 'em there is a glim showing."

It chanced that he was to hear more concerning the Lemon "light spotting" the very next day. "Judge" Tipton, the Boston bachelor who rented the Crawley cottage on the Bluff Road, dropped in at Bradshaw's to order supplies—cocktail crackers, anchovy spread, cheese, olives, and other necessary adjuncts to the little stag parties which he was in the habit of giving to his friends down from the city over the weekend.

Zenas Bradshaw was not an admirer of the "Judge," who, like the character in one of Damon Runyon's stories, "was not a judge, never had been a judge, and never would be a judge." There was a good deal of him, in circumference as well as in height; his hair, clipped mustache and eyebrows were white, and his face florid. Zenas did not fancy him particularly, but he was a good customer and paid his bills promptly, a habit to be counted in his favor just at present.

Zenas waited upon him and, after the purchases had been made, noticed that the "Judge" was regarding him with what seemed to be a speculative look in his eye.

"Say, Bradshaw," he said, after a moment. "Can I have a word with you in private? Want to ask you a thing or two."

Zenas, wondering what the thing or two might be, said, "Sure—come along." He led the way to the back room which, as Willie Snow was away on his delivery round, was untenanted. Tipton, his hands in the pockets of his checked sport-jacket and a cigar in the corner of

301

his mouth, followed. When Zenas turned, the Judge asked his first question.

"Say, Bradshaw," he queried, lowering his voice, "you've got a fellow named Lemon living down at your place, they tell me. Is that so?"

"Why—in a way," was the qualified reply. "His wife keeps house for me, has for years. Jake lives with her, in their part of the house."

"Um-hm. Well, what sort of a guy is he?"

"Why— I don't know's I get what you mean. His wife is a good cook and a good woman."

"I don't give a hang about her. I want your opinion of him. Is he a straight shooter? Would you trust him— as far as the corner, say?"

It was on the tip of Zenas Bradshaw's tongue to reply that he might, if the corner was not too far away. He did not say it, however, but he hesitated. Tipton noted the hesitation and, apparently, drew his own conclusion.

"I see," he granted. "You figure him about as I do."

"Now look here, Judge—"

"That's all right. I've got it in for that baby. But there was a bare chance I might be wrong, and I thought I'd talk to you first. He's one of those—what-do-you-call-'em?—Air Wardens, and he's been making a damn nuisance of himself. Probably you've heard that before. From other people, eh?"

Zenas had, of course, but he did not choose to admit it. His own opinion of Judge Tipton was not much higher than his estimate of Jacob Lemon.

"We-ll," he drawled, "I suppose likely, if you are an Air Warden and on your job, you can't help being a nuisance once in a while. Been bothering you about your blackouts, has he?"

Tipton snorted. "Don't dodge, Bradshaw," he ordered. "I'm talking straight to you because everybody tells me you are straight; even the Big I–Ams that don't like you say that. And don't you get me wrong about this blackout nonsense, either. I'm a good American, and if foolishness with window curtains will help win the war I'll be as big a fool as the next. I can put up with a rube Air Warden getting me over to the telephone to crab that I've got a light showing. It may make me mad, but —well, what of it? I can stand that. What I can't stand is a cheap-skate double-crosser. And I think this Lemon guy has double-crossed me. This is all under your hat, of course; you are to keep it to yourself. . . . Now let me tell you."

On a Saturday evening two weeks before Mr. Tipton had entertained a few masculine friends at his Bluff Road cottage. "Giving a little party to some of the boys from the city," he explained. "Just half a dozen of them, all good fellows, and as fine A–1 Americans as you'd want to meet."

Early in the evening, about nine or thereabouts— "Just as things were beginning to liven up, you understand"—the Judge's houseman called him aside to say that a person named Lemon, who said he was Air Warden for that section of the town, was on the telephone, and wished to call Judge Tipton's attention to the fact that a light was showing in one of the windows on the second floor.

"I told Thomson, that's my houseman's name, to tell the Lemon guy that there weren't any lights showing, and, anyway, they would be put out. Naturally I supposed that settled it. But no, an hour or so later, right in the middle of the party, card game going and all that, in comes Thomson again to whisper that this condemned Lemon was at the door—the *front* door, mind you. 'What the devil is he doing there?' I wanted to know. Well, according to Thomson, he was there to say that lights were still showing and that it was his duty, as what he called 'a duly appointed Air Warden of this township,' to see that blackout regulations were obeyed or he would have to report me to the authorities.

"Well, sir, I was sore. The boys had heard some of this, and they were beginning to josh me, you understand. So I told Thomson I'd handle the thing myself and headed for the door. When I got there this fellow was in the hall—inside my house, by the Lord! What do you think of *that* for nerve? I asked him what he meant by it, and he started in again on the 'duly appointed' stuff. Not quite so fresh as he had been to Thomson— he knew better than to try that with me—but fresh enough; only, this time, the freshness had a sort of under layer of grease, if you get what I mean. I listened to him, and I looked him over, and thinks I: 'Baby, I've got *you* sized up. I've dealt with your kind before.' So I took a ten-dollar bill out of my pocket and— See here, Bradshaw; this is under your hat, remember. It mustn't go any farther."

Zenas's "All right" was curt, but the Judge seemed to find it satisfactory. He went on.

"I held that ten spot where he could see it. 'Are you dead sure about that light?' I asked him—something like that, anyhow. Well, he didn't know as he was exactly sure. He *thought* he had seen one, and, being a duly appointed Air Warden—he certainly had that by heart— he felt he must do his duty. I said I was strong for duty, myself; only—well, the friends I was entertaining were from away, and, not being as used to strict blackouts as he and I were, they didn't understand. 'Which makes it kind of embarrassing for me, the host, having to get up and leave a little friendly game right in the middle of the draw, to say nothing of the explaining I have to do when I come back—if you get me.' He cut in then to say that making me unnecessary trouble was something he wouldn't dream of doing. He was sorry; perhaps he had been mistaken, anyway. I told him that everybody made mistakes once in a while, and— Oh, well, when he said good night I was afraid he was going to kiss me.... Bah!"

He shrugged in disgust.

"And he took the ten dollars?" queried Zenas, incred. ulously.

"I'll say he took it!"

"Taking bribes! Why, that's—"

"Here, here, Bradshaw! Wait a minute! W-a-ait a minute! Who said anything about bribes? To make a person a little present isn't bribery, is it? I didn't ask him to do anything in return for the ten, did I? You bet I didn't. And he didn't promise not to do anything, either. Bribery! You must have an evil mind. I'm surprised at you."

He was very solemn, but, catching Zenas's eye, he grinned. "I told you I had sized him up, didn't I?" he went on. "And that I knew his kind? Well, I do; have known them ever since I first broke into ward politics."

Zenas pulled at his upper lip. "He hasn't bothered you since, I presume likely," he surmised.

Tipton's grin disappeared. His chin thrust forward, and he frowned.

"That's just it," he declared, grimly. "*He* hasn't—no.

305

But the next time—last Saturday night, that was—the Coast Guard rang me up and they said a light was showing. So, after all, I had to send Thomson and a maid from cellar to garret pulling every shade down to the sill. And the boys—some of them from the same bunch I had down the week before—laughing their heads off and guying me about sending me flowers when I was in jail and asking me if I knew the regular visiting days, and all that sort of rot. I pretended to enjoy the joke as much as they did, but I was boiling inside. And I am yet. You see why, don't you?"

"Can't say as I do, exactly. The Coast Guard—"

"Coast Guard be hanged! Who tipped off the Coast Guard? That's what I want to know. I'm betting our Lemon pal did it. Taking my money and then saving his own 'duly appointed' face by double-crossing me. The rat!"

"Oh, I don't hardly think—"

"You don't have to. I have done the thinking already, and I've come to the conclusion that that is just what happened. Prove it? Of course not. How could I prove anything without getting myself in Dutch? Only—well, nobody ever double-crossed me yet without getting some of their own back. Somehow or other I'll squeeze *that* Lemon—flat."

He looked as if he meant it. Zenas Bradshaw was vaguely troubled, not on Jake Lemon's account, but because of Betsy. And he could not understand why Tipton had come to him with the story. The Judge hinted a possible explanation in his next sentence.

"Bradshaw," he said, "I've been given to understand that this Lemon bird is manager, or partner—anyhow is high resident muck-a-muck—of this Genuine Antique place across the street yonder. You needn't tell me; I know that much about it. But I'm told that the person behind him and it, putting up the money for the building and the stuff in it, is a woman named Bodley. She lives in Boston, when she is at home. That so?"

"Yes."

"Um-hm. Well, there are plenty of Bodleys up there. What I want to be sure of is which particular Bodley she is. Those that told me the rest of it thought they knew, but they said you were the one who would know the most. What is the rest of her name?"

"Her first name is Luella, or seems to me it is. She is the widow of—let me see—Carleton Bodley, that's it."

Judge Tipton struck his right fist into the palm of his left hand. His grin was back again now, broad and triumphant.

"I thought it might be," he crowed. "I hoped it might be. Carleton Bodley! I knew him like a book. He and I were in a dozen deals together. I knew her, too, or used to. Well, well, well! And it is her money that Lemon has been blowing right and left for the junk in that Shoppe thing."

Zenas was surprised at the word.

"Junk?" he repeated. "Why, Mrs. Bodley has the name of being a judge of antiques and such. She and Jake used to ride from Dan to Beersheba, picking out what she called 'choice bits' for that—er—Shoppe. When you say 'junk' it seems to me—"

Tipton did not wait for him to finish. His grin became a laugh.

"Ho, ho!" he roared. "Listen to me, Bradshaw. I do know antiques: they have been one of my pet extravagances for years. And, if what I can see through the windows of that— Humph! Oh, well, never mind. I'm much obliged to you. You'll keep what I've told you to yourself?"

Zenas's shoulders straightened. "I said I would," he replied, stiffly.

"Sure! Sure! You are no double-crosser, I'll swear. All right. Keep mum and maybe we'll all see some fun one of these days. So long."

This call from Judge Tipton and the latter's revelation concerning Jacob Lemon's acceptance of the "present," left Zenas Bradshaw in a mood divided between anger, disgust, and mild amusement. He was not surprised, exactly, to learn that Jake could be bribed or that the price of his perfidy was as low as ten dollars. Nor was he interested in the question as to whether or not Tipton, the briber, had been "double-crossed" by Lemon, the bribed. If that were true, in his estimation it served the Judge exactly right. Both parties to the transaction were crooked and, worse than that, were traitors to their country in time of war. Tipton had, at least twice in his narrative, taken pains to proclaim himself a "good American." And Jake was eternally orating, in Defense meetings and on street corners, concerning his own patriotism and sense of duty to his country. A grand pair of Americans, they were!

Zenas, however, on reflection, could not see that he could do anything toward giving them the public "showing up" they deserved. He could not for at least two reasons. His interview with Tipton had been in private, there were no listeners, and both Tipton and Lemon, if the story was told, would promptly deny its truth. Moreover, before he heard it, he, Zenas, had promised to keep it to himself. He fumed inwardly, but he could

308

do nothing. He might—later on, he would—take Jake aside and drop a few pointed hints concerning certain indefinite rumors which had reached his ears. This might, possibly, put the fear of the Lord into the scamp and perhaps prevent his acceptance of another ten-dollar "present." But the next one might be fifteen, and then—

A half-dozen good swift kicks in the right place and with the proper force behind them ought to accompany the hints, but there was Betsy to be considered. Oh, blast the Tiptons and Jakes and all their nasty breed. Mark, and thousands and thousands of fine young chaps like Mark, were fighting over yonder, while here at home there still were a few—skunks? No, that was not fair to the four-legged skunk: he never pretended to be a rose—an American Beauty, anyway.

As to the latter part of the Tipton remarks, those dealing with Mrs. Bodley and "Ye Genuine Antique Shoppe," Zenas paid no attention to them. He was not interested. His own store, its business, and how it was to be kept afloat, were anxieties sufficient for one seventy-year-old man. He did not mention, even to Emily, the subject of his back-room talk with the Judge, and she did not ask him about it.

So, a week later, when she and Zenas came home to supper one evening, both were surprised to find Betsy in an excited frame of mind. The excitement itself was not surprising: Betsy could get excited over a cake which had "fallen" or a pan of biscuits which had not "come out right." This time, however, the cause of her excitement was not so commonplace. She lost not a minute in disclosing it. Who in the world did Zenas suppose had come to that very house that very afternoon? Mrs. Bodley, that was who! Yes sir, Mrs. Luella Bodley, herself. What did Zenas and Emily think of *that?*

Emily did not appear to think much about it, one way or the other. And Zenas Bradshaw's reception of the news was disappointingly placid.

"Well, well," he observed. "So she is down here again, is she? Luella, eh? When that fellow asked me the other day I said I thought that was it, but I wasn't quite sure. Your memory is better than mine, Betsy."

Mrs. Lemon's comment was made in a tone which caused Emily to look at her.

"That's the name all right," snapped Betsy. "Luella. *I* haven't forgot and I ain't likely to. Luella! O-oh, yes!"

"What is she after?" asked Zenas. "More antiques? Thought she and Jacob had bought up all there was in the county already. Jake was glad to see her, I guess likely. Cry for joy on each other's shoulders, did they?"

"They did not. And if they had tried it I—" She paused, and then added, "Jacob wasn't here. He had a chance to ride down to Trumet this forenoon in somebody's car, and he went. Some sort of war-meetin' there to-day, so he told me. He hasn't got back yet."

She went on talking as she brought the supper in from the kitchen. Mrs. Bodley had not been alone when she called. There was a man with her. Mrs. Bodley said his name was Anderson and that he came from Fall River.

"I've seen him before," said Betsy. "He was around town considerable last summer. Seems to me Jacob told me he was an antiquer, too."

Zenas stirred the tea in his cup. "Probably Freeling Anderson," he surmised. "There is a Freeling Anderson who runs a big antique shop in Fall River. One of the top-notchers in the trade, so folks say. He and Jake never hit it off very well. What's he doing down here with the Bodley woman? And how could she spare time to come, anyhow? According to the newspapers she is superintending the war these days. Country was liable to go to smash if she left her job for more than ten minutes, I judged."

Betsy did not know about that part of it. All she knew was that Mrs. Bodley and the Anderson man had come to the house about one o'clock and asked for Jacob. When told that the latter was out of town Mrs. Bodley had demanded the key to Ye Genuine Antique Shoppe.

"I didn't know what to do," went on the housekeeper. "Jacob always keeps that key hid away behind the daguerreotype of my grandmother on the shelf in our bedroom, and he is dreadful particular that nobody, not even me, should so much as touch it. I declare I didn't know what to do when she ordered me to give it to her. But, after all, that Shoppe place is almost as much hers as it is my husband's. Wouldn't you say so, Zenas?"

Zenas Bradshaw nodded. "Why, yes, Betsy," he agreed, gravely. "Almost, or pretty nigh, or next door, something like that. So you let her have the key?"

Betsy had, and it had troubled her ever since. Mrs. Bodley and Anderson left at once, with the key in their possession. They had not yet returned.

"And I do hope she'll fetch it back before Jacob comes," she continued. "He won't like it if it isn't here. I told her so, and she said: 'Oh, I shall be back, Mrs. Lemon. You may be sure of that. I shall want to see your husband. I *imagine* I shall want to see him very much indeed.' Maybe it's just my nerves, but the way

311

she said that 'I imagine' part sounded—well, kind of spiteful. Oh, dear! I'm so worried! I do wish she'd bring back that key."

But Mr. Lemon made his appearance before the key was returned. He entered at the back door, and the trio in the dining-room heard him shouting his wife's name. She hurried out to greet him, but, before she reached the kitchen, the knocker on the front door clanked loudly. Betsy came rushing in again to answer the knock. A moment later Emily and Zenas heard her say: "Oh yes, Mrs. Bodley, he's here. I'll—I'll go and tell him. Er—er—won't you come in?"

The invitation was a trifle superfluous, for Mrs. Bodley was in already. It was she who led the way into the sitting-room, Betsy fluttering nervously at her heels, and Anderson, a thick-set, middle-aged man, with a smile at the corner of his lip and a twinkle in his eye, sauntering in the rear. The door between the dining-room and sitting-room was open, and Emily and Zenas Bradshaw could both see and hear. They rose from their chairs at the table.

Betsy continued to flutter. "Won't you sit down, Mrs. Bodley—er—I mean both of you?" she stammered. "I'll run and tell Mr. Lemon you've come. . . . Oh, I forgot! You know Mr. Bradshaw? Yes, of course you do. And Mrs. Bradshaw—that is, I don't mean she's this Mrs. Bradshaw, she's the other one. Well, anyhow, she's— she is—"

Emily came to her rescue. "I am Mrs. Marcellus Bradshaw," she explained. "Mr. Zenas Bradshaw's grandson's wife. How do you do, Mrs. Bodley?"

Mrs. Carleton Bodley nodded. "How do you do?" she said stiffly. She was a large woman, wearing clothes which seemed to contain all of her with difficulty. Her hair was white, her chin prominent, and she wore rimless eyeglasses. Just now the eyes behind those glasses had a frosty gleam, and her face—there was a good deal of it—was flushed.

Zenas said, "Good evening, Mrs. Bodley," but, if she heard him, she did not respond.

Mr. Anderson, however, was more cordial. Judged by his expression, he seemed to be enjoying himself. He waved a hand and said, "Hello, Zenas. Good evening, Mrs. Bradshaw."

Zenas said, "Hello, Freeling. Haven't seen you for some time. How is antiquing these days?"

"Not so good." Then, noticing that Betsy had left the room, he turned to Mrs. Bodley and asked: "Better shut the door, hadn't I? These folks are having supper."

He was reaching for the knob, but Mrs. Bodley interposed. "I think," she said, slowly, "yes, I think it might be better if there were—er—disinterested witnesses." Then, turning toward the pair at the table, she said: "Mr. Bradshaw, I am very sorry to delay your meal, but if you and your—granddaughter, is it?—will be kind enough to remain and hear what is said in this room, I shall be very much obliged. Thank you."

Zenas and Emily exchanged puzzled glances. It was more of a command than a request, and the lady evidently took their consent for granted. To quote Zenas, "She said 'Thank you' before we could say aye, yes, or no." And at that moment the kitchen door opened and Jacob and Betsy entered.

It was Jacob who came first, and he came in a hurry. He strode into the sitting-room, his face beaming and his hand outstretched.

"Well, well, well!" he gushed. "This *is* a surprise! Mrs. Bodley, ma'am, how do you do? When Mrs. Lemon said you were here I could scarcely believe my ears. I can't begin to tell you how glad I am to see you here. I am delighted. I am honored. I—I—"

He stammered and stopped, probably because of the expression on his partner's face. She did not appear to be either delighted or honored. She dashed the proffered hand aside with a push of her own. The glare she bestowed upon the resident manager of Ye Genuine Antique Shoppe was, to quote Zenas once more, "like the Orham lighthouse on a clear night." Jacob did not wither, exactly—no one had ever likened him to a sensitive plant—but he did look tremendously taken aback, also not a little alarmed.

"Why—why, Mrs. Bodley," he gurgled. "I— Mrs. Bodley—"

"Mr. Lemon," pronounced Mrs. Carleton Bodley, with venomous emphasis, "you are a cheat."

She paused, but only momentarily.

"You are a cheat," she repeated. "A miserable two-faced double-dealing— Oh, *what* shall I call you!"

Again she paused, this time either from lack of the fitting word or from lack of breath. If she had expected to cause a sensation her expectations were realized. Betsy's mouth opened and shut, but no speech came from it. Zenas Bradshaw and Emily stared, wide-eyed. As for Jacob Lemon, at whom the volley had been fired, he stepped slowly backward, the color fading from his cheeks.

Mr. Freeling Anderson was the only one of the group who appeared to be completely at ease. He stepped into view from the shadow of the Bodley bulk.

"Hello, Jake," he said cheerfully, and laughed.

Mr. Lemon did not laugh. It was evident from his expression that Betsy, when hastily informing him of the Bodley surprise visit, had made no mention of the lady's companion. He turned toward the latter, gasped, and choked. And Mr. Anderson laughed again.

Mrs. Bodley, however, was not in a laughing mood. Having fired the opening shots and noted their effect, she proceeded to blast her victim with the fury of a machine-gun.

"When I think how I trusted you," she declared, "I am ashamed—ashamed! I had been warned, but I would not listen. Hints had been dropped, but I paid no attention to them. In—in my innocence, I believed that I knew honesty and—and capability and loyalty when I met them, and so I trusted you. When my duties, my important duties, kept me in the city I left everything here to you. I gave you authority and money—much money! I permitted you to buy and buy and buy, and I paid and paid and paid. Oh, I was such a perfect fool! You must have laughed in your sleeve." She added, with sarcastic acidity, "Which you probably did."

Again she paused for breath. Anderson cleared his throat with a mild "Ahem." She turned momentarily in his direction.

"You are right, Mr. Anderson," she said. "I am wasting words, and he is not worth it. I want him to understand, however. I want him to understand perfectly."

The Anderson lip curled. "Wouldn't wonder if he did," he observed dryly. "Looks so, don't you think? How about it, Jake?"

Jacob Lemon's plump cheeks were whiter than ever, but this taunt, coming from the source it did, was too much to bear. He was evidently very much frightened, and, up to that moment, had not ventured an interruption. Now, however, he broke in.

"What are you doing here, Free Anderson?" he demanded, furiously. "What business is it of yours? If you've been lying about me to—to her, I—I'll—"

Anderson lifted a hand. He was quite unruffled. "My business," he said, mildly, "is buying and selling antiques. I've been in that line most of my life. Sometimes, same as now, I'm hired to look over a collection and pick out the good stuff from the bad. As to lying—well, in this case I judge there has been some, here and there, but not by me—no."

Mrs. Bodley took over at this point. "Mr. Anderson came to Harniss," she stated crushingly, "at my request. I am paying him for his services. I was told, by the friend who suggested my coming here at this time, that he was thoroughly reliable and thoroughly honest and perhaps as good a judge of genuine antique Americana as any one in the state. He and I, together, have been looking over the—the trash which you have bought with my money and put into my Shoppe. And—and, oh dear, I was so *proud* of that Shoppe! It was almost my dearest possession."

For just an instant she looked as if she were going to cry, which, as Zenas said later, "would have been about as much of a miracle as seeing the Statue of Liberty turn into sprinkling cart." She did not cry, however, and while she was fighting for composure, Jacob attempted his first move in the case for the defense. His tone, when he spoke, was that of one deeply wronged and even more deeply wounded.

"Mrs. Bodley, ma'am," he began, sadly, "I can't tell

you how much these—er—surprising accusations hurt my feelings, coming from you. From anybody else"—with a savage sidelong glance in the direction of Mr. Anderson —"I should treat them with—er—contempt. Yes, ma'am, contempt. A competitor in business—your business and mine, if I may say so, Mrs. Bodley—might be expected to do everything he could to run me down, to slander me to you. He would do that to make himself solid with you, and—and from spite and jealousy. But coming from you—well, as I say, I can't begin to tell you—"

That was as far as he was permitted to go. The stamp of the Bodley foot shook the prisms of the Sandwich lamp on the table. "I am very glad you can't," she snapped. "I shouldn't listen to you if you tried. The fact that, in spite of all your airs and—and ridiculous self-importance, you really know nothing whatever about antiques, I might, perhaps, excuse. I say I might excuse that. But dishonesty, plain downright dishonesty, I will not excuse. Take that—er—duck-foot maple table, for example, the one you bought at that house in South Bayport. It will be interesting to hear what you have to say about that table, Mr. Lemon. As well as about other things."

That Jacob Lemon was surprised to hear the maple table mentioned was plain. That the surprise was a pleasant one was just as plain. A look of at least temporary relief spread over his countenance, to be succeeded by one of injured innocence and righteous dignity.

"Mrs. Bodley," he loftily orated, "I don't understand. I am afraid you have forgotten that you and I inspected that particular table together. You went into that South Bayport house with me. That table is a very fine piece, a museum piece." Then, dropping the oratory, he added: "I happen to know"—with another sidelong snarl at Anderson—"that that very—er—sneak who is with you now was trying to buy that table, had been trying hard to buy it for months. If he has the *gall* to tell you it isn't a fine piece, then—then"—triumphantly—"why was he so anxious to buy it? He seems to have told you a lot of things: maybe he'll tell you that."

Anderson, the unperturbed, smiled. "Glad to," he said. "Fact is, I've told her before. That duck-foot table *is* good: it's one of the half-dozen really good things you've got in that Shoppe. I did try to buy it, but the people who owned it wouldn't sell. Finally I left a standing offer of forty dollars with them, which was all it was worth—to me. If they changed their minds they were to let me know. To-day I saw it in the Shoppe. So that's that. You outbid me, Jake."

Jacob sneered. "Mrs. Bodley and I outbid you—yes," he proclaimed. "When she and I bought that table—"

And now Mrs. Bodley interrupted. "I had no part in the buying," she broke in, indignantly. "I looked at it with you, yes, but you told me you wanted to be a little surer that it was entirely original. You said you didn't feel quite certain about one of its legs. If I would leave the matter to your judgment, you said—"

Again emotion choked her, but not for long. "And I did leave it to you," she went on, her voice rising. "Oh yes, I left it to you, just as I left so many other matters. You bought that table yourself, after I had gone back to the city. And you sent me a bill for seventy-five dollars. Do you dare deny that?"

Mr. Lemon looked as if he were tempted to deny it, but he did not. His chin trembled, but he fought on.

"It—it was—was worth all that, and—and more," he

318

stuttered. "I don't care what Free Anderson offered for it. It was worth—worth a hundred, anyhow. And"—desperately—"those South Bayport folks wouldn't take his forty bid, would they? No, of course they wouldn't. I had to keep going higher and higher, until finally . . . What are you grinning at, you—you *crook?*"

The epithet and question were addressed to Mr. Anderson, who was smiling broadly. His reception of both was placid.

"Crook, did you call me, Jake?" he asked. "Well, well! That's interesting, coming from you."

Mrs. Bodley once more moved into the driver's seat. "This has gone far enough," she announced, with finality. "I did not come here to take part in a—a brawl. Mr. Lemon, it is time you knew that Mr. Anderson and I visited those people in South Bayport this afternoon. They tell me that they sold the table to you for exactly forty-five dollars, just five dollars more than Mr. Anderson's standing offer. Now perhaps you can explain why you wrote me that you paid seventy-five? And sent me a bill for that amount and accepted and cashed my check for it, too? I have the bill, and I have the canceled check with your endorsement. . . . Well?"

If any one present had been looking at Zenas Bradshaw just then—which no one was—he would have seen his eyebrows lift in surprise. Emily put her hand to her lips as if to prevent an exclamation. Betsy gasped faintly. As for her husband, he also gasped, and swallowed several times. Mrs. Bodley, having her opponent on the ropes, proceeded to deliver the finishing punch.

"And that isn't all," she added. "I may as well tell you that Mr. Anderson and I called on no less than three other families from whom you have bought other high-priced articles for my Shoppe, and, in each case, in *each* case, the price which they are ready to swear you paid them is much lower than that which you wrote me you paid. And, which, like a trusting idiot, *I* paid to you. . . . I think that is all, Mr. Anderson. Now we may go."

She was turning toward the hall, Anderson in her wake. Jacob Lemon, reeling, but still partially conscious, attempted one more pitiful swing.

"You—you— Mrs. Bodley, ma'am," he pleaded, "you— you've forgotten again. I hunted up all those things and bought 'em on my own time. I had to have—seems to me I was entitled to some—"

"Nonsense! Your time! You know perfectly well that I have been paying you a regular sum—an amount we agreed upon before I went away—for that 'time' you talk about. I have paid it regularly each month."

This was the knockout. Jacob was speechless.

Now Betsy, for the first time during the proceedings, now uttered an articulate word.

"Why—why, Jacob Lemon!" she cried, in horrified amazement. "That ain't true, is it? She hasn't been payin' you wages right along? I asked you once and you said— I don't believe it. It isn't so."

Mrs. Bodley regarded her with a sort of Olympian pity. "Certainly it is so," she retorted. "No doubt he hasn't told you about it. He kept that money in his own pocket, just as he kept the other sums which he swindled from me."

Then, as if suddenly aware that an audience was present, she turned to the Bradshaws.

"I am sorry," she said, "that you two were obliged to sit here and listen to this disgraceful exposure, but, as

I think I said at the beginning, I thought the presence of disinterested witnesses advisable. And, as you are witnesses, I hope you will note that I am retaining the key to my Shoppe and warning this—this Lemon person that if he dares so much as step a foot on its premises I shall have him arrested. . . . I shall probably do that, anyway."

Anderson had gone into the hall and opened the outer door. Jacob was still speechless, but again it was his wife who spoke. And what she said was most unexpected. She was breathing rapidly, and there was a look in her eye which neither Zenas nor Emily had ever seen there before.

"Mrs. Bodley," she demanded, "I want you to tell me one other thing. Have you and—and him"—pointing to her cowering husband—"been callin' each other by your first names?"

Mrs. Bodley stared. *"What?"* she gasped.

"I'm askin' you if he's been callin' you 'Lulie' and you've been callin' him 'Jacob'? And, when you've been writin' each other back and forth lately, has it been 'My dear Lou' and 'My dear Jacob'?"

Mrs. Carleton Bodley did not answer. She looked as if she were going to, but instead she said, "My heavens!"

"Have you been callin' each other those pet names? I want to *know*."

"I—*I*—call him . . . or permit him to address me . . . Woman, you are crazy!"

"But have you?"

"Certainly not. Good heavens! *No!*"

She swept out of the room and out of the house. Betsy Lemon turned toward her husband. She looked him over from head to foot and nodded slowly.

"Hm-m!" she observed, between tightly compressed lips. "Hm-m!"

Jacob did not return her look. He stumbled toward the kitchen door, opened it, and disappeared. Betsy's gaze followed him. Emily rose and approached her. "Never mind, Betsy," she said soothingly. "Don't—"

But Betsy pushed her aside. Her lips twitched, and her eyes opened and shut rapidly. Then she burst into tears and rushed after her husband.

Emily turned toward Zenas. "Grandfather," she began, but stopped.

Zenas was not there. He had gone, too, but in the other direction, leaving the front door ajar behind him.

Chapter 15

EMILY was in the sitting-room when Zenas came back. "Where are they?" he asked, with a jerk of his head in the direction of the kitchen door.

"The Lemons, you mean? In their room, I think. We could hear them if they were in the kitchen."

"You haven't been out there?"

"No. How could I? If Betsy were alone I might have tried to say something comforting, at least tried to tell her how sorry I was. For her, I mean. I can't be very sorry for him—the scamp."

Zenas nodded. "Darned fool," he commented. "Well, this ought to shake some of the pompous stuffing out of him, if it does nothing else. Poor Betsy, though: it was tough on her. Sort of a tragedy. And yet"—with a quiet chuckle—"being Betsy, she couldn't help making it funny, there at the end. 'Dear Lou' and 'Dear Jacob'! I suppose likely he had been giving her to understand that he and sister Bodley were figuring on eloping together."

Emily smiled. "Did you notice Mrs. Bodley's face when Betsy asked if they called each other by their Christian names?"

"Notice it! It was blazing so I thought it might set the house afire. Oh, dear! Well, quite an evening we've had, so far, wouldn't you say?"

"I should, decidedly. But where have you been,

Grandfather? When the others had gone and I turned to speak to you, you had vanished, too."

"Um-hm. I ran out to catch the old girl before she got off the premises. What she said about putting Jake in prison bothered me. We couldn't have that, you know. There is enough chit-chat connected with this Bradshaw bunch as it is; that they've started dragging us off to jail would make some of the chatterers *too* happy. And, besides, there is Betsy again."

"Yes—oh, yes. But Mrs. Bodley isn't really going to put Jacob into prison, is she? You don't think she meant it?"

"She may have meant it then, but she won't when she thinks it over. No, no. You see, no matter how she blusters, the fact is that she and Jake were together on a lot of those antique hunts, and she is pretty near as much responsible for the 'junk' as he is. And she used to sing his praises from one end of the town to the other. Wouldn't listen to a word against him and called him a 'genius' and 'talented' and 'distinguished' and Lord knows what all. Oh, no, clapping him in jail would mean showing herself up, and, if there's one thing that woman wouldn't like, it is being laughed at."

"Did you speak to her about it?"

"No, but I talked with Anderson for a minute or so. He's got a level head. He is expecting to have the job of cleaning out the trash in the Genuine Shoppe and he'll probably be running it himself, by-and-by. He didn't say that, but you can bet it's so. He agrees with me that the sane thing to do is hush all this hurrah up. He'll make her see it that way. A smart fellow, Free Anderson is—and straight—which is worth a medal, considering the temptations in his business."

324

Emily was thinking. "How do you suppose he happened to be here—with her, I mean? She hired him as an expert—she said so—but why? Why did she lose confidence in Jacob Lemon so suddenly?"

Zenas Bradshaw stroked his lip. "I think she was tipped off," he replied. "Somebody—somebody she knew was a top-notcher in antique collecting—put a flea in her ear about the kind of stuff Jake had been spending her money for. That set her thinking about how much money it was. She got suspicious, hired Anderson, probably at this same other somebody's recommendation, and started on the warpath. That's my guess."

"Have you any idea who this somebody was?"

"Why—yes," slowly. "Maybe I have, but I can't tell even you. I got the notion on account of some other news that was handed to me, but not until I had promised to keep it dark. Or 'under my hat,'" he added with a twinkle. "So I'm afraid it will have to stay under, for a spell."

A silent and saddened Betsy served their breakfast. Jacob did not appear, but Emily, just after she and Zenas left for the store, imparted an astonishing bit of information.

"I looked out in the back yard just now, Grandfather," she said, "and what do you suppose I saw?"

"Give it up. Not the sheriff coming after Jake, I hope."

"No. Something much more remarkable than that. I saw Jacob himself, out there, with a hatchet in his hand splitting wood for kindling."

Zenas whistled. "Whew! Well, well, well! Jake Lemon working! I wish I could have a photograph of it. Do you suppose his wife is responsible? I can't believe she has waked up, after dreaming all this time."

"I don't know. It looks as if she had, for the present, at least. Oh, if it will only last!"

"I'm afraid it won't. Jake Lemon is something like that man who used to give the Mesmerism show once a year in the town hall when I was a boy. Jake is some mesmerizer, himself. After his scare wears off I imagine he'll begin making passes before Betsy's nose and put her to sleep again. Well"—with a satisfied nod—"if he starts making 'em too soon I've got a little reminder of my own to whisper to him, one that may make him glad to reach for the kindling hatchet. We'll wait and see."

A few days later Judge Tipton again dropped in at Bradshaw's, and again Zenas waited upon him. After making his purchases, which was, as always, a lengthy and fussy procedure, the Judge asked a question. It was asked quite casually.

"How is our duly appointed Lemon these days?" he inquired. "Happy and satisfied with life, is he?"

Zenas Bradshaw turned to look his interrogator in the eye. "Why, no," he replied, with deliberation. "Now that you mention it, it don't seem to me that he is— altogether."

Judge Tipton's expression, perhaps because of its years of training in "friendly little games," changed not an iota. "Well, well," he observed. "Now isn't that too bad."

That was all. He walked away without another word. Zenas, watching his departure, was smiling as he hastened to serve the next customer.

When he was thinking it all over afterward, this unexpected Lemon-Bodley-Tipton affair reminded him of the old-fashioned melodramas he had seen in Boston theaters when, as a young man, he had gone to the city on business trips for the store and was, as he would have called it, filling in his evenings. In those melodramas, *Alone in London, Harbor Lights,* and their like, the hero and heroine, alone or together, were persecuted and robbed and threatened with murder by the wicked villain and his assistants until the feelings of the audience had been harassed to the limit of emotional strain. Then the tension was temporarily eased. Two flat sections of scenery, usually painted to represent the rear wall of a room, slid in from the wings and met in the middle, leaving only a few feet between that wall and the footlights. In that shallow strip the "funny folks," the hero's faithful manservant, who joked always, with or without provocation, and the pretty servant girl, who, just as like as not, was even funnier than he was, upset the table, or tripped over each other's feet, making uproarious love and "carrying on" until the audience was laughing its head off. A sort of tonic, this was, to brace a person up and get his constitution in condition to swallow the dose of horrors to be administered in the scene to follow.

A salesman who had accompanied Zenas to one of these plays and who knew, or pretended to know, all about the theater, said that the proper term for this kind of break in the prevailing misery was "comic relief." Well, in a way, the tumbling of Jake Lemon from his pedestal had, to every one but the principals in the act, been a comedy and, while it lasted, provided a bit of relief. For a little while he, Zenas, had been led to think of something besides his own present anxieties and ever-growing fear of the future.

327

That little while was now at an end. The comedians had left the stage, and the persecuted and their persecutors were back again. More and still more regulations and restrictions for the small businessman were imposed, new and often contradictory ones succeeding each other. One week it was permitted to sell this and not that and the next neither that nor this. Buying was as difficult as selling. Bradshaw's orders were accepted, and, just before the promised date of delivery, word would come that those same orders could not be filled. There was a gasoline shortage, and rationing of that commodity had already begun. It was not yet exacting —car owners still drove, although not as much or as far —but it was prophesied that the delivery of goods to retail customers must soon be discontinued. All right for "cash and carry" companies, like the chain stores, but ominous for independents like Bradshaw's, whose patrons—especially the summer cottage colony—had never cashed nor carried.

Money, ready money, was Zenas Bradshaw's chief lack. The store's working capital was drawn upon almost to depletion. Taxes were high and were to be much higher. Wages were going up. Willie Snow, as he would have said, "struck for a raise" and got it, a small one, for, if Willie left, how could Zenas fill his place? Abner Hallett was faithful and uncomplaining. He was for Bradshaw's first, last and all the time. But Zenas was quite aware that, with living costs continually rising, Abner and his family must find the going hard.

Thoughts like these hurt. Bradshaw's had always had the reputation of being liberal with its employees. "If you work for Bradshaw's you've got a fine job and a steady one"—that was what used to be said. Zenas Bradshaw was as proud of that reputation as his forebears had been.

True to his resolve, he kept his own council, even with Emily, although he knew she must be aware of the dwindling bank account and that she could not help noticing the scarcity of stock on the shelves. Hallett, too, noticed the latter and spoke of it to her.

"We're runnin' out of this-or-that," confided Abner, naming the missing items. "I wish you would call Zenas's attention to it. Maybe he'll pay some mind to what you say: he don't to me. What ails him, anyhow? Gettin' careless in his old age? I hope not."

Emily's tone was very serious. "He isn't well, Abner," she replied. "Can't you see he isn't? I'm dreadfully worried about him."

Abner nodded. "So am I," he agreed. "If only Mark was here 'tendin' to his job, instead of runnin' flyin'-machines somewheres at t'other end of creation. Where's Zenas gone to now? Know, do you?"

"He didn't tell me. He said he would be back before very long, that is all I know."

If she had known where Zenas Bradshaw had gone, and upon what errand, her worry would have been even greater. Zenas was, at that moment, in the private office of the Harniss National Bank, in conference with George Godfrey, its cashier. And Godfrey was saying: "I'm sorry, Zenas, but, as I told you before, we have to be so very careful how we make loans nowadays. We've got about all the money out that we ought to have. So the directors feel, anyhow."

"I see. Well, then, how about taking the mortgage on my house property? I own that house and land free and clear, you bank folks know that. I'll guarantee regu-

329

lar interest payments, and I hope, in a little while, when things get a little easier and the money that is owed me comes in—"

He paused. Then, with a shrug, he added, "I've told you all that before. I told you that what I need just now is a drawing fund, some ready cash to tide me over. You people used to be only too happy to lend Bradshaw's money. Jumped at the chance, you did—then. Now I'm asking you to take a first-class first mortgage on property that should be, and is, worth a darned sight more than the figures I named. You had your weekly meeting last Saturday. What did your directors say about taking that mortgage? You were to let me know, and you haven't done it. Why?"

George Godfrey looked very uncomfortable. His fingers tapped the desk behind which he was sitting, and when he replied, it was without looking at the man opposite.

"Zenas," he stammered, "Zenas—I—oh, we might as well get it over with, I suppose. I haven't let you hear from me because—oh, because I feel so confoundedly sick about the thing. You and I are good friends, have been since I was a kid. If I owned this bank, instead of being its hired man, I—"

Zenas Bradshaw's wave of the hand silenced him. Zenas nodded slowly.

"I see," he interrupted. "The vote was no, eh?... Humph! Unanimous, was it?"

"No-o. No, it wasn't. This is between ourselves, but I'm going to tell you I honestly believe you would have got the money you asked for and the bank would have taken the mortgage, except—"

"Except what, for the Lord's sake?"

"Except that there was a very definite objection in—in certain quarters. On the part of certain directors, I mean."

"The majority of them?"

"It was a minority to begin with, but the objectors were important people and their opinion has a big influence. This—er—these objectors felt that, for the present, now, in wartime, the bank had more than enough real estate, was holding too many mortgages as it was. That to take on another, even for a person with as good a reputation as yours, Zenas, would be a mistake. There was a good deal of talk, but in the end the minority came to be a majority. I said all I could, as much as I dared, but—well, that is how it stands."

Zenas Bradshaw tugged at his lip. "George," he said, "if I ask you a straight question will you give me a straight answer? Who was the head of this objecting bunch? John Thacher, was it?"

The cashier hesitated. Then he leaned forward. "I may be risking my job," he answered, lowering his voice, "but that's just who it was."

Zenas said "Hm-m." He rose to his feet. Godfrey also rose and came around the desk to stand beside him.

"I'm sorry, Zenas," he said. "I am awfully sorry. It's a shame, if you ask me. And some of the others feel the same way. Look here, is this spot you are in a very tight one? You've got a few war bonds, haven't you? I know you took some. Now, maybe, if you care to have me, I could manage—"

But Zenas stopped him. "No, George," he said. "Even if there was enough of those bonds to be any real help I wouldn't let go of 'em—not yet, anyhow. Maybe it's foolish, but those few dollars I put there represent, as

I see it, about all I've done to help Uncle Sam. God knows I'd like to do more, and God knows I meant to, but—well, as things turned out, I couldn't, that's all. With Mark and all the rest of 'em doing so much, I feel mean enough as it is. I'll keep those bonds till the last plank's afloat. . . . So long."

"Wait a minute. If a little bit of money would be any use, a couple of hundred or thereabouts, I—well, I'm pretty sure I could fix that up. Just as a personal loan between friends. Understand?"

"Security?"

"That be hanged! Your word would be security enough, for a pair of us, anyhow."

Zenas put a hand on his shoulder. "No, thanks, George," he said. "Nice to know that I've still got friends whose friendship doesn't stop at the top edge of the pocketbook, but I won't take advantage of 'em. In the first place, I need considerable more than a couple of hundred, and, in the second, I'm not borrowing that way. Thanks again. . . . Well, I must get back to the store. Don't worry about me. I'll get along."

Emily went home at closing time that afternoon, but Zenas remained, saying he would follow her in a few minutes. After she had gone he began a letter to the president of the Ostable Savings and Trust Company. In it he repeated the statement he had made to the Harniss bank, that he needed money to use in his business, and he suggested the possibility of securing a loan by a mortgage on his Pond Road property. Every word of that letter was a stab at his pride, and he did not finish it. He was strongly tempted to tear it up. He sat there, his head bent, desperately trying to think of some

332

other means of averting, or at least tiding over, the crisis that was so near.

The fifteen hundred dollars he had paid Seymour would have made a tremendous difference. With that in reserve he would have felt free to order necessary items for stock: he would have had breathing space to wait for what was due him. It was a bitter reflection, the idea that a mere fifteen hundred could mean so much to Bradshaw's of Harniss. What would his father have thought? Or his grandfather? What would he himself have said to any one who, even two years before, had hinted at such a possibility?

He did not regret paying Seymour the money, and he would not permit himself, even for a moment, to think resentfully of Mark's action. Who knew where Mark was now, at that very moment? He might be ill, or wounded—yes, he might even be dead. The papers were already printing the names and photographs of boys, sons or grandsons of New Englanders like Zenas Bradshaw, who had died in this war which was only beginning.

This kind of brooding and speculating did no one any good, of course. It did not help any. He must stop it. He rose wearily from the chair. Was the light over the desk really spinning in circles? No, it was steady enough, but it was strangely dim. Bulb was wearing out, probably. He must not stop to change it now. He must go home, for it was past suppertime.

A wave of vertigo engulfed him as he left the office. The partially written letter lay forgotten on the desk. His head cleared as he came out into the cool evening air, and he walked more briskly. As he passed the windows of the chain store he glanced at their display. They were well filled and the variety seemed to advertise prosperity. The old idea, the idea which he had persistently refused to consider, returned once more. He could, if he wished, sell out to those people.

Think what it would mean! No more nights and days of close figuring, no more worries about bills to be paid or accounts to be collected. No more humiliating experiences like the one he had undergone at the bank. They, the chain-store crowd, would probably pay in cash, and, if what Thacher had hinted was true, they would pay enough to keep him fed and housed for the few years of life likely to be allotted him. He could rest. Rest! He had almost forgotten what the word meant.

And then, as always, the case for the opposition presented itself. Sell Bradshaw's! Why, the ghosts of all the dead and gone Bradshaws would arise and haunt him. What would Emily say? What would Mark say when he heard of it? Besides—this was secondary, but a possibility to be considered and remembered, nevertheless—John Thacher's hints had been dropped some time ago. They had not been repeated, and none had since come from other sources. Very likely the chain-store group might not care to buy now. They would know, for Thacher would tell them, that he, Zenas, was trying to borrow, was even trying to mortgage his home to raise money. Why pay for what, by waiting, could soon be had for nothing? Bradshaw's was bound to quit, to give up as a competitor, to put up its shutters or fail, go into bankruptcy.

Those shutters might be put up, but there would be no failure. When, or if, they went up, no creditor should have cause to shake his fist at them and declare himself cheated. Before that happened every debt should be paid and—and—

Here! What had happened? Where was he? That was his house back there, behind him. He had walked past it, had not seen it at all. He could not see it very clearly now. The whole neighborhood seemed to be in a whirl. He was talking, but there was no one to talk to. Out in the road and talking to himself. Reciting poetry, speaking a piece, like a young-one in school. That was funny. He laughed aloud.

He was still laughing and still reciting when he staggered into the sitting-room. Emily, after one glance at him, sprang from her chair and ran toward him.

"Grandfather!" she cried. "Grandfather!"

Zenas groped for the arm of the sofa and propped himself against it.

> " 'He does his job, which is to squirm,
>   And squirms—but doesn't squeal.' "

"*Grandfather!*" cried Emily again. "What is it? Betsy! ... Oh, Betsy, come—quick!"

Betsy came, running, but before she reached the spot where her employer had been standing, he was standing no longer. His hand had slipped from the sofa back. He had toppled forward and slid limply to the floor.

Chapter 16

TO the person who has been ill, seriously ill, especially when the illness has come suddenly and without warning, memory, when it returns, is a curious mixture, a jumble of vague realities and equally vague imaginings, neither distinct from the other. Zenas Bradshaw's memories of the days and nights which followed his unconventional entrance to his own sitting-room that evening, were, even later on, when he began trying to pick out fact from fancy, still a hodge-podge. Of the first few hours he remembered nothing. They were a blank, completely wiped from his calendar. Then, and for a week afterward, they were a succession of glimpses, impressions, little pictures and many dreams. The pictures were scattered amid dreams, and he could not be sure which was which.

John Thacher and Laurie Davidson and the manager of the Harniss branch of the chain store, dancing hand in hand and singing the chorus of "John Brown's Body" —"Glory, glory hallelujah!" That was a dream, certainly, but it had seemed real enough. And Mark, flying his plane in and out of the dining-room windows. And George Godfrey, the bank cashier, telling him that it was a rule of the institution never to lend money to a worm.

Those were silly, the nonsense of delirium, but there

were others, the pictures which came and went, and they were different. Of a woman in a gray-and-white uniform stooping over him and making him drink this or swallow that, stuff he did not want at all. And of Emily, and of Betsy, once of Jake Lemon. He seemed to remember ordering Jake to get to the devil out of there, but that, too, was probably a sort of wishful dreaming, not a reality. And always, very often, there were snapshots of Doctor Ben Stevens, fussing over him, pawing at his wrist, prodding at his chest with that rubber hose contraption of his. A ridiculous performance which made him laugh, and to laugh was a crime, judging by the disturbance which followed.

Little by little, the dreams—the silliest, at least—faded away, but the pictures came more often and remained longer. And, at last, he knew that he was in his own room, in his own bed, that he had been sick but was ever so much better. Emily told him that. "And," she added, "the doctor is sure that if, as he says, you will take it easy and behave yourself, you are going to be all right again. Isn't that wonderful!"

Zenas said he guessed likely it was. "How long has this darned circus been going on?" he asked. "What day is it?"

Emily told him it was Sunday. He made an effort at concentration and remembered that it was on Tuesday he talked with Godfrey at the bank. "Humph!" he muttered. "About four days. Seems all of four years, but four days is too long. I ought to be in the store this minute."

"Shh! You mustn't talk any more. Remember the doctor said you must behave yourself. Now rest."

"Rest! The store—"

"Shh! Please be still. The store isn't open to-day. Have you forgotten I said this was Sunday?"

That quieted him for the time, and he dropped asleep. But the next morning he was ready with more questions.

"Why am I so everlasting weak?" he demanded. "Look at that arm. Feel as if I'd need a derrick to hoist it as high as my chin. Who was that woman that was here yesterday? Feeding me with a spoon, she was. What was she doing here?"

"She was the nurse. Doctor Stevens brought her from the Wapatomac Hospital. She has gone now, and the doctor says you won't need her any longer. You are well enough so that Betsy and I can take care of you. Isn't that splendid?"

"A nurse! Why in blazes did Ben Stevens fetch a nurse down here? Whose money does he figure he is spending? . . . Say, look here, Emily: how long *have* I been sick? No fooling."

"We'll talk about that to-morrow."

"Here! Come back! We'll talk about it now. . . . Oh, Lord! Here is that nuisance again, and always at the wrong time. Clear out, Ben! What did Betsy let *you* aboard for?"

Stevens took the chair by the bed. "Shut up, Zenas!" he commanded. "Yes, I mean it. If you don't I'll fix you so you'll have to. I'm your skipper now, and you take orders from me."

"You sound more like a bucko first mate. Oh, my soul, there you go, waving that speaking-tube! I didn't dream it, after all. Ben, when I get out of this bunk I'm going to lick you."

"I may give you the chance to try, later on. Just now

I've got you where I want you. Zenas, old boy, will you give me a chance to prove that I'm the best doctor in Ostable County? I have always admitted that I was, but nobody believed it. Now, if you will do as I tell you—"

"Be quiet, can't you? How long have I been sick? Tell me that, and I won't say another word. You can shove that—that hose thing down my throat, if you want to. Just tell me that much, like a good fellow."

The doctor and Emily exchanged glances. The former nodded. "Might as well," he said. "Go ahead and tell him."

Emily bent forward. "Grandfather," she said, quietly, "you have been sick a long time."

"How long? You said four days, didn't you?"

"You said that, I didn't. You have been in bed for"— another glance at the doctor—"for almost three weeks."

She spoke the words and then drew back, fearful, dreading their effect. Doctor Stevens rose, his watchful gaze fixed upon his patient. But the immediate effect was not what either had expected. Zenas Bradshaw did not cry out, did not protest. He lay quiet, almost as if stunned.

"Grandfather," whispered Emily, anxiously.

Zenas drew a long breath. "Three weeks!" he repeated, slowly. "Three whole weeks! And just now, of all times! The store—"

"Now, now, Zenas," cautioned the doctor. "Take it easy. The store is getting along nicely; everything there is O.K. Emily knows. She can tell you. I'll let her tell that much."

Zenas looked at the girl. Emily put her hand on his as it lay outside the coverlet. "The store *is* all right, Grandfather," she declared earnestly. "Truly it is.

339

Everything there is—this is the truth—better than it was when—when you were there last. Much better. Please—oh, do please believe me."

Zenas weakly shook his head. "I'll have to believe it, if you say so, Emmie," he sighed. "Only—only, you don't know—you can't know what—"

"But I do know, Grandfather, I know about every-thing. Everything. And it has been attended to, all of it."

Doctor Stevens broke in. "That's all," he announced, with decision. "That is absolutely all—for now. Zenas, confound you, you heard what she said, and I'll add my word to hers. There is no reason whatever for you to worry about Bradshaw's Store, or Bradshaw's business. Or about anything else, except getting back your strength, and, if you'll do your part of that, we'll attend to ours. The less fuss you make for Emily and Betsy and me, the sooner you'll be able to go to your precious store and see for yourself. Now will you do that? Will you obey orders and behave?"

Zenas Bradshaw's answer was, for him, amazingly docile. "All right, Ben," he agreed. "Only—oh, well, I suppose likely I'll know more by-and-by. Go ahead and enjoy yourself. Don't mind me, I'm tired. . . . Pshaw, that's ridiculous, now, isn't it? I recollect thinking the other night—that Tuesday, or whenever it was—that if I could just go to bed and stretch out for a couple of hours I'd feel fine. Now, according to Emmie, I've been in bed and stretched out for three weeks and I don't feel any finer—if that. Well, you two can figure it out, if you want to, only don't ask me for the answer. I never was much good at arithmetic."

The next day, however, he felt better, and the day

340

after that, better still. Doctor Stevens was much pleased with his patient and said so.

"You've been a pretty good little boy, so your grand-daughter tells me," he observed. "Knowing you, I am surprised. Just keep it up, that's all I ask."

Zenas grunted. "It isn't all *I* ask," he declared. "I warn you that I'm set to ask a whole lot. Emily won't tell me a blessed thing. The only word I can get out of her is 'Wait.' I'll wait until to-morrow. Then, if I can't strike oil any other way, I'll start pumping Betsy. *Her* well hasn't run dry, I'll bet."

Stevens chuckled. "I'll guarantee you would have been pumping Betsy before this if you thought she knew anything worth while. You want to hear about the store, of course. She can't help you there. I'll make a bargain with you, Zenas. If you will rest contented until after I see you to-morrow I'll let Emily tell you a little. She won't tell you the whole all at one time: you'll have to get it in parts, like a serial story in a magazine, but you'll get the first instalment to-morrow. Provided, that is, I find you have picked up in the coming twenty-four hours as much as you have since yesterday. How about that? Satisfy you, does it?"

"Huh! Course it doesn't satisfy me. But a man that can't get a square meal is thankful for a mouthful—or had better be, I guess likely. All right, Ben, it's a deal. Only don't you, or Emily either, come tiptoeing in to-morrow saying 'Wait' again. If you do—well, if you do you'd better order that nurse to come back, because one of us going to need her."

The improvement continued, and when the doctor next called, which was early the following morning, he expressed himself as satisfied. "You get another good

341

mark, Zenas," he said. "How you did it I don't know, but you are going to get well, after all."

"After all?" indignantly. "After all what? In spite of your doctoring, do you mean? Of course I'm going to get well. I am next door to well now. See here, I've kept my part of our bargain, but how about yours? Where's Emmie?"

Emily had been standing in the doorway. Now she came forward. "Here I am, Grandfather," she said. Zenas looked at her; she had her hat in her hand.

"What you hanging on to that thing for?" he demanded. "Put it down this minute. Now how about all those things you were going to tell me?"

She turned to Doctor Stevens.

"Yes," he said. "You may tell him. A little, not too much. A serial story, remember, and the first instalment a short one. Good-by, both of you. I'll leave him in your charge, Emmie. See you later, Zenas."

He went out. Emily took the chair he had vacated. "Grandfather," she asked, "what do you want to hear about first? Where shall I begin?"

"At the beginning.... No, wait a second. First about Mark. Heard any more from him?"

Yes, she had. Another letter had come from Mark. It was not in answer to those she and Zenas had written but was dated only a day later than the one she had received just before Zenas was taken ill. Mark had written that he was well and as happy as he could be so far away from them. "He likes his commanding officer very much and says his squadron is the best bunch of boys on earth."

"Humph! Pretty short letter, was it?"

"No-o, it was quite long. Eight pages."

"Wouldn't take eight pages to put down what you've told me, I wouldn't think. What else did he say? Been doing any fighting?"

"Not up to that time, or so I judged. There was just one line which makes me think he expected to very soon. He said it began to look as if business might begin at any minute. I have been watching the papers, but they print so very little."

"I know. Only what the Washington folks let out. . . . Hm-m. . . . What else was in the letter? More than that, wasn't there?"

Emily hesitated. "Yes," she admitted. "There was. Something he had not told me before, although he hinted at it in his other letter. I—I think I won't tell you what it was now. Suppose we leave it for what the doctor would call the next instalment. It is time I was at the store, and I know it is the store you want to hear about. You and I mustn't think too much about Mark. I mean—I mean—oh, of course we can't help thinking of him always, but—"

Zenas's thin hand reached from the bed to take and hold hers. "Sure, certain," he interrupted, hastily. "I know what you mean. Too much thinking doesn't do him any good, and it won't help us. Go on, about the store. You say it is all right. How on earth it can be I can't understand. With me laid up here and—and things as they were, I vow if you'd said we had shut up shop I wouldn't have been too surprised."

"Hush! Don't say such things. Of course we haven't shut up shop. We are getting on pretty well. I don't dare say very well, but ever so much better, truly. Now listen."

Bradshaw's had been "short-handed" before its proprietor was stricken. Deprived of his services for no one could be sure how long, the short-handedness became acute. Emily herself could leave her bookkeeping at occasional intervals and help Abner Hallett wait upon customers, and she did so. Even Willie Snow was called from the back room to assist.

Zenas interrupted here. "Willie must have been about as much help as an extra tail on a cat," he observed.

"I know, but he helped as well as he could. Abner was scouring the town every evening to try to find somebody who could be hired, if only for a few hours a day, but he was almost in despair. And then, not because of his hunting but just as a—a happening, we had our first bit of good luck. Mr. Gammon walked in one morning and asked if he could have his old job back."

"Eh? What? Eli Gammon? Thought he was making a thousand a week or so out of the Government. What in the world?"

"I don't know. Abner says that, as near as he can find out, the defense work was too hard, or—or something."

"Or Eli was too soft. You took him on, anyway?"

"Indeed we did. And he saved that part of the situation for us. And business began to improve a little, it really did. Some of our former customers, people who had been buying at—at other places—"

"Chain store: you don't have to cover up. You don't mean they began trading with us again?"

"Why—yes. I don't mean they give us all their orders, but they do give us a share."

"Well, well! What was responsible for that, do you suppose?"

"I don't think it was a 'what.' I think it was a 'who.' And you were that 'who,' Grandfather. Every one knew

344

how sick you were, and every one was sorry, or almost every one. You are liked in Harniss—oh, yes, you are. And these people, I think, realized how much Bradshaw's meant to you and that we, Abner and I and the others, were trying to carry on for your sake. Even though they could, I suppose, buy some things cheaper at the other place, they—well, I *hope* they felt ashamed to do it while you were so ill. At any rate, they have given us orders and have kept on giving them. You will be surprised when I tell you that even Mrs. Simons—"

"*What!* Abbie Simons? Why, that 'damn' I said to her blew her out of Bradshaw's like one of those depth bombs we read about. *She* didn't come back?"

"Yes, she did. And she gave a small order, too. You see, she hasn't been very well, and Doctor Stevens has been calling regularly—professionally, I mean—"

"Lord, I hope so! I'd hate to think he was calling on Abbie any other way. Humph! So Ben has been around passing the hat for me, has he?"

"Now, Grandfather, you mustn't think that. Mrs. Simons adores Doctor Stevens, and he is a good friend of yours, a very good friend. It is possible that she may have made some unpleasant remark about you, about all of us, and the doctor told her what was what. She would take it from him, you know."

"Humph! Well, maybe. Anyhow I can't afford to be too particular. Never mind Abbie. Money—that's what I want to hear about most. Those bills, you know. The ones we owe and those that are owed us. What about them?"

"No, Grandfather. The first instalment is ended. Here is where I must say 'Continued in our next.' I must get to the store."

"But, Emmie, you can't quit now. Those bills—There is next to nothing in the bank and—"

"Hush! To-morrow I shall tell you a lot more. Perhaps this evening, if the doctor is willing. Yes, I will say just this now. Every bill we owe—every pressing bill, that is—has been paid. That is the truth. Now, good-by."

He called after her, but she had gone. Betsy came in to ask what he wanted. "I'm nurse now," she announced, "and you better be thankful that I am. You are savin' money. Oh, I don't mean just wages, either. I never saw a person waste vittles the way that nurse woman did, never in my born days."

There followed a long day of waiting and wondering and guessing. Emily's assurance that Bradshaw's bills had been paid was almost unbelievable, too good to be true. Where had she found the money to pay them with? And yet she had said it was true. No, wait a minute. Her exact words were that every pressing bill had been paid. That "pressing" must be the joker in the deck. And yet, as far as he could remember, each one of the lot was pressing, or would have become so in a week or two.

He figured and refigured and muttered and frowned. Betsy scolded him and threatened to tell the doctor. She did tell Emily, when the latter came home to dinner, with the result that Emily, too, scolded.

"If you don't behave, I know Doctor Stevens won't let you hear my next instalment this evening," she warned him. This had the desired effect. He resolutely put the puzzle from his mind, and when Stevens entered the room at five that afternoon Zenas was asleep.

He was wide awake, however, at eight o'clock, when Emily again took the chair by the bed.

"Going to get the rest of it now, am I?" he asked, grimly. "I better had, for all hands' sake as well as my own."

She smiled and nodded. "Yes," she replied. "The doctor told me I might go on with our serial. Let me see. It was about money and bills you were anxious to hear, wasn't it?"

"I'll say it was. And I haven't got over it. Don't ask me—tell me."

She resumed her story by saying that, after his sudden seizure and the realization of its gravity and the certainty that he would not be in condition to attend to business for some time—

"Or forever. Yes, yes, I know. Well, I'm going to fool you. We're a tough lot, we Bradshaws. My granddad used to say the average Bradshaw was Injy-rubber and rawhide from the neck down, and bone up aloft. Never mind that. Go on, go on!"

Realizing, from the doctor's report, that Zenas was out of the picture, as far as the store was concerned, she, Emily, realized just as keenly that the present, as well as the future, of Bradshaw's was on her shoulders. To carry that responsibility she must know all; there could be no more secrets. She went through her grandfather's drawer in the desk and his locked drawer in the safe.

In that drawer she found an envelop bearing her name in Zenas Bradshaw's handwriting. The enclosure was a brief note. It was, in effect, a power of attorney, giving her, Emily Bradshaw, authority—in the event of Zenas Bradshaw's incapacity, owing to illness—to carry on the business of Bradshaw's Store as long as that incapacity lasted. By it she was empowered to draw upon or deposit to the account of Bradshaw's in the Harniss bank, to sign checks, to pay bills—in short, to handle the store and its affairs until its owner should again take over.

"Finding that was a great surprise, Grandfather," she said. "And a tremendous relief to me. It made things so easy."

"Didn't make any fuss over it at the bank, did they?"

"Not the least. Mr. Godfrey was very kind and understanding about it all. Your signature was as familiar to him as his own, and he had known me all my life. A big city bank might have required a more formal, sworn-to, certification, but it was not necessary here. When I signed your name I added 'Per Emily Bradshaw, Attorney,' as Mr. Godfrey told me to do."

Zenas nodded. "Good!" he exclaimed. "Some advantage in being a small-town man. I'm glad I fixed up that power thing."

"But you never told me you did. I certainly had not expected to find anything of the kind when I opened that drawer. When did you put it there, Grandfather?"

"Week before I was knocked out, or thereabouts. I did it kind of—well, on impulse, as they tell about. I hadn't been feeling any too fit and I got to thinking 'Suppose this' and 'Suppose that.' Not about dying—no, no! I couldn't afford to die just now, anyhow, and if I did, Bradshaw's estate, such as it is, would have had to be settled under the terms of my will. It was another spell of sickness I was afraid of—although I certain didn't expect such a spell as this one turned out to be. My writing out that power of attorney was what you might call a 'hunch,' I suppose. Mighty lucky hunch, too."

He chuckled. Emily stroked his hand. "It is nice to know you trusted me so very much, Grandfather," she said. "Thank you."

"Eh? Heavens and earth, child! Why should you thank *me* for anything? The thanking is the other way around.... Well, well! Go on with your yarn."

The power of attorney was not the only important item in the contents of that safe drawer. There, too, she had found Zenas Bradshaw's personal check-book with the stub showing he had drawn a check on the Ostable Savings and Trust Co., to the order of Frank Seymour, for fifteen hundred dollars.

"That explained what Mr. Seymour came to Harniss to see you about, Grandfather," she continued. "But it did not explain why you should pay him all that money. You had told me, remember, that he did not borrow from you. And it was absurd to think you had ever borrowed from him. There was another possibility. I couldn't believe it, and yet—well, there was something Mark said in his letter to me—not this latest letter, but the one before, the one I read a part of to you—which had troubled and puzzled me very much. I knew Frank Seymour and Mark were—"

She hesitated, then hurried on. "Oh, well," she said, "that makes no difference now. Mark's letter, the one you haven't seen, cleared it all up, and the letter from Mr. Taylor, which came a few days after you were taken ill, explained—"

"Wait!" Zenas broke in. "Letter from Mr. Taylor? What Taylor?"

"Mr. Edmund Taylor, the one who was such a good friend of yours years ago. The one Mark wrote he had come to know so well at the training camp before he was called to active service, and who had been so kind to him. That Mr. Taylor."

"For the Lord's sake, what did Ed Taylor write you about? I kind of expected he might write me again, but why you?"

She told him why. Mr. Taylor had not, himself, written the letter. He had dictated it to a stenographer in the sanatorium in the South, where he was slowly recovering from a severe illness. In this letter he stated that Mark, whom he had grown to know and like immensely, had come to him just before leaving for his unknown destination. Mark had told Taylor of his marriage, that the marriage was a secret even from his grandfather, but that the fact that he might be called away at a moment's notice and that his wife might need the money—

Zenas once more interrupted. "What money?" he asked. "Shh! All right, all right. I understand. *That's* what he did with it. Gave it to Taylor to take care of. Just like him. Wonder if he bothered to take a receipt. He and Frank Seymour are a grand pair of businessmen, I must say. Why didn't he send it straight to you, instead of making Ed Taylor trustee?"

Emily flushed. "Because, if he did that, he would have had to tell me that he borrowed it of Frank. And he knew perfectly well how *I* would have felt about that."

"Humph! And how I would have felt, too. That's why he didn't tell me, either, of course. Well, why *did* he borrow it—of anybody?"

"He explained that in his latest letter, the one you haven't seen, Grandfather. At the time when he and I said good-by, no one but ourselves and the town clerk and Doctor Stevens and the Ostable minister knew of our marriage. I was living with Uncle John and Aunt Etta, but he knew, as I did, that I couldn't continue to live with them very much longer. They were bound to find out. There was Laurie, and—and—"

"Sure! I can see all that. Seymour told me Mark said just about that to him when he borrowed the money. Let that go, for now. Get back to Ed Taylor. How did he come to write you he was holding the fifteen hundred?"

Taylor, or so the latter had written, was asked by Mark to keep the money until notified by him, Mark, to forward it to Emily. But Taylor's unexpected illness and delayed convalescence prevented his attention to business matters, even to correspondence. Now that he was well enough to pay a little heed to such things, he learned that no word of any kind had come from Lieutenant Bradshaw. So, feeling that he must not assume the responsibility any longer, he had dictated the letter to Emily, stating that the fifteen hundred dollars was in his hands, awaiting her orders concerning it.

"I sent for it right away," she said. "The check came a few days later."

"I see. You've got it. That's fine."

Emily smiled. "I had it," she corrected. "Of course I deposited it in the Harniss Bank to Bradshaw's account. It helped to pay those bills we were talking about."

Zenas frowned uneasily. "Now, look here, Emmie," he protested. "That money was yours, not Bradshaw's. Mark borrowed it for you, not for me."

"Yes. And you paid Frank Seymour for me—for Mark and me—not for yourself. And didn't tell me one single word. Oh, I know all about it now. I wrote Frank, and he answered my letter. Good heavens, Grandfather! You

351

didn't suppose I kept that fifteen hundred dollars, do you? After all you have done for me—for both of us."

"Shh! Shh! There, there! It is only that Mark borrowed it so you might have it handy in case you needed it. To put it into the store don't seem hardly the square thing."

Her eyes were wet as she bent to kiss him. "You know perfectly well I don't need it. You have given me a good home and a—yes, work to do and a salary for doing it. You can't do *all* the square things: I mean to do some of them. I am a Bradshaw, myself, now. You mustn't forget that."

Betsy came into the room. "Doctor's orders," she announced, importantly. "He said twenty minutes, and you two have been hard at it for half an hour."

Emily rose. "I know," she agreed. "Good night, Grandfather. See you in the morning."

"Hi! Hold on! There's a lot more I want to know. About the store."

"That's for the next instalment. Good night."

She went out. Betsy shook her head. "A man that's been sick as you have, Zenas Bradshaw," she declared, "ought to know better than to swear. Takin' chances, that's what *I* call it."

Chapter 17

ANOTHER fortnight slid by. To Zenas Bradshaw it was much more of a crawl than a slide. He was gaining strength daily and, considering his age, remarkably fast, but, as Doctor Stevens put it, his ambition was always a length ahead of his physical fitness.

"Confound you, Zenas," complained the doctor, "you want to sprint before you can creep. Have a little patience. I'll let you go to that blessed store of yours when I decide you are able to go. You don't want to be lugged into it on a stretcher, do you?"

"No, and I don't want to be wheeled there in a baby-carriage, either. I'm nigh enough to my second childhood as it is. Keep me boxed up in this bedroom much longer, and I'll be playing with a rattle and cooing at you. Oh, for the Lord's sake, Ben, have a heart!"

"If I didn't have one I should make you stay here another month. More heart than brains, that's my trouble."

"Humph! I won't argue with you there. Only—"

"Shut up! Now listen. One more week and then—well, we'll see."

That week was the longest of all. As it crawled to its end, Emily, in conference with the doctor, expressed her feeling. "I honestly think we had better let him go," she said. "He is strong enough to stand the ride in the

353

car, I am sure, and if he could have just one look at the store I believe it would do him more good than harm. He talks about nothing else, and he won't let me talk of anything else, either."

In their evening conferences she had told him much more concerning Bradshaw's and the Bradshaw business. The news, some of it, was surprising, with almost all the surprises pleasant ones. Zenas's illness had, apparently, stirred some consciences in Harniss. The owners of those consciences had not previously crossed the Bradshaw sill in months, but now they dropped in to express sympathy and inquire concerning the sick man's chances of recovery.

"Truly, Grandfather, I think they were ashamed of themselves. One of them said that Bradshaw's Store and you were landmarks in Harniss and that the town would not seem the same without both, or either."

"Humph! First time I ever was called a landmark, as I know of. They'll be hanging a bronze tablet on me next. Who said that?"

"Mr. Seabury."

"So? Clem Seabury, eh? Well, old Vernon Seabury and his family traded with Father before I was born, and the younger sons traded with me—until this season, anyhow. Then they switched to the chain store, or I heard they did. Young Mrs. Clem—that's old Vernon's grandson's new wife—is a sharp buyer, I guess, and of course she hasn't been summering in Harniss very long."

"I know. But her husband, Mr. Clement, told me that he used to come into Bradshaw's, when he was a little boy, to buy nonpareils. You know, those little flat chocolate candies with the round dots of white sugar sprinkled on top."

"Certain he did. I've sold 'em to him, myself. So Clem Seabury remembered that. Well, well!"

"He did. And, before he went out, he gave me a good-sized order for groceries and supplies to be sent to the house. And his wife has ordered almost every day since then!"

Zenas chuckled. "Never was a Seabury yet that didn't have an eye for a good-looking girl," he observed. "Ought to have set you to selling long ago, Emmie."

"Nonsense! It was you—you and Bradshaw's—he remembered and liked. I had nothing to do with it."

The most surprising item of all was that Mr. Barbour, the retired head of the Boston wholesale grocery firm, had called at the store.

"He was down here with some friends on a motor trip, he said," she went on, "and dropped in to see you, Grandfather. He was very sorry to hear how sick you were and wanted to know if he could help in any way. I told him I thought perhaps he could."

"You did! How on earth could Jim Barbour help a sick man? Hasn't taken to mixing pills in his old age, has he?"

"No, no"—with a laugh—"I didn't mean help you get well, I meant something else entirely. I'll tell you. It was just an idea that came to me."

It had occurred to her to wonder if Barbour knew of her visit to his former place of business and of the curt refusal of Mr. Philips, the "active manager," to be a bit more lenient in the matter of Bradshaw's term of credit.

"I didn't tell you, Grandfather," she continued, "but when I was there, I explained to the man who took my order that our bills—the Bradshaw's customers' bills, I mean—were, many of them, not paid until the end of

355

the summer season, which usually meant three or four months, or sometimes even longer. These were our best customers and they had always been in the habit of paying that way, and to ask them to settle each month, as we were now asked to do by the wholesale firms, would be a great mistake on our part. We would be misunderstood and—oh, well, I won't repeat all I said. To sum it up, I asked if it might not be possible to allow us, say, sixty days' leeway, instead of thirty. That would be a little help, at least. The salesman took the matter up with his superiors, or said he did, and the answer was a decided no. An ironclad rule, thirty-day limit—that was his report to me."

Zenas would have interrupted here, but Emily would not listen. "Wait," she said, "I haven't finished. This is what I am leading up to."

While Barbour was in the store she told him all this. It was, as she could see, news to him, and as she went on with her story, his face, so she declared, grew redder and redder. When she finished, his statement was brief and to the point.

" 'You tell your grandfather,' he said, 'that, although I'm not actually head of that concern any longer, I still have a fairly heavy interest in it, and my orders or—well, recommendations—aren't chucked into the waste-basket, even yet. You tell him that Bradshaw's name has been on our books for something like a hundred years, that we never lost a dollar by having it there, and that I know we never will. Tell him—and I tell you, young lady—that so long as we sell goods Bradshaw's can buy them and, more than that, pay for them when it gets good and ready.' ... What he actually said was 'damned

356

good and ready.' He said he wrote you that once; that he meant it then, and meant it now. What do you think of *that*, Grandfather?"

"Glad Abbie Simons wasn't around to hear that damn," Zenas observed, with a grin. "Two of 'em in the same store would have snapped her moral fiber, as the books tell about. What do I think? Well, I think there have been some pretty good Bradshaws, but the best one has lately married into the name. I get prouder of you every day, Emmie. And I'll give Jim Barbour a good mark, too. *He* hasn't lost his eye for the girls, either."

At last the great day came. The car, with Willie Snow at the wheel, was drawn up by the front gate of the Pond Road house, and Zenas, escorted by Doctor Stevens, Emily, Betsy, and—yes, even by Jacob Lemon— was carefully put aboard it. The doctor and Emily saw to the stowage of the passenger on the rear seat; Betsy fluttered about, hen-like and cackling as usual, and Jacob, his pomposity only a trifle deflated, superintended the embarkation.

Doctor Stevens, saying he would see them later, got into his own car and drove off. Emily rode beside Zenas. The Lemons waved farewell.

"Jake is coming around to normal all right," commented Zenas. "I was afraid he would. Got his wife trotting in harness already, I judge likely. I have been trying to tip her off, telling her now she'd got him in his place to keep him there, but I know she won't. It isn't in her. So long as she imagined Mrs. Bodley was trying to charm her husband away from her she was actually getting mad. Now she's sprouting a new set of rabbit ears. Too bad."

357

"She is still angry at Mrs. Bodley," said Emily. "Calls her 'that designing woman.'"

"I know, but that is because the Bodley one didn't appreciate the worth of what she was trying to steal. If she had shown signs of heartbreak at losing Jake, Betsy might have forgiven her—after trying to scratch her. But now, as it is, Jake is tagged with a ticket labeled 'Misjudged Merit and Injured Innocence.' He goes around looking like one of those martyrs in a Sunday-school picture-book. If he would tear the top out of his straw hat and wear the brim like a halo he'd be perfect. I gather, from what his wife says, that he has gone back to his old job, hanging around the park at the water-front, telling the summer crowd what's what and who's who. All right. Some of these days I'll tell him a what's what I know about *him*. That will put a reef in his mizzen tops'l, I shouldn't wonder."

They passed Ye Genuine Antique Shoppe. Its doors were still closed and locked. Mr. Freeling Anderson had been looking over and appraising its stock, but Emily said the rumor was that the Shoppe would not open during the present summer, if it ever did. Apparently Mrs. Bodley's "pet" was in danger of death by slow starvation.

At Bradshaw's Store the welcome accorded its proprietor was hearty, if not spectacular. With Abner Hallett on one side and Emily on the other, Zenas was assisted up the platform steps and enthroned in an armchair before the bookkeeper's enclosure. Eli Gammon came forward to shake hands and tell him how glad he was to have him with them once more.

"You look natural as ever, Zenas, darned if you don't," declared Eli.

Zenas sighed. "My, that's a relief, Eli," he said, solemnly. "I was afraid you wouldn't know me. Been an awful shock to have you take me for a new customer, or something."

Willie Snow, standing by, was very earnest. "Oh, we'd have known you anywheres," he vowed. Then, after thinking it over, he added, "If you had been a new customer we wouldn't have helped you up the steps. You'd have come in yourself."

Abner Hallett made one of his rare jokes. "Not by an almighty sight," he asserted. "If he had looked like a new customer we would have *dragged* him in, wouldn't we, Emmie?"

"Yes," agreed Emily, "and locked the door."

Zenas's first stay in his beloved store lasted but an hour. Doctor Stevens and Emily saw to that. But he came again the following day and was permitted to remain twice as long. It was pleasing to note that the place was at least as trim and orderly as before his long absence. The stock on the shelves was not plenteous, but it was not noticeably meager. There seemed to be as many, perhaps a few more, customers, and some of them were persons who had not traded at Bradshaw's for months. They shook hands with him, as did the regulars when they came. Every one said pleasant things. That second day was even happier than the first.

When the next week began he was permitted to leave his chair and move about a little. One of his first moves, when the opportunity came, was to go into the office and examine the books, the accounts paid and unpaid, and, of course, the Bradshaw bank account. The latter was in far better condition, he discovered. The amount in the checking account was by no means as large as it should be, but the record of deposits showed that a dozen good-sized bills—bills which usually remained unpaid until fall—had been paid at the end of the month just past. And the accounts of those who had paid them were, apparently, still open and active. Emily must have actually asked these people to pay, or at least suggested that they do so. He, Zenas, could never have done that, he would not have dared. And if he had, they—some of them, certainly—would have been insulted by the suggestion. They would not have taken it from him, but they took it from Emily. And kept on buying at Bradshaw's, just as if nothing had happened.

Bradshaw's own bills, even that of the firm formerly headed by Mr. Barbour, had been paid when due. The fifteen hundred dollars retrieved from Edmund Taylor helped here, of course, but the prompt payment of the bills owed the store was even more of a help, and the implied hint that the Calloways and the other "slow payers" might, somehow or other, have been maneuvered into a willingness to "settle up" at more frequent intervals was the brightest hope for the future.

All this was the result of Emily's effort and diplomacy and management, he realized that. Bradshaw's had had one of those things the papers were beginning to print so much about—a blood transfusion. New blood, that was what it had needed, and now it had it. And mighty fine blood, too. Mark was indeed a lucky boy to get such a girl for a wife. And when Mark came home after the war—why, then there would be more new blood. He, Zenas, ought to be able to step down—or out—then, with a clear conscience.

It was high time they heard from Mark again. Not a word had come from him, although his latest letter—

that which Emily told Zenas she had received during the first week of his illness—bore a date almost six weeks gone. Of course, mail from the men in active service was subject to all sorts of delays, especially when it came from the South Pacific, which, they were almost certain, was where Mark was stationed. Waiting was an anxious business. Emily was sure her husband was safe and well; she—perhaps almost too frequently—proclaimed herself confident of that. And Zenas was, outwardly, just as confident. He quoted the ancient bromide about no news being good news and pretended to feel no anxiety whatever.

Nevertheless, each knew that the other was anxious and worried, and that, as the days passed without a letter, the worry increased. The newspapers were printing more and more tales of hard fighting "down under."

And when, at last, word concerning Mark did come, it was from an unexpected quarter and was phrased so oddly as to be both reassuring and alarming. Emily came out of the little office in the store one morning and hurried over to where Zenas Bradshaw was standing, talking with Abner Hallett.

"Grandfather," she said.

Zenas turned. There had been a tremble in her voice which caused him to look quickly at her face. She was pale.

"What is it?" he asked. Then, to Hallett, "Run along, Abner, I'll see you later."

Mr. Hallett, with a surprised glance at both of them, moved out of hearing.

"What is it, Emmie?" repeated Zenas. "Something wrong? . . . What's that?"

He pointed to a slip of paper which she was holding in her hand. She seemed about to give it to him, then hesitated.

"Grandfather," she said again, "I— I—"

"Yes, yes. Go on."

"The man at the telegraph office just 'phoned. He said he had a—a message."

"Message? For me?"

"No, for me. It is for both of us, really. It is about—about Mark."

Zenas Bradshaw's heart, still by no means strong, skipped a beat. Unknowingly he put out a hand and groped for the edge of the counter.

"About Mark?" he said slowly. *"About* him! . . . Good God! You don't mean—"

"Oh, no, no!"—hastily. "It isn't *that*. I have frightened you. I am— I am sorry. It is only— No, no! Listen. The message is from Mark, himself, truly it is. Please—oh, please, Grandfather, sit down."

"Sit down nothing! From Mark, eh? . . . Whew! That —that is different. . . . Well, what's wrong with him? Something, or you wouldn't look like that."

She shook her head. "He doesn't say anything is wrong. He says—oh dear, I am *so* silly! Here, read it yourself. This is the message the man read to me on the 'phone. I wrote it down."

Zenas took the slip of paper and read the words she had hurriedly penciled.

AM GETTING ON TIPTOP. DON'T WORRY. MAY BE SEEING YOU SOONER THAN WE EXPECTED. LOVE TO YOU AND GRANDFATHER.

MARK.

Zenas read the message and then read it again. He looked at Emily, and she returned the look.

"Hm-m!" he mused. "That's a funny thing to cable half across creation. No news, nothing he couldn't have put in a letter. 'May be seeing you sooner than we expected.' What—"

Emily interrupted. "Grandfather," she broke in, "you haven't noticed. That message never was cabled. It is just a telegram, and—see—it was sent only yesterday, from San Francisco."

"Eh? From San Francisco? Why, that's a fact, so it was. What does that mean? What is the boy doing back in San Francisco, for mercy sakes?"

"I can't imagine. Unless—this is what frightens me —unless something had happened to him, and they took him back there."

"Happened to him? ... You mean—"

"I am afraid to think what I mean. Why should he telegraph us that he was 'getting on tiptop' and for us not to worry? He must know that we always worry. Of course, if he thinks we have heard ... but we haven't heard."

Zenas pulled at his lip; his fingers were unsteady.

"No," he agreed, "we haven't. And if anything—anything that amounted to much—had happened, we would have heard, I should think. I understand that the Government folks always notify soldiers' and sailors' families. But this is from Mark, himself. It does look as if he thought we had heard something."

"But, Grandfather, what can we do?"

"Nothing much, I'm afraid. We must send an answer to this telegram, sending it to the Army address there in New York where we've been sending his letters. We

363

can't telephone to San Francisco because we don't know how to reach him there, or even that he is in the place at all now. Fact is, we can't be sure he has ever been there; somebody else may have sent the wire for him. ... Well, we'll try and think of something, or some way. ... Keep your chin up, Emmie. Don't forget that 'getting on tiptop.' That's comforting, so far as it goes."

Neither Emily nor Zenas Bradshaw could remember much of what went on in Bradshaw's store the remainder of that day. They stayed there until closing time, however, because, as Zenas expressed it, it was just as good as any other place.

And that evening came another telegram, this time from Washington. It was a formal notification, worded as is customary in such cases, and signed by an Army official of high rank. It stated simply that the War Department regretted to be obliged to inform Mrs. Marcellus Bradshaw that her husband, Second Lieutenant Marcellus Bradshaw, had been seriously wounded in action, date as of June 13th.

That was all, no report of his condition, of his chances of recovery, nothing but those few words. The telegram was not telephoned this time, but delivered by messenger. Emily tore open the envelop, read the enclosure, and sank into the rocking-chair by the table in the sitting-room, the paper rattling in her trembling hands. She did not cry out nor speak. Zenas Bradshaw, too, said nothing. He was watching her, waiting—waiting— for what? He dared not think.

At length he could wait no longer.

"Well? ... Well, my dear?" he faltered.

She started and, still without speaking, handed him

the telegram. He read it. There was another interval of silence. Suddenly Zenas uttered an exclamation.

"Why!" he shouted. "Why—why, look here! *Look!*"

His tone was elated, almost exultant. Emily, for the first time, raised her head. His expression caused her to spring from the chair and come to his side.

"What? What is it, Grandfather?" she cried.

Zenas was pointing to the telegram.

"Look!" he repeated. "Look at that! That there! See what it says. 'As of June 13th.' That's when—when it happened."

"Yes. Yes, but . . . oh!"

"Yes, that is it. He was wounded on the thirteenth of June. More than a month ago. And day before yesterday—that's less than *three days* ago—Mark, Mark himself, wired us from San Francisco that he was getting on tiptop. Don't you see? Don't you *see*, Emmie? This thing"—shaking the telegram—"is just one of those regular notices the Government always sends out. Since then —a whole month—Mark has been getting better. Well enough to be brought back to this country and, probably, put in a hospital here. There's where he is now, and—yes—doing well enough to be let send us a telegram of his own saying he is next door to all right again. Thank the good God, Emily, girl! . . . Here, here, here! Don't *do* that! Stop crying. If—if you don't I vow I'll start crying myself, and I haven't done that for so long I've forgot how."

He was so sure, so certain, that Emily began to share his confidence. She could not understand why the official telegram had been so long delayed, but he had an explanation for that.

365

"It's just one of those things," he declared. "You read about 'em in the papers time and again. Folks get word that some one of their men who has gone soldiering or sailoring is dead, or missing—which amounts to the same thing—and then, a good while afterward, they hear that he's fit as a fiddle. This telegram, this thing here, may have been held up for what they call 'information to the enemy' reasons, or by red tape, or mistake, or on account of there being so many like it to send—or—or— Oh well, it *was* held up, anyhow. And our Mark is all right, or pretty soon will be. I'll bet on it! I tell you I know it! Just wait and see."

"How *can* we wait? I feel as if—as if I must know now, this minute. Don't you think I ought to go to him? If he is in San Francisco, I mean?"

"Can't start to-night. And to-morrow morning we'll begin stirring all creation to find out where he really is and all about him. Gosh!"—as the thought flashed to his mind, "What a mercy Mark's own telegram got here before this one, instead of afterward. That was luck for certain."

A long sleepless night for both the Bradshaws, and then, in the morning, more surprises and even more sensational developments.

Emily and Zenas were breakfasting, or making a pretense of doing so, when the telephone bell rang. Betsy answered the ring. She came back to announce that the call was for Mrs. Marcellus Bradshaw.

"It's a man," she added, "and he said he was telephoning from Boston."

Emily turned to Zenas. "It must be for you, Grandfather," she said. "Who would call me from Boston?"

Betsy, however, was positive.

366

"No, it ain't for him," she declared. "I asked if it wasn't Mr. Zenas Bradshaw he wanted and he said no. He said again that 'twas Mrs. Marcellus Bradshaw. You better go, Emmie; them long distance calls cost money."

Emily left the room and was absent several minutes. When she returned she looked puzzled and excited.

"It was a man from one of the Boston newspapers," she said. "He is coming down to interview me—that is what he said, to interview me—and he wanted to make sure that I would be at home. I told him I expected to be at Bradshaw's Store, as I always was on weekdays, and he said he would see me there. He said he was bringing a photographer with him."

"A photographer? What for? Didn't he say what he wanted to interview you about?"

"I asked him that, of course. He seemed very much surprised. 'You are Lieutenant Marcellus Bradshaw's wife, aren't you?' he asked. I told him I was. What he said next was the queerest thing of all. 'Well, your husband is very much on the front page just now, Mrs. Bradshaw,' he told me, 'and, naturally, every one is going to be interested in his family.'"

"Eh? Front page!" exclaimed Zenas. "Front page of what?"

"I asked that, too. He seemed more surprised than ever, I thought. He whistled between his teeth, I could hear him. 'Look here, Mrs. Bradshaw,' he said. 'Would you mind telling me when you last heard from the Lieutenant?' I said that I heard only yesterday; that I received a telegram from the War Department saying he was wounded, and another from him, Mark, sent from San Francisco, saying he was recovering. 'And that is all?' he asked. It sounded as if he could hardly believe it. 'You don't know any more than that? Nothing of what he did? No particulars?' "

Zenas was by this time sitting on the edge of his chair. "Particulars?" he broke in. "What particulars? What is the fellow talking about?"

"I'm sure I don't know. He said only one more thing before he hung up. 'Look in our morning edition, Mrs. Bradshaw,' he said. 'I'll see you later.' "

Zenas's hand was at his lip. "Morning edition," he repeated. "Hey, Betsy!"

But Betsy had gone. A moment later they heard the back door slam and, from the window, saw Jacob Lemon hurrying out of the yard. Before they were ready to leave for the store he came back, a copy of a Boston daily in his hand. He and his wife burst into the sitting-room.

"Here it is!" shouted Jacob. "All about it. Right on the first page, too! ... Let it alone!"—savagely: this to Betsy, who was trying to take the paper from him. "Emily Bradshaw," solemnly, "you ought to be a proud woman this day. *All* of us Bradshaws can be proud."

Betsy was fizzing like a soda bottle. "It's about him," she spluttered. "It's about Mark—our Mark. He—"

Zenas Bradshaw snatched the newspaper from Jacob's hand. He read one of the head-lines and gave a hasty glance at the printed words in the column beneath it. Then, without reading more, he handed the paper to Emily.

"Just wanted to make sure it was all good news," he exclaimed. "Looks as if it was. You read it first, Emmie. He belongs to you, you know."

He sank down on the sitting-room sofa. "Whew!" he panted. "Well, well, well! ... *Gosh!*"

Emily was reading. The tears were running down her cheeks, but they were happy tears this time. Zenas impatiently waved the Lemon pair to silence.

"Quit it!" he ordered. "Leave her alone!" Then, a little later, he offered a suggestion. "If you feel like it, Emmie," he suggested, "you might read it out loud. When you are up to it, that is. No hurry. Be still, Betsy! Hush up!"

After another brief interval Emily declared herself "up to it" and began to read aloud. Hers was a rather choky reading, but she read the article to the end.

The head-line's black letters proclaimed: "New England Flier's Heroism. Lieutenant Marcellus Bradshaw of Harniss Distinguishes Himself in Air Battle in South Pacific."

The story was not a long one, merely an Associated Press despatch, amplified by the newspaper's California correspondent. It described how a squadron of United States Army fliers had engaged a much larger force of Japanese airmen who were attempting to bomb and strafe a small port in Northern Australia and had not only beaten off the enemy but destroyed the greater part of the attacking force. The hero of the battle was Second Lieutenant Marcellus Bradshaw of Harniss, Massachusetts. He, so the despatch stated, had shot down six of the enemy planes and, although his own plane was riddled with machine-gun bullets, his gunner killed, and he himself severely wounded, had brought his ship back to a safe landing.

"The fight took place early in June," the account went on, "but the story has just been released in a communiqué from the War Department. Lieutenant Bradshaw was invalided home to the United States and is now in a California base hospital, where he is reported as making a rapid recovery. He is quoted as being eager to return to active duty. He has been recommended for immediate promotion, has earned the Purple Heart for wounds received in action, and will, so it is confidently asserted by those 'in the know,' be awarded the Distinguished Flying Cross. Lieutenant Bradshaw is married. His wife, before their marriage, was Miss Emily Thacher of Harniss, niece of the Honorable John Thacher of that town. His father, Zenas Bradshaw, died, fighting in the Argonne, in 1918. His grandfather, who bears the same name, is still living and is in business at—"

But here Zenas Bradshaw interrupted. "To blue blazes with all that!" he shouted. "Recommended for promotion! The Distinguished Flying Cross! . . . Mark! Our Mark! . . . Emmie, come here to me!"

And Emily came.

Chapter 18

SO again the Bradshaws of Harniss were in the public eye and on the public tongue. And this time the eye was an approving one and the tongue wagged in praise instead of censure. The United States was only beginning to take an active part in the war. Our boys had been in combat but a short time, and the tales of their heroism were but beginning to be printed and applauded. Heroes were not as plentiful then as they have become since, and Mark Bradshaw was Harniss's first hero to be publicly acclaimed.

So, in the light of Mark Bradshaw's heroism, Harniss felt that it shone by reflection and could and should be proud. Newspapers were even more widely read than usual that morning, and the stock of extra copies at the stationery, candy, and notion stores was exhausted before ten o'clock. Many townspeople called at Bradshaw's. Emily's hand was shaken many, many times, and Zenas declared his back needed padding. "If they wouldn't all thump the same place I could stand it better," he complained. "Send Willie out for a bottle of horse liniment or something, won't you, Abner? I'm getting bone spavin between my shoulder-blades."

Abner wore a wide grin as he served customers. Eli Gammon's facial expression showed bland satisfaction. Eli had had to endure a good deal of irritating nagging

371

because of his leaving the "defense job" to come back to putting up groceries at Bradshaw's, and the store's sudden burst into the limelight was, he considered, a vindication of his judgment. Willie Snow delivered orders with a flourish. He drove the small truck as if he were piloting a plane.

The Lemons were swollen with pride. Betsy, when Zenas came home for his noon meal, was wearing a small flag pinned to the bosom of her dress.

"Think it's Fourth of July, do you?" inquired her employer.

"It's Fourth of July in this house," announced Betsy. "I'm just waiting for that Ryder woman to ask me what I'm wearin' it for. That good-for-nothin' son of hers is trying to sneak out of the draft on account of his bein' threatened with consumption. Doctor Stevens says he won't get away with it, though. Consumption of vittles is all that ails *him*."

That afternoon came the Boston reporter and the photographer. They planned, so the former said, to make up a "special" for the Sunday rotogravure section. Emily was photographed, Zenas was photographed, and there were to be pictures of the store's exterior and interior, with Abner and Eli and Willie prominently displayed. Pictures of the Bradshaw home were taken, with Betsy and Jacob in the foreground. Copies of the photographs were sent in advance to Emily by the good-natured cameraman, and Zenas was hugely amused when he saw the likeness of Mr. Jacob Lemon, one arm negligently resting upon the fence post and the hand of the other tucked between the upper chest buttons of his coat.

"Looks like a combination of Saint Who's–This and

372

Napoleon, doesn't he?" was his irreverent comment.
"They tell me it's worth crawling down to the park on
your hands and knees to hear Jake lecturing to the
summer folks about how he helped bring up Mark as
if he was his own son. Tut, tut! Pshaw! I must show that
picture to Judge Tipton some time. The Judge will
appreciate the sanctimoniousness of it."

Emily smiled. "You don't take all this very seriously,
do you, Grandfather?" she observed.

Zenas shrugged.

"Take what Mark did serious enough," he replied.
"But all this back-thumping and brotherly-loving needs
considerable salt to help me swallow it. It is like a
young-one's chicken-pox: it broke out sudden but it
won't last long. By next fall some of those folks who
have always known that Bradshaw blood was bound to
tell will be dropping each other hints about being
ashamed to say *what* it tells. . . . Oh, I don't mean all
of 'em, of course—there are as many nice people in
Harniss as any other place—but when I have to listen to
somebody praising Mark to the skies to-day and remember what that same somebody was saying about
him a year ago, I—well, that's when I reach for the salt
shaker."

Then, with another shrug and a grin, he added:
"Emily, when you've lived a hundred or so years, same
as I have, you come to realize that jealousy and spite
are considerable like clams. At high water you'd never
know there was any around, but when the ebb is under
way they commence to spout. It's high tide for us Bradshaws just now, but the turn is bound to come. We
mustn't forget that."

There was truth in this bit of philosophy, of course.

There were some whisperers and sneerers even now, when the tide was at flood, but the fact remained that to Emily, and to Zenas, in spite of the latter's professed cynicism, there were many pleasant reminders that all friendship was not a sham and that the real friends were rejoicing with them.

For example, there was the long letter from Frank Seymour. "I told you that boy was all right, didn't I, Zenas? He will fly high, and not in airplaning altogether, either. He is a great kid, and, considering what kind of wife and grandfather he has, he ought to be."

Another from Mr. Barbour, the Boston merchant. "Great stuff, Bradshaw," wrote Barbour. "Congratulations. Send mine on to your grandson, please, when you write him. By the way, there is nothing wrong with your granddaughter-in-law, either. Tell her, for me, that there will be no more trouble about Bradshaw's credit with my old firm. I have attended to that."

George Godfrey, the bank cashier, took Zenas Bradshaw aside and imparted an item of news.

"Your name came up again in our directors' meeting Saturday," confided Godfrey. "One of the directors—one who voted against you before—brought up the question of the mortgage you asked for. He said he was ashamed of the way he had voted the first time and that Mark Bradshaw's grandfather ought to have practically anything from our bank that he asked for. We took another vote, and this time it was all your way. Unanimous. You can have the money, and we'll take that mortgage any time you say the word."

Zenas Bradshaw turned to look at him.

"Unanimous?" he repeated. "John Thacher? How about him?"

Godfrey chuckled. "Thacher went with the rest of us," he said. "He was pretty fine about it, too; have to give him credit for that. He said that young Bradshaw had distinguished himself in his country's service and that, as a patriotic American—"

Zenas interrupted. "Meaning himself, naturally?" he queried.

"Why, yes, sure. As a patriotic American he did not feel that any one bearing the Bradshaw name should be refused a reasonable favor, particularly as he had looked into the matter and the amount of the mortgage asked for was not in excess of the value of the property."

Zenas's hand stroked his upper lip. "Excess, eh?" he observed. "What I asked was less than two-thirds of what that house and lot would bring at a forced sale.... 'Young Bradshaw,' that's what he called the boy, eh? Didn't call him Mark?"

"No. But he will before long. I tell you, Zenas"—lowering his voice—"John Thacher and his wife know which way the wind is blowing. It is one thing to have one of your family marry a young fellow who ran away to enlist when there was no war and something else to have her married to a—well, a hero that is being talked about and printed about all over this corner of the U.S.A. Wait until next fall. John will be making political speeches then, and 'My nephew, who has received the Distinguished Flying Cross for bravery in action' won't hurt those speeches any.... Say, for heaven's sake, don't tell anybody *I* said that, will you? Now, how about that mortgage?"

Zenas Bradshaw's reply was quietly given, but he derived much personal satisfaction from it. "Why, thanks,

George," he said, "but I have decided not to do anything in the mortgage line. For the present, anyhow."

One more ironically amusing incident—seeming to hint at least partial fulfilment of the Godfrey prognostication—was described to Zenas by Emily a day or two later. She came into the store with an odd expression on her face.

"What's the joke?" asked Zenas. "You look as if something funny had happened."

"Perhaps it has. It was surprising enough, certainly. I met Aunt Etta just now, as I was coming back from lunch. Up to to-day she had passed me by with the snippiest of bows. This time, if you please, she stopped and talked with me."

"To you—or with you?"

"Both. She asked if I was well, and—this *is* unbelievable—actually congratulated me on what she called my husband's gallantry. We shook hands when she left. *What* do you think of that?"

Zenas Bradshaw laughed aloud. "Think?" he repeated. "I think George Godfrey ought to be in the Old Testament along with Isaiah and Ezekiel and the rest of 'em."

Emily demanded to know what he meant, and he told her of Godfrey's prophecy.

Best of all the letters was one from Mark, himself, which came within the week following his telegram. He was still in the California hospital, but was, or so he declared, "almost as good as new" and was permitted to sit on the lawn a part of each day. He said little about his battle with the Japs, but he did say that he was now a First Lieutenant and that there was "talk" of his being given the Flying Cross. "I won't believe it until it happens," he wrote. "A dozen fellows in my squadron

376

deserve it more than I do. The nurse says I mustn't write any more now, but I am hoping that I may be given leave to come home for a week or so before going back to report for duty. That would be something for all of us, wouldn't it? That leave, I mean. It certainly would for me. Thanks for the telegram and letters. Keep them coming. Love to both of you."

There was a separate sheet for Emily alone. That she did not show to Zenas.

So there was great rejoicing in the Bradshaw home and a wonderful hope. More than a hope, really, for Emily was sure Mark would not have mentioned the leave if he had not been confident of getting it.

Zenas Bradshaw's health continued to improve. He was thinner, and he looked a little older, but his spirits were higher than they had been for more than a year. He no longer spent the greater part of his days in the store sitting in the chair by the office. He walked about now, superintending, attending to customers, almost as active as before his illness. Doctor Stevens shook his head as he regarded him.

"He is a wonder," declared the doctor. "I wish I could take the credit for pulling him up like this, but I can't. The great news from Mark and the way you kept things going here at the store have been the bracers. I hardly know which has helped most. He idolizes his grandson, but he worships this Bradshaw business almost as much. It is an obsession with him. Pride, I suppose, pride in the name. Bradshaw's may be forced under some day, as so many other small business concerns have been and are being, but I sincerely hope it won't happen until after Zenas has left us."

Emily was very serious. "It shan't happen if I can

help it," she declared. "So long as Grandfather lives Bradshaw's must live, too. It shall. Mark and I will keep it alive, for his sake."

The doctor nodded. "And after that?"

"I don't know."

She did not know, of course. It was more than probable that Mark, when the war was over, if he were well and still as keen for flying, would not be contented to live in Harniss and manage a small retail business. There would almost certainly be other, more ambitious and more congenial opportunities for him elsewhere, and she, his wife, would be the last to advise against his taking advantage of them. Nevertheless, she had meant what she said to the doctor. So long as Zenas Bradshaw lived, Bradshaw's, too, must live.

Doctor Stevens had gone. Emily's glance turned toward Zenas, who was standing by the end of the counter, looking out of the window at the people passing on Main Street. Her eyes grew moist as she looked at him. Those weeks when he was so ill and the care and responsibilities of Bradshaw's had been shifted to her shoulders, when she had been forced to look into the state of his own and the store's finances—those weeks had brought to her a revelation of the soul of this good-natured, quiet, uncomplaining man whose grandson she had married.

She had always liked him. Later she had learned to love and respect him. But never, until those weeks had afforded her that insight, had she appreciated and understood him as she now did. She had come to realize and understand what a blow Mark's sudden relinquishing of his part in Bradshaw's future must have been to his grandfather. Zenas had taken it for granted that

Mark would carry on as those other Bradshaws had done. It was a settled, fixed certainty in his mind. And yet, when the blow fell and his card castle fell to pieces, he had not outwardly rebelled or upbraided. There had been no "scene." Mark himself had told her how sensibly and comprehendingly the old man had accepted the announcement. He had, to quote Mark's own words, "made no row." Instead he had picked up the cards and begun rebuilding alone.

And how he had defended Mark against the local critics, who, as he knew, were voicing the town's opinion! When Frank Seymour came with that fifteen hundred note— Oh, how *could* Mark have borrowed that money? Of course he had done it to help her, but he should not, he should not. . . . When Seymour came with the note, Zenas Bradshaw had not told her, Emily. He knew it would trouble her, so he had kept the secret and paid Seymour the fifteen hundred, paid it because it was a Bradshaw obligation and Bradshaws always paid.

And this, as she now knew, was at a time when Zenas was at his wits' end and close to the end of his resources. No, Bradshaw's—the Bradshaw store and the Bradshaw business—must and should go on while Zenas Bradshaw lived, no matter what sacrifices she and her husband might have to make to keep them going.

"The newspapers don't tell of all the heroes. Indeed they don't!"

She said it aloud, without realizing that she did so. Abner Hallett, who was near the office enclosure, turned. "Eh?" he asked. "What heroes are you talking about now, Emmie? Got 'hero' on the brain, I guess likely. Well, we all have, far as that goes."

379

Emily smiled. "Was I talking, Abner?" she said. "I didn't mean to. I was thinking, thinking about him."

She nodded in the direction of the figure by the window.

Abner was hugely tickled. "Him?" he repeated. "Your grandfather, you mean? Ho, ho? That's a good one! If anybody said Zenas Bradshaw was a hero, how Zenas would laugh!"

Emily did not laugh. She nodded, gravely.

"Yes, Abner," she agreed. "I know. He would, wouldn't he?"